Money for M
and
Borrowed Time

Valentin Rasputin

Money for Maria and Borrowed Time

Two Village Tales

translated by
Kevin Windle and Margaret Wettlin

QUARTET BOOKS
London   Melbourne   New York

First published in Great Britain by Quartet Books Limited, 1981
A member of the Namara Group, 27/29 Goodge Street, London W1P 1FD

Originally published in Russian, 1967, 1970

English translations © University of Queensland Press, St Lucia, Queensland,
1981

ISBN 0 7043 2274 9

Typeset by Press Etching Pty Ltd, Brisbane
Printed and bound by Southwood Press Pty Ltd, Sydney

Contents

Foreword

The stories presented here have been printed in Russian more than once, with some stylistic revision in later editions. The text used for the translation of *"Poslednii srok"* ("Borrowed Time") is that in the volume *Povesti* (Moscow, 1976). The translation of *"Dengi dlia Marii"* ("Money for Maria") first appeared in the monthly *Soviet Literature* (no. 4, 1969), and has been revised in accordance with the Russian text as printed in *Povesti* (Moscow, 1976).

As yet little has been written about Rasputin in English. "Money for Maria" is briefly studied in Deming Brown's *Soviet Literature since Stalin* (Cambridge, 1978), and a helpful commentary on his other major works may be found in Geoffrey Hosking's *Beyond Socialist Realism* (London, 1980). In German a concise introduction is given by Wolfgang Kazack, *Osteuropa*, no. 7, 1975. Selected critical articles in Russian are referred to in the introduction to this volume.

Thanks are due to Craig Munro and Robert Woodhouse for a great many valuable observations on the first draft of the translation of "Borrowed Time". Responsibility for any remaining flaws rests with me.

K.W.

Introduction

Valentin Rasputin was born in 1937 in the Siberian village of Ust-Uda on the River Angara, about halfway between the cities of Bratsk and Irkutsk. He later studied at the university in Irkutsk, where he has lived in recent years. In the early 1960s, after graduation, Rasputin worked as a journalist and also published his first short stories in Siberian journals.

With the appearance of "Money for Maria" and "Borrowed Time" in 1967 and 1970 he attracted a wide readership, and his popularity increased with the publication of "Live and Remember" (1974) and "Farewell to Matiora" (1976). His other major publications include "Going Downstream" (1972) and "Unexpected Trouble" (1969), the latter written jointly with V. Shugaev.

In an interview in September 1976 Rasputin stated that his favourite writers were Dostoevsky and Ivan Bunin, a novelist and memoirist who spent most of his life in exile, but who has found favour with Soviet readers since the fifties.[1] In a later interview, in answer to a question about the role of the writer, Rasputin quoted the words of Lev Tolstoi: "An artist is an artist only because he sees things not as he wishes to see them, but as they are."[2]

Rasputin's choice of this quotation tells us much about Russian literary attitudes: about the sense of continuity which exists in Russian writing despite the upheavals of the twentieth century, and about the seriousness with which Rasputin regards his calling. The preoccupation with "eternal questions" — so apparent in the works of Tolstoi, Dostoevsky, and their contemporaries — endures to this day, although the social context is greatly changed.

Rasputin's predilection for Dostoevsky and Bunin, however, seems to have less to do with matters of philosophy than with themes and technique. He confesses his admiration for Bunin as a stylist, and it may be that he is also drawn to Bunin as a meticulous memoirist, for Bunin, throughout his years in Paris, never forgot his youth in rural Russia, and wrote with penetrating accuracy about a way of life which was passing. Bunin's intimate knowledge of rural society, its *mores*, and his memory of the details of peasant life provide one of the mainsprings of his art.[3]

Rasputin shares with Bunin a profound feeling for the Russian village and an interest in the problems of rural life. In this he is anything but alone, since "rural prose" or "village prose" has been perhaps the strongest current in Soviet writing throughout the sixties and seventies, and many of the most gifted Soviet writers display the same preoccupations. These include Fiodor Abramov, Viktor Astafiev, Vasily Belov, Boris Mozhaev, Evgeny Nosov, Vladimir Soloukhin, and the late Vasily Shukshin, among others. Most of these are, like Rasputin, of peasant origins themselves, and thus well equipped to present the village, its social history, and its problems to their readers.

Since the main events of recent history which figure

in the works of these writers are the collectivization of agriculture, the famine of the early thirties, the war, and the famine of 1946-48, one might suppose that these writers could find little to be nostalgic about. Yet everything points to a traditional feeling of community which survived these catastrophic events and has only recently, in the 1960s and 1970s, lost ground before the advance of modernity. It is this passing of traditional values which is recorded and sometimes lamented by these writers.[4]

The appeal of Dostoevsky, says Rasputin, lies in his "psychological tension [*napriazhionny psikhologism*], the passions of his characters, and his ability to tell everything about a person". Here again the influence of Rasputin's reading shows in his work. No nuance, however subtle, is overlooked in the psychological interplay between Kuzma and the villagers who are asked to help him, nor in that between the four children of Anna Stepanovna, who have lived apart for so long. Ugly scenes, known to Russian readers of Dostoevsky as *skandaly*, have their place in Rasputin's work too.

It is possible that Rasputin also inherits from Dostoevsky one of the organizing structural principles of his stories. In his four major works to date Rasputin's characters find themselves in dire predicaments from which there seems to be little or no escape. In "Money for Maria" the heroine is faced with the inevitability of a prison sentence and in "Borrowed Time" the death of the old lady cannot be long delayed, nor can the tensions within the family be held in check for long. Nastiona, in "Live and Remember", cannot conceal her pregnancy indefinitely. She can escape the ostracism of the community only by disclosing the whereabouts of her husband, who has deserted from the army and is the prospective father of her child. Refusing to betray her husband to the authorities, she drowns herself in the Angara. In "Farewell to Matiora" the death of a whole village is imminent, as the island on which it stands is shortly to be flooded by the newly dammed waters of the Angara, and some of the old folk would apparently prefer to stay and perish with their ancestral home. (The island's name, "Matiora", suggesting the word for "mother" brings together much of the symbolism which is latent in Rasputin's other stories: the doomed mother figure, and the threat to home and family life from outside forces.)

In each case the circumstances, the terrible finality of an impending crisis, provide the tension which is the driving force in Rasputin's stories, and the tension can only increase as time runs out. Thus psychological and personal conflicts are sharpened and brought increasingly to the fore.

Anna Stepanovna's middle-aged sons and daughters have grown into very different people in the many years they have lived their separate lives, mostly away from the village. There is little the four can share in common beyond reminiscences of childhood in the village, and their feelings for their mother, which are expressed more than sincerely felt. Tensions are apparent from the first brushes and misunderstandings and these are soon followed by more serious clashes. The eruption of full-scale hostilities at the end effectively shatters all remaining bonds and leaves the old lady to die without the comfort she so much hoped for.

It is significant that Mikhail is the one who has given most thought to the question of his mother's death and takes the most compassionate view, for

Mikhail has lived most of his life with his mother and remains a peasant, and one of the themes of this story, as of "Money for Maria", is the contrast between townsfolk and countryfolk.

One of the social consequences of modernization in the Soviet Union has been the movement of the population from rural areas to the cities. The process began in the late nineteenth century, when the industrial revolution began to make itself felt, but its momentum was greatly increased by the crash programme of industrialization, together with collectivization of the land, inaugurated by the first five-year plan of 1928. In the early years many peasants had no alternative but to leave the land and seek a livelihood elsewhere, but in more recent times the young have found city life more attractive than the *kolkhoz*, and seized every opportunity to migrate to a new way of life.

The process of assimilation, however, is inevitably gradual. The differences between city and rural life are substantial, as can be seen from Rasputin's stories. Kuzma sets off on his journey to the city as if he were going to a foreign land. Anna Stepanovna, who has never ventured far from her native village, wonders how people manage to survive in the cities if they cannot keep a cow, a pig, or any hens. Varvara's and Liusia's vastly different notions of fashion illustrate, if only superficially, how widely city and country differ. This being so, the newly arrived peasant is unlikely to make a complete transition to city life, and for much of his life will probably feel more like a transplanted countryman than a settled townsman. Ilia, as seen from his mother's viewpoint, falls into this category, resembling neither a townsman nor a countryman, and seeming to have lost his personality along with any sense of belonging.

The problems posed for ordinary people by this migration have been studied more than once in modern Russian writing. Return visits to the country by people now resident in the city are also a stock feature of "village prose". Stories by Belov, Nosov, and Abramov could be cited as examples. Typically, the young writer who is the hero of Rasputin's "Going Downstream" (*"Vniz po techeniiu"*, in *Nash sovremennik*, no. 6, 1972) returns to his Siberian village and his family and can find no place for himself there. Soviet writing of the decades preceding the rise of "village prose" offers at least four stories in which a first-generation city-dweller makes a belated return visit to his birthplace on the occasion of his mother's death: N. Zhdanov's "Journey Home", Konstantin Paustovsky's "Telegram", Andrei Platonov's "Third Son", and Iury Kazakov's "Smell of Bread". In each case the experience is profoundly disturbing for the hero or heroine.

In "Borrowed Time" Rasputin takes this same situation as his starting point, but carries his study very much further. Anna Stepanovna's children all represent different stages in the process of breaking with traditional rural life. Mikhail may still live in the village, but he has left the *kolkhoz* for the sawmill. Varvara has moved away, though only to a nearby provincial town. Ilia lives in the city, but it is perhaps fitting that he should be a lorry driver, as he remains in an uncomfortable limbo, uncertain were he really belongs. In Liusia the integration into city life has been most complete (although it might be argued that Tanchora, whom we never see, has made the cleanest break, having gone furthest away and not once returned). Liusia has at the same time become distinctly middle-class in her ways. The very idea that the village was once "home" to her is now strange, for the country has become in her mind a place for holidays and weekend outings, and little else. Her clipped, grammatically correct speech seems to betray a superior attitude to her less sophisticated siblings. Rasputin clearly differentiates the members of the family by their speech habits, and the difference between Liusia and the others is given added emphasis when Varvara complains that Liusia now speaks another language, which she (Varvara) does not know.

Rasputin is directing attention to the misplaced sense of inferiority suffered by the more simple-minded country people. Its converse is a crude snobbery on the part of some city-dwellers towards the peasant. This is forcefully shown in the mocking attitude Kuzma encounters when forced to buy a first-class ticket on the train. His speech, his clothes, and his "boots like tractor treads" immediately proclaim him a peasant, and to some on the train he is a figure of fun, made to feel ashamed of his appearance, and not accorded the respectful treatment extended to those who *look* like first-class passengers. Gennady Ivanovich, a representative of the managerial classes, ignores Kuzma and tactlessly sets forth his view that the village is not pulling its weight in the national economy. Kuzma's brother, we learn, is determined to put his youth in the country behind him, as something shameful, even if this means spurning his own family and old friends.

The question of identity is pondered by Stepan Kharchevnikov in the course of his drunken conversation with Mikhail and Ilia. Nobody, he says, should be ashamed to call himself a *muzhik* or a *baba*, on the contrary, these titles should be used with pride. In standard Russian these words are usually applied disparagingly, to stress the boorish nature of a man or woman from the country, as opposed to the stylistically neutral nouns *muzhchina* (man) and *zhenshchina* (woman). In peasant speech, however, (and in Rasputin's narrative throughout these two stories), *muzhik* and *baba* mean simply "man" and "woman", with no pejorative overtones. Stepan's personal preference in women is for the *baba* of the country, *zhenshchiny* being creatures of the city, an inferior breed, and he opines that Anna Stepanovna has been a *baba* all her life and an example for all to follow.

It seems, then, that those who aspire to grander titles, shedding the appellations *muzhik* and *baba*, are set on a path which leads them away from the finer qualities of their forebears. Since the older generation have no such aspirations, it is important to consider this other opposition, the line dividing generations. It is made quite plain that Anna Stepanovna's children, and presumably succeeding generations, lack something which is of inestimable value in life. A loss has occurred either at home in the changing village, or in long years spent away from it. The younger generation is less confident in its surroundings, less certain of itself, whereas the old people, who have lived close to their roots all their lives and known no other life, do not suffer from this uncertainty, and have an unfailing sense of the harmony and one-ness of all life.

Nowhere is this more apparent than in the differing attitudes to death which emerge in Anna Stepanovna's last days. While most of her children feel obliged to seek refuge in pretence and deny the reality of death, the old lady can freely joke about it with Mironikha. Anna regards a "good death", with all her children at her bedside and one daughter to keen over her, as the happy and desirable consummation of a long life. The little we see in "Money for Maria" of Aunt Natalia, who might almost be a sketch for the portrait of Anna Stepanovna (who in turn seems to have been further developed as Daria in "Farewell to Matiora"), reveals exactly the same point of view, including a similar personification of death.

The contrast between this peasant outlook and the fear and deep sense of injustice as death approaches, examined so clinically and ironically in Tolstoi's celebrated study of death, *The Death of Ivan Ilich*, could not be more complete. Anna Stepanovna is a fuller, more credible embodiment of all the intuitive attitudes which Tolstoi instilled in the peasant youth Gerasim, to provide a counterpoint to the ambitious, cerebral lawyer Ivan Ilich. Exemplifying, as she does, the idea of "life for others", she is surely a character who would have met with Tolstoi's unstinting approval.

Of course, Anna Stepanovna's children have little in common with Tolstoi's highly educated representative of the middle classes in late tsarist days, but in losing touch with their roots, and with the traditions and rituals for which the late twentieth century has no time, they have become just as spiritually poor and vulnerable as Ivan Ilich.

Similar themes and similar conflicts can be traced in the work of most of the "village writers" named above. Also not uncommon is a marked preference for elderly women as central characters — for example, in Abramov's "Wooden Horses", Astafiev's "Last Respects", and Viktor Likhonosov's "Kinsfolk". In the absence of men, women for many years had to fill roles normally regarded as more properly those of men, in addition to their own traditional roles in society. Stepan's remarks about the heroism of the peasant woman on the home front during the war are something of a truism. In a speech largely devoted to defending "village prose" against the charge of being backward-looking, Fiodor Abramov adduced much the same arguments (also using the word *baba*)⁵.

The choice of elderly women rather than young women often reflects a concern for a Russia which is fast disappearing, taking with it, it is said, much that ought to be saved, a part of the spiritual life of the nation which cannot be preserved without conscious effort. Here both writers and critics slip easily into clichés about "external values" and the old village as the "real Russia", the home of the "truly Russian spirit". (Some "village prose" is characterized by a strain of fervent nationalism.) However the point will frequently be made that Russia, having been a predominantly rural and agrarian nation for most of its history, cannot in the space of two or three generations turn its back on its past. It will be implied, at least, that the dislocation of society caused by sudden change, has disrupted the natural process by which the sterling qualities personified in old people like Anna Stepanovna are normally passed on.

This case is clearly set out by Fiodor Abramov, as the following extracts from his speech at the Sixth Congress of Soviet Writers show:

. . . The age-old foundations are crumbling, the ancient soil on which our whole national culture grew to maturity is disappearing: its ethics, its aesthetics, its folklore, its literature, its marvellous language. We can say, paraphrasing the well-known words of Dostoevsky, that we all came out of the village. The village is our roots, our origins. It is to us the mother's womb, where our national character was conceived and shaped.

And now that the old village is living out its last days, we look with particularly close attention at the sort of person the village produced — our parents and grand-parents . . .

We have talked a lot lately about the conservation of our natural environment and examples of our material culture. Is it not time we showed the same energy and determination in the matter of preserving the eternal treasures of our spiritual culture, accumulated by the experience of the people over the centuries?[6]

Sceptical and "progress"-minded critics writing in Soviet literary journals at times exaggerate these arguments in order to attack them more effectively, refuting any suggestion that "eternal values" are to be found only in the fastnesses of Vologda province, or the Siberian *taiga*, where the industrial revolution, and indeed the Soviet revolution, have made least impression.

Naturally, in the debate about "village prose", much hinges on the portrayal of the representatives of old village life. The nineteenth-century tendency to idealize the peasant has now receded, leaving the writer less restricted by desirable models and making for more diversity of character. Despite this, a common outlook on life, which is closely bound up with a firmly grounded religious faith, may tend to dominate all else and give the characters a kind of similarity. In the minds of some critics they may be reduced to a stereotype — a meek, god-fearing, warm-hearted old lady of passive disposition and limitless inner resources, who is out of place in this age of socialism and high technology. At least one Soviet critic has reacted with irritation on descrying yet more specimens of a species he feels has become too prevalent in recent Soviet literature. A. Bocharov describes Rasputin's Anna Stepanovna, not without irony, in the words of a Russian saying, as "one of those righteous folk who keep the country going", thereby immediately reminding his readers of another well-known heroine in the same tradition, Solzhenitsyn's Matriona, for the story "Matriona's Home" also ends with this saying. While acknowledging the exceptional talents of Rasputin, Nosov, and Belov, the critic has no patience with their "passive" heroes, nor with other Soviet critics who find them admirable: "How dreadful it must be to believe in their reality, to accept it, to become resigned to it! And even more dreadful to dote on it."[7]

The typology here is not wholly accurate, for two of the characters used as examples, Anna Stepanovna and Belov's Ivan Afrikanovich, are hardly "passive" or "meek". If they were, they could not have brought their families through the extreme hardships of village life and maintained their own integrity at such difficult times, as other critics have pointed out. In the defence and sustenance of their families they have been extremely active, steadfast, and hard-working, but industry and determination with such modest aims are no qualification for the title of "positive hero". Kuzma and Maria, whose aims in life are equally modest, would not qualify either.

Certain critics, including the editors of *Voprosy literatury*, claim that Rasputin's viewpoint needs to be more clearly differentiated from that of his heroes (an objection heard not for the first time in critical discussion of the works of popular Soviet writers).[8] It is felt that Rasputin's narrative technique, in which the third-person narrator often submerges his own identity in order to convey from within the thoughts and feelings of a character, is detrimental to objectivity, allowing only the viewpoint of that character to emerge. In support of Rasputin, however, it must be said that this technique need not always be used to enlist sympathy for a character, and that Rasputin is objective at least to the extent that he is careful to eschew any schematic over-simplification. In "Money for Maria" the arguments point to the moral superiority of the country over the city, but Rasputin's villagers are not all of a piece, any more than the townsfolk on the train. Though we may in the end conclude that some of Anna Stepanovna's children are heartless, and that Kuzma's neighbours are on the whole too concerned about themselves to make any real sacrifice on Maria's behalf, we are also given at least some indication that the situations are more complex than they may seem, and that an examination of the motives of those who appear "guilty" is called for.

The most extensive exposition of mitigating circumstances is supplied in the case of Liusia in "Borrowed Time", who draws general condemnation from readers as being harsh, snobbish, and unfeeling. But to simply dismiss Liusia with these or similar pejoratives is to ignore much of what the author tells us about her, particularly in the chapter devoted to her walk in the forest and the fields of the abandoned *kolkhoz*. Objectivity is heightened in much of Rasputin's writing by a shifting point of view in the narrative, and in this chapter the narrative voice closely follows Liusia's train of thought.[9] We see the village, and the history of the family, as perceived by Liusia, not, as earlier, as perceived by her mother. As Liusia's returning memories take possession of her and actually direct her steps against her will, we are brought to a fuller appreciation of what it means to be a member of this generation which has lost its roots in the countryside by moving to the city. Her walk becomes a painful sort of trial by memory, in which she is made to feel some responsibility for the neglected state of the land she once tilled.

Mikhail's compulsive drinking, with a Gargantuan bout even while his mother is on her death-bed, his premature consumption of the liquor purchased, as he assured everybody, for the funeral feast, can only be seen as thoroughly reprehensible. His sisters look on his drunkenness and his irresponsibility as unforgivable, but Rasputin nonetheless takes pains to present him as a more attractive character than his brother and sisters. He and Nadia have long borne all responsibility for the old lady, something of which the others have no experience and little understanding (as illustrated in the embarrassing dispute over her bed-linen). Mikhail's drinking bouts provide his only release from the pressures of life, and, for all his irresponsibility, he retains a great deal more basic humanity than the rest of the family, and more real compassion towards his mother. Above all Mikhail has the capacity for heartfelt remorse and repentance. Not unlike some of Dostoevsky's noted sinners, he enjoys his sinful pleasures to the full while he can, but is a greatly humbled man after the public display of his vice, even refusing Ilia's suggestion of "one for the road". He is all too painfully aware of what he has done.

Liusia, on the other hand, finally stands condemned,

not so much for forgetting the *kolkhoz* and her youth as for her actions in the last chapter, when she departs without waiting for her mother to die, putting her own hurt feelings above all else, and refusing to be reconciled with Mikhail even for her mother's sake. Here she causes her mother as much pain as Mikhail did in his outburst of the previous day, and also gives a lead for Ilia and Varvara to follow. At this point we are given no hint of any twinges of guilt on Liusia's part. Unlike Mikhail, she is able to deflect a looming personal crisis by saying to herself that others are more blameworthy than she.

It is less easy to speak of guilt and justification in "Money for Maria", since those who declare themselves unable to help Kuzma and Maria are mostly minor characters in the story, and are not under the same obligation as Anna Stepanovna's children. However, we have no reason to disbelieve the claim of the veterinary sugeon's wife that she and her husband have a real need for the wage-packet which is theirs by rights, to cover their own debts. Selfish she may be, but if she hardly knows Kuzma she cannot be expected to take kindly to the thought of all her husband's earnings going to him while she remains in debt. The mechanic's claim for twenty roubles back is given less foundation by Rasputin, and the man takes the proffered notes without any obvious embarrassment. Kuzma, on the other hand, feels so deeply ashamed at depriving people of their wages (for whatever reason), that he is almost relieved to be able to return the money he so desperately needs.

In all these instances the question of a feeling of guilt is central, and it comes as no surprise to hear Rasputin making special mention of this when asked in an interview which qualities he particularly values in people. "Many of our vices stem from the absence of a feeling of guilt," he says, pointing once again to the importance which adheres to the individual conscience.[10] Much has been written about the therapeutic effects of literature as the national conscience in Russian writing — old and new — and there is no need to repeat it here. Suffice it to say that, having the idea of conscience, and duty dictated by it, as a vital theme, Rasputin stands firmly within a venerable tradition. The view of literature which he enunciates in the same interview, as "education of the emotions" (*vospitanie chuvstv*), confirms this.

But a belief in the ennobling aims of literature, and a determination to serve these aims in his own writing would not by themselves make of Rasputin a writer who merits serious attention and an audience outside his own land. It is beyond the scope of this introductory essay to examine in detail the literary form and technique which give flesh to Rasputin's themes, but some mention should be made of his mastery of that genre particularly favoured in Russian writing, the *povest* or novella. While the modern Russian novel tends to be somewhat diffuse, often having its story line partly obscured by intertwining sub-plots, the more compact novella has tighter organization within a narrower framework, a clearer plot line, and more direct, logical movement in its development. Rasputin gives us as much information about his characters as we need, but no more. Anna Stepanovna's biography remains sketchy. Only selected episodes are recounted from her own memories and those of her children. We learn very little about the children who died young, and there is much we are not told about those who have survived: is Liusia married? What is her job? has Ilia any children? We are told little of Kuzma's and Maria's lives before the misfortune with which the story begins, and yet these characters stand before us with the utmost clarity.

Never does Rasputing carry his story to its conclusion, always leaving the reader to give the story an ending. "Money for Maria" ends as Kuzma reaches his brother's doorstep. It is left to us to imagine what his brother will say. Anna Stepanovna's death, when it finally comes, is communicated by one laconic sentence in what amounts to an afterword. We can only imagine the further fate of the deserter Andrei after his wife has chosen to drown rather than disclose his hiding place, in "Live and Remember". We are spared the actual rising of the waters over the village of Matiora. In each case, however, enough pointers have been given for an informed guess to be made about the ending which the author leaves open, and his plots move logically and inexorably towards it.

There is sufficient material in these stories for much longer works, but Rasputin prefers the shorter genre, with plots hinging on a single event, enclosed within a narrow time-frame — a matter of days in the two stories offered here. Situations and relationships are swiftly established at an early stage, and these then develop through their own logic. The present is given depth and background by tight interweaving of "flashbacks" to the recent past in "Money for Maria", memories of childhood and youth in "Borrowed Time", and of dreams, including the one which gives the title and the point of departure for "Money for Maria".

Dreams also form part of the technique by which Rasputin modulates the reader's hopes for his characters. In one of Kuzma's dreams the required thousand roubles are collected, but then snatched away again, in partial anticipation of the outcome of the story. Against this stands Komarikha's prophecy that Maria will not go to prison, but the ominous parallel with the story of the *kolkhoz* chairman is probably stronger. The chairman *did* go to prison, for a minor offence committed for the good of his collective, in circumstances not unlike those in which Maria is trapped. Such parallels and premonitions, carefully arranged, serves as a useful aid in the manipulation of tension.

When there seems to be a danger of his plot becoming too predictable, Rasputin sometimes gives it a wry twist, adding a leavening of humour. The grim procession of events in "Money for Maria" seems about to be pushed along another step after the veterinary surgeon's wife has called to reclaim her husband's wages. We fully expect the next visitor, the agronomist's daughter, to reclaim her father's contribution, but in fact she only wants Kuzma to keep his little boy from pestering her.

A darkly humorous touch of a quite different nature occupies a similar place in the closing pages of "Borrowed Time". By having Varvara remind Liusia of her promise to leave her the (unused) black dress, Rasputin adds to our picture of Varvara, and provides some humour by the sheer incongruity of the request at this particular moment. Though obtuse, Varvara has as sharp an eye for her own interests as five-year-old Ninka, and as little tact and sense of timing in defending them. Just when Anna Stepanovna's need for moral and spiritual support is greatest, her eldest daughter is defending her own material interests, her younger daughter is nursing her bruised feelings, and both are about to abandon their mother to her fate.

Although Rasputin's narrative blends closely with the thoughts of his peasant characters this does not mean that the text as a whole is heavily salted with local dialect. In the later stories, "Live and Remember" and "Farewell to Matiora", where the setting is stated precisely as being the author's home country, on the Angara, dialect is freely employed. In "Money for Maria" and "Borrowed Time", however, geographical location is not specified, perhaps to allow more general application, and dialect forms are less in evidence, though those that do occur belong to the same part of the world. Dialect words and expressions help to differentiate the speech of the older generation from that of their children, and, to some extent, to separate the country people from the city-dwellers. The conversations between Anna Stepanovna and Mironikha draw colour and humour from their use of dialect, which is richest of all in Mironikha's speech.

Unfortunately, such distinctions as these cannot be faithfully reflected in translation. It has been found preferable to rely on a generalized form of uneducated English, where appropriate, rather than select at random a dialect variation of English. In any case Rasputin's characters are distinguished not only by the extent of dialect in their speech, but also by speech mannerisms unrelated to dialect, some of which can be conveyed, if only approximately, in English.

A feature of Rasputin's style which the reader cannot help but notice is a taste for animism and anthropomorphism. The elements, the sky, the night, and Anna Stepanovna's house are all endowed with independent life, especially in the thoughts of the old lady herself. Liusia's memories, Anna Stepanovna's limbs, the deficit in "Money for Maria", and even human sensations have a mind and purpose of their own, such as Mikhail's hangover, with which he does battle as with an animate and cunning adversary. The process is carried to its extreme in "Farewell to Matiora", where what can only be described as the spirit of the doomed island is embodied in a unique, surrealistic animal, referred to as "the Master". This has much to do with the conception of life held by Rasputin's characters, who tend not to divide the phenomena of nature into the familiar categories of human, animate, vegetable, or mineral, instead finding life and a capacity for feeling in everything around them. It is perfectly natural for Anna Stepanovna, like Gorky's Akulina Ivanovna, to treat Igrenia the horse and Zorka the cow as if they were as human and as intelligent as the members of her family, and she evokes a human response in them. It is no accident that summer persists longer than usual, keeping Anna Stepanovna company in the Indian summer of her life, nor that a ceaseless autumnal wind buffets the bus and the train carrying Kuzma to town, easing only to let the first snow fall as he reaches his destination.

There is much in Rasputin's writing which deserves close study, for he has proved himself as able an exponent of the genre of the *povest* as any now writing in Russian, a deft creator or characters, and a gifted student of the human psyche *in extremis.* These talents have brought him to the forefront not only of "village prose", but of modern Russian writing as a whole. At the same time, in possessing a deep sense of the writer's responsibility to society and to his readers, he is the heir to a literary tradition and to the literary attitudes upheld by those earlier writers for whom he has expressed admiration. He writes with deep understanding and compassion for the unassuming, ordinary man and woman, and yet, in spite of the tradition, remains a less tendentious writer than many of his predecessors. He tells a taut, powerful story, with little that is superfluous, without preaching, and without passing judgment. In a relatively short span of years he has secured a wide following, which ensures that his future career will be watched with intense interest.

K.W.

NOTES

1. "Byt samim soboi", *Voprosy literatury*, no. 9, 1976, p. 145.
2. "Ne mog ne prostitsia s Matioroi", *Literaturnaia gazeta*, no. 11, 1977.
3. The relevance of Bunin in this context may be seen in D.J. Richards, "Memory and Time Past: a theme in the works of Ivan Bunin", *Forum for Modern Language Studies*, vol. 7, no. 2, 1971, pp. 158-69.
4. A fuller study of this question is made by P. Lewis, "Peasant Nostalgia in Contemporary Russian Literature", *Soviet Studies*, 1976, pp. 548-69.
5. F. Abramov, "O khlebe nasushchnom i khlebe dukhovnom", *Nash sovremennik*, no. 11, 1976, pp. 170-72.
6. Ibid.
7. A. Bocharov, "Mera otvetsvennosti", *Voprosy literatury*, no. 2, 1972, p. 24.
8. Editors' concluding remarks to round-table discussion of Rasputin's works, *Voprosy literatury*, no. 2, 1977, p. 81.
9. This narrative method is widely practised in modern Russian writing. A useful study of it, with some reference to

Rasputin, may be found in M. Chudakova, "Zametki o iazyke sovremennoi prozy", *Novy mir*, no. 1, 1972, pp. 212-45.

10. "Ne mog ne prostitsia s Matioroi", *Literaturnaia gazeta*, no. 11, 1977.

Money for Maria

Kuzma was woken up by a lorry that flashed on its headlights as it turned the corner, flooding his room with light.

The wavering beams felt their way over the ceiling, climbed down the wall, turned to the right and disappeared. A minute later the sound of the engine had died away. Again it was dark and still and in this darkness and stillness it seemed as if the invading light had been a secret signal.

Kuzma got up and lit a cigarette. He sat down on a stool by the window, gazed out into the night and puffed as vigorously as if he himself were signalling. With each flare of the cigarette the dark glass would give back the reflection of his face, grown worn and haggard in the last few days, and each time the flare died the reflection would vanish, dying with it, leaving nothing but the fathomless darkness beyond. Not a single light or sound. Kuzma's thoughts turned to the weather: by morning it would probably be snowing and would go on snowing — on and on, like God's blessings.

Then he went back to bed, lay down beside Maria and fell asleep. He dreamed he was driving the lorry that had woken him up. The headlights were turned off, he drove in the dark. Suddenly the lights snapped on and he saw a house in front of him. He stopped, climbing out of the cabin and knocked at the window.

"What do you want?" came a voice from inside the house.

"Money for Maria," he answered.

The money was brought to him and once more he set out in the dark. Whenever he passed a house in which there was money, a mysterious mechanism turned on the headlights. He would knock at the window and another voice would ask:

"What do you want?"

"Money for Maria."

He woke up a second time.

Darkness. It was still night, still not a light, not a sound; so utterly lightless and soundless that he felt something extraordinary was about to happen; it was hard to believe that dawn would come in its proper time and day would follow.

Unable to sleep any more, Kuzma lay awake thinking. From overhead, like a sudden shower, came the whistling scream of a jet plane. Swiftly it died away, leaving silence again, but an ominous silence it seemed, as if something were about to happen. He could not throw off his sense of alarm.

He weighed the question: should he go or not? He had weighed it yesterday and the day before, but then he had not been pressed for time, he could ponder without making a final decision. Now his time was up. If he did not go this morning it would be too late. He must decide: yes or no? Of course he must go. He must. Enough of this torture of indecision. There was no one else here to turn to. As soon as he got up in the morning he would take the bus.

He shut his eyes — now that his mind was made up

he could sleep. Sleep, sleep, sleep . . . He tried to cover himself with sleep as with a blanket, burying his head, but to no avail. It was like sleeping beside a fire: turning over on one side left the other cold. There he lay, neither asleep nor awake, the vision of the lorry flicking through his mind, but he knew very well that he had but to open his eyes to be fully awake. He turned over. Still night, night untamed even by the familiarity of working on night shift.

Morning. Kuzma got up and looked out of the window. No snow, but a leaden sky suggested it might begin coming down any moment. A pale, unfriendly dawn seemed to be forcing itself through the clouds against its natural inclination. A dog with hanging head slunk past the window and turned the corner. Not a soul in sight. A gust of wind struck the wall from the north and died away at once. It was followed by another. Then another.

Kuzma went into the kitchen and said to Maria, who was busy at the stove: "Pack me a little lunch. I'm going."

"To the city?" she asked, suddenly alert.

"Yes."

Maria wiped her hands on her apron and sat down in front of the stove, narrowing her eyes against the heat of the flames.

"He won't give you anything," she said.

"Do you know where that envelope is with his address on it?"

"In the next room, if it's still around."

The boys were asleep. Kuzma found the envelope and came back into the kitchen.

"Find it?"

"Yes."

"He won't give you anything," she repeated.

Kuzma sat down at the table and ate in silence. He too had no idea whether he would get anything or not. It became very hot in the kitchen. The cat rubbed against Kuzma's leg and he gave it a little kick.

"Will you come back?" asked Maria.

He pushed away his plate and considered the question. The cat arched its back and sharpened its claws in the corner, then returned to Kuzma and rubbed its back against his legs. He got up, paused for a moment, trying to think of something to say in parting but went to the door without saying it.

As he put on his things he heard Maria crying. He had to hurry, the bus left early. Let Maria cry if it helped her.

The wind was blowing. Everything was groaning, rattling, rocking.

The wind struck the bus head-on and entered through the cracks round the windows. The bus turned its side to the wind and instantly the window-panes began to rattle and ring from the dry leaves and sand lifted off the ground and flung against them. It was cold. This wind was sure to bring frost and snow, and before you knew it winter would be here — it was already the end of October.

Kuzma was sitting on the very last seat, next to the window. There were not many passengers, he could have moved to a seat nearer the front but he did not feel like getting up and moving. He slumped down, hunched his shoulders and stared out of the window. For at least twenty kilometres there was nothing to see but wind, wind, wind — wind in the woods, wind in the fields, wind in the villages.

The passengers did not talk. The bad weather made them glum and taciturn. If anyone happened to speak it was in a voice too low to be understood. They did not even want to think. They did nothing but sit, clinging to the backs of the seats in front when the bus went over bumps in the road, shifting and nestling into more comfortable positions, preoccupied with the journey to the exclusion of everything else.

As they were climbing a hill Kuzma tried to distinguish the roar of the wind from the roar of the engine, but the two sounds merged. One compound and continuous wail. At the top of the hill was a village. The bus stopped at the *kolkhoz** administration building but nobody got in or out. Kuzma looked out of the window and saw a long empty street down which the wind rushed like water through a pipe.

The bus started up again. The young fellow who was driving glanced over his shoulder at the passengers before he risked taking a cigarette out of his pocket. Kuzma joyfully seized the opportunity to do likewise — he had forgotten all about his cigarettes. Presently little blue clouds of smoke were floating in the air inside the bus.

Another village. The driver drew up at a café and climbed out from behind the wheel.

---

* *Kolkhoz:* collective farm, whose members (*kolkhozniki*) live on its shared profits and the proceeds of their small individual plots.

"Time out," he said. "Whoever's hungry can get some breakfast here. We've still got a long ride ahead."

Kuzma was not hungry; he only got out of the bus to stretch his legs. Next to the café was a general shop just like the one in his own village. Kuzma mounted the steps and went in. Exactly the same: to the right a grocery department, to the left clothes and haberdashery. Three women were standing and gossiping at the counter while the salesgirl, arms folded, stood listening to them languidly. She was younger than Maria and her job seemed to be causing her no trouble; she certainly looked unperturbed.

Kuzma went over to the stove and warmed his hands on the hot tiles. From there he could see out the window; he would have plenty of time to reach the bus when the driver came out of the café. The wind banged the shutters. The women turned and looked at Kuzma. He felt an urge to go over to the salesgirl and tell her they had exactly the same sort of shop in his village and that his Maria had been standing behind the counter of it for a year and a half. But he did not. Again the wind banged the shutters. Again the women turned and looked at Kuzma.

He knew very well that the wind had arisen only that morning; when he had got up and gone to the window during the night there had been no wind. Yet he could not free himself of the feeling that it had been blowing for a long time, all these last days in fact.

Five days before this, a man of about forty, neither townsman nor countryman in appearance, wearing a cap, a light raincoat and imitation leather boots, had knocked at their door. Maria was not home. The man left orders that she was not to open the shop the next day, he had come to take inventory.

The inventory began in the morning. At lunchtime, when Kuzma dropped in to see how things were going, everything was upside-down. Maria and the man had pulled all the jars, packages and boxes off the shelves and put them on the counter to be counted and re-counted a dozen times. They had brought the big scales from the store-room and weighed sacks of sugar, salt and cereals; they had scraped butter off its waxed-paper wrappings, counted empty bottles, carried them from one corner to another, prised free the lozenges stuck to the corners of boxes. The man ran nimbly among the mountains of boxes and crates, a pencil behind one ear, counting out loud, making calculations on the abacus almost without looking and using most of his five fingers. Having announced a sum out loud, he would give a little toss of his head that shook the pencil into his fingers so that he could put the number down on paper. It was clear he was a past master at this business.

Maria came home late looking worn and haggard.

"How are things going?" Kuzma asked cautiously.

"Don't know yet. Tomorrow we count the clothes and things. Then we'll see."

She shouted at the kids who had been up to mischief, and went straight to bed. Kuzma stopped outside. Somebody was singeing the carcass of a freshly stuck pig and the air was filled with the appetizing odour. The harvest was over, the potatoes were dug, people were making ready for the autumn holidays and for the winter. All the hum and bustle was behind them, they were now in that pleasant in-between season when they could rest, think, and look about them. Things were still quiet, but in another week they would be lively: the villagers would remember all the holidays, old and new; would stroll from house to house, arms entwined; would shout, sing, recall their war experiences; and at the guest table make up old quarrels.

Kuzma went back into the house, told the kids not to sit up late, and went to bed himself. Maria was sleeping so soundly he could hardly hear her breathing. Kuzma dozed off but was roused by the noise of the children in the next room and had to get up and quiet them. Silence fell. Then dogs barked at somebody, but soon stopped.

When he woke up next morning Maria had already left the house. He had breakfast and went off to spend the day with the second field team. On the previous evening the *kolkhoz* chairman had asked him to go and see what was wrong with this team's vegetable storehouse and what materials were required to repair it. Kuzma was so busy he quite forgot about the inventory; he remembered it only as he approached his house in the evening. Vitka, his eldest son, was sitting on the porch and ran into the house on catching sight of his father. "What's up with him?" Kuzma wondered, quickening his steps.

They were waiting for him. Maria was sitting at the table with red and swollen eyes. The accountant, who was sitting on a stool by the door, greeted Kuzma with guilty embarrassment. All four of the children were lined up against the stove according to size. Kuzma instantly guessed what had happened. Without asking any questions he took off his dirty boots and shuffled barefoot into the bedroom for his slippers. They were not there. He came back and looked for them behind the door; not finding them, he said to the boys:

"Any of you seen my slippers?"

The strain was too much for Maria, she burst into tears and ran out of the room. Kuzma watched her go with a dull gaze that showed no surprise, then he shouted at the boys:

"You going to find my slippers or not?"

He watched the four of them dash into corners, crawl under beds, run single file from one room to another as if tied together, and as he watched he felt more and more at a loss.

The slippers were found at last. Kuzma thrust his bare feet into them and went in to where Maria was lying on the bed whimpering, her hands over her face.

"How much?"

"A th-thousand."

"What? New money?"

Maria made no reply. Turning to the wall, she again covered her face with her hands and sobbed bitterly. The sight of her shaking shoulders, so dreadful and unexpected, made him forget what had happened for a moment. When the reality of it returned to him, as though in a dream, he went to the man in the next room and nodded him to a seat at the table. The man obeyed. Kuzma took out a cigarette and lit up unhurriedly. He had first of all to get a grip on himself. He drew the smoke into his lungs in quick little puffs, like swallowing water. From the boys' room came a sudden loud burst of radio music. Kuzma started.

"Turn that off!" he bellowed.

The boys wrenched themselves away from the stove without changing the order in which they stood, dashed into their room and stifled the radio. When

Kuzma raised his head they were again lined up against the stove ready to fulfil his least command. His anger subsided and was replaced by pity for them. They were not to blame. He said to the man:

"I'll be as honest with you as if I was confessing to the priest: not a grain of anything have we taken from that store. I'm telling you this in front of the kids, and I wouldn't lie with them to hear it. You can see for yourself we live poor, but what we have is our own."

The man said nothing.

"Tell me how it could be so much. A thousand is it?"

"Yes, a thousand."

"New money?"

"Nobody counts in old money any more."

"But that's a crazy sum," said Kuzma musingly. "I've never held a sum like that in my hands. We borrowed seven hundred roubles from the *kolkhoz* when we were building this house and that seemed an awful lot. Haven't been able to pay it back to this day. And now — a thousand. I know anybody can make mistakes, and these mistakes might mount up to, say, thirty, forty, maybe even a hundred roubles, but not a thousand. I can see you're an old hand at this game, maybe you can tell how it happened."

"I don't know," said the man with a shake of his head.

"Could the people at the supply base have cheated on all those invoices and accounts?"

"I don't know. Anything could have happened. She doesn't seem to have had much of an education."

"Education? You're joking. Can't do much more than count her pay, let alone the till. How many times did I tell her: don't try to do something you're not fit for. But there was nobody else to take the job and they talked her into it. At first it looked as if she was getting on all right."

"Did she go for supplies herself or have somebody bring them to her?" asked the accountant.

"She didn't go herself, trusted anybody who happened to be going to town."

"That's bad. Can't do that."

"I suppose you can't."

"But the main thing is there hasn't been an inventory taken for a year."

Their conversation broke off and in the silence they could hear Maria whimpering in the next room. From out of a neighbour's door flew a song, which sounded a while, like a bumble-bee flying along, and died away. After that Maria's crying grew louder and she gulped with the noise of stones dropping into water.

"What'll happen now?" said Kuzma to nobody in particular.

The accountant stole a glance at the children.

"Get out of here," commanded Kuzma, and they marched in single file into their own room.

"I'm moving on to the next place tomorrow," said the accountant in a low voice, hitching his chair closer to Kuzma's. "I've got to go over the books of two more shops. That'll take me about five days. When I finish I'll come back here." He fidgeted uncomfortably. "In other words, if you can find the money by that time . . . Get what I'm saying?"

"I get it," Kuzma replied.

"I see what it means to you. The kids. They'll take her to court . . . give her a sentence . . ." said the accountant.

Kuzma looked at him with his lips twitching in a pitiable smile.

"Only don't forget — nobody's to hear of it. I have no right to do such a thing. I'm taking a risk."

"I know."

"Collect the money and we'll try to hush everything up."

"A thousand roubles," said Kuzma.

"That's right."

"A thousand roubles. One thousand. Well, we've got to find it. Can't have her put in prison. I've lived with her so many years. We've got kids."

The accountant got up.

"Thank you," said Kuzma, taking his hand and nodding. The man went out. The gate squeaked as he closed it. His steps passed under the window and he was gone.

Kuzma was alone. He went into the kitchen, sat down beside the stove that had not had a fire in it since the preceding day, dropped his head on his hands and just sat. He did not think — that would have taken too much strength. He just sat as if turned to stone, except that his head drooped lower and lower. In this way an hour or two passed and night came on.

"Daddy!"

Kuzma slowly lifted his head. Vitka was standing in front of him barefoot and in his vest.

"What do you want?"

"Daddy, will everything be all right?"

Kuzma nodded, but Vitka did not go away. He had to have his father put it in words.

"Of course it will!" said Kuzma. "We'll turn the whole world upside down before we let them take your mother away. There's five of us men, we're up to it."

"Can I tell the others everything'll be all right?"

"Tell them just that: we'll turn the world upside down before we let them take your mother away."

Reassured, Vitka went out.

The next morning Maria did not get up. Kuzma woke the elder boys, poured out yesterday's milk for them and sent them off to school. Maria lay quite still on the bed, her eyes fixed on the ceiling. She had not even undressed in the evening, but simply thrown herself down in her shop clothes. Her face was puffy. Before he went out Kuzma stood looking down at her and said:

"When you feel a little better get up. Don't worry, everything'll be all right. People'll help us. Don't let it kill you before your time."

He went to farm headquarters to warn them he would not report for work that day. The chairman was alone in his office. He got up and held out his hand to Kuzma and gave him a long look that ended in a sigh.

"What's wrong?" asked Kuzma, puzzled.

"I've heard about Maria," said the chairman. "I suppose the whole village knows by now."

"Let them. Can't hide it," said Kuzma with a hopeless wave of his hand.

"What're you going to do?" asked the chairman.

"I don't know. Don't know where to turn."

"You've got to do *something*."

"I know."

"You know yourself I can't advance you the money now," said the chairman. "Time to turn in the year's accounts. When that's done we'll talk it over, maybe we can let you have it. Of course we'll let you have it, no question about it. Meantime borrow it somewhere with the promise of our loan behind you — better than no security at all."

"Thanks."

"To hell with your thanks. How's Maria?"

"Bad."

"Go and tell her what I said."

"I will." At the door he turned to say, "I won't turn up for the job today."

"What a thing to bring up! A lot of work I'd get out of you if you did!"

Maria was still lying on the bed. Kuzma sat down next to her and squeezed her shoulder. She made no sound, did not even stir, as if she had felt nothing.

"The chairman says as soon as the year's accounts are turned in he'll lend us the money," said Kuzma.

She made a scarcely perceptible movement.

"Didn't you hear me?" he asked.

Suddenly something came over her. She leaped up, locked her arms round Kuzma's neck and pulled him down beside her.

"Kuzma," she gasped, "Kuzma, save me! Do something, Kuzma!"

He tried to tear himself loose but she fell upon him, half choking him, and covered his face with her own.

"My own, my love," she whispered hysterically. "Save me! Don't let them take me away, Kuzma!"

He wrenched free of her grasp.

"Don't be silly," he said gruffly. "Do you think I would?"

"Kuzma," she murmured weakly.

"What's got into you? I tell you they're giving us a loan, and you go off like a lunatic!"

"Kuzma!"

"What?"

"Kuzma!" Her voice grew weaker and weaker.

"Calm yourself. I'm here."

He kicked off his boots and lay down beside her. Maria was trembling all over and her shoulders jerked spasmodically. He put his arms around her and began stroking her shoulders with his big palm, up and down, up and down. She pressed closer to him. He went on stroking her shoulders, up and down, up and down, until he felt the tremors subsiding. For some time he lay there beside her, and when he got up she was asleep.

Kuzma racked his brains. He could sell his cow and his hay, but then the children would be left without milk. He had nothing else to sell. But selling the cow must be a last resort, when there was no other way out. He had not a kopeck of his own, the whole sum must be borrowed, and he could not imagine borrowing a thousand roubles. The sum seemed so enormous that he kept confusing it with the old money, one-tenth the value of the new, and when he caught himself making this mistake he forced himself to face the truth though his heart sank. He supposed that such an amount of money actually existed, as millions and billions actually existed, but he could not conceive of its being in the hands of a single person, especially himself, and he felt that to put such a sum into the hands of a single person, particularly if that person was himself (in the event of his obtaining the money), would be an irremediable error. For a long time ~~he stood motionless, as if awaiting~~ a miracle, as if he expected someone to come and tell him it was all a joke, that the missing money had nothing to do with him and Maria. And indeed why should it? All these other people in the village — it had nothing to do with *them!*

Happily the driver brought the bus to the station entrance and Kuzma did not have to make his way against the wind, which was still blowing unabated. Loose sheets of tin on the station roof were beating a tune, papers and cigarette ends were whirling above the ground, people were rushing about so strangely he could not tell whether the wind was sweeping them along or they were running about their business despite it. The voice announcing the arrival and departure of trains over the loudspeaker was so torn and blurred and clotted that nothing could be understood. The hoots of shunting steam engines and the piercing whistles of electric engines sounded like warnings of impending peril.

An hour before his train was due Kuzma took his place in the queue for tickets. The ticket office was not open yet and the people stood impassively, throwing belligerent looks at anyone who walked past them to the head of the queue. The minute hand on the electric clock above the ticket office jumped forward with a little click every sixty seconds, and at each click the people in the queue could not help raising their tired, strained faces to look at it.

At last the ticket office opened. The queue contracted and a hush fell upon it. The first head bent
down to the tiny window. Two, three, four minutes
passed without the head lifting.

"What's going on there?" called out a voice from
behind. "Haggling over the price?"

The head at fault pulled itself out of the opening in
the window and the woman it belonged to turned and
announced to the others:

"There's no tickets."

"No second- or third-class tickets, citizens," shouted
the cashier.

The queue went into a huddle but did not disperse.

"Anything to get money out of us," blustered a fat
woman with a red face framed in a red shawl. "Who
wants their first-class carriages? Why, even if you go
by plane all the tickets are the same price."

"Then take a plane," said the cashier blandly.

"So I will," retorted the woman. "Play this trick
once too often and you'll not have anybody using the
railways. You ought to be ashamed of yourselves!"

"Fly to your heart's content. A lot we care."

"You'll care all right when you find yourself out of a
job!"

Kuzma walked away from the ticket office. The next
train was in about five hours' time. Should he go first-
class? The hell! Why not? There might not be second-
or third-class tickets for that train either. Why waste
five hours? Once your head's cut off, no sense in crying
about your hair. An extra five roubles won't make any
difference now — It's a thousand I need, why worry
about a fiver?

Kuzma went back to the ticket office. The queue had
dissolved, the cashier was poring over a novel.

"A ticket to the city," said Kuzma.

"Nothing but first-class tickets," answered the girl without raising her head, as if reading the answer out of the book.

"Give me whatever you've got."

She inserted a ruler into the book to mark her place, snatched a ticket from the rack on the wall, and slipped it into the punch.

Kuzma's whole attention was now centred on hearing the announcement of his train. When it arrived he would take his place in a first-class carriage and ride to town in comfort. Get there in the morning. His brother would give him the money needed to make up the thousand. Take it out of the savings bank, he supposed. They'd sit down together over a bottle in parting and then Kuzma would hurry away so as to be back before the accountant returned. After that life with Maria would resume its usual course, they'd go on living like everybody else. When this crisis was over and Maria was once more her normal self they'd go on bringing up their children, taking them to the pictures — they had a whole *kolkhoz* of their own: five men and a mother. All of them had long lives ahead. Once more when they were going to bed at night Kuzma would tease Maria, would slap her on the bottom and she would scold him sharply but not seriously because she liked him to fool with her. It didn't take a lot to make them happy.

Kuzma came to with a jolt. It was a lot. An awful lot. A thousand roubles. No, not a thousand now, he had managed to scrape together more than half the sum. God knows at what price. He had gone begging, made promises, cravenly mentioned the loan he was to be given, shamefully accepted money that burned his hands. And still it was not enough.

As any other of the villagers would have done in his place, he appealed to Evgeny Nikolaevich first.

"Ah, Kuzma!" said Evgeny Nikolaevich as he opened the door. "Come in, come in. Take a seat. You haven't been to see me for so long I thought you must have a grudge against me."

"What grudge could I have against you, Evgeny Nikolaevich?"

"I don't know. A man doesn't always say what's on his mind. Sit down. How's life?"

"Not bad."

"Come, come. Moved into a fine new house and all you've got to say for it is 'not bad'?"

"We've been in the new house for over a year. Too late to boast about it."

"Perhaps, I don't know. You don't come round and tell me the news."

Evgeny Nikolaevich took some open books off his desk and put them on a shelf without shutting them. He was younger than Kuzma but everybody, even the old folks, always addressed him respectfully by his name and patronymic because for fifteen years he had been headmaster of the school. Evgeny Nikolaevich was born and bred in this village and on graduating from teachers' college came back to it. He did not abandon farm work completely. He helped with the haymaking, was a good carpenter, had a big garden and barn-yard, and in his leisure time went hunting and fishing with his neighbours. Kuzma applied to him first because he knew Evgeny Nikolaevich had money. He and his wife were childless, she too was a teacher, they both received good salaries and had few expenses since they produced their own meat, vegetables and milk.

Seeing Evgeny Nikolaevich gather up his books, Kuzma got up as if to go.

"I'm afraid I chose the wrong time . . ."

"Sit down, sit down. What do you mean, the wrong time?" said Evgeny Nikolaevich. "I'm free. When I'm not at school my time's my own so I've got a right to do what I like with it, haven't I?"

"I suppose you have."

"Why 'suppose'? If I say I have, I have. I'll put the kettle on."

"No, thanks," said Kuzma. "I've just had breakfast."

"As you like. If your guest's had dinner he's easier to please, as the saying goes. That right?"

"That's right."

Kuzma fidgeted on his chair, then broached the subject that had brought him here.

"I've come to ask a favour of you, Evgeny Nikolaevich," he got out at last.

"A favour?" Stiffening perceptibly, Evgeny Nikolaevich sat down at the table. "Well, out with it. I can't give you an answer until I know what you want. Don't stall; take the bull by the horns, as the saying goes."

"I don't know how to begin," stammered Kuzma.

"Speak up, speak up."

"It's money I want to ask you for. A loan."

"How much?" said Evgeny Nikolaevich, stifling a yawn.

"I need a lot. As much as you can give."

"To be exact? — ten, twenty, thirty roubles?"

Kuzma shook his head. "I said a lot. Here, I'll tell you what it's for so you'll understand. My Maria has been found with a deficit, a big one. Perhaps you've heard about it."

"No, I haven't."

"Yesterday the accountant finished taking inventory and sprang this little surprise on her."

Evgeny Nikolaevich tapped on the table with his knuckles.

"A nasty business."

"Eh?"

"A nasty business, I say. How did it ever happen?"

"It just happened."

They both remained silent for a while, and in this silence Kuzma became aware of the thunderous ticking of an alarm-clock. He looked round but could not discover the clock. It clicked with a frenzied impatience. Evgeny Nikolaevich tapped with his knuckles again. Kuzma stole a look at him. There was a slight frown on his face.

"They may take her to court," said Evgeny Nikolaevich.

"That's why I want the money — so's they won't."

"They can take her anyway. A deficit's a deficit."

"No, they can't. She didn't take the money, I know that for a fact."

"You don't have to tell me that," said Evgeny Nikolaevich with an offended air. "I'm not the judge. Tell him. I just said it to warn you you've got to be careful. You can turn all this money over, put yourself in debt for life, and have her taken to court anyway."

"No!" Kuzma realized it was his fear that this might be true that made him deny it so vehemently, more to himself than to Evgeny Nikolaevich. "They're careful not to make innocent people suffer now. We had no use of that money, we don't need it. It's her ignorance got her into trouble, nothing else."

"A lot they care about that," said Evgeny Nikolaevich with a wave of his hand.

Remembering the loan the *kolkhoz* chairman had promised him, Kuzma spoke before he had regained his composure and in a plaintive entreating tone that he himself found repellent:

"I won't keep your money for long, Evgeny Nikolaevich. Only two or three months. The chairman has promised to give me a loan as soon as he's turned in the year's accounts."

"He won't give it to you now?"

"He can't now. We haven't paid back our old loan yet, the one we took when we built the house. He's doing us a big favour as it is, there's not many would go so far."

Again the clock sounded its loud alarm, and again Kuzma failed to discover where it was. Perhaps it was standing on the window-sill behind the curtains, or on the shelf behind the books, but the sound seemed to be coming from directly overhead. Kuzma caught himself looking up at the ceiling and cursed his idiocy.

"Have you asked anybody else for it?"

"No, you're the first person I've come to," said Kuzma.

'Well, looks as if there's no way out, have to give you some," said Evgeny Nikolaevich with sudden animation. "If I don't you'll say, Evgeny Nikolaevich didn't give me anything, the old skinflint! Won't the gossips just lap that up!"

"Why should I say such a thing about you, Evgeny Nikolaevich!"

"I don't know. I'm not talking about you, just in general. There's all sorts of people in this world. But my money's in the savings bank in town. I keep it there on purpose, so's not to be tempted. I'll have to make a special trip. And I have no time now." He frowned again. "Yes, I'll have to go specially. Can't be helped. I've got a hundred roubles there. I'll take it out. That's the only decent thing to do. We've got to help each other."

A sudden feeling that all the strength had drained out of him prevented Kuzma from saying a word.

"That's why we're human beings, so's we can help one another," went on Evgeny Nikolaevich. "They say all sorts of things about me in this village, but nobody can say I ever refused a person help. They often come to me for a fiver, or a tenner, and often it's the last one I've got. True, I expect to get paid back. Nobody wants to work for nothing."

"I'll pay it back."

"I'm not talking about you. I know you'll pay it back. I'm talking in general. I know you've got a conscience. But not everybody has. You know that very well without my telling you. There's all sorts of people."

Evgeny Nikolaevich talked on and on until Kuzma got a headache. He was tired. When he finally went out the fog which had lasted until noon had dispersed and the sun was shining. The air was crisp and translucent, as it always is on fine days in autumn. The forest on the outskirts of the village seemed close at hand and instead of looking like a solid wall was distinctly composed of individual trees, each stripped of its leaves and flooded with light.

Kuzma felt better out of doors. He enjoyed the sense

of walking even though a deep-seated pain gnawed at him like an ulcer. He knew this would go on for a long time.

Maria had got up and was sitting at the table with Komarikha beside her when Kuzma entered the house. Kuzma instantly realized what was going on.

"Came running, didn't you?" he growled at Komarikha, whom he would gladly have thrown out. "Sniffed trouble. Like a crow sniffs carrion."

"I didn't come to see you and don't you try to put me out," chirped Komarikha. "I came to see Maria. Her and me's got business together."

"I know what business that is," scoffed Kuzma.

"Whatever it is, that's what I came for."

"Don't we know it!"

Maria, who had not moved a muscle so far, now turned to him.

"Don't butt in where you're not wanted, Kuzma. If you don't like it, go away. Don't be afraid of him, Komarikha. Go on."

"I'm not afraid." Komarikha pulled a pack of cards out of the folds of her skirt and, one eye on Kuzma, began shuffling them. "I'm not robbing anybody, what's there to be afraid of? If a person got upset every time a puppy barked at him he wouldn't last long."

"Now she'll tell you exactly how everything will turn out," sneered Kuzma.

"I'll tell her just what the cards say, no more no less."

"And here was me thinking you'd give her cold facts."

Maria turned her head to say in a pained voice:
"Go away, Kuzma."

Kuzma said no more. He went into the kitchen, but even there he could hear Komarikha spit on her fingers and tell Maria to pull three cards out of the pack.

"Thank God you didn't draw the lock and key, sweetie. That's God's truth, I wouldn't lie to you. Here's the card, see? But you'll take a long journey — an unexpected gain."

"That's a journey to Moscow to have a medal pinned to your chest," Kuzma could not resist calling out.

"And there's worries coming, big worries. See? — here it is. Got to check this three times." He heard Komarikha sweep up the cards. "Here, take the top one off, sweetie. No, not you. Somebody else. Somebody you can be sure won't bewitch the cards. The kids home?"

"No."

"Too bad."

"Come, I'll take it off," said Maria.

"No, no. Spoil everything if you do, the cards won't come right. Kuzma!" she called in a placatory voice. "Come here a minute. Don't scold us, you've got your beliefs, we've got ours. Take this top card off, that's a dear."

"A plague on you!" grunted Kuzma, but he flicked the top card off.

"That's right. My son-in-law didn't believe in it either. He couldn't, he was a Party member. But when he got a summons back in forty-eight, that very evening he comes running to me for a prayer."

She dealt out the cards face down.

"You all come to it sooner or later. It's only when things are going good you laugh at us. Soon as trouble comes, not just little upsets but real trouble, then you remember the Lord God and His servants, the ones you spat on before."

"Rave on, Komarikha," said Kuzma with a weary wave of his hand.

"I'm not raving. I'm telling you God's truth. You don't believe in this fortune-telling? You just *think* you don't. If a war was to start tomorrow you might want to know if you was going to get killed."

"Let's see what the cards say, Komarikha," put in Maria impatiently.

Komarikha turned away from Kuzma and went on explaining what the jack of diamonds and the six of spades meant. Kuzma listened. The card signifying the lock and key didn't turn up this time either.

When Komarikha went home they were left alone in the house. Maria sat with her back to Kuzma gazing out of the window. Kuzma smoked. Maria did not stir. Kuzma tried to discover what she was looking at so intently but could not. He was afraid to speak to her, afraid he might inadvertently say the wrong thing and be unable to right it. But neither could he bear to go on sitting there in silence. His head had begun aching again, sharp little hammer-beats at his temples, each one of which he anticipated and dreaded.

Maria said nothing. But he could sense her every movement; in that silence the least rustle of her dress would have been conveyed to him. He was waiting.

At last she stirred. He started.

"Kuzma," she said, still looking out of the window. Seeing this, he dropped his eyes.

Suddenly he heard a little ripple of laughter. He kept looking at the floor unable to believe it was she who had laughed.

She laughed a second time, but this time it came from a distance. He raised his eyes. She was gone. Looking about him, he got up and cautiously went to the bedroom door. She was lying on the bed.

"Come here," she said without looking at him.

He went to her.

"Lie down beside me."

Gently he let himself down beside her and found she was trembling like a leaf.

Half an hour later she said to him:

"You must have thought I was crazy. I guess I am. First I cry, then I laugh like that. I remembered what somebody told me women do to each other when they're in jail. God, how foul! The very thought of it made me sick. Then I remembered I wasn't there yet, I was still here."

She pressed hard against Kuzma and began to cry.

"Here I am crying again," she whimpered. "Don't let them take me, my darling, don't let them take me, I don't want . . ."

The train drew slowly into the station, gave one last grinding jerk and came to a halt. Kuzma was frozen but he did not climb into the carriage at once. He stood watching. A few passengers jumped out and rushed from one kiosk to another, as if the wind were whirling them about. A ray of light, fragile and transparent as a withered leaf, forced its way through the clouds, testimony to the existence of the invisible sun. It trembled precariously upon the platform and the roofs of the carriages, but presently the wind seized it and drove it away.

On the rare occasions when Kuzma took a journey he was always filled with anxiety. His feeling was that of one who has lost all his possessions and has set out on a hopeless search for replacements. This time the feeling was more acute than ever. He knew the journey must be made but he feared to make it. And then there was this wind. Obviously the wind could in no way be related to Maria's misfortune, nor to his journey, it blew as it had blown in previous years when all had been well with him and Maria. And yet he could not throw off the impression that there was some connection between these apparently unrelated things, that it was not for nothing the wind did not subside. And his being unable to buy a third-class ticket also seemed to have a hidden meaning, as a warning to turn back and go home.

The loudspeaker announced that his train would leave in two minutes. Kuzma hurried to his carriage, but before getting in he cast a look at the station behind him and thought to himself: what will I come back with? Strange though it seemed, the posing of the question calmed him, as if he had murmured a prayer and entrusted his fate to someone else, thereby relieving himself of all further responsibility. He stood at the window watching the station buildings slide into one another, and it seemed incredible that he had been at home that very morning. Aeons of time seemed to have passed since them. He drew a deep breath. Soon his worry about this money would be over — for better or for worse, it would be over. In two days' time the accountant would come back and everything would be decided. Two days was not long. He felt tired, dreadfully tired, and the more dreadful for not being physically tired — he was used to physical tiredness.

"Your ticket, please," said a voice behind him.

Kuzma turned round. A middle-aged carriage attendant, the worse for many years of travelling, was standing at his shoulder. She took his ticket and turned it in her fingers, glancing from the ticket to him and back again several times as if she thought he must have stolen or forged it, and as if she regretted that railway tickets did not carry the passenger's photograph, for nothing could be proved without a photograph. She looked down at his boots and Kuzma looked down at them too. Against the bright glass-clean carpet his mud-stained, outsize, imitation-leather boots looked like tractor treads in a flower garden. He felt ashamed and murmured apologetically:

"I couldn't get a second- or third-class ticket."

"And ain't you glad," she said viciously. Unable to put him out yet unwilling to continue the conversation, she made a sign that he was to follow her.

She knocked at one of the blue doors, slid it back and stood aside so that those within the compartment could get a full view of Kuzma and his boots, his sweater and army bag, then said in a voice as apologetic as the one in which Kuzma had just addressed her:

"Sorry, but here's another passenger . . ." She paused before adding in self-justification: "He's got a ticket."

"Not really!" exclaimed a military man, shutting one eye. Later Kuzma observed that he was a colonel.

"Impossible!" said a man in a white vest that spanned a protruding belly. "Impossible!" he repeated in feigned horror.

The carriage attendant smiled stiffly.

"Yes, he's got a ticket."

"Do you mean to say you couldn't have found us a passenger without a ticket?" chided the colonel with a shake of his head and a cluck of his tongue. "We did ask you, you know."

At that the man in the white vest broke into unrestrained laughter, making quick little chuffs like a motorcycle at half-throttle and the colonel, his bluff called, grinned broadly.

"You're just joking," said the carriage attendant in obvious relief. "I really haven't anywhere else to put him, all the compartments are full." As she went away she herself made an attempt at levity: "But he's got a ticket all right."

"Come in, come in," said the colonel to Kuzma.

Kuzma stepped forward and halted in the doorway.

"That's your bunk," said the colonel nodding toward an upper berth. "Let it down and settle in if you want to. Don't mind us."

"I won't."

"Were you in the war?"

"Yes."

"All the better. Nothing can frighten you after that."

"As to all the compartments being full, she exaggerated, to put it mildly," came the unexpected comment of a man stretched out on the second lower berth. "Next door in No. 9 there are only three passengers too, but she didn't put him in there."

"Oh, no," replied the man in the white vest with meaningful emphasis. "You couldn't expect her to be on such easy terms with *them*."

"And she can be with us?"

"She's used to sizing people up, Gennady Ivanovich. She doesn't need identification papers. Take you, for instance, she saw at first glance you were nothing more than the director of some radio station." The man in the white vest winked at the colonel.

"Not the director of a radio station but chairman of the regional committee for radio and television," Gennady Ivanovich corrected him frostily.

"It's all the same to her you may be sure."

"I can't understand it," and Gennady Ivanovich pursed his lips without specifying what he could not understand. He was lying in pyjamas, with socks pulled up over the bottom of the legs, a small man with a handsome if effeminate face, the most striking feature of which was his big cold eyes. He wore his hair long and slicked down and he turned his head slowly and with dignity. Once it was turned he adjusted it to a graceful pose.

Kuzma was still standing in the doorway. He wanted to take off his sweater but both hooks on his side of the compartment were occupied and he didn't dare hang it on top of that expensive brown coat; not that the sweater was dirty, but he'd worn it, after all. He had no trouble with his army bag, he just put it on the floor near the door.

If he let down his berth he might find a place on it for his sweater — at the foot, say — but he did not know how to let it down. He tried pulling it, but on turning round he met the scornful eyes of Gennady Ivanovich.

"Wait a minute," said the colonel, getting up and shooting the bolt that held the berth. "That's how you do it. The technical age, man. You're a big fellow, a few more pulls like that and you'd have this carriage apart."

"You from the village?" asked the man in the white vest.

"Yes."

"Your bedding must be somewhere up there," said the colonel, pointing to the niche above the door that resembled the stove bunk in a village house. It was into this niche that Kuzma stuffed his sweater because his berth had a white cover on it that he dared not contaminate with his sweater. Thank goodness he had found a place for it. He felt easier. Now all he had to do was to find a place for himself.

"How do you suppose I guessed our friend here was from the village, Gennady Ivanovich?" asked the man in the white vest.

"The country aroma."

"Not at all. If you observe closely you will note that the faces of countryfolk almost without exception are browned by wind and weather."

"And I thought you had scented him out," said Gennady Ivanovich mockingly.

The colonel moved over and Kuzma sat down, first on the edge of the berth, then, seeing that Gennady Ivanovich was aware of his awkwardness, he settled back into a more natural position. The three of them occupied one lower berth, Kuzma next to the door, the man in the white vest next to the window, the colonel between them, while Gennady Ivanovich lay with his knees drawn up on the opposite berth. Kuzma lifted his eyes to Gennady Ivanovich's face and instantly dropped them. Gennady Ivanovich was studying him intently. It seemed to Kuzma that he did not take his eyes off him, but surely that was impossible; it must be that his eyes just gave that impression. It's clear, said Kuzma to himself, he's been bossing people about for a long time and he's not got much softness of heart; he's got a puny voice, can't get very far with a voice like that, so he falls back on his eyes — strikes fear into their hearts with his eyes.

"How are things in the country? Got the harvest in?" asked the man in the white vest.

"Oh, yes."

"A good harvest?"

"Not bad this year. In our district we never have a very big harvest but this year we took in twelve hundredweight of wheat to a hectare."

"It's been a good year for crops in general," said the colonel. "The village will breathe freely this year."

"The village always breathes freely," said Gennady Ivanovich with emphasis. "If the villagers need money they borrow from the state, and to pay it back they borrow again, and that's how it goes until there's nothing left for the state to do but spit on their debts and wipe them off the slate."

"That's hardly a sign of affluence in the village," observed the man in the white vest. "You know that as well as I do."

Gennady Ivanovich sniffed.

"How many workers does your factory lose every autumn when they're sent to help the farmers gather in the crops?" he asked.

"Can't be helped. Apparently there's no other way out. The farmers can't cope with the work themselves."

"Humbug. But even if that was so, why is it that at the end of the year when you're sweating to fulfil your plan at the factory and the village folk have practically nothing to do, they don't send their people to help you as you did them? On an equal footing, like good neighbours."

"Factory work requires special qualifications."

"There's lots of jobs in a factory that can be done without special qualifications."

"You talk as if you knew the work better than I do."

"I don't, of course, but that's not the point. Once a man who had tuberculosis made an interesting confession to me. He said he could have been cured long ago if he'd wanted to be, but he didn't. Sounds crazy? I thought so too until he explained. He spends four or five months every year in hospital completely supported by the state; or in a sanatorium where the patients go fishing and take walks in the woods while the state goes on paying him his salary in full. All his medical treatment is gratis, his food is the best, he's the first to be given a good flat — all the blessings, all the privileges, just because he's sick. So when he comes home from a sanatorium he intentionally begins to drink and smoke, especially if he finds a great improvement in his health. Anything not to lose his privileges. He's got so used to them he can't imagine how to live without them . . ."

"So what?" said the man in the white vest.

"Nothing," replied Gennady Ivanovich with a condescending smile. "Surely you won't deny that the villagers enjoy a rather privileged position. We sell them machines at reduced prices and buy their wheat for inflated prices. With the cunning and hard practical sense typical of country people, they have decided it is not to their advantage to do everything themselves. They could if they wanted to, but they know only too well that at harvest time the towns will send them workers and machines and the government, if necessary, will give them money."

He seems to know more about it than all the rest of us put together, Kuzma thought to himself.

"We all eat their bread," said the man in the white vest.

"So far as I know, your factory doesn't make machines for its own consumption either," observed Gennady Ivanovich, and the man in the white vest conceded the point with the slightest of nods. "You're right when you say we all eat bread, but we must demand from everybody the best they can give in the particular field entrusted to them, and be inflexible in demanding it. It's required of us, why shouldn't it be of them? But for some reason we handle the village with kid gloves, as if it wasn't a part of our state at all. We make deals with it."

"Why are you so set against the village?" asked the colonel calmly, but behind his calmness one sensed he was politely if firmly requesting that this tedious quarrel be ended.

"Set against it? I'm not. I'm only trying to get to the root of its backwardness," said Gennady Ivanovich, loath to give in. "It's my opinion that we ourselves are to blame. People are beginning to realize this. A few towns refused to send workers and students to help the farmers with the harvest, and the farmers, it seems, managed very well without them."

"I dare say there are people a lot better equipped to solve this problem than you and me, Gennady Ivanovich. Why should we waste time on it?" said the colonel, narrowing his eyes good-naturedly but preserving his firmness of tone. "Let's turn to something we're more competent at — a game of preference, for instance."

The man in the white vest instantly perked up.

"That's right. High time to stop this talk or before you know it we'll be quarrelling about God knows what. Who do you think we are, the Council of Ministers?" Turning to Kuzma: "Do you play preference?"

"Preference?" Kuzma did not even know what it was.

"He only plays 'fool'," said Gennady Ivanovich.

"I do know how to play 'fool'," confessed Kuzma innocently.

There was a burst of laughter. The chuff-chuffing of the man in the white vest could be heard from one end of the carriage to the other; Gennady Ivanovich only grinned; the colonel shook all over, and when he stopped he patted Kuzma on the shoulder and said:

" 'Fool' is a good game too, but we need a fourth for preference. We'll play 'fool' next time." He turned to the man in the white vest. "You'll have to go and get that friend of yours again."

"Aye, aye, colonel!" saluted the man, springing to his feet.

They began moving about and talking in loud voices and the compartment was suddenly very crowded. Only Gennady Ivanovich remained lying where he was undisturbed. The man in the white vest pulled on his jacket and buttoned it over his bulging belly, then, clowning, scratched his nose and cocked an eye at Gennady Ivanovich.

"How much did we check to your account yesterday, Gennady Ivanovich?"

"Not much."

"Not enough?"

"Oh, it's enough, but . . ." Gennady Ivanovich glanced at his watch. "The bar's closed, can't buy anything now."

"That can be arranged."

The man in the white vest left the compartment whistling a merry tune, and presently his voice rang out in the corridor:

"Madam! Be so good as to come to our compartment!"

The next moment the carriage attendant appeared in the doorway and fixed her tired eyes on the colonel. He gestured toward Gennady Ivanovich, who addressed her in a brusque manner, not at all as if he were asking a favour:

"One good deed deserves another, my good woman. We took in your passenger with the ticket, and now we should like to ask you to do us a favour in return." He held out some money. "A bottle of cognac if you have no objections. Those people in the bar are your friends, they'll do it for you."

"Very well," she said in a habitual tone of acquiescence.

Kuzma wondered whether he ought to get out of the way by climbing to his upper berth or by standing out in the corridor. In either case he would have to take off his boots, for the carriage attendant would scream at him for dirtying her carpet in the corridor. She puts on airs but she's no better than me, Kuzma said to himself; it's only that she's got a different job. Just see what a job can do to a person!"

As Kuzma pulled off his boots and folded up his linen foot-wrappings he again felt the eyes of Gennady Ivanovich on him. This disconcerted him and excited mixed feelings of shame and anger. There on the floor beside him stood the colonel's polished leather boots. Kuzma hastily shoved his own under the berth and went out into the corridor in his socks. Let them find fault now if they can, he thought viciously.

Standing there at the window he could hear the voice of the carriage attendant delivering the bottle of cognac, then there was a blending of voices, among them the voice of the man who had come to make a fourth for preference. Their laughter and discussion of scores was interrupted by a brief pause during which Kuzma heard the familiar gurgling of poured liquor and a smacking of lips.

The wind had not died down. The sky was grey with dirty streaks, like the surface of a stream in flood. Little settlements of five or six houses were scattered along the railway as if the wind had broken a big station into bits. Kuzma could see the quivering and the tension of the telegraph wires and seemed to hear them humming frantically in their effort to tear themselves loose and find peace.

"Hey, friend!" called out the man in the white vest, causing Kuzma to turn round. "What if you exchange compartments with this fellow here?" indicating the fourth for preference. "His ticket's in the next carriage, second-class; we'd like to be together."

"If you agree I think you'll be even more comfortable there," put in the fourth for preference.

"It's all the same to me," said Kuzma indifferently.

The colonel looked intently at him.

"You don't have to go if you don't want to, it's not obligatory, you know. We just thought we might disturb you if we stay up late playing."

"It's all the same to me," repeated Kuzma.

"Splendid," said the man in the white vest. "I told

you he'd agree. All we've got to do now is tell the two attendants. You can come and visit us if you like," he said to Kuzma. "Right next door, in the next carriage. We'll fix you up in a jiffy."

A minute later Kuzma was wrapping up his feet and pulling on his boots again; with a little leap he caught hold of the sleeve of his sweater and pulled it down from the niche; he picked his bag up off the floor, and there he was, ready to move. Here or there — it really was all the same to him. The only thing he cared about was getting to his destination. If he could move to a third-class carriage he would be happier still. Who knew, perhaps somebody would make such a proposal.

The fourth at preference was waiting to see him to his new compartment.

"Goodbye," said Kuzma, turning round.

"Good luck," said the colonel.

The door of the shop was locked and sealed, the shutters on the windows were bolted down, the paper announcing that the shop was closed for inventory remained pasted to the door. On seeing the paper people would climb the high porch and stand reading it painstakingly. It ought to have been removed but it was left there for Maria's sake. Let people think the inventory was being taken as long as Kuzma was collecting the money, as if this act of generosity could influence her fate.

The shop was a bogey in the community: how many people had suffered because of it! Fortunately they had had Ilia Innokentevich before the war; he ran the shop for nearly ten years without mishap. But Ilia Innokentevich was an experienced trader, his father before him had owned a shop which he himself had inherited; from earliest childhood he had been used to waiting on customers.

After Ilia Innokentevich the trouble began. The first person to suffer was Marusia, a woman whom the vicissitudes of war had brought to their village. Everybody laughed at her Ukrainian accent, but everyone liked her and felt sorry for her. She had confronted war face to face, and had escaped unhurt with her two little children. Marusia had more schooling than many of the women in their village and even so she got caught. Nobody remembered how much money she had been short. They gave her five years, her children were put into a home and nobody had heard anything more of them since.

One-armed Fiodor was found with a surplus, but he was smart enough to find an explanation for it. He said he always kept his own money in the till. At first nobody believed him and he was handed over to the district centre. There, too, he stuck to his story and in the end they let him go, merely forbidding him to run the shop any more. But that, as he never tired of saying afterwards, was the last thing he wanted to do.

Maria's predecessor had been a girl named Rosa, a teenager who had been discharged from a shop in the district centre and sent here. Rosa worked according to her mood: she would open the shop if she felt like it, keep it shut if she didn't. On Sundays and holidays she would go home to the district centre and often stay there for three or four days. When she came back she would bring some semblance of new stock and assert she had been busy in town receiving goods. Try to prove she had been playing truant! The village people did not like her, nor did she conceal from them her contempt for their village and that shop. Time and again she tried to be released, but they could not let her go until someone was found to replace her. Often young boys from the school for mechanics in Alexandrovskoe came to see her and they had a gay old time together. No doubt those boys played no small part in earning Rosa the three-year sentence she was given for a deficit.

After that the shop was closed for four months. Nobody would take the job. The villagers had to go to Alexandrovskoe, twenty kilometres away, even for salt and matches, and sometimes they would find the shop there open, sometimes closed. It is not hard to imagine how irate they felt; there they were with their own shop, ten minutes' walk there and back, and they had to spend an entire day, perhaps even two, buying groceries! The village soviet phoned the trade centre but the only reply they got was: "Find somebody in your own village;" to which the villagers replied, "We've over-filled our prison supply plan, thank you." Everybody was afraid. They had seen with their own eyes what this job led to and the money paid to the shop-tenders was not sufficient to justify the risk.

In the spring there seemed some hope that the shop would be reopened. Nadia Vorontsova, pregnant with her third child, agreed to take over when she was delivered. She still had two months to go, and after the child was born she would have to be home another two months at least. And so they began looking for someone to fill in for those four months. They called one person after another to the village soviet and tried to talk them into it. Maria was among those summoned.

At that time things were not going well for Maria.

Her youngest son was sickly and needed the best she could give him. Maria herself was in poor health; the doctors had warned her not to do any heavy work, but that was easier said than done: what light work had the kolkhoz to offer? She was ashamed even to ask for such a thing. And so she went on lifting and carrying, unsparing of herself. So far no harm had come of it but she feared she wouldn't be able to keep it up for long. If only the kids would hurry and grow up!

At that time they still lived in their old house, which, being next to the shop, was another point in favour of the job. She could keep an eye on the kids and go home and dig the garden when business was slow; any customers who came while she was absent had but to hail her and she would be on the spot in an instant. The job seemed made for her. And they certainly could make good use of the extra income; it would be a long time before she and Kuzma would be out of the woods now that they had borrowed so much money for the new house.

Despite all this, Maria flatly refused the job when she was offered it.

"Better heads than mine have fallen there, I'm taking no chances," she said and went away.

Knowing that Kuzma would be at home the following day, the chairman of the soviet came and spoke to him. He knew what line to take. He began by saying the villagers could not go on without a shop — how long could they go on making the trip all the way to Alexandrovskoe for all their provisions? — Someone had to be found to stand in for Nadia Vorontsova until she could take over, and the best candidate was Maria.

Kuzma said:

"Decide for yourself, Maria," adding jocularly: "If

the worst comes to the worst we can sell our cow, and very glad I'd be; I'm sick and tired of cutting a winter's supply of hay for her every summer."

Marial realized very well that somebody had to be found and so, folding her hands in her lap, she stopped shaking her head obstinately as she had done when the chairman first broached the subject, and listened to him in silence, a pained look on her face. She felt it would be wrong on her part to go on refusing, yet she was terrified by the thought of accepting.

"I don't know, I don't know," she kept repeating.

In the end the chairman got her consent. A week later the shop was opened and four months later, when it was time for Nadia Vorontsova to relieve her, Nadia said she had changed her mind. Maria, frightened to death, closed the shop and demanded that an inventory be taken. Evidently there was no avoiding one's fate. The inventory was satisfactory, the difference amounted to only a few roubles, Maria was reassured by the results and went on working.

That was how it all began.

Compared with work on the *kolkhoz*, work in the shop was easy — dangerous, of course, but easy; if something heavy had to be brought from the storehouse Kuzma would do it, as would any of the other men if asked. Maria opened the shop at eight in the morning and worked until twelve, closed it for lunch until four, opened again at four and worked until eight in the evening. But she was not bound to these hours. She always opened on time, but when business was slack she left one of the boys on duty and came immediately at their call, never causing anyone to wait long for her. Not all the village women understood time according to the clock and even those who did would forget sometimes and come shopping during the interval in the middle of the day. If Maria was home at such times she always opened for them. It didn't do her any harm and might save some old lady from having to slop through the mud from one end of the village to the other a second time. The men, on the other hand, would come at nine or ten at night and ask for a bottle of liquor. Explain as she would that all the bottles were inside the shop and the shop was barred and bolted for the night, they knew only one tune: "Grudge us a little drink, do you?" For such occasions Maria began keeping a case of vodka at home under her bed and in the summer would sell it through the window. If Maria was not at home they would apply to Kuzma and once even Vitka sold three bottles of it.

Maria, however, was very strict about payment. She knew very well that if she let the men have it on credit it would be the women who would suffer. A drunken *muzhik** is certain his impecuniousness is a thing of the moment, tomorrow he will be rich; and so he goes on drinking with no thought of his family. No money, no vodka. There was a time when, by agreement with Mikhail Kravtsov's wife, who had wept herself dry over her husband's drunkenness, Maria refused to give him drink even for money. Mikhail shouted and threatened but Maria was firm; then he brought the chairman of the village soviet and made a scene in front of him:

"Here, you represent soviet power," Mikhail had said to him, "tell me this: is there any law as says a man can't buy what he wants with his own money? Does

---

* *muzhik:* peasant. May be used pejoratively, but in the speech of the peasants themselves it commonly means simply "man".

she think she can make her own laws? Who give her the right, tell me that — who give her the right?"

"Oh, let him have a bottle, and be rid of him," said the chairman.

"Then," said Maria, "bring me an offical paper."

"A paper? What kind of paper?" asked Mikhail, astonished.

"An official paper from your wife saying she doesn't object. Then I'll give it to you."

The chairman shrugged his shoulders and went away. Mikhail went on shouting a while longer, threatened to burn down the shop, stomped out and slammed the door behind him. Later his wife recounted how he had demanded the paper from her and when she refused to give it to him had run after her shaking his fists. Even so he was seen drunk that very evening. Apparently he had bought the liquour through an intermediary, but this was beyond Maria's power to control.

She knew that people enjoyed coming to the shop when she was in it. Women would come even when they had nothing to buy, merely for the pleasure of grouping together to confide their secrets or haul somebody over the coals. The old women sat on wooden boxes that Maria left in the store for that express purpose. In winter the men would drop in for a smoke before work in the morning and Maria would get them to lay a fire in the stove for her. During church holidays whole groups of merry-makers would charge into the shop if it was open, Maria would climb up on the counter to get a better view of their antics, they would lift her off it when they were finished, make her lock up the shop and go off with them.

She found satisfaction in the knowledge that the

village could not do without her. There were not so many it could not do without: the chairman of the village soviet, the chairman of the *kolkhoz*, the doctor, the teachers, the trained specialists, — and Maria. Why, even if the agronomist went away for a month his absence was scarcely noticed, but when the shop had been closed for three days that time she was sick the villagers were at their wits' end. Maria was aware that many would like to become friendly with her, but she tried to keep them all on an equal footing. During the first month of her work in the shop she had received a consignment of oilcloth tablecloths. The village had not seen such tablecloths for a long time and, since there were not enough to go round, some women had come to her house and asked her to supply them "for friendship's sake". Maria had lightly (so as not to offend) but firmly put each of them off with:

"What are you talking about? It's only in the big towns people get things through friendship. There most of the shoppers are strangers to the saleswomen and so naturally they save things for their friends, but here in our village, you're all my friends. How would I look you in the face if I gave to one and didn't give to another? You just get up a little earlier tomorrow morning and take your place in the queue."

When Kuzma stepped outside at dawn the next day there was already a queue on the porch of the shop. Maria leapt out of bed and ran to the shop without doing any of her household chores because she was in no state to do chores with those women standing there waiting for her, and long before the eight o'clock opening hour all the tablecloths were sold.

From almost the first day Maria kept a notebook with the names of debtors in it. Soon the pages were covered with figures, to one figure was added another, then these were crossed out and new ones entered. What else could Maria do when Klava, whom she had grown up with and who was now bringing up two children without a husband, came to her and said her Katia could not go to school without a uniform and she had no money to pay for it at present? Maria rarely gave expensive goods on credit, and when a debt had grown to a big sum she refused further credit until it was paid. Recently, in view of the anticipated inventory, she had collected from all her debtors with the exception of the Chizhovs, who owed her four roubles and eighty kopecks.

As early as the summer she had asked them to make inventory of her stock, when they would send an accountant. She did not know how to press her demand, they made promises, she went away, and in this way the inventory was put off from one month to another. Soon she felt she could not go on working any longer in the dark, without knowing how things stood. When at last the accountant put in an appearance she was dazed rather than frightened by the thought of what the inventory might reveal — so dazed, in fact, that she could hardly answer the man's questions. But not in her worst moments could she have foreseen what actually happened. When the calculations were over and Maria was shown the result she nearly choked and all that evening and the following day she was in a state bordering on suffocation.

She wept, pitying and cursing herself and longing to die. The thought of death brought relief, she seemed to withdraw to another world from where she looked down upon her children and Kuzma, imagining how they would live without her. In pity for herself she forgot her immediate sufferings. But these moments did not last long. The thought of the deficit, like a hangman who released her briefly to go in search of a natural death, always returned to proceed with the execution. Whatever she thought of, wherever she turned, all was painful and horrifying, and she lay prostrate hour after hour.

Later Kuzma came home and told her the *kolkhoz* chairman had promised to lend them the money. At first she did not grasp the meaning of his words but suddenly salvation seemed so close that she feared Kuzma might let it slip through his fingers, and flung her arms round his neck, pulled him down on the bed and begged him to save her with the frenzy of one possessed. At first he shouted at her, then he lay down beside her and stroked her gently until, worn out by a sleepless night, she lost consciousness; it was not sleep she fell into, rather a comatose state induced by exhaustion and relief.

She was awakened by Komarikha. Maria was glad to see her and asked her to tell her fortune. The cards boded well. All will yet turn out right, God willing, thought Maria to herself. Once more hope revived within her and she resolved that she too must canvass the village for money.

Vitka ran home from school with four roubles and eighty kopecks. The Chizhovs had stood waiting for him along the way and told him to give it to his mother.

After the lunch hour Maria went to see Klava, who had been her friend since childhood. Klava sat Maria next to her on the bed, threw her arms about her and began wailing in a loud voice, as village women do at funerals. Maria was so terrified that she broke into tears. Hearing her cry, Klava wailed louder than ever. Maria suddenly realized this was the wrong thing to do so she got up, dried her eyes and left the house, to Klava's great chagrin.

At the turn of the road leading to the river Maria met Nadia Vorontsova, who told Maria she must have been out of her mind when she consented to take over the shop, must have *wanted* to go to prison. Anyone could see what a job like that would lead to.

Without hearing her out, Maria turned and went home. She made no more sallies into the village after that.

Nor did she any longer believe that Kuzma would be able to collect the money.

In the compartment Kuzma had moved to as a favour to the preference players he found an old man and his wife, each with snow-white hair and snow-white faces, as if hair and faces had blanched together. The bedding on one of the upper berths was rumpled so there must have been a third passenger in the compartment who had gone out.

As Kuzma was pulling off his boots again, before climbing up on his berth, a drunken young man lurched in. For a moment he stood staring at Kuzma in astonishment and, after sitting down next to the old lady and getting up again, he grinned, held out his hand to Kuzma and said:

"What's your name?"

Kuzma told him. The grin on the young man's face broadened and vanished.

"I see. Kuzma. We'll remember that. This," he said,

gesturing to the left, "is Grandpa, and this" — to the right, "is Grandma. And this is me. No relation," folding his arms on his chest and laughing.

"Tut, tut, tut!" clucked the old lady with a shake of her head. "First time you've set eyes on the man and you behave like a blinking idiot. Don't pay any attention to him, just make yourself at home," she said to Kuzma. "He's been to the bar again."

"What did I say that I shouldn't?" roared the young man. "Did I hurt his feelings? Kuzma, did I hurt your feelings?"

"So far you've not said anything to hurt my feelings," said Kuzma diffidently.

"Hear that? Kuzma has no complaint to make. Ah, Grandma, Grandma, always finding fault with me!"

He sat down next to her and, winking at Kuzma, put his arms round her.

"Get away!" she said angrily. "Goodness, how much longer will this journey take! I'm sick to death of him."

"Come, come, are you really sick of me? Lived with your old man all your life and aren't sick of him and I put my arms round you just once and you're sick to death of me. Grandpa!" he called out. "Shall I take her away from you?"

"If you can," replied the old man serenely.

The young man made no reply. For a little while he contemplated the old man drunkenly, then the old lady, and he recited in a tired voice:

"Once upon a time there lived an old man and an old woman . . ."

"Tut, tut, tut," the old lady clucked indignantly.

"The old man got angry with his old woman and gave her a whack in the belly."

The young man broke off and said with animation:

"Did you beat your old lady when you were young, Grandpa?"

"Never in my life have I laid a finger on her," said the old man with dignity.

"Not once?"

"Not once."

"You'll not find men like my husband nowadays," said the old lady.

"Oh, no, of course not," scoffed the young man. He expected somebody to take him up on this but all were silent. With his face all screwed up he studied each of them in turn, then said to Kuzma with obvious effort:

"So you're riding in our compartment, are you?"

"Yes."

"Good."

He dropped his eyes and sat staring at the floor between his feet. The carriage rocked with gentle regularity. The young man's hands and head drooped and he closed his eyes. A passing train went roaring by but he seemed not to hear it.

Kuzma climbed up on his berth. Down below the old lady shook the young man.

"Lie down, you're uncomfortable. Here, lie on my berth."

"Haven't I got one of my own?"

Slowly, clumsily, he managed to climb up, and there he lay mumbling to himself.

Kuzma turned to look at him. The young man's eyes were closed and there was nothing written on his face but sleep.

Kuzma, too, closed his eyes, but he did not fall asleep at once. The clicking of the wheels grew louder and softer in turn and Kuzma, frightened, opened his eyes and listened. The wind was still blowing. He huddled under the blanket and tried once more to fall asleep. As last he succeeded.

He had a strange dream. He seemed to be at a *kolkhoz* meeting where the question of collecting money for Maria was being discussed. There were so many people that the hall was overcrowded. Some were standing in the doorway, others had brought stools with them. And still they came.

"*Kolkhozniks!*" called out the chairman. "The suggestion has been made that we shut the doors. The hall won't hold everybody who would like to attend anyway.

The doors were shut.

"First we must elect a presidium," said the chairman. "The administration nominates Maria and Kuzma, we can't nominate their children because they're not of age. All those in favour, raise your hands."

All were in favour. Amid general applause Maria and Kuzma took their places at the table on the platform. Kuzma looked at the audience and for some strange reason could not find a single familiar face. "Maria," he whispered in alarm, "look, these aren't our people." "What are you talking about, Kuzma?" she replied. "They're all ours." When the applause died down Kuzma again studied the faces and this time recognized them.

"*Kolkhozniks!*" went on the chairman. "The suggestion has been made that we help Maria."

Another burst of applause.

"The administration has considered the question and

decided the best thing to do is to count how many of us are here and then, knowing how much money Maria needs, calculate how much each of us has got to pay. Any other suggestions?"

"No."

"Then count how many people in each row. But I warn you anybody who tries to pass himself off for two will be put out."

While they were counting, Kuzma tickled Maria in the ribs for joy. She jerked away and laughed. "Shame on you," she whispered. "People don't do things like that on the platform. Behave yourself." He grew quiet.

"Two hundred and twenty-five people," somebody cried out.

"Divide one thousand roubles by two hundred and twenty-five people," figured the chairman on the platform, "and it comes to four roubles and forty kopecks each."

"Let's round it out to five roubles each," called out several people at once.

Suddenly the table at which Maria and Kuzma were seated was turned into a coffer into which innumerable hands threw money from all sides. In five minutes the coffer was full. Maria was so touched she burst out crying and tears the size of green peas fell with a sharp ring on the money and rolled inside the heap.

"Everybody paid?" called out the chairman. "If so, the counting committee can begin its work."

A few people stepped out of the audience and began counting. They sorted the money into five, three, and one-rouble piles, writing the total sum of each pile on top as in the bank.

"One thousand one hundred and twenty-five roubles," they announced at last.

The chairman shook his head disapprovingly:

"That one hundred and twenty-five is extra. What are we to do with it?" he said.

"Let them take it all," somebody suggested.

"Can't do that," said the chairman. "A hundred and twenty-five roubles is a lot of money. Here's what I say: let's put all the money in the music room and each of us will go in separately. Those who need money will help themselves to a rouble or two. Don't make a lot of noise or raise a howl. We're not millionaires. You don't have to take any money at all if you don't want to, but everybody's obliged to go in so that we won't know who took it and who didn't. Anybody got a better suggestion?"

"No!"

The money was taken out. One by one the people got up, went into the music room and returned to their places. The last person to go was Komarikha. Kuzma watched her jump up, look furtively around and close the door behind her. The next moment a scream came from the music room and Komarikha came running out with wild eyes, shouting:

"There's nothing there! Not a single kopeck! I wanted to take just a rouble!"

The audience burst out laughing. People rocked and roared and held their sides, some of them pointed gleefully to Komarikha who was standing in front of them with her mouth open. Presently she too burst out laughing. Kuzma watched them in horror and astonishment. Unable to understand what was going on, he glanced at Maria. She was sitting on her haunches, writhing with laughter.

Kuzma woke up and heard the old lady say to the old man:

"Give me the hot-water bottle, Sergei, I'll fill it."

She went out of the door hugging the bottle to her chest. All was quiet. You couldn't hear the clicking of the wheels on the rails unless you listened for it. The light which entered through the window was grey and weary, lashed by the gale outside. Once inside the gently swaying carriage it was still, suffusing the compartment with the cosiness of evening. The young man was sleeping, with his chin on a Gargantuan fist.

The old lady came back with a bulging hot-water bottle and thrust it under her husband's blanket. In the mirror on the door Kuzma could see the old man stretch out his legs and lie still.

"Does it hurt today?"

"No, not today."

"Good."

They talked in quiet, intimate voices that seemed almost part of the silence. Kuzma knew he could not go back to sleep again but he did not want to admit it to himself; if he did he would have to think or occupy himself in some way. He lay with his eyes closed. He was afraid above all to think about his dream, to speculate on the meaning of it. Why in the world should he have dreamed such a thing? It meant nothing, of course. His mind had been dwelling on one thing for so long that when he slept it crept back into his head, that was all. Yet he was more disturbed than ever. Everything had sinister meaning: the wind, his bad luck with his railway ticket, and now this dream. Could it be that all his efforts would come to nothing?

"Sergei," he heard the old lady say, and Kuzma was glad of something to distract him from his fears.

"Sergei, do you suppose they've had our wire by now?"

"Oh, yes. They must have," replied the old man.

"And they're expecting us."

A smile of unconcealed joy made her broad face broader than ever. The smile lingered a while before fading away.

On the same day that Kuzma went to see Evgeny Nikolaevich the headmaster sent a boy to Kuzma's house.

"Evgeny Nikolaevich said to tell you he's busy tomorrow and can't go to the centre, but he'll go the day after tomorrow and do what he said."

"That's all right," said Kuzma.

Old Gordei was visiting Kuzma at the time, sitting cross-legged on the floor in front of the stove.

"Did he promise you much?" asked the old man.

"A hundred roubles."

"Could have given more, he's got money."

"He says he hasn't."

"*He* says!" jeered the old man. "Oh, of course, where's *he* to get money from? He's got learning, he has, the old goat. But he's got more tricks in his bag than learning in his head. You and me don't know how to play tricks, we give ourselves away right from the start, but when Evgeny Nikolaevich plays tricks on the likes of us we start wriggling like we was the guilty ones and not him. Oh, he's a learned one, he is!"

Kuzma said nothing.

Old Gordei had been sitting there for an hour and a half. Kuzma had things to attend to and there he was sitting and listening to the old man's babble. He could not offend him by telling him he was in the way, and so Kuzma just sat and held his tongue, hoping the old man would get sick of doing all the talking himself and go home.

Old Gordei was over seventy but not too much the worse for age. True, in the last year he had developed a lean to one side, for which the villagers nicknamed him Lieutenant Schmidt, after the steamboat *Lieutenant Schmidt* which had been plying their river for thirty odd years and had developed a list to starboard after the war. Several times the old boat had been put up for repairs but each time it reappeared on the river with the same list, to the secret delight of the villagers along the banks.

Old Gordei's crookedness seemed no handicap to him for he hopped about as lively as ever. At night he served as watchman in the *kolkhoz* workshops and in the daytime, for want of anything better to do, went wandering about the village. Whenever he settled himself on a neighbour's floor, and took out his ancient pipe with a hole burnt in the bottom, you could be sure it would be a long stay. There was nothing urgent in his life. He lived alone in a little neglected hut at the edge of the village, having left his big house to his son and his son's big quarrelsome family, with whom he could not get on. When Gordei's wife had died he left and moved into the "henhouse", as he called his hut. It really was as dirty as a henhouse. The old man was not used to cleaning up after himself and the only person who did it for him was Komarikha, a distant relative of his, who came to sweep out the accumulated refuse no oftener than once a month or even once in two months. But old Gordei did not notice her efforts.

Now he settled himself more comfortably in front of Kuzma's fire, pulled up one knee so that he could rest an elbow on it, and said:

"Confound it all! — me without a kopeck. You'd have no trouble if I had any money."

"Don't worry about it," Kuzma waved the suggesting aside. "Of course you've got no money. Where would you get it from?"

"That's it; you and me wouldn't be sitting here twiddling our thumbs if I had it, you'd just come and take it from me."

"I'll manage somehow," said Kuzma, trying to reassure the old man that he could get by without him. "Why should I drag you into this?"

The old man took this as an insult and said nothing. He knocked the ash out of his pipe onto his knee, blew it off and filled his pipe again, diligently packing the tobacco in the bowl with his thumb. He had no intention of going away, and as he smoked another pipeful he forgot his resentment.

"So you say you went to see Evgeny Nikolaevich?" he began all over again.

"Yes."

"He's got money, he just didn't want to give it to you. Want me to go and ask him for it?"

"No, I'll find it. It's my worry, not yours. You'd do better to go home and take a nap."

This time the old man really did take offence.

"You talk like a baby, Kuzma. Think it's myself I'm worried about? I've lived all my life without money and can live without it to the end. I've got my own tobacco and a crust of bread and I can light my pipe from a coal. As for money — makes no difference to me whether I have it or not."

"I know," said Kuzma in a conciliatory tone.

"And I've got rags enough to cover me till the day of my death. If it's a drink I want I can fit up a still and turn out liquor that'll burn like pure alcohol. How often have these hands of mine had money in 'em? Could count the times on me ten fingers. Ever since I was a kid I was taught to make things myself and live by my own labour. If need be I can knock a table together or make felt boots as good as any. Back in 1933, during the famine, I even got salt from the salt marshes. It's nowadays people can't live without the shops; time was when they only went to them twice a year. Lived on their own food. And they lived, mind you, didn't die. Now a person can't take a step without money. Money everywhere you turn. Trip over it. Everybody's forgot how to do things themselves. And why should they? They get everything in the shops. As long as they got money. Lucky the family as hasn't got money, their kids won't forget how to use their hands, and they'll learn to rely on themselves instead of on money. Makes spongers of everybody. Big folks and little folks alike."

"Don't get so excited, Grandad."

"It's God's truth I'm telling you. Who ever heard in the old days of village folk helping each other for money! Need help building a house? Resetting a stove? Plenty of volunteers, and that's what it was called — 'help.' If the owner had home-brew he'd give his neighbours a treat, if he hadn't they knew he'd help them in his turn. Not so nowadays. All for money. Plough your potato patch — ten roubles; bring you a load of hay — another ten, and if he turns away so's not to sneeze in your face — that's another rouble. Everybody works for money and lives for money.

Looking for gain in everything. That's what we've come to."

"Drop it, grandad, we could go on like this forever."

"I've said all I had to say. You think I've gone soft in the head just because I'm old? I know what I'm talking about. I've lived longer'n you on this earth and seen all sorts of people."

His pipe had almost gone out and he hastened to suck it back to life. This done, he smoked in silence, with his eyes shut. Kuzma hoped he would go now. Night was falling, the unmilked cow out in the yard lowed plaintively from time to time, but Maria had gone out after dinner and the cow complained in vain.

"If you start from the top of the village," resumed the old man suddenly, "I'm thinking who you'd ought to speak to," he continued by way of explanation. "Who's got money up there at the top of the village? You've spoke to Evgeny Nikolaevich. Ekh! You don't want to put your finger in *that* man's mouth. That man lets out a fart up there on his hill and the whole village stinks, but when it comes to offering a neighbour help he'll kiss a rouble ten times before he'll part with it, as if he was giving away his life's blood. And so he is. He'll die early, straining himself like that."

"To hell with him, I'm sick of hearing about Evgeny Nikolaevich," said Kuzma crossly.

Old Gordei appeared not to hear him.

"Piotr Larionov's got nothing to give. He's a simple soul, he is. He'd give you the whole world if it was his. Funny thing: there's Evgeny Nikolaevich living next door to Pior Larionov, and the two of them as different as heaven and earth. Born in the same place, speak the same language, and don't understand each other." The old man shook his head in mute astonishment, then:

"You might speak to our agronomist, but he's just come back from a sanatorium. No harm in asking, maybe he didn't spend everything on his treatment. They say he earns a lot; gets a salary from the government and the *kolkhoz* pays him workday units as well. That true?"

"Yes."

"Then go and speak to him. He may give you something. If he don't, go to his neighbour Misha." The old man gave a little laugh like a cough. "A lot you'll get from him! He's drunk up all his money for the next three years to come. There's a drunk for you! Let's see now, who else could you ask?" the old man mused. "I'm stumped, Kuzma. Like as if folks don't live bad, but daily living eats up all their earnings. Nothing left over to lend. They've all got kids to look after. Lucky for you your trouble came at the fat season, so to speak; if it'd waited till spring you might be going from house to house begging seed and potatoes instead of money. And who would you sell them to? For a hundred kilometres all around — nothing but *muzhiks* like yourself."

The old man had put into words Kuzma's own fears. There was very little money in the village and probably no surplus at all. The *kolkhoz* members had received their workday payment in grain alone; there was nobody to sell this grain to, and even if there had been the price was trifling. But Kuzma could not accept the old man's conclusions that things were hopeless. He had no right to think so, and he said:

"We'll find a way out, Grandad."

"A way out," scoffed the old man. "The way out's hid under the mare's tail, that's where to look."

"Some folks have got money."

"You think so?"

"You mean to say Stepanida has no money when she sells a cow or a bull to the *kolkhoz* every blessed year? If you ask me she's got thousands put away."

"You're right there. Stepanida's got money."

"So there you are. Stepanida's got money. The tractor drivers ought to have some, too. During the harvest season they get bonuses and extra pay."

"That season's long past now."

"Folks've got money, Grandad. You mean to say I can't collect what I need from this entire village? You mean to say they won't see me through my trouble? I don't believe it, Grandad; they will."

"I never said they wouldn't."

"Good," said Kuzma, taking heart from his own words. "You and me aren't going under, Grandad. You go to your job now and I'll do the rounds — take a sack with me and put my gleanings in it. A pittance here, a pittance there. It all adds up. Then I'll hire you to guard my sack."

"You *are* a joker, Kuzma," said the old man, his face creasing into a smile. He rolled over onto his hands and knees and from that position pulled himself to his feet.

"I'll drop in to find out how things are going with you," he said as he rubbed the side he sagged on.

"Do, Grandad. Better to watch my money-bags than those heaps of old iron you guard. As a watchman you suit me: you smoke a pipe, so you won't be tempted to roll yourself cigarettes with my banknotes."

"Khe-khe-khe," laughed the old man, and immediately began to cough.

When a man is getting on for fifty it is hard to say

whether he has friends or not. So many and such varied people have passed in and out of his life as friends, like guests to his home, that he has learned to look upon even those closest to him with equanimity and reserve. He may see them no oftener than others and share no secrets with them, and yet in his heart of hearts he feels (if precariously, hardly trusting his own judgment) that there are those who, in time of need, will understand and support him.

That evening Kuzma went to see Vasily. Directly after the war he and Vasily had worked in shifts loading and driving the *kolkhoz*'s only truck. Later Kuzma was given an American Studebaker and the old truck was left to Vasily, who, to everyone's astonishment, kept it going a remarkably long time before it fell to pieces. Still later the farm had bought two new ZIS'es, one for each of the drivers, but Vasily did not work on his for long. His sight began to fail, a check-up was made at just this time, and he was disqualified. For the last four years he had been working as leader of a field team growing vegetables.

He and Kuzma saw each other almost every day, as did most of the members of the *kolkhoz*, but with the years they grew apart. Their only intercouse was the few words they exchanged during chance meetings. Nevertheless nothing had supplanted the old feeling of friendship Kuzma had for Vasily and he cherished this feeling, nourishing it on kindly thoughts of him. Deep in his heart Kuzma was sure he could count on him now. The only other man he regarded as a friend was the chairman of the *kolkhoz*, but Kuzma usually kept his distance lest he be accused of currying favour with the bosses.

Vasily received Kuzma with no show of surprise or

joy, simply shaking his hand in silence as men do and asking how things were. It was evident he had heard about Kuzma's trouble and did not know what to say, not being one who oh'd and ah'd and offered useless advice. So they sat and smoked. Vasily's wife kept coming into the kitchen and looking with awe and pity at Kuzma, but, hearing nothing of interest, she did not stay. Neither she nor her husband found the courage to ask him questions and Kuzma himself volunteered no information. He felt like one spending the night among strangers in a strange village: it is still too early to go to bed and there they sit, he the wayfarer and they his hosts, not really making each other's acquaintance, merely sitting and killing time.

At last Kuzma got up and took his leave. Vasily saw him out. They stood a while at the gate shifting uncomfortably, each aware of the embarrassment of the situation. Vasily said:

"Drop in again when you've got time, Kuzma."

"I will," said Kuzma.

It was then that Kuzma first thought of appealing to his brother. If worst came to worst and he did not collect the money in the village he could make the long trip to the city and ask Alexei for it. He had heard that his brother was well off. Kuzma had never visited his brother. The last time they had seen each other was seven years before, at their father's funeral. That had been in the autumn, at the very peak of the harvest season, and Alexei had spent only two days in the village, going home directly after the funeral. He promised to come back for the forty-day memorial feast when all the family would gather, but he did not come and the feast was held without him. Two months or so later he wrote that he had been away on a business trip.

Kuzma rarely thought about Alexei. Only when he recalled his father and mother. When he recalled them it was only natural for him to remember that he was not an only son, that he had a brother. But he and his brother had lost contact so completely that the very thought of Alexei seemed unreal to Kuzma, as if it was a thought prompted by somebody else, not the natural issue of his own mind. And again he would forget all about him. It seemed they were not permanently brothers, but only on their occasional meetings, and also far back in their childhood when they had grown up together in the village.

Three years before, Maria had gone to consult a physician in the city and had spent two nights at Alexei's. When she came back she said she would have felt better staying with strangers. That Alexei and his wife were well off she reported without surprise or envy. "They have a TV and a washing-machine and all that, and they watched me as if they were afraid I'd break something, and his wife followed me about with a rag, wiping up my tracks after me. They weren't interested in anything I said. You and me are nothing to them, Kuzma. I wouldn't go back there, not for a mountain of diamonds!"

The previous year Kuzma had given his brother's address to Mikhail Medvedev, who had studied with Alexei in the same factory school after the war. The *kolkhoz* was sending Mikhail to the city for a study course in agriculture, and he expressed a wish to see his old friend. When he came back to the farm Kuzma said:

"Well, did you go and see my brother?"

"Yes, I dropped in."

"How is he?"

"Oh, he's all right. Healthy. Works as foreman in a factory," was his evasive reply.

Later, when Mikhail was in his cups, he said:

"He didn't deny knowing me, but that was all. Didn't accept me as a friend. Didn't so much as offer me a drink."

As he reflected on these things Kuzma concluded that, as far as the village was concerned, his brother was a slice severed from the loaf. Nothing would induce him to come back and see how his kinsmen and friends were getting on and to stir old feelings by roaming through scenes connected with his childhood. It would give him no pleasure to talk to the villagers, finding out from them what had become of Grandpa Fiodor, who had once switched him with nettles, or of the girls he had once seen home from a village hop. In his heart Kuzma was hurt with Alexei, but it was a mild sort of hurt. After all, Alexei answered for what he did, he was no longer a child. And the village paid him back in kind: as he forgot the village, so did the village forget him.

But surely if Kuzma came and asked for his help Alexei would not refuse it. He was his brother, his own flesh and blood. He must have some savings put by. Kuzma would explain that the loan was not for long, in a little over two months the *kolkhoz* would advance him the money and Kuzma would instantly pay him back. How was it Kuzma had not thought of applying to his brother sooner?

To reassure Maria, Kuzma said:

"If I can't collect as much as I need here I'll go and get it from Alexei."

"He won't give it to you," said Maria after a little pause.

This was enough to shatter Kuzma's conviction that he ought to apply to his brother.

All his life Kuzma had maintained a very simple attitude towards money: when he had it, well and good; when he didn't, he must do without. This attitude was the natural result of his never having enough money. His family did not suffer from lack of food. Kuzma always earned more than enough wheat and grain even in times of bad harvest, and they got their meat and milk from their own barnyard. But money . . . He had heard of *kolkhozes* that paid their members as much as a rouble and a half or two roubles a workday, and he did not doubt that this was so. But in their *kolkhoz*, cut out of the northern forest, with scraps of field spread all over the place, nobody had ever been paid more than half a rouble a workday. For the last three years, ever since Kuzma had borrowed all that money from the *kolkhoz* to build his house, his salary in money amounted to almost nothing. All that Maria made in the shop was spent on the boys. When there are four of them in a family the clothes go as if devoured by flames. The remarkable thing was that Maria managed to make ends meet and her sons always looked neat and clean and were dressed as well as the rest of the village children. The older ones were supplied with new clothes when they needed them, the younger ones, as had been the custom from time immemorial, wore their hand-me-downs.

Kuzma never looked upon himself as poor. His family had all the essentials of life, none of them went unclothed or unshod. There was no one he envied. He regarded people who had more than he did with the same serenity with which he regarded those who were taller than he was. Was he to walk about on his toes to make up the difference in height? To each man his own destiny.

Kuzma could not understand and made no effort to understand how people could have money left over. For him money was something to patch the holes, a bare necessity. One had to put by stores of meat and grain, one could not raise a family without them. But a store of money seemed silly, even ludicrous. He was content with what he had.

On the wall of the post office, which also housed a savings bank, hung a poster portraying a rosy-cheeked young man (as unlike anyone in their village as the man in the moon), who kept urging everybody to "Watch your roubles mount: Open a bank account!" It had been there for years. When Kuzma entered the post office the man's eyes looked past him. Just for the fun of it Kuzma took various positions in front of the poster, but no matter where he stood the eyes looked past him. Kuzma found this amusing.

And now he suddenly needed a lot of money. Why had money picked him for its victim? He had never had serious dealings with money. Perhaps it was for precisely this reason it was taking revenge on him. Like it or not, he was forced to think of only one thing: were could he get money? He had applied first to **Evgeny Nikolaevich** because it was the common opinion that the schoolmaster had money. To whom was he to turn now? Even before old Gordei's visit he had, in imagination, canvassed the entire village and come home empty-handed. Some of his neighbours had more, some had less, but all had their own needs, their own holes that needed to be patched.

He could not bear the thought of asking them for money. He would simply pay them a visit and say nothing. The mere fact of his coming ought to speak for him. But when he actually went to them, they, too, kept silent and their silence in its turn said more, and said it more clearly than the most eloquent words could have done. He would take his leave and go to the next house — not the next in line, there was no sense in going to every house, only to the houses where he thought there might be money. But you couldn't spot money from the front door; it is always hidden away — in crevices in the wall where cockroaches nest, in the pockets of old jackets, at the bottom of trunks. They say money fears the light of day. If banknotes, like family photographs, were hung up on the wall, Kuzma would know what houses to enter, and he would also know how much to take without inconveniencing the owners. But his position was as puzzling in houses where there was no money at all as in those where it was hidden away. The owners of both met him in silence and he had no means of telling what lay behind that silence — poverty, parsimony, or reluctance to put themselves in his shoes.

And yet Kuzma hoped things would turn out differently. If one neighbour said nothing, another would understand what Kuzma was going through and say simply: "We've saved up fifty roubles towards an outboard motor, but you need it now. Here, take it." He would hand over the money casually and just as casually Kuzma would take the warm, thin bundle of notes and slip it into his pocket and he and his friend would go on chatting about this and that, neither of them even mentioning the word money again.

Kuzma went to Vasily first so as to get some idea of his chances; he wanted to begin with success. Kuzma went home and sank rather than sat down on the stool next to the window, at a loss as to what to do next. It was then that he remembered his brother, and cheered up.

He knew very well there was money in the village — not much, perhaps, but some. Everybody was trying to better his circumstances. A *muzhik* would walk about in ragged trousers so as to save up money for a motorcycle. What did he care about patches when his heart's desire was to own a motorcycle?

It was on these savings Kuzma had counted. As long as the price of a motorcycle had not been saved, the money lay useless, doing nobody any good. Why, then, should not Kuzma have it to save Maria? Surely nobody would refuse it him!

Somebody knocked on the closed shutters of the window.

"Who's there?" asked Kuzma, getting up.

"Come outside a minute."

Maria came running out of the bedroom, her hands clutching her throat.

"Who is it?"

"Sounds like Vasily. What are you afraid of?"

"I don't know."

Vasily was standing at the gate, a tall broad silhouette against the darkness.

"Won't you come in?" asked Kuzma.

"I'm sorry for what happened," said Vasily. "You didn't mention what you wanted when you came to see me. What was it?"

"You know without my telling you."

"I s'pose I do."

"So what's there to say? I know you've got no money," said Kuzma with feeble hope.

"I haven't. The old lady's got twenty roubles stowed away somewhere and that's all."

"Come inside."

"No. We can't talk in there. Let's sit down here."

They sat down on a bench beside the gate, lit up and stared into the darkness without speaking, but it was an understanding silence they preserved, not a strained one. To the right of them could be seen lights in village windows and sometimes a voice would be carried to them, sometimes a burst of laughter from the direction of the club-house. Though it was not yet late the village, gradually adjusting itself to the shortening days, was settling down for the night. Sounds and voices became fewer and fewer.

They finished their cigarettes and almost simultaneously ground the ends under their feet. Again they sat in silence until Kuzma shifted his position and said:

"Funny how a person can get struck down without even suspecting the blow's waiting for him."

"True," said Vasily.

"Why, even yesterday everything was all right."

"And tomorrow it'll be the next fellow's turn. Maybe not in our village, in another, and then back to our village — my turn or somebody else's. That's why we've got to stick together."

"H'm."

"I know Evgeny Nikolaevich is giving you something. Who else?"

"Nobody so far. I want to go to Stepanida tomorrow but I haven't much hope."

"Stepanida?" Vasily shook his head doubtfully, then, after a brief pause: "Let's go and see her now. The two of us'll squeeze her. She's in my team, maybe she'll be ashamed to turn you down in front of me."

"Come on. Before we change our minds."

"How did you know about Evgeny Nikolaevich?" asked Kuzma along the way.

"My old lady told me. Guess he spread the news himself. He likes to brag about his good deeds."

"I'm as good as an astronaut these days," said Kuzma wryly. "The whole village is talking about me."

"Naturally. Watch out when you go out to the privy. Somebody may be lying in wait to snap your picture. Well, a joke's a joke, but it's true: everybody's counting your roubles."

"You don't have to tell Stepanida what we've come for. She's probably been expecting me since morning."

"And found a safe place to hide her fortune in."

They laughed. With Vasily beside him Kuzma felt better; no longer was his trouble a hard lump pressing on one spot; it had softened and spread out, making it easier to bear. And while he had little hope of getting anything out of Stepanida, he knew he and Vasily would leave her house together and would talk it over together before they parted and perhaps draw up a plan for the next day. That steadied his nerves and kept him from thinking of one and the same thing all the time.

Stepanida lived in a big two-storey house with her niece Galia, who had moved in with her after Stepanida's sister died. Galia was not yet seventeen years old but had long outgrown Stepanida in height and width. They could not get on together, indeed they quarrelled like cat and dog, and when the big house became too small to contain them they ran outside and shrieked at each other so loudly that the neighbours' dogs would glance cautiously round, put their tails between their legs and slink to the other side of the street.

When the two men came in Stepanida began fidgeting and uttering little cries of pleasant surprise, but her face assumed a guarded expression, as much as to say: what can have brought them? Time and again the smile fell off her lips, but she always jerked it back and went on fidgeting, biding her time. The men took off their things and sat down on a bench. On hearing their voices Galia came out of another room in a tight short skirt that revealed her sturdy rounded knees.

"Who invited you?" Stepanida barked at her, happily seizing upon this outlet for her emotions. To the men: "Ain't she a beauty, eh? You might at least cover your nakedness!"

"There's nothing to show they haven't seen already," replied Galia languidly.

"Phoo, have you no shame at all?"

"Have you?"

"Get out of here!"

With a wink to the men, Galia went out.

"She's wore me out," began Stepanida plaintively. "The little beast! I wouldn't wish her on my worst enemy. Sucked the last drop of blood out of me, that's what she has!"

"As if there was any blood in you to suck!" called out Galia from the next room. "It's swill that runs in your veins."

"Hear that? To your one word she'll answer ten, to your ten — a thousand. How I stand it is more than I can say. A fine thing to have to put up with in my old age!"

"You wouldn't quarrel all the time if you had something better to do," said Vasily. "Look here, Stepanida, are you going to give us something or not?"

Stepanida, taken unawares, screwed up her eyes.

"You *are* a foxy one, Vasily."

"Foxy? I'm putting it straight enough. Me and Kuzma kept thinking to ourselves on the way here: Stepanida's our one hope; whatever she's got she'll give."

"Oh, Vasily, aren't I good to those as are good themselves? Can anyone say I grudge the little I've got? That's what I keep it for; a nice one I'd be if a good man came to see me and I had nothing to offer him."

"Exactly."

Stepanida gathered up her skirts and climbed down into the cellar, from where she handed up a green bottle with sealing-wax and dirt clinging to it. Kuzma took it from her and held it up to the light, peering at it with one eye.

"It's the real thing," said Stepanida.

"That's what you should have begun with instead of that quarrel with Galia," said Vasily in a lighter vein.

"Don't speak of her!"

Stepanida wiped the bottle on her skirt, stood it in

the middle of the empty table, and hurried out to the shed to fetch some food to go with it.

"Don't bring up the question of money yet," warned Vasily. "All in good time."

"Best if you tell her."

Galia came out of the next room and the bottle caught her eye.

"Oho! How did you ever make the old bitch cough up!"

"What a little snake you are, Galia," said Vasily angrily. "Anybody ask you for your opinion? No. So shut up. You aren't big enough to talk to me like that."

"Oh, is that so? How would you like me to talk to you? 'Yes, sir; no, sir; by your leave, sir'?"

"There's no talking to you, you're too dumb."

"So don't talk to me, I haven't asked you to. A lot of difference it makes to me! D'you think I don't know what you've come for?"

"Shut up!" hissed Vasily.

"Aha! That scared you! Don't worry, I won't tell. But don't make me mad. I might even help you if you behave decent." She looked at Kuzma sentimentally: "Poor Maria!" Then to Vasily: "You've got no right to shout at me just because you're older. Shout at your wife. Thank God I'm not under your heel."

"We've had enough lip from you," said Vasily, choking back his anger.

"You've picked the wrong lady to bully this time."

"That'll do now," put in Kuzma in an attempt to make peace.

Stepanida came hurrying in and fussed about the table. When she had seated the men she began intoning her usual lament, which took the place of grace.

"I've got nothing to offer, it's a disgrace to invite

you to such a table, if I'd known you were coming I'd have got something ready but all unexpected like this, it's a disgrace, a disgrace . . ."

"You don't have to make excuses, Stepanida. A person could feast a week on this food," Vasily reassured her.

"You do say such things, Vasily!"

Three glasses of vodka were poured out. At just the right moment, when the three had touched glasses and were taking a deep breath before gulping down the fiery liquid, in came Galia.

"And what about me?"

Stepanida almost jumped off the bench in fury.

"Now what do you call that? Was there ever another like her? At that very moment she had to come in to spoil our appetites! Oi, oi, oi! What have I done to have such a plague put on me?"

With a gloating smile Galia placed an empty glass in front of Stepanida and helped herself to her aunt's full one.

"Put it down, blast you! Put it down, I say!"

"Fill that one and I'll put this one down."

"If I wasn't ashamed in front of these men I'd teach you how to talk to your own aunt! I'd show you!"

"Wouldn't you just!"

"A she-devil, that's what she is!" cried Stepanida, but she poured some vodka into the empty glass. Galia took it, filled it to the brim from her aunt's glass and held it out to clink with the men's.

"Isn't it rather early for you to be taking a man's size drink?" said Vasily. Galia studied him with half-closed eyes as he added: "If you can drink like this while you're still wet behind the ears, what'll you do next?"

"Hear that? Listen to what clever people have to tell

you if you won't listen to what your poor aunt's got to say."

Galia did not take her eyes off Vasily:

"You know where you can go to with your sermons," she said tranquilly. "I can take care of myself without your help, thank you."

"How dare you talk like that?" shrieked Stepanida, trembling all over. "Do you think he's your uncle that you can be so familiar with him? You must be mad!"

"Let him hold his tongue, or I'll give all his secrets away."

Kuzma nudged Vasily under the table as a warning to leave Galia alone. "Some poor bastard's walking around without knowing there's a noose waiting for him to stick his head through," said Vasily. "Doesn't know what he's in for."

"It won't be *you* at any rate."

"That's something to be thankful for."

"Is that why you licked you lips when I came in in that short skirt?"

Kuzma interrupted:

"Perhaps we'd better pour the drinks back and just sit and listen to your smart remarks?"

They drank. Galia winked at Kuzma and rolled her eyes in Stepanida's direction. Kuzma gave a little shake of his head. She couldn't wait to see them get the money out of her aunt, the little snake. Volunteered to help, but, with her brains, she was sure to do them more harm than good.

"Why aren't you at the club tonight?" he asked her unexpectedly.

"Why, am I in the way? I've told you already, I'm on your side — if he —" nodding in Vasily's direction, "— don't get on my nerves too much."

"What's that, what's that?" asked Stepanida warily.

"None of your business," snapped Galia.

Kuzma shut up like a clam. He found it dangerous to talk to Galia. She did not suspect that a problem could be attacked in a round-about way; or perhaps she considered tactics superfluous in dealing with her aunt, who was not to be coaxed or persuaded but ruthlessly caught and held and plucked on the spot. Kuzma frowned and made a sign that Galia was to hold her tongue. The girl turned away from him.

"Why don't you drink, Auntie?" she asked. "Want to have the advantage over us?"

"We can't have that," said Vasily. "What's the idea, Stepanida? That's no way to receive guests."

"It's my health. My health don't let me drink," she said.

"You're a funny one, Stepanida; it's as if you said, 'Look, friends, I'm not drinking and don't you drink either.' That's how it looks."

"What a thing to say, Vasily! I'm not like that. You do like to twist things. I'm sure I don't grudge it you. Drink it all up, that's what it's here for."

"We can't drink unless you do."

"I will, I will," and she hurriedly drank it down. "My, but you did hurt my feelings, Vasily. I'll not forget what you said very soon. Me, as would do anything for a neighbour."

"We'll see about that," said Galia.

"What'll we see, you little gutter-snipe?"

"I guess she wants money for a ticket to the pictures," put in Kuzma hastily. "She hasn't found a young man to pay for her tickets yet."

"Her? Why, all the projectionists let her in free of charge. All the bucks in the village are after her. A decent girl can't get a ticket for love nor money, but she just wags the place her legs grow out of and no money needed! You'd think she was Vasilisa the Beautiful! That's why I never go to the pictures myself, I'm ashamed to face people on her account."

Galia's nostrils were quivering but Kuzma did not give her a chance to explode.

"Let's have another," he said. "Pour one for you, Galia?"

"I'll drink to spite her, to make her burst with greed!"

"The little bitch! It's my death she's longing for, me as has been a mother to her since she was nine. Fed her, clothed her, and look what she's grown into! Gave her all I had and not a kind word do I hear from her! There's gratitude for you!"

Stepanida reached for her skirt to wipe her tears away.

"Stop it, Stepanida. Come, here's to you! May you live another hundred years and never know a trouble!"

"What do I want with another hundred years? I've wore myself out and the sooner I go to my rest the better. I can't do a day's work any more and nobody believes it. I look healthy but my insides are all wore out. Laugh, you hussy; time will come when you'll know what it means to be wore out. Oh, yes, you will, my fine lady. Go ahead and laugh." Stepanida's voice had hardened again.

"How many workdays did you earn this year?" asked Vasily.

"Two hundred and fifty."

"And the number of days you put in no work at all?"

"I'm ailing, Vasily."

"I just want to make sure you've got no complaint against me as your team-leader?"

"Complaint? Indeed I have not, Vasily. Who else would give me credit for so many days? How can I thank you?"

"And the management has no charge to bring against you, you've done your minimum."

"That I have. I'm not worrying this year, nobody can bring anything against me. And all because of you and your cabbages. I'd gladly give you the shirt off my back, and you say I begrudge you this bottle. How could you ever think such a thing, Vasily?"

"Do you know what we came here for, Stepanida?" he asked.

"N-no." She could not keep herself from darting a glance of suspicion in Kuzma's direction. "I thought you just came to see me."

"Call her bluff," said Galia harshly.

Vasily rounded on her.

"Shut your trap! We don't need you to butt in!" He went on, "That's one thing — to come and see you. But Kuzma and I have another matter in mind too. Have you heard that Maria has a big deficit charged against her?"

"Some rumours reached me."

"Help them out of their fix, Stepanida. It's a serious matter. If we don't find the money in the next two days they may take Maria away. I'm sure you've got something saved up."

"How should I have anything saved up?"

"Give it to them, Stepanida. I'm asking you in the name of the whole village. You can't let us down."

"We'll soon give it back to you," said Kuzma. "As soon as the _kolkhoz_ has turned in its year's accounts they'll give me a loan. I'm not asking for the money for long."

"See? It's not for long," went on Vasily. "You can trust them. Give it to them, Stepanida."

"Do you think I wouldn't give it to them if I had it to give?"

Galia cried out:

"She's got it; she has I tell you. Don't believe what she says. You've got it, Auntie. Why do you lie?"

"Have you seen it? Have you counted it?" shrieked Stepanida, jumping to her feet.

"I haven't seen it and I haven't counted it, but I know you've got it! You'd have killed yourself to get it. You'd steal it. You're a *kulak*,* worse than a *kulak*, they ought to set the law on you!"

"You'll answer for those words! You'll answer to the court! You'll answer to me!" Stepanida was fairly dancing with rage.

"Don't try to scare me! We'll see who'll do the answering! *Kulak! Kulak!*"

"Quiet!" shouted Vasily. In the silence that followed Vasily said calmly: "Think about it. Think it over, Stepanida. Maybe you can do something. Maria's got four kids, don't forget."

"Let's drop the whole thing," said Kuzma.

Galia looked and him and burst out crying:

"Poor Maria!" she wailed. Copious tears ran down her fat, flushed face and into the neck of her dress. Stepanida bent over and wiped her own eyes on the hem of her skirt, saying in maudlin tones:

"Maria's like a sister to me. I'd give my last kopeck

* *kulak:* before collectivization, a prosperous peasant. The literal meaning is "fist", hence the connotations of meanness.

to her and gladly. All the favours she's done for me."

Again there was a pause. Stepanida kept bending down and wiping her eyes, as if she was polishing them like buttons. From her bending position, almost under the table, she glanced up at the two men and let out noises that were something between a whimper and a moo.

"Stop crying, Galia,"said Vasily. "It's too soon to weep over Maria."

"She's lying, she's lying," burst out Galia again. "I know. I can't bear the sight of her!"

"Then get out if you can't bear the sight of me!" shouted Stepanida. "I won't cry over *that*, you can be sure! Get out this very moment! You've gnawed me to the bone!"

"Let's go, Vasily," said Kuzma.

"Right."

They put on their things and went out. A crescendo of shrieks came from Stepanida's house behind them and it was answered by fierce barking from both ends of the village. As he clumped along beside Kuzma, Vasily threatened to throw Stepanida off his team. Kuzma felt indifferent to everything. When the question of money had been brought up at the table he had suffered acutely for Maria and the boys, but this had passed and now the deficit seemed to him as innocuous as the barking of the dogs. Let come what would. The only thing he wanted now was to get to sleep. Nothing else mattered.

"I'll come and see you tomorrow," said Vasily as he turned into the gate.

"Good."

Kuzma was alone. He walked to the very edge of the village, where his new house stood, the new house meant for them to live and prosper in. Except for the barking of the dogs, the village was silent. People were sleeping, and with them slept their problems, gathering strength for the oncoming day when they would develop in one or other direction. For the time being, everything stood where it was, motionless.

Kuzma went to bed the moment he reached home. He fell asleep almost immediately and slept soundly, oblivious of everything on earth.

This was the end of the first day.

The train rushed on, throwing back on either side of it the lights that were dulled and shaken by the wind. When the lights vanished nothing could be seen outside the window but the paleness of gathering night. Then again a lone light would appear in the distance, blossom sadly for a moment and withdraw; it might be followed by two or even three in a cluster, lighting up a patch of earth, a very small patch with a tiny house on it and perhaps a wood-pile, or the corner of a shed. Instantly it would be swept away by the darkness and Kuzma waited for the next light and the next house because he felt uncomfortable without them.

Kuzma lay looking out of the window. He was sick of lying there staring at the darkness as at a wall, but he could think of nothing else to do. It was a good thing that the train kept going on and on and the city kept coming closer and closer. While watching for the next light he didn't need to think. It was a sort of game that took his mind off his troubles.

The young man across from him tossed in his sleep

and ground his teeth. Down below the old lady opened her eyes and looked at her watch.

"Sergei," she said softly. "Wake up, Sergei."

"I'm not asleep," said the old man. "Just lying with my eyes closed."

"Time to take your medicine."

"Very well."

"Does it hurt now?"

"No."

Kuzma turned over on his back. He could turn from the window now and listen to the old man and woman. Wakened by their voices, the young man gave another toss, frowned and sat up with his legs hanging over the side of his berth.

"Oho!" He had caught sight of the old man drinking out of a glass. "So Grandpa's taking a little nip, is he? Not bad, not bad."

"You've got a one-track mind, young man," said the old lady without malice. "That's all you can think of even when a man washes down his medicine with a glass of water."

"I bet it wasn't water he drank when he was young, eh, Grandpa?"

"Sergei never drank much," said his wife. "He might take a drink now and then but I never saw him drunk."

"That's what they all say when the time's past. I suppose when I'm an old man, if I live that long, I'll also say I never drank anything but *kvas*."*

"You tell him, Sergei."

"What's the use?" replied the old man reasonably.

"You're right. The young folks today can't understand."

* *kvas:* rye beer.

At another time the young man might have taken up the argument, but he was in no condition for it now. Gingerly, with much grunting and groaning, he let himself down. When he was standing on the floor he said:

"What a head! Banging away like a sledge-hammer."

"What do you expect if you're so cruel to it?" said the old lady.

"Cruel to what?"

"Your head."

The young man forced a smile:

"Cruel to my head," he repeated. "My wife says I'm cruel to her, and you say I'm cruel to my head."

"If only you could see yourself! I don't know what you look like, but certainly not a human being."

"That's easily remedied, Granny. Kuzma, there, I bet he knows what a hangover is; worse'n death." The young man pulled on his boots slowly, straightened up with a groan and thrust his hand into the pocket of his jacket. "We'll just say the magic words, then we'll be as good as new. Not the first time."

He went out. The old lady shook her head and heaved a sigh as she watched him go. In the mirror Kuzma saw the old man glance at her and smile faintly.

"What is it, Sergei?" she asked.

"Nothing."

"Have I done something I shouldn't?"

"Nothing at all. Don't worry."

"Tell me if I have."

"I will, I always tell you, don't I?"

"You do."

Kuzma enjoyed listening to their talk, and yet he felt uncomfortable, as if he were listening in to a private conversation between man and wife. He shut his eyes and pretended to sleep, but soon he felt stiff and wanted to turn over on his side and open his eyes. He wriggled like a child and squeezed his eyes shut. Presently the door was opened. It was not the young man; it was the carriage attendant.

"Will you have tea?" she asked.

"Tea, Sergei?" said the old lady.

"Let's have some. A fine thing, tea."

Kuzma slid down off his berth.

"Think I'll have some too," he said.

"You surely must," said the old lady. "I was just going to wake you up."

They sat round the little table drinking tea and the old lady treated Kuzma to home-made buns. Kuzma had a bag of hard-boiled eggs and pork fat on his berth, but he could not make up his mind to reach for it. What did they want with his pork fat? They were cultivated people, who talked to each other as if they had met only yesterday and were still discovering each other, still falling in love, though in reality they had shared a long life together. The old lady told Kuzma they were on their way to visit their son in Leningrad. Their son usually came to visit them in the summer but this year he had been sent abroad. In her turn she asked Kuzma where he was going and he said to visit his brother whom he had not seen for seven years. The old man made few remarks but listened attentively. Kuzma felt at home with them, especially with the old lady, who, it turned out, came from the country and had the greatest respect for country people. She told Kuzma that when you got right down to it, all people came from the country, some sooner, some later; the thing was, not everybody admitted it. Kuzma was pleased to hear her say this and turned to see how her husband took it, but the old man made no comment. Human kindness, respect for one's elders, industriousness, all the best human qualities, said the old lady, come from the village, and this time it was she who turned to her husband.

"Isn't that so, Sergei?" she asked.

"Very likely."

At this moment the young man came back. They had heard him singing when he was still at the other end of the corridor. He shut the door of the compartment behind him and went on with his song:

> *The very best place to find some skirt —*
> *Is on the Black Sea shore,*
> *The Black Sea sho-o-ore!*

"What a song!" said the old lady with a reproving shake of her head. "Whoever taught you a song like that?"

"Don't you like it, Granny?"

"What's there to like about it?"

"No pleasing you, Granny. Always finding fault with something. A fine song if you ask me; no bad words in it; could sing it in a concert hall and nobody'd have anything to complain of." He sat down next to Kuzma and shook his head as one shakes a bottle of medicine. "Almost back to normal," he said cheerily. "Just a bit heavy still, but that'll pass soon. What's that you said, Granny? — that I was cruel to my head?"

"And so you are. Drinking like you do. I should think you'd be sorry to waste your money."

"Money. What's money? You can always get more where the last came from."

"A person ought to have respect for money, too. It

isn't got for nothing. You have to work for it, give of your strength and health."

"I've got lots of money. It comes running after me, Granny. Money's like the girls: the less attention you pay them the better they like you. A person who counts every kopeck'll never have money."

"Why won't he if he doesn't throw it away and doesn't drink it up like you do?"

"Well, he won't, I tell you. Money'll see he's stingy and run in the opposite direction."

"I'm not so sure of that."

"It's the honest truth. Money's not as dumb as you think, Granny. It knows a skinflint and gives him the skin, but with a big-hearted fellow like me it's just as big-hearted. We understand each other. I don't grudge it and it don't grudge itself. Comes and goes, comes and goes. If I tried heaping it up it would see I wasn't the right sort and all kinds of things'd happen to me — I'd get sick or have my tractor taken away. I know what I'm talking about."

"An interesting point of view," observed the old man. "One has only to be big-hearted to have money?"

"Oh, no! You've got to work," said the young man earnestly. "I like to work. I earn two hundred and fifty or three hundred a month — as much as four hundred in the winter time when timber-hauling begins. There's not many can keep up with me. If a fellow don't work, where's the money to come from?"

"Where do you make all that money?" Kuzma could not resist asking.

"In the timber business. They pay us drivers well."

"And what's the good of it?" said the old lady. "You only drink it up."

"So I do. What of it? Can't I allow myself a drink

after freezing on the job all day long? What sort of a life is that? I've got a right to some fun too."

"I suppose your wife serves you up a bottle every evening?"

The young man laughed.

"Being funny, Granny? What wouldn't I give for a wife like that!"

"In other words, yours isn't so happy about your drinking?"

"She don't understand. But it doesn't matter now. We've parted."

"Parted?"

"Yeah. Not long ago. Parted. I up and left."

"What for?"

"She's dumb, didn't understand me. That's why. Born in a barnyard and never learned better. Oh, to hell with her!" The young man was trying to bolster his spirits. "There's lots of other women in the world."

"None of them likes a man who drinks. They all want to live like human beings, and you, no doubt, come home hardly able to stand on your feet and begin ranting and raving and throwing your weight about."

"Not me. I'm quiet when I'm drunk. If nobody touches me I just fall asleep. But you mustn't touch me. I don't like that. You can say anything to me in the morning and I'll swallow it, but not when I'm drunk. Better leave me alone when I'm drunk."

"Lack of respect for women also comes from the village," remarked the old man to the old lady.

"No, it doesn't, Sergei."

"What's that?" said the young man.

"Sergei says more respect is shown to women in the town than in the village."

"You don't want to respect a woman too much.

You'll just bring a lot of trouble on your head if you do. I know. You want to keep a tight rein on her and not give her her head. Once she senses you're a weakling you're done for. Start telling you what to do. Ride you like a donkey."

"A fat chance any woman would have riding you!" said the old lady.

"Sure, I wouldn't stand for it. But there's some that would. They're the ones who get it."

"What nonsense you're talking. Utter nonsense. Defending your weak brothers! You're the ones who drink and the women are to blame!" said the old lady half in anger, half in astonishment. Well, you've made your bed. You'll have to live by yourself now."

"Why will I? I'll find somebody else."

"Who wants a drunk like you?"

"Granny," said the young man with a look of gentle rebuke. "All I've got to do is whistle. The world's full of left-over women. All looking for a man. They're the weaker sex, aren't they? They can't live without us men. Take me, I'm from the country myself, but whenever I go to town I find a woman. They say you got to give them money and things. Nothing of the sort. Maybe it was like that before the revolution but not now. They've all got consciences these days. It's just a little loving they want. Just don't be rough with them, know how to touch their hearts and you're sure to get what you want."

"It's a very good thing your wife parted with you," said the old lady crisply.

"Why?" asked the young man in surprise. "Because I had other women? What's wrong with that? Everybody has."

"Don't measure everybody by yourself."

"What are you trying to tell me, Granny? Somebody once pointed out a place in a book to me; the man who wrote it — I don't remember his name — he says a person — a man, that is — who don't know anybody but his own wife, is a fool, has no interest in life. And he's right. A man gets sick of living with one and the same woman all the time. Gets you down."

"Hear that, Sergei?" said the old lady with a smile.

"Yes."

"Tell him your view of the matter."

"What for?"

"Tell him. He thinks that's the way to live. He doesn't know the first thing about living."

"That's his business."

"Come on, tell me, Grandad. Is it a secret or what?" said the young man.

" 'Come on, tell me, Grandad,' " mocked the old lady. "That old Grandad there, the one in front of you, he's never in his life, not one single time, been untrue to me. And you say everybody does it. There he is, take a good look at him if you've never seen another like him."

The young man winked at the old one.

"Do you think I'd talk about my affairs in front of my wife?" The thought of the consequences made the young man burst out laughing. "A hell of a row there'd be! Why, she'd . . ."

The old lady watched him with a tolerant smile.

"But he really has *not* been unfaithful," she said with the same smile. "Why is it you can't understand such a thing?"

The young man went on laughing.

"How do you know, Granny?"

"I trust him."

"Oh, so you trust him."

"Tell him, Sergei. He can't understand."

"Why should I have been unfaithful to her?" the old man asked the young one.

"That's for you to know, she's your old lady, not mine."

"Why are you unfaithful to your wife?"

"Oh, just for the fun of it."

"What fun is it?"

The young man gave a suggestive little laugh:

"Oh, you know . . . a new woman and all . . . no two women are alike, you know."

"Sergei was happy to be with me," she said seriously. "He would have been unhappy if he'd gone to anyone else."

The young man looked at the old one with frank curiosity, as though he were an incomprehensible foreigner.

"Am I to believe that?"

"As you like."

During the pause that followed the young man switched his gaze from the old man to the old woman and back again. Suddenly he became aware of Kuzma.

"What about you, Kuzma? Haven't you ever been unfaithful to your wife?"

Kuzma grinned uneasily. During this conversation his thoughts had kept turning to Maria, and with a pang he realized how badly he needed her. All the good and the bad moments of their life faded from his memory, leaving the two of them alone and as if they were just setting out together, and Kuzma knew without doubt that there could be no life for him without Maria. He tried to find an explanation for the way two people cling to each other, and could not. Was it children who held them together like nails? No. While the old couple had been arguing with the young man he had forgotten all about his children, but it was as if Maria had been sitting on his knee, so that he felt her breath upon his cheek, and she heard everything.

"Come on, have you ever deceived your wife, Kuzma?" asked the young man.

"I did once," confessed Kuzma.

"See? Kuzma too . . ." began the young man, but Kuzma interrupted him:

"Wait a minute. It was different with me, I lived with another woman before the war but we never got married. After the war I married Maria, but just once I had an affair with this other woman for old time's sake. She met me one evening . . ."

The old lady looked at Kuzma sorrowfully:

"And did Maria find out?"

"Yes. She left me, but I got her to come back. Promised it would never happen again. And it never did."

"Do you believe what I said about us?" asked the old lady.

"I do. There are plenty of couples like you in the village."

"In the village!" burst out the young man. "Everyone knows everybody else's business there. If a man so much as looks at another man's wife the whole village knows it. They're afraid to misbehave."

"That's not the reason," protested Kuzma. "People there get married so as to spend their lives together."

"Like Sergei and me. We've spent our whole lives together," said the old lady as she looked at her husband. "Wherever he goes I go too. We've never been apart for long. I couldn't get on without him and he couldn't without me, isn't that so, Sergei?"

"When we were young we decided that was how we would live, and we have. We decided to share everything, the good and the bad, even death itself." Her voice was calm and quiet. "Now Sergei's got a bad heart and mine's still good, but his bad heart belongs to both of us."

"You ain't them . . . what do they call 'em? . . . Baptists, or something, are you?" asked the young man incredulously.

"Baptists? You're joking!" said the old lady with a mirthless laugh. "Hear that, Sergei? We've joined the Baptists."

Meanwhile the train went on and on, bringing the city closer and closer.

The second day began with a visit from old Gordei very early in the morning, before the boys had left for school. He sat down on the floor in front of the stove as usual, lit his pipe, and sucked on it in silence without taking it out of his mouth. Kuzma did not begin talking to him. What was the old man doing here before sunrise? Couldn't he sleep? Who needed his advice? What good did it do? Kuzma remembered how, on getting up, he had told Maria not to go blabbing about her trouble to the village women, to which Maria had replied irately:

"Teaching me what to do! As if I hadn't had a lesson to last me a thousand years and more! No, everybody's got to teach me!"

When the older boys had gone to school and Maria was busy about the house, Kuzma said to old Gordei:

"What have you come for, Grandad?"

"Eh?" The old fellow began fidgeting and tried to struggle to his feet. "Here," he said holding out some money. "Yesterday I wangled fifteen roubles out of my son; I have no use for money myself . . ."

"I don't need it, Grandad."

"You don't need it?" echoed the old man in puzzlement. "Then what did I bring it to you for? Don't worry. I didn't tell him it was for you."

He stood in front of Kuzma, holding out his hand with three five-rouble notes rolled up in it. He looked at Kuzma, clearly afraid he would not accept them, but Kuzma took them.

"Don't you worry about it," said the old man joyfully. "If you've got the money you'll give it back, if you haven't — what does an old man like me need with it?"

He made to go out, which was not at all his habit.

"Stay a while, Grandad."

"Got to go."

"Listen . . ."

"What?"

"Don't bring me any more money."

"Why not?"

"I'll find it myself. I know you. Next thing you'll be going round the village taking a collection for me."

"I won't if you say I'm not to."

"Don't, Grandad, I'd rather you didn't."

The second person who came to see him was the little boy who had come before — Evgeny Nikolaevich's neighbour.

"Evgeny Nikolaevich told me to tell you he's going to the centre today and will be back this evening."

Kuzma said:

"Does he have you announce to the village every time he goes out to the privy?"

The boy giggled, and ran out.

Then Vasily came and said briefly:

"Put on your things and come with me."

"Where to?"

"To see my mother."

Kuzma had not seen Aunt Natalia for a long time, not since she had taken to her bed three or four years before. Kuzma could not imagine her lying in bed instead of running about, busy with a thousand tasks; could not imagine her lying there like any other old woman waiting to die, ponderously turning her body from side to side, gazing at those who came to see her with weak and watery eyes. He could imagine almost anyone else in this situation, even himself, but not Aunt Natalia. As long as Kuzma remembered her she had worked like a machine on the farm where she earned as much as six hundred workdays a year, or at home where she raised three boys, the eldest of whom was Vasily, with no husband to help her. It was an understatement to say that she was hard-working. There were plenty of hard-working women in the village, but none of them could compare with Aunt Natalia. She never walked at a normal pace, and when her neighbours saw her dashing down the street they would call out good-naturedly:

"Where are you off to?"

And she would call back, without stopping, "Nowheres special but I'm in a frightful hurry."

This became a sort of saying in the village, and it perfectly characterized Aunt Natalia.

All the farmers remembered how she stacked the hay during the hay-making. Her stacks withstood the worst weather, the rain slid off them as off a duck's back and they stood undisturbed as if painted — until the snow came. She also loved to go fishing and was as good at it as any man. When she took her boat out in the autumn and got ready to start fishing, the men would swear and row their boats further away.

And so, never having learned to walk at a leisurely pace, she ran to her bed on her last legs and fell upon it, never again to rise. There she lay, so unlike herself, as if she had outlived herself, never getting up, in a tiny room partitioned off the big one. Old women came and sat beside her and complained of life, and she, who had never had a moment to spare for conversation, lay and listened and nodded.

When Vasily and Kuzma came in she was asleep. The room was dark, one window was curtained entirely and one leaf of the shutters was closed over the other window. Kuzma could not make her out at first.

"Mother!" said Vasily.

She woke up and looked at them without a trace of surprise, as if she had been expecting them.

"Vasily," she said. "And the other's Kuzma. I haven't seen you for a long time, Kuzma."

"Yes, Aunt Natalia, it's been a long time."

"Come to see what I look like? I'm ailing, Kuzma. There's nothing left to look at."

She had grown thin and wizened, her voice was feeble and she spoke slowly and with an effort. Her shrunken face seemed to have hardened; when she spoke it remained immobile, even her lips did not move and this gave the impression that her voice did not come from her, but from somewhere beside her.

"I'm not so old, not seventy yet. Others live longer. But I've got this thing," she said, so slowly and painfully that her hearers felt they ought to busy themselves with something.

"Are you in great pain?" asked Kuzma.

"No pain at all. Only I can't walk. My legs give under me when I stand up. No strength in them."

"If nothing hurts, just you lie and have a rest, Aunt Natalia. You've done enough running about. Take it easy now."

"Easy to say, Kuzma. I want to get up. I could still walk last summer, went outdoors all by myself."

"If you could do it then, you'll do it again."

"Ah, no, I won't. My breath's getting shorter and shorter."

Vasily broke in with:

"Have you any money, Mother?"

"A little. But I'll not give it you, Vasily. Let it lie."

"Not to me but to Kuzma, Mother. Give it to him. For Maria. He's having trouble collecting it."

Aunt Natalia turned her eyes to Kuzma and blinked at him for some time. Kuzma waited. Vasily got up and went out of the room to say something to his sister, who lived with his mother. Presently he came back.

"That money's saved for my death," said Aunt Natalia.

"What? Does a person have to pay to die these days? It always used to be free," said Kuzma in surprise.

"No-o." A faint sparkle came to her eyes. "I want to

pay for my own funeral and funeral feast. Not to burden my children with it."

"As if it would be a burden," muttered Vasily.

"I know. But I want to pay for it myself. So that more people will come, and remember me longer. I never did anybody a bad turn. And I always did everything myself. I want to do this myself, too."

She rested a little without speaking, without stirring. Thinking he had better go, Kuzma glanced at Vasily. But just then Aunt Natalia said:

"Does Maria cry much?"

"Yes."

"If I give you the money and then die, what then?"

"Still harping on that, Mother," said Vasily making a face.

"I've given in already," said Aunt Natalia and the two men understood she was speaking of death.

Kuzma started and looked at her with fear in his eyes.

Every day, every hour, men are confronted by death, but for Aunt Natalia, as for a saint, Death had stepped aside to admit her to the threshold separating this world from that. Aunt Natalia could not go back, but she could linger before taking the final step. So there she stood, contemplating both sides of the door. Perhaps she had run so hard all her life that she had even worn out Death, who now waited to catch his breath.

With a feeble motion of her hand she pointed under the bed.

"Take it, Vasily."

Vasily pulled out an old battered suitcase and took a little package tied up in a red rag out of it. She said as she untied it:

"Many a year I've been saving this. But I must give it you. I'll try to hold on. Don't keep it long, Kuzma. My strength is going fast."

"Try to get better, Aunt Natalia," said Kuzma.

She did not answer him.

"If I can't hold on, give the money back to Vasily. Give it back at once. I'll not give it you if you don't. I want to die on my own money."

"I promise to give it to him, Aunt Natalia."

"Will you come to my funeral?"

He could not find words for an answer.

"Do come. Drink and remember me. There'll be lots of people. You come too."

She held out the money and he took it as if it were a gift from the other world.

Although he had told Aunt Natalia that Maria cried, the fact was she had stopped crying. She was silent. When asked a question she would answer in monosyllables and grow silent again. Sometimes she did not even answer, pretending not to have heard. She went about her household tasks, but she didn't seem to see anything, as if she were being led about and shown what she must do. When her chores were done she would drop on the bed and lie without moving a muscle. When the children came and asked for something to eat she would get up and prepare it for them like a sleepwalker, unconscious of her actions.

The children, too, were different. They no longer played roughly and shouted. They listened to every word spoken by the grown-ups and were in a constant state of suspense, waiting for something to happen.

And they clung to one another, afraid to be separated. They would stand silently in a row staring at their mother, who seemed not to see them.

Their big, new house was so quiet it might have been deserted.

Kuzma was sorry he had come home. Hoping to cheer Maria, he showed her the money Aunt Natalia had given him, but she just looked at the banknotes as though they were blank pieces of paper and walked away. Kuzma waited but she made no further response. He realized that nothing mattered to her now. On the previous day, the first day, the shock of fear had made her cry and implore him to save her. Now she was turned to stone. She looked without seeing, heard without understanding. No doubt she would remain in this state until her fate was decided: either they would lead her away, or tell her everything was all right and she would go on living as she had before the misfortune. When that happened the tears would begin to flow again and, if all went well, her heart would gradually soften.

Oppressed by the atmosphere at home. Kuzma went out again.

It was a dark, grey day, heavy and ragged at the edges. All was quiet. The world looked abandoned and neglected, as if one owner had moved out and his successor had not yet moved in. That was exactly how it was: autumn was leaving, winter had not come. Chimney smoke crawled low over the roofs, not daring to rise into the sky until the season for that arrived. Unhappy dogs roamed aimlessly through the streets. Children's faces appeared at the windows but there were no children, or grown-ups either, outside. The streets were empty. The forest beyond the village looked dreary and deserted.

Everybody was waiting for something. Waiting for winter when they would undertake new tasks and assume new cares. Waiting for the holidays and the festivities they promised. Waiting for tomorrow, bringing both winter and holidays nearer. Today was a blank. Nobody wanted today. It was just something to be got through with. For Kuzma alone, it seemed, this day had begun luckily, and so he wanted it to continue, in the hope that his luck would last.

As he walked down the street he considered in his mind whom he had best call on now; unable to settle on anyone and reluctant to return home, he stepped into the *kolkhoz* office.

The chairman asked, "How are things?"

"Not so bad."

"Collected much?"

"Not very much so far."

"How much? — do you mind telling me?"

"If Evgeny Nikolaevich brings me what he promised today I'll have almost two hundred and fifty."

"And that's all?"

"So far."

The chairman began leafing through the papers on his desk with a disgruntled air. He frowned, he sighed. He shut one folder, put it away and reached for another. He asked, without raising his eyes:

"Where do you think you'll get the rest? Have you anything in view?"

"I just go around asking," replied Kuzma with a shrug of his shoulders.

The chairman became absorbed in his papers and made no reply. Fearing that he was in the way, Kuzma got up.

"Sit down," ordered the chairman.

Then he seemed to forget all about him.

As Kuzma sat there he recalled what had happened in September 1947. The corn was ripe, the harvest season was at its height, and all the machines for gathering it in were standing idle for lack of fuel. Five days a week the chairman lived at the district centre, running from the local Party committee to the machine and tractor station begging, borrowing and buying fuel rations, which lasted two days at the most; then the machines stood still again. The weather could not have been more perfect for harvesting. Not a cloud in the sky. The corn, not too abundant as it was, began spilling out of the ear. It was hard to see this, after all the suffering the war had brought and the two famine years following the war. Sickles were brought out and horse-drawn harvesters, but they could gather in little, especially since there were only one third as many horses and hands as there had been before the war.

It was Satan himself who arranged for that barge to moor on the banks of their river that September. The captain, a *muzhik* as fat as a woman, rolled up his trouser legs and spent the day fishing, and in the evening he built a camp-fire and made fish soup. To get the fire going he sprinkled petrol on the wood. It was at this moment the chairman came strolling up.

Quickly they made their bargain. In the morning two drums of petrol were rolled onto the river bank and the barge set out. That day a tractor towed the harvesting machine out into the field again and Kuzma drove his lorry to the harvester to load it with reaped grain. Everybody in the village knew the petrol had been bought from the barge captain, but only the chairman knew the risk to himself involved in such a transaction.

He was arrested at the beginning of November, as though the authorities had waited to give him time to take in the harvest. He asked to be allowed to spend the November holidays at home. His request was not granted. And so the holidays were not holidays for the village that year. At first no one could understand the reason for his arrest: he had not stolen the petrol, he had bought it, and bought it not for his own use but for the use of the *kolkhoz*, because there was no fuel at the machine and tractor station and the grain could not wait. Later it was explained to them that the petrol belonged to the state, the barge captain had no right to sell it nor the chairman to buy it. Some of the villagers understood, others did not. At a meeting of the *kolkhoz* they elected a committee of three who were to try and get their chairman back. They did everything in their power; went time and again to the regional centre and the district centre; they even wrote to Moscow, but their efforts were in vain. Indeed, their efforts may even have damaged the chairman's cause, because he was given fifteen years. They were stunned by the news.

Thanks to an amnesty, he returned to them in 1954. They wanted to make him chairman again but were not allowed to: a man who had served a jail sentence and been expelled from the Party. So he was given a job as a team-leader. Only five years ago, after a good dozen chairmen had tried and failed and half the members of the *kolkhoz* had run away, the remaining *kolkhoz* members had written to the regional Party committee asking that he be made chairman again. This time their request was granted. He was invited to resume his old duties in the autumn after the harvest season, at just the same time he had been arrested. He might have been taking up where he left off, if it were possible to forget the more than ten years that had intervened.

The chairman tore his eyes away from his papers and called out in the direction of the door:

"Polina!"

Polina came in from the book-keeping room.

"Polina, look and see how much the monthly salaries of our specialists amount to — my own included."

"The sum total do you mean?"

"Yes, the sum total."

"I know without looking. Six hundred and forty roubles."

The chairman considered a moment before asking:

"Has the book-keeper come back?"

"No, he won't be back before evening."

"Very well, you may go. Tell them to come here."

"Who?"

"Everybody on the payroll. Tell them it's urgent or they'll come trailing in one by one. I haven't got two hours to waste on them."

He said to Kuzma:

"You stay where you are."

He went back to his papers.

The specialists began coming in.

The first was the agronomist, who had just come back from a course of treatment. During the harvest season his stomach ulcer had given him trouble and he was sent off to a health resort.

He had come to their village as an agronomist two years before from the agricultural administration department. Of his own accord he had chosen a remote *kolkhoz* and for this he was respected, though at first he was looked upon with distrust: he had been an office worker, a boss used to giving orders; nobody knew quite how to talk to him, perhaps in the guise of an agronomist he was just another of those agents sent to every *kolkhoz* at one time. But he proved his genuineness by his work as agronomist and these suspicions were forgotten. He loved his work, he was out in the fields from dawn to dusk during the summer and very soon was fully accepted in the village.

He came in, spoke a greeting and looked enquiringly at the chairman, who, without answering his look, said:

"Sit down, we'll wait for the others."

The next to come was the veterinary surgeon. He had worked at this *kolkhoz* for so long that few remembered he was one of the specialists assigned to it. Then the livestock expert came in. She was a big woman with a man's voice. She spoke little and rarely lost her equanimity but even so people were afraid of her, as if they felt that strength like hers and a voice like hers must vent themselves before long, and there'd be trouble when they did.

They waited some time for the mechanic. The chairman began to grumble and throw impatient looks at the door.

"Beneath his dignity to come when he's called, got to be asked a dozen times."

At last he came, a young man still wearing his college badge in his buttonhole. With the assumed weariness of one who has been hard at work while others have been shirking, he slouched over to the sofa and sat down on the edge of it.

The specialists were all sitting on the sofa on one side of the room, Kuzma on a chair facing them. Only now, it seemed, did the chairman realize the proposal he intended making to these people was not such a simple one. He shifted in his chair, cleared his throat, and could not begin. They sensed his uneasiness and waited in silence.

At last he began:

"This is what I've called you together for. Tomorrow is pay day. If the book-keeper brings the money this evening you have a right to get it tomorrow. But here's how things stand." He paused significantly, indicating that it was a weighty matter he was drawing their attention to. Presently he went on in an even, unperturbed tone. "Here's how things stand. This summer, and in the spring too, there were times when we held up your pay. Nobody died, you found a way out somehow. Seems to me you can find a way out now too, if we hand over our pay to Kuzma, which is what I suggest. You know yourselves he's up against it. In three days he's got to find one thousand roubles; where's he to find it if we don't help him? Later on the

administration will advance him the money, but he
can't wait. It'll be too late then. As for us, we'll manage
somehow, we won't die. The *kolkhozniks* can do it.
That's the proposition I make. It's up to you to decide.
We can't force anybody."

Kuzma said with a groan:

"Think of the position you're putting me in. You
might have warned me it was this you were going to
talk about."

"Nobody's asking you. Time enough to object when
they do." The chairman turned away. "Well, what
about it, comrade specialists?"

The specialists made no reply.

"Kuzma could not bring himself to look in their
direction. He fancied his shame made him translucent,
so that they could see all that was shameful and con-
temptible inside him. He sat in front of them like a
prisoner in the dock, and he could not have said
whether he wanted them to show him mercy or not.
The only thing he felt was shame, the bitter, biting
shame of a mature, middle-aged man. Heedless now of
the consequences, he actually hoped they would reject
the chairman's proposal, because then he would not be
indebted to them. But someone said:

"Of course we'll give it to him."

"That's right, we've got to give it to him," said the
chairman firmly. "As I say, nothing will happen to us,
but something very serious may happen to him. I know
very well you've been counting on this money but in
November we'll think of something — try to get the
bank to let us have our salaries earlier. So that's that.
Tomorrow you'll come and sign for your pay and we'll
give it to Kuzma. If there's any of you who objects let
him say so now."

"Nobody objects," spoke up the agronomist for everybody. The rest said nothing.

"Good. So tomorrow morning you come and get it, Kuzma. Polina says it'll come to six hundred and forty roubles. Not enough, I know, but it's all we've got. I'll tell the book-keeper, he'll be informed."

"I didn't quite understand, have we got to turn over our entire pay or only part?" asked the vet, throwing anxious glances at his colleagues.

"You haven't got to turn over anything at all," said the chairman sharply. "It's voluntary. You can keep your whole pay if you want to. Why didn't you speak up sooner, when the question was being decided? The rest of us are giving up our entire pay; you can do as you like."

"Oh, I will too, I will too," replied the vet hurriedly.

"As you like."

"Of course I will."

"Why should they give it all to me?" said Kuzma to the chairman, getting up. "What do you take me for — a highway robber? They've got to live too, and me taking all their money away from them. Look, if you've no objections, give me half and keep the other half for yourselves." He was speaking to the specialists now. "Let's decide on that. A fine thing that would be — you work and I —"

The chairman cut him off:

"Stop bargaining. Take what you're given and be thankful."

"I've got a conscience, haven't I?"

"Stuff your conscience!" he exclaimed. "So you've got a conscience, and we haven't, I suppose. You'd do better to use your brains thinking where to get the rest of the money, instead of carrying on about your conscience. You're so tight with that conscience of yours you won't give any of it away. You think the money's going to be brought to you on a silver platter? You'll have a long wait! You were counting on that conscience when you went to Stepanida. Well, did it bring you much?" In his irritation the chairman kept moving the papers on his desk from one place to another. "Either you come here tomorrow and take all that money or you can start saving crusts for Maria's food parcels. I need money too, if you want to know, but I'm giving my pay to you because I'll manage somehow without it and you will *not*. The rest feel the same way. If you've got a conscience, so have we."

"Surely you don't think I —"

"That's all, we've talked enough. You can go now, anyone who wants to."

The mechanic left immediately. As soon as he had gone the livestock expert got up and, after asking the chairman something in a low voice, went out too. The vet cast quick glances about him and slipped through the door. Three were left: the chairman, the agronomist and Kuzma. Kuzma sat down again in his old place, which was opposite the agronomist.

Nobody spoke.

Presently the agronomist got up, shook hands with the chairman and Kuzma and said to Kuzma, nodding towards the chairman:

"Don't think we're doing this because he made us. He was right to raise the question. Don't have any qualms about taking the money. Count it as yours."

He gave him a nod of encouragement and went out. Kuzma made ready to follow him and seeing this, the chairman said:

"Wait for me."

He cleared his desk of papers and folders, tested the safe to make sure it was locked and began putting on his things.

It was growing dark. Faint yellow lights glowed in some of the windows, the rest were dark. The village lay close against the river bank, like a camp of tired travellers resting for the night before moving on in the morning.

It was hard to realize that this impression was just the result of one's own weariness, that the village was not really sleeping but simply passing through that aimless, idle period between afternoon and night; later, when darkness fell, people could go on with their work, do something useful until bed-time. For the present they could do nothing but wait out the aimless twilight hour.

Kuzma and the chairman walked along without speaking until they reached the chairman's house.

"Come in if you're not in a hurry," he said.

They turned in at the gate. The chairman opened the door and switched on the light. They were alone in the house. The chairman produced a bottle, half filled two glasses with its contents and brought a dipperful of water. Pointing to the bottle, he said:

"Pure alcohol."

"Where did you get it?"

"I've had it a long time. Bought it last spring when I went to the mines. Not much left. Here, let's drink to Maria — to her staying where she is instead of setting out on a trip."

The words made Kuzma's heart sink. Swiftly he gulped down the burning liquor to swamp the ache within him. He washed it down with water, took a deep breath and said simply, without pain:

"Looks as if I'll come out on top now. You've certainly helped me."

"I'll teach that bitch of a Stepanida a thing or two! Just you wait till the new year begins," said the chairman grimly.

"Maybe she really doesn't have anything."

"Didn't we pay her for her cow in September? What did she do with the money, eat it? You can be sure it's lying in some trunk tied up in a rag.

"Leave her alone. What good'll it do, once she's like that?"

"Oh, no, I'll teach her a lesson. What's she thinking of anyway? She'd die rather than put that money to use though it's no good to anybody just lying there, not even to herself. Just think! Her own money, and she daren't use it. People would see and know she'd lied. So she'll just dribble it out, one rouble at a time. Punished herself and lost her neighbour's trust. It'd have cost her less if she'd given you the money. But no, she couldn't; she was stingy even before she was born."

"The devil with her. I never expected to get anything from her. But those specialists, I feel rather bad about them. Here they were counting the hours till pay day and I come along and collect. They'll hold it against me, and against you, too; you made them do it."

"That's all right, don't you worry about them, they'll manage. But if you'd gone to the agronomist and asked him for something tomorrow — well, he needs the money, of course — he might have given you something, but not much, and what good would a little do you? As for the vet, he wouldn't have given you a kopeck. It's easier to refuse when you're alone. That's why I got them all together." The chairman gave a little laugh. "I know them; it's not so simple to refuse in front of everybody, nobody wants to show his wrong side to everybody, but when he's alone he can be cunning and nobody'll notice, there's no witnesses. I got wise to that a long time ago."

"Now that I think of it, you're right," said Kuzma in surprise.

"Of course I'm right. In the prison camp where they sent me that time there was a queer bird, he wrote a whole notebook about it, a big thick notebook. Lots of things in it were just made up out of his head, but I remember this particular thing because I'd learned it myself from experience."

"I've always been wanting to ask you," said Kuzma, "Did you hold it against us when they arrested you that time?"

"Against who? You?"

"Yes, me, and the rest of us here in the village. We got the benefit of that petrol but you were the only one held to account for it. It wasn't for yourself you bought it."

"Why should I have held it against the villagers? You had nothing to do with it."

"In one way we didn't, in another way we did. All depends on how you look at it."

"Forget it, Kuzma," said the chairman, waving the matter away with an impatient gesture. "What's the sense in bringing that up now?"

They poured out the rest of the liquor and drank it down. The chairman fell into a reverie, looking very unlike a chairman now that his face was red, all slack and fleshy, without a trace of its usual firmness, and with that look of misery in his eyes Kuzma would have thought he was drunk had he not known how little he had consumed.

"You ask me if I held it against you," he said a little later, looking steadily at Kuzma and speaking in a sober voice. "You people here of course had nothing to do with it. Maybe at the very beginning I did, I thought you could have worked a little harder in my defence. After all it wasn't for myself I did it, it was for the *kolkhoz*. I thought they ought to take that into account; I thought the *kolkhoz* would write a letter on my behalf and they'd fine me and that would be the end of it. That would have been bad enough. But at the trial what do they do but accuse me of sabotage! Believe it or not," he said with a little laugh, as if he himself could not believe it to this very day. "I held it against somebody, but not you. I was to blame for buying that petrol and I don't deny it. But if you think it over it's easy to see I wasn't the only one to blame. It wasn't sabotage that made me do it, it was need. The grain was spilling out. Somebody higher up must have been to blame too, somebody higher up must have neglected his duty, if there was no fuel. But nobody wanted to answer for it. I was the only who was taken to court."

"I remember."

"When they asked me to become chairman again I didn't want to at first. And then I said to myself: Who am I spiting — the *kolkhoz*? The *kolkhoz* wasn't to blame. The state? Why bring the state into it?" The chairman was silent for a moment then smiled and added firmly: "I'm only sorry those seven years were taken out of my life for nothing."

When he got home Kuzma found Evgeny Nikolaevich waiting for him.

"Well, no one can accuse you of sitting at home moping, Kuzma. I've been saying to myself as I sat here, 'If the mountain won't come to Mohammed, Mohammed will go to the mountain.' "

"Have you been waiting long, Evgeny Nikolaevich?"

"Pretty long, but I decided to sit it out. I'm that sort: once I make a promise I have to keep it. When I got to the savings bank today I found it closed for repairs. I rushed from one office to another but the only answer I got was there's nothing we can do for you. Finally I went to the bank manager's house. Fortunately he knows me. Gave me the money. Just your good luck, Kuzma."

"I am a lucky one all right."

"You are. So here I sat thinking, maybe I needn't have troubled myself, maybe you don't need it. You didn't come for so long. I thought you might have found the money. But I sat on, didn't budge. Once I'd promised, I had to see it through. So's you wouldn't take offence."

"I'm very grateful."

"So you need the money, do you?"

"Indeed I do, Evgeny Nikolaevich."

"Then here you are. The full sum. Count it."

Kuzma took the money and stuffed it into his pocket. "Why should I count it? It's all here."

"Just as you say. I wouldn't cheat you. What I said

I'd give, I've given. Do I get a bottle of vodka for my pains?"

"That goes without saying, Evgeny Nikolaevich."

"Oh, I'm just joking. We'll wait till everything's over to have a drink. Every kopeck's needed now, I know that. A person's got to have a conscience. We've got to help each other without thinking of ourselves. Like the Russian princes stuck together against the Polovsty* in the old days. That's how we've got to stick together when trouble comes. Know what your trouble is? It's the Polovtsy, the Polovtsian host. Remember your history, Kuzma? We've got to stand against them all together, like the Russian princes. Just try and hurt us then! There's lots of us and we'll not give up without a fight. Eh, Kuzma? Am I right?"

"Right you are," laughed Kuzma. "That's one way of putting it!" and he laughed again.

Vitka peered through the doorway and, seeing their merriment, smiled happily.

"Am I right, Vitka?" Evgeny Nikolaevich called out to him. "Have you got to the Polovtsy yet in your history lessons?"

"I read a book about them."

"And isn't it like that now?"

"Yes."

"See? Your headmaster knows a thing or two after all."

Embarrassed, Vitka escaped. Evgeny Nikolaevich heaved a deep sigh, though the expression of his face

---

* Polovtsy: Nomadic Turkic tribe whose incursions caused great disruptions in the twelfth century, before the main Tartar invasion.

indicated he was more than satisfied with himself. He got up.

"I must be going. Takes a lot out of you, fighting those Polovtsy. I'm tired. I'll go and take a little nap."

"I've put you to a lot of trouble, Evgeny Nikolaevich."

"That's all right. I don't hold it against you. Once it had to be done, I did it. You're not a stranger here. Another time you'd do as much for me. A person's got to be decent to his neighbours if he wants to win their esteem. Am I right?"

"You're right."

"That's how it is." Evgeny Nikolaevich glanced round. "Where's Maria? Sick?"

Kuzma did not know where Maria was, but he said:

"Yes, she's sick."

"What's the matter with her?"

"Got a headache."

"That's nothing."

As he was going out Evgeny Nikolaevich turned round to ask in lowered tones:

"That loan you spoke of — have they promised it to you?"

"Yes, they have."

"Good. Well, when you get it you can pay me back. I won't press you. I know you can be trusted. It'll be safe in your hands."

Maria was sitting on the bed looking at the photographs in an old dog-eared album lying in her lap. When Kuzma came in she was studying a picture of herself taken thirty years or so before. There she was with a heavy plait over one shoulder in the manner of those days, with a round-cheeked face — a maiden waiting for her mate, innocent of suffering, of the pains of childbirth, unacquainted with tears, other than the easy tears of childhood. She knew nothing about herself but her name, and that she had been born and raised in this village and would go on living here forever. She knew nothing of war, of her children, of the shop, of the deficit; with so many people in the world she never supposed that trouble would seek out an ordinary country girl for the lion's share; her mind had always rejected the thought of a life full of tears and sorrow. And now in her wretchedness she gazed in wonder at this other girl, the one who had had no experience of life, and she envied her and said farewell to her forever. Until that moment her life had been too busy to do so, but now she had time, and she sat down and realized that nothing was left of that girl, nothing but her name and her memories. Everything else had vanished as completely as a soldier on the "missing" list. She dared not let herself contemplate the future.

Kuzma went over to her and said:

"Things went fine today. I've collected almost the entire sum."

Maria did not answer. She put the album on the window-sill and went out. He did not follow her. He sat down on the bed and suddenly felt exhausted. He wanted nothing so much as to go to sleep.

He felt somebody's eyes on him. He looked up. It was Maria. She was staring at him from the other room as if trying to recall what he had said to her. He went out to her. She passed into the kitchen. Again he felt her eyes upon him, as if she were making a desperate effort to remember what he had said. He waited but she did not utter a word.

He got undressed and went to bed.

The second day had come to an end.

Long ago, when still a young man, Kuzma had come to realize that each new day is born only for him to whom it brings luck. If a person has no luck, if day after day luck is against him, that means those days were not his; his day is yet to come.

As he fell asleep Kuzma knew for certain that this day had been his. When he had got up in the morning he could not have dreamed of such good luck. First old Gordei had brought fifteen roubles, then Aunt Natalia had given him over a hundred, then the chairman had gathered the specialists together, and there you were — a whole pile of money in one fell swoop; he only had to go and take it in the morning. In the end Evgeny Nikolaevich had brought him the hundred he had promised. To think of such a dull, dreary day turning out to be so rich, so lucky! And how fortunate that such a day should have turned up just at a time when Kuzma felt there was nothing left for him to do but go outside and howl like a wolf.

Kuzma fell asleep filled with gratitude to his day, and to the people who had so kindly rallied to his cause. He fell asleep happy, forgetting that his day was over.

On the train Kuzma was awakened in the middle of the night by the young man.

"Kuzma! Kuzma! Are you asleep?"

"What is it?"

"Give me a smoke. I'll die if I don't smoke and I'm out of cigarettes."

Kuzma raised himself on one elbow, felt for his cigarettes on the shelf over his berth and handed them to the young man.

"Oh, what a relief!" he groaned as he took them. "I thought I was done for."

Kuzma had no desire to go back to sleep. He and the young man both climbed down. The shuffle and rustle woke the old lady, who lifted her head and looked at them.

"It's all right, go back to sleep, Granny, it's only us," whispered the young man.

They went out into the corridor. It was empty of people and filled with a sleepy, cosy sort of half-light. The pink curtains shutting out the darkness stirred slightly at the windows, the floor trembled slightly under the carpet.

They lit up. One on either side of the window, they stood and smoked: the young man hastily, with noisy satisfaction; Kuzma slowly and methodically as was his habit. The smoke floated down to the far end of the corridor and dissolved in a whirl.

Having satisfied his initial craving the young man smoked more calmly. He said to Kuzma:

"Do you mind me waking you up?"

"I wasn't really asleep, just dozing."

"Why's that?"

"Because I slept in the daytime, I s'pose. I'll soon reach my station."

"H'm. I always sleep bad after I've been drinking." Then with a sidelong glance and in a voice of calculated indifference: "Funny old pair, that old lady and her man. What do you reckon?"

"Yeah."

"Are they really like that or just putting it on?"

"I think they're really like that. There's all sorts of people in this world."

"She's always coming to him: Sergei, Sergei. Strokes his head. And he stands for it, like it was natural. I'd rather die, especially in front of people."

"They've probably always been like that."

"He's lying when he says he's never had other women."

"Who knows? Maybe he hasn't. Seems to me he hasn't."

"Well, she trusts him anyway. You only have to look at her to see that, don't you?"

"Yeah."

"And if she trusts him she won't go cheating on him either. Waited for him right through the war. Can you beat it?"

The young man even stopped smoking and began chewing his lips thoughtfully:

"She deserves a medal for that," he observed after a little. "They ought to think up some sort of medal for faithful women."

The sound of their voices brought the carriage attendant out of her compartment. She came up and stood staring at them without speaking.

"We're just having a smoke," said the young man.

"Couldn't you find a better place?"

"Got to yell at somebody, haven't you? You're all the same. You ought to take a lesson from that old lady in our compartment. She's never yelled at her old man in her life, not once, and you — you start yapping at the slightest excuse. That's just like your sort. Women never used to be like that."

"All you're looking for's a chance to insult me."

"Who's insulting you? As if I'd take the trouble. I'm just telling you."

There really was not anything insulting in his tone, it was rather the injured, plaintive tone of one who has endured countless trials. The attendant considered his words a moment and walked away. The young man lit his second cigarette and leaned against the wall deep in thought. A moment later Kuzma ran down the corridor after the attendant and asked her how much time was left before they got to his station. Only three hours. No point in going back to bed. Kuzma sauntered back to his companion.

The young man looked past Kuzma as he said:

"My woman wasn't such a bad sort, but somehow we couldn't make a go of it."

"Maybe it was your fault."

"How shall I put it, Kuzma? It was, and again it wasn't. True, I drink, but I'm not the only one. Another would have got used to it and made the best of it. That's what most women do. Grumble just for the sake of it and then go on as if nothing had happened. Don't I see it all around me? But that harpy of mine, she's got principles, she has, so she up and left. It's not as if I drank every day. I'm not an alcoholic. I just drink when I'm in the mood, when I'm with the boys. And I earn enough to pay for everything — vodka and the family as well. I said to her, 'damn your principles!'" He paused and went on in a calmer voice, "I was a fool in the first place. I ought to have known who I was marrying. Another'd have taken me as I am, but not her. Got to toe the line with her."

"Got any kids?"

"A little girl. Soon be four."

"Then you'd better go back. How's the kid going to get on without a father?"

"I don't know. She left me once before but I knew she'd come back that time. Can't say how I knew it, but I did, I knew she was just trying to scare me, show me she had the guts to leave me. Well, go ahead and show me if you want to so badly, I thought. That's your right. and I didn't lift a finger to bring her back. This time I don't feel that way about it. This time she's in dead earnest. I can see that."

"Haven't you gone to her and talked it over?"

"No. Soon as she left I took my holidays and left too. Tit for tat. She's not the only one who's got guts."

"H'm."

Everybody else was asleep. They spoke in low voices so as not to disturb anyone and it was as if they had been posted there on purpose, so that there would be somebody, at least, to talk and think about life, and not miss the best of it during sleep. From time to time the engine whistled in the night; it would be repeated soon, they must listen for it. Nothing is simple at night, everything evokes fear and anxiety, next morning seems infinitely far away and one even doubts that it will come at all; perhaps there will be a breakdown in the eternal order of day and night and the world will remain in darkness or come to a standstill. Who would take it upon himself to assert finally that this is impossible?

The young man said:

"There again, she won't find it easy all by herself with the kid. She'll come to her senses when she sees how hard it is. She's still too young to know the world. It's when we quarrel the women think they can get along without us. Call us all the names in the book.

Then when it's over and they've had time to think about it they're just the opposite — call us pet names and do us favours. We humans need our kind. What'll she do all by herself? Take my word for it, she won't stick it out."

"Why should she be all by herself?" said Kuzma meaningfully. "She'll find somebody else."

"Just let her try," said the young man with spirit. "Find somebody else! Think I'll stand and watch? It'll be just too bad for him and her too."

"But once you've parted . . ."

"Then let her go off somewhere where I can't see her. I don't care who he is, do you think it's pleasant to see another bloke living with your wife, even if you've divorced her? Like cutting a piece of the living flesh off you. I know one thing, nobody in our village would dare live with her. They know damn well I wouldn't stand for it."

He went to drop his cigarette in the rubbish can, stepped on the pedal, but the lid jumped up and fell back with a crash.

"Damn!" said the young man.

The noise brought the attendant to the doorway again and she threw them an angry look. From one of the compartments came the sound of a sleeper turning over, no doubt roused by the crash. Meanwhile the train went on and on.

The young man rolled his cigarette end between two fingers and bits of tobacco spilt on the floor. With a furtive glance around he stooped down and blew them off the carpet, gently lifted the lid of the rubbish can with two hands and threw in the cigarette end, all of this in glum silence.

Again everything was calm and quiet. It was not

possible to see or hear the wind — perhaps it had subsided — nor to see where the train was going. One
could not even see the earth under one's feet. Better to
sleep at such a time. On waking it would be morning,
perhaps the sun would be out, and sunshine was a comfort.

Kuzma thought to himself that soon he would reach
the city. He wished he could just go on travelling
forever and never find out the answer, but soon he
would be there and learn everything.

The young man said:

"Damn it all, maybe I ought to turn round and go
back. A woman loves to have a man give up pleasure
for her sake. Maybe I ought to go back and say, 'Look,
here's how it is . . .' What do you think, Kuzma?"

"I don't know," said Kuzma cautiously. "It's up to
you to decide that."

"Oh, I know," he said, sniffing like a child in his excitement. "But it's not so easy . . ." While he reflected,
the train carried him farther and farther away. At last
he burst out with: "The hell! It's too late now. I've
started out and that's that. We'll see what happens
when I get there. If it's no, it's no. She's not the only
woman in the world." He tried to turn it into a joke.
"If I go back what'll I do with all my money? Have to
drink it up. Better spend it on a holiday."

A little later he made a confession:

"It's all because of that old man and his old lady.
They upset me, they did. Made me go all soft. I'm a
softy in lots of ways. Born that way I guess. It's all I
can do to keep myself from bawling when they show
something sentimental at the pictures. So I always try
not to sit next to the boys. Ashamed to. They laugh

and I bite my lip to keep from crying. I must've been born with a woman's heart."

The train gave a little shudder and there was a grinding of brakes. The attendant came out of her compartment with a lantern in her hand and went unhurriedly to the exit. In other words, nothing was wrong, they had just come to a station. The young man pushed back the curtain and looked out. He saw a few lights in the darkness and said:

"People living even in this godforsaken place."

It would not be long before they reached the city now.

The third day began.

Kuzma got up with that contented feeling one has when all goes well. He himself woke the boys in time for school, stood watching them hurry into their clothes and said to himself he ought to tell them about the money to cheer them up. When they sat down at table Maria poured out milk for the boys as usual and tea for herself and Kuzma. Kuzma winked at Vitka, pointed to his glass and said:

"Let's swap."

Vitka was surprised and delighted.

"Let's," he said.

"Are we short of milk that you must take it away from the child?" said Maria testily. "I'll give you some if you want it."

"I don't."

Far from minding Maria's sharpness, Kuzma was secretly glad she was displaying some feeling: if she could be angry she could also be glad; she had not gone completely numb and soon would be her old self again. All the while they sat at breakfast he and Vitka kept exchanging conspiratorial glances, and Kuzma knew the boy had got his message. Vitka set off for school with a hop, skip and jump.

When it was full daylight Kuzma began dressing to go out, forcing himself not to hurry. And as he passed Maria he said casually:

"I'm off to pick up that money."

She made no reply, but he had not expected her to; he had said the words, the important thing was that they should sink into her consciousness and do their work.

Again it was a grey day like the previous one, Kuzma's day. This, too, would no doubt be his day. Everything pointed to it. As he walked along he was aware of the pleasant weight of his body on his legs; every step begged the next one. He often found such pleasure in walking. It always gave him rest.

And still he fancied there was something strange. The day was as fragile as thin, brittle glass. It must have been the time of year — neither autumn nor winter. Oddly enough, the first flurry of snow had not come yet. Well, they had not long to wait now.

When he had almost reached the administration office the mechanic met him and shook his hand. Kuzma felt embarrassed: after all, he was on his way to collect the mechanic's pay. Not a very pleasant situation. It made him ashamed to look the man in the eye.

The mechanic said:

"Listen, Kuzma, I hope you'll forgive me for what I'm going to say to you. I know I oughtn't to, but I can't think of any other way out. You see, I invited a friend to visit me for the holidays, a classmate from the institute, and I haven't got a kopeck. Not even the price of a bottle of vodka."

"Lord, man, I'll give it to you," said Kuzma with relief. "What're you apologizing for? It's your own money."

"Twenty roubles, if you can spare it. I hardly know anybody here, there's nobody I can borrow it from."

"I'll give it to you of course. As if there could be any question about it."

They went into the office and the mechanic nodded in the direction of the room where the farm specialists gathered.

"I'll wait in there," he said.

Kuzma went to the book-keeper. On catching sight of Kuzma the book-keeper threw himself back in his chair and contemplated him, every line of his body expressing his anticipation. Like all book-keepers, he was mean and meticulous, and suddenly it dawned on Kuzma that he might not get the money after all. Why had he been so sure of it? The chances were all against his getting it; few had ever received money from this man's hands the first time they came for it. That was too easy; he made them come back for it three and four times.

Kuzma was amazed with himself for having assumed all he had to do was go and collect it. As he approached the book-keeper his belly contracted into a hard ball and he prepared himself for the worst.

"Good morning."

"Good morning to you," replied the book-keeper provocatively. "So you've come?"

"Yes."

"To get the money?"

"If you'll give it to me."

The book-keeper felt how deeply aware Kuzma was of his dependence upon him, the book-keeper. And so, to prolong Kuzma's sufferings, he did not speak immediately. At last he said:

"There's been an unpleasant little misunderstanding." Another pause, during which he frowned and gloated. "I didn't know about the arrangement and I went and spent my salary."

"Spent it?"

"That's right. Spent it. In a shop. I can give you an account: bought the wife a jacket for the winter, bought myself felt boots."

When the fact sank into Kuzma's consciousness he nodded.

"And the rest?"

The book-keeper watched Kuzma for some time, savouring the pleasure of keeping him in suspense, before he said:

"The rest is in the safe. Polina's in charge of it. Not everybody's signed for their pay. If Polina wants to give it to you at her own risk, that's her business."

As Kuzma turned to go over to Polina, he heard the book-keeper say:

"Make a note of how much you owe everybody. You've got to pay it back, don't forget.

The book-keeper could hardly bear to let him go, to have the little scene over so soon.

Polina whispered to Kuzma:

"I'll give it to you, only go and find the livestock expert and the vet and tell them to come here at once."

"I will."

She began counting the money with expert deftness, and still it took her an age; it was all in three and one-rouble notes, and when she had gone through them

once she began all over again. Kuzma stood there waiting, watching the flash of her fingers, feeling nothing,
caring nothing. As she handed him the money she
whispered again:

"Have you still got a lot to collect?"

"I have now."

Kuzma stuffed the notes into his pockets, making
them bulge. He patted them down and suddenly
remembered that he had to give the mechanic twenty
roubles. He took out the top pile of three-rouble notes
and counted out thirty roubles instead of twenty
because twenty is not divisible by three. From his corner the book-keeper watched him with cold curiosity
and Kuzma returned his stare until the book-keeper
was obliged to drop his eyes. In revenge he said:

"Don't drink it all up."

"Get away!" replied Kuzma without malice.

He went into the room where the mechanic was
waiting for him and inconspicuously, as if slipping him
a bribe, gave him the thirty roubles. Without turning
round the mechanic murmured:

"Uh-huh."

In the corridor Kuzma saw the vet's wife, but he did
not notice the look of greed and evil intent in her eye,
the look of a beast pursuing its prey. He thought of
going in to see the chairman, opened the door of his
room, found it full of people, and shut it again. What
could he say to him anyway? Better to go home.

The day was still grey, the glass as yet unbroken;
now it appeared to be pasted together out of old
wrinkled transparent paper. Blow on it and it would
crumble. But there was no wind and no one to blow on
it. All about him were rustling, crackling, barking
sounds, like the crackling of the walls of this paper day.

The distances hung there vague and misty. This day thought Kuzma, is the book-keeper's day — and very well it suits his scowling mug.

His bulging pockets prevented him from striding freely ahead. He walked with restraint, as if afraid the money would spill over. He did not rejoice in it; something had happened to joy, it did not stir within him. He knew that he needed the money, but there was no sweetness, not even any gratification in the possessing of it. His only desire was to put it away somewhere, free his pockets of it.

As soon as he got home he stuffed it into a big lemon-drop tin he had brought from Austria after the war, and stood the tin on top of the wardrobe. Now he felt better. As a means of improving his mood he told himself that nobody else in the village had so much money as the tin contained. He had done everything in his power; in the remaining two days he must obtain what was left to make up the thousand. How he would do it he had no idea. But he would think of something; it was impossible that things should end here. If it was a thousand he needed, a thousand he would get. But not now, not today. He could not ask anybody for money today, he had expended all his inner resources. Today he must have a rest.

Steps were heard in the entrance. Kuzma's mind registered the sound as merely steps, not as an indication that someone had come. And so it was with surprise that he looked up to see the vet's wife. How had she got here? Only then did he remember that he had not found the vet and the livestock expert and told them to go and sign.

The vet's wife stood in the doorway with tight lips that quivered in the corners. She was a flat, plain-faced woman and Kuzma could never decide what it was in her that roused his pity at times. He knew she and her husband did not get on together and her appearance demonstrated what happens to a woman when there is no harmony in the home. More from habit than desire Kuzma said:

"Come in, come in; what are you standing there for?"

She did not move. Her lips quivered more than ever.

"What are we going to live on, Kuzma? Have you thought of that? How could you do such a thing?"

Kuzma did not comprehend immediately, and when he did he found nothing to say.

"We've been waiting a whole month for that money." Her voice trembled and broke off so as not to disgrace itself. "We're fifty roubles in debt. What are we going to do?" Kuzma got up and took the tin down from the wardrobe. He upturned it on the table, found the paper telling the salary of each of the specialists, and carefully counted out what was due to the vet.

The vet's wife drew closer, and as he handed her the money he caught sight of Maria. She stopped for only an instant on her way to the kitchen, but her presence made Kuzma feel miserable and ashamed, as if he were stealing from her and she had caught him in the act.

The vet's wife went away.

Kuzma put the remaining money back in the tin and replaced it on top of the wardrobe — nearer the edge this time. With so much money in it someone else was sure to come begging. He must wait.

And he began to wait.

Several times Maria went past and glanced in his direction but he did not look up.

He was waiting.

One hour passed, another, and Kuzma wondered why nobody came; then he heard steps in the entrance and this time the sound told him somebody was coming. He had not waited in vain.

A little girl came in — the agronomist's daughter, and Kuzma said to himself disapprovingly: why can't they come themselves? Why must they send their wives and children? This child may lose the money and then who will be to blame?

"Hullo," said the child shyly, glancing up from under her brows.

"Hullo," returned Kuzma, getting up and reaching for the tin. A good thing he had put it on the edge this time and not against the wall.

"Uncle Kuzma," said the little girl hurriedly, "tell your Vitka to stop following me about."

"What's that?" Kuzma stopped and his raised hand dropped to his side.

"Tell your Vitka not to follow me about. All the kids are teasing us, say I'm his girl. 'Vanka and his girl, went fishing for a pearl' — that's what they shout after us."

Kuzma gave a little laugh.

"You don't say!"

"Why does he do it? I told him not to but he don't listen to me. Let him pick another girl."

"The little rascal!" This time Kuzma laughed heartily. "So he follows you about, does he?"

"The kids make fun of me and it's not my fault."

"You just leave it to me, I'll show him when he comes home! So he follows you about, does he? The little gander!"

"You tell him. He ought to listen to you, you're his father."

"I'll tell him."

"Then I'll be going."

"Off you go and don't worry. You'll see, he'll not so much as look at you again."

She bent her head, almost bowing to him, and ran off. Kuzma chuckled as he watched her go but presently he felt that same cold emptiness coming over him again. He glanced at the tin and sat down. He ought to count the money but he did not want to get up. He was afraid very little was left and the confirmation of his fears would only make him feel worse.

He tried to console himself by saying that only yesterday, twenty-four hours ago, he could not have hoped to have even that much money. He decided he must think about what to do next, whom to appeal to next.

Then he fell into a sort of trance and thought of nothing at all. He just sat there by the tin like a watchman who knows there are no thieves about and are not likely to be. He sat smoking restlessly.

The boys came running home from school and Kuzma tried to remember something he had to say to Vitka but he could not.

The children ate alone in the kitchen, neither Kuzma nor Maria went out to them.

The house was quiet; everybody was at home and yet it was quiet and frightening.

Just before evening old Gordei arrived out of breath. He called Kuzma and went pattering about the room, unable to get a grip on himself. At last he beckoned to

Kuzma from the door and drew him out into the entrance, where he whispered:

"You don't need any money at all, Kuzma. Get me? You can do without that money."

"What are you raving about, Grandad?" said Kuzma with a grimace of annoyance.

The old man tittered merrily:

"Raving? Not me. This old man don't rave, he knows what he's talking about. Listen to what I have to tell you."

Kuzma listened.

"Here's how it is. You can do without that money. Without one single kopeck. And they won't touch Maria. And it'll all be right and lawful." Old Gordei pushed his face close to Kuzma's ear and whispered: "Give her a baby and they can't touch her. It's written in the law: a woman with a baby can't be put in jail."

"What? Are your serious?" cried Kuzma, starting back.

The old man went on with increasing vehemence:

"It's a good man as told me, not one to fool a person. What I'm telling you is God's truth. Give Maria a baby and there's an end to it. What's that for you? Easy as snoring."

"Run along, Grandad, and don't come back with any more of your bright ideas. A fine councillor, you!"

"What!?" exclaimed the old man, incredulous.

Kuzma turned and went into the house.

"Here I am telling you a way out and you go darting into the first hole in the ground!" old Gordei shouted after him. "Very well, do as you like; I've done my duty by you. But don't complain later that I didn't tell you."

The more Kuzma thought about it, the more feasible

the old man's proposal seemed. It offered a solution to all his problems. He himself had heard that the law was merciful to pregnant women, but he had forgotten about it — perhaps because he was not sure it was true. If they could feed six mouths they could feed seven; if they could raise four children, they could raise five. But probably it was too late now. If only he had known sooner! Still, he might suggest it to Maria. No, better not; she'd only think he was unable to raise the money and that would kill her — she was half dead as it was. Every avenue was a dead end. What was he to do? Whom to ask for money tomorrow? As if there was anybody to ask! Nobody. Perhaps he ought to just write off the village and set out early the next morning to see his brother. But had his brother any money? And if he had, would he give him any?

Well, there you were, a pretty mess if there ever was one.

The third day also came to an end. Its hour struck and it went into the ground as into the grave — not a bone of it left. Now there were only two days, three at the outside, before the accountant came back.

Kuzma fell asleep rather early but in the middle of the night the headlights of the lorry woke him up and frightened sleep away. Kuzma got up and sat by the window. Pitch darkness lay upon everything, annihilating all the living, extending endlessly. Kuzma lit a cigarette to steady his nerves, and the very fact that he could still light up made him feel better. All kinds of fears enter a person's mind at night; that is why people try to sleep the darkness away.

Later he went back to bed and had the good fortune to fall asleep again. He had an odd dream: he seemed to be travelling in the lorry that had woken him up, canvassing money for Maria. The lorry knew where to stop for it, Kuzma had but to get out and knock at the window and ask for money. Invariably it was given to him and he went on his way.

He woke up again but it was still night, the darkness had not let up in the least. Again all sorts of fancies entered his mind and one of them was particularly disconcerting: he imagined he was alone in the world, a dark, desolate world that had nothing in common with the one he was used to. But this fancy was shattered by the scream of a plane that seemed to be falling apart; the scream soon died away, as if the plane really had fallen apart, and Kuzma lay listening for other sounds to emerge from the darkness. They did not for a long time, but at least Kuzma now knew he was not alone in the world and could let his mind stray to other things. Out of the depths of his consciousness the thought of Maria rose with an aching pain, dragging with it a chain of other thoughts, the last link of which was the thought of his brother. Then and there he decided to go to his brother early in the morning.

The next morning a high wind was buffeting the walls of the house. Kuzma knew he must hurry. He told Maria he was going to the city and she, silent and immobile of late, passed sentence on his project: his brother wouldn't give him any money. Kuzma, however, had no alternative. Fearing to be left alone and defenceless, Maria said over and over again that his brother would not give him any money. Then she cried. Kuzma made no attempt to comfort her — let her cry, he welcomed her tears, anything was better than that silence.

In the bus he sat watching the furious dance of the wind. Kuzma felt this was only natural, what other sort of weather could one expect when he and Maria were in such a fix? But the wind was blowing with such force that he began to fear the situation might get worse. All day long he waited for it to abate, but in vain; even with closed eyes he could see the earth struggling and groaning under its blows.

Only with the coming of darkness did Kuzma grow more tranquil. He could no longer see what was going on about him and he did not wish to guess what awaited him. He was glad to be able to do nothing, to let the train do everything. He rested, but it was the rest of a man in the dock waiting for his sentence to be pronounced, and Kuzma was keenly aware of this.

He would have liked to travel on and on, but the train had almost reached the city. With horror he realized that he must ask for money again. He was not prepared to. He was afraid of the city, he did not want to enter it. And when he heard a grinding of brakes he shrank, remembering the wind, telling himself it was all a matter of the wind.

Kuzma climbed down the steps of the carriage and stood stockstill in surprise. Snow was falling. Big ragged flakes were coming down, whitening the ground in the growing light of early morning. Not a puff of wind was blowing. A soft, unearthly silence descended along with the snow and blotted out the rare sounds of that early hour.

Kuzma tried to step in other people's tracks so as not to trample the snow as he made his way across the rails to the station building. He was filled with a desolate sense of the inevitability of whatever was about to happen. He forced himself to remember that it was to his brother he had come for aid, not to a stranger, but the idea of his brother coming to his rescue found no purchase in his mind; it kept slipping away, leaving only the word "brothers" which was too short and intangible to bring him much comfort. He thought of the snow and decided it was a good omen. It ought to be. His thoughts were back in the village, now he saw himself coming home and Maria meeting him, with eyes shining with hope. She probably thought Kuzma had seen his brother and collected the money by now, and that the snow was a sign to her, to calm her fears. She was capable of thinking anything.

Kuzma walked over to the bus stop, took out the envelope with his brother's address on it and asked how to get there. He was told which bus to take. He got in. At this early hour, it being Sunday besides, the bus was almost empty. Kuzma felt lost and alone among these strangers; it was as if he had not come into the city of   his own accord but had been brought here by force. The money matter seemed a trifle to him compared with the trial he was facing. He glanced at the people; all of them were looking out of the window, unaware of his presence. He inwardly cursed himself: how in the world could he ever have come to the city for this wretched money! — surely he could have got it in the village!

At last he climbed out of the bus and went down the street looking from side to side, the envelope with the address on it held in front of him. The snow kept coming down, covering his head and shoulders and getting into his eyes as if trying to keep him from going ahead.

He found his brother's house, stopped in front of it to catch his breath, and pushed the wet envelope into his pocket. Then he wiped the snow off his face with his hand, took the last few steps to the door and knocked. Here he was — pray for him, Maria!

In a moment the door would be opened.

Translated by Margaret Wettlin

Borrowed Time

I

Old Anna lay on her narrow iron bed by the stove and waited for death to come for her. It was time, she thought. She was nearly eighty. For a long time she had battled against old age and refused to lie down, but three years ago, completely weakened, she gave in and took to her bed. In summer she felt a little better. She could drag herself outside to warm herself in the sun, and even totter across the road, with pauses to get her breath back, to see old Mironikha. But by the first snowfall the last of her strength had left her, and she could not even carry out the chamber-pot she had inherited from her grand-daughter Ninka. After two or three falls on the porch in as many excursions, she had been forbidden to get up at all, and now she was reduced to sitting up and lowering her feet to the floor for a while, and raising her feet onto the bed and lying down again.

The old lady had borne many children in her time, but only five were still alive today. In the early years, death had called on the family as regularly as a stoat visiting a henhouse, and then came the war. But still, five had survived — three daughters and two sons. One of the daughters still lived in the district centre, another in the nearest provincial town, and the third in faraway Kiev. The elder son had lived in the north, where he had ended up after his military service, then moved back to their provincial town. Anna was living out her last years with her younger son Mikhail, the only one who had not left the village, and his family, doing her best not to get in their way.

This time it looked as if the old lady would not see the winter out. She had been failing since the last days of summer and only the district nurse's injections kept her in this world. On waking she would moan in a thin voice, quite unlike her own, tears would trickle from her eyes, and she would lament: "How often do I have to tell you: leave me be, let me go on my way by myself. If it weren't for your district nurse I'd be there now." And to Ninka, whose task it was to fetch the district nurse, she would say, "Don't you go running for her no more. When Mummy tells you to fetch her, you just hide in the bath-house and wait, and then say the nurse was out. I'll give you a nice sweet!"

At the beginning of September a new affliction struck: the old lady could not stay awake. She no longer ate nor drank. She did nothing but sleep. When disturbed she would open her unseeing, lacklustre eyes for a moment, then fall asleep again. The family disturbed her fairly frequently to make sure she was still alive. She grew wizened, and eventually turned sallow all over, so that she looked ripe for her funeral, but still there was breath in her body.

When it finally became apparent that she had no more than a day or two to live, Mikhail went to the post office and sent telegrams to his brother and his sisters, telling them to come. He then shook his mother and enjoined her, "Hang on till they get here, Mother. You must see them."

The eldest daughter Varvara was the first to arrive

the very next morning. Since she had only fifty kilometres to come, it wasn't hard to hitch a lift. She had no sooner opened the gate than she started wailing, "Ma-a-a!" as if she'd simply pressed a switch, oblivious to everybody.

Mikhail sprang out onto the steps. "Hold on! She's still alive, just sleeping. Scream indoors if you must, or we'll have the whole village down here in a moment!"

Without looking at him, Varvara went into the house, fell heavily to her knees at the old lady's bedside, shook her head and again began to wail, "Ma-a-a!"

The old lady did not wake, and her face remained as sallow as before. Only when Mikhail lightly slapped his mother's sunken cheeks was there any sign of eye movement, as if her eyes were trying to open, and could not.

Mikhail shook her. "Mother! Varvara's here. Look!"

"Ma!" Varvara kept on. "It's me, your eldest. I've come to see you and you won't even look at me. Ma-a-a!"

The old lady's eyelids hovered like the pans of a balance, and fell still, tight shut. Varvara got up and went over to the table, where she could cry in a little more comfort. Here she went into fits of uncontrollable sobbing, knocking her head against the table-top. Five-year-old Ninka stood close to her, stooping down and stepping this way and that to see why Varvara's tears weren't falling to the floor. Her parents chased her away, but she managed to steal back to the table.

That evening Ilia and Liusia arrived from town by the steamer which plied the river. It only made the journey twice a week, so they were lucky to catch it when they did. Mikhail met them at the jetty and led them to the house where they had all been born and in which they had grown up. They walked in silence — Liusia and Ilia on the shaky, narrow boards of the footpath, Mikhail beside them stepping over dry clods of mud. Passing villagers greeted Liusia and Ilia, but did not stop to talk. They looked back curiously when they'd passed. Old women and children stared out of their windows at them. The old women crossed themselves.

At the sight of her brother and sister, Varvara could not restrain herself, and again took up her lament: Ma-a-a!"

"Now hold on," Mikhail stopped her. "Time enough for that."

They all gathered at the old lady's bedside, including Mikhail's wife Nadia, and their daughter Ninka. Old Anna lay still and cold, to all appearances at the very end of life, or the onset of death.

"She's dead!" Varvara gasped.

Nobody hushed her. Instead all were stirred into anxious activity. Liusia hurriedly raised the palm of her hand to her mother's open mouth, and could feel no breath.

"A mirror," she suddenly remembered. "Get me a mirror!"

Nadia leapt to the table, took a piece of broken mirror from it, and handed it to Liusia, having wiped it on her skirt as she ran. Liusia raised it to the old lady's bloodless lips and held it there for a minute or so. A trace of film appeared on it.

"She's alive," she said with a sigh of relief. "She's alive."

Varvara, who had stopped crying, now hurriedly started again, as if she'd misheard her sister. Liusia also shed a tear before walking away. Ninka got hold of the mirror. She started blowing on it and looking to see what would happen. Seeing that nothing very interesting happened, she seized her chance to hold it to the old lady's lips, just as Liusia had done. Mikhail saw her, smacked her soundly in front of everybody, and sent her out of the room. The little girl's yells drowned Varvara's weeping, and Varvara was forced to be quiet.

"Oh, Mother, dear Mother," she sighed.

Nadia asked where she should lay the table — in the living-room, where the old lady's bed stood, or in the kitchen. They decided the kitchen would be better, so as not to disturb their mother. Mikhail brought in a bottle of vodka and a bottle of port. He poured some vodka for himself and Ilia, and port for his wife and sisters.

"Tatiana won't make it today," he said. "No point waiting."

"No, no more transport at this time of day," agreed Ilia. "If she got your telegram yesterday, she'll be on the plane today. Change planes at the city airport. She might even be in the district centre now, but there she'd have to stay. No buses leaving in the evening."

"Or she could be in the city still."

"She'll be here tomorrow."

"Yes, tomorrow for certain."

"If she gets here tomorrow, she'll be in time."

Mikhail, as host, raised his glass first: "Come on. Let's drink to our reunion."

"Can we clink glasses?" asked Varvara anxiously.

"Of course you can. We're not at a wake."

"Don't say that!"

"Say it or not, we . . ."

"It's ages since we were all together round this

table," said Liusia suddenly, in a wistful but agitated voice. "Only Tatiana's not here. When she comes it'll be as if none of us had ever gone away. We always used to sit round this table, and only lay the living-room table when we had visitors. I'm even sitting in my old place. Varvara's not in her old place, nor are you, Ilia."

"As if you'd never been away? Come off it!" Mikhail's hackles began to rise. "You left all right, and for good. Varvara's the only one who calls in now and again, when she needs some potatoes or something. The rest of you might as well have died."

"Varvara hasn't far to come."

"And you've got to come all the way from Moscow, I suppose," Varvara fanned the flames. "One day on the steamer, that's all. You might keep quiet if you've disowned your family. No time for us country yokels now you've become city folk!"

"You've no right to talk like that, Varvara!" said Liusia angrily. "What's all this about city folk and country yokels? Just think what you're saying!"

"Oho! So I've no right to talk, have I? Varvara doesn't count. What's the point talking to her? Might as well talk to yourself, is that it? She's no sister of yours. But might I ask you how long you've been away from here? Varvara might not count, but Varvara's visited our mother lots of times every year, although Varvara's got a bigger family than you. And now it turns out Varvara's in the wrong!"

"When was she last here?" Mikhail asked, backing up Varvara. "Before Ninka was born. And Ilia was last here when he came back from the north. Nadia was weaning Ninka, smearing mustard on her nipples. Remember how you laughed?"

Ilia nodded.

"I didn't come because I couldn't," said Liusia in a hurt tone.

"If you'd wanted to you'd have managed it," retorted Varvara sceptically.

"I tell you I couldn't. In my state of health, if I don't look after myself during my holidays I have to spend the whole year running from one hospital to another."

"Not short of excuses, are we?"

"What do you mean — excuses?"

"Oh, nothing. There's no talking to you at all now you're up on your high horse."

"That's enough now," said Mikhail. "Time for another glass. Can't let the stuff go sour on us."

"You've had plenty," Varvara admonished him. "You men can't think about anything but getting drunk. Your mother's at death's door and here you are boozing. Don't you dare sing any of your songs!"

"Nobody's said nothing about singing. And there's no reason why we shouldn't have a drink. We're old enough to know when to drink and when not to."

"Oh, what's the use of talking to you!"

And so they sat on talking round the long, wooden table their late father had fashioned fifty odd years earlier. Now that they had lived apart for some time there was little resemblance between them. An outsider might have taken Varvara for their mother. Although she was only just out of her forties, she looked much older, and unlike anyone else in the family she was stout and slow in her movements, like an old woman. She took after her mother in one way: in bearing lots of children, one after another. And since death in infancy was rarer by the time she started her family, and since there'd been no war to take them away, her children were all alive and well, although one of the boys was in prison. Her children had brought her little joy. She had fought with them while they were growing up, and gone on fighting with them afterwards, which was why she looked old before her time.

After Varvara, the old lady's second child was Ilia. Then came Liusia, Mikhail, and finally Tatiana, whose arrival from Kiev they expected.

Before joining the army, Ilia had acquired the nickname "Short Ilia," on account of his height, and it had stuck, although there was no "Long Ilia" in the village. He had lost most of his hair, having lived in the north for over ten years, so that his naked head, like an egg, shone in fine weather as if it had been polished. There in the north he had married, not altogether happily: his bride was a woman of normal proportions, but, after they'd been married some time, she blew up to almost twice his size and became as bold as brass with it. Even in the village it was said that Ilia had to put up with a lot from her.

Liusia was also over forty, but nobody would ever have said so to look at her. Unlike the village people, she had a face as smooth and clean as a photograph, and she dressed with care. She had left the village straight after the war, and in her years of city life had learned how to look after her appearance. But then of course she hadn't had all those family worries: God had not blessed her with children.

Mikhail, unlike Ilia, had thick, curly, gypsy locks, and a beard that curled into ringlets as well. His complexion was also dark, chiefly from the sun and the frost as he was out in the open all the year round, logging in the forest in winter, and at the riverside loading in the summer.

They sat on talking at the long kitchen table, so as

not to disturb their dying mother, for whose sake they had gathered in their old home for the first time in so many years. Only Tatiana was missing. Mikhail and Ilia still had some vodka left. The women had pushed back their glasses, but still they sat, languid from the reunion and the conversation, and from everything that had happened to them that day, and fearful of what might happen tomorrow.

"I should have sent young Volodia a telegram straight away," said Mikhail. "He could have been here with us by now. It'd be good to see him again, see how he's grown up."

"Where is he?" asked Ilia.

"In the army. Serving his second year. Promised to come home on leave in the summer, but it looks as if he's got into trouble and they won't let him. He says somebody in his unit deserted his post, and he got the blame because he was in charge. But I wouldn't be surprised if he'd done something himself. What do you think? Would they let him out to see his grandmother?"

"They ought to."

"I should have sent a cable yesterday. Instead of fooling around, wondering how to word it so they wouldn't ask questions. After all, a grandson's not a son."

"You should have just said: Granny's very ill. Come at once," said Varvara.

Nadia was looking strained at being cheated out of the joy of seeing her son again. "That's what I told him. But do you think he'd listen?"

"Best to wait a bit," said Liusia.

'Yes, best to wait. Or we might just make things

worse. We'll let him know right away, when the time comes. They ought to let him out for the funeral."

Varvara heaved a sigh. "Oh dear! Who would have thought it? Our one and only Ma!"

"How many do you want?" enquired Ilia.

"Fine brother and son you are!" said Varvara indignantly. "Always sneering. Always trying to make me look stupid. I'm no stupider than you, so you can stop your sneering."

"What's biting you? Did I say you were stupider?"

"Didn't you?"

Liusia asked Nadia softly, "Have you got a sewing machine?"

"Yes, but I don't know if it works. I haven't had it out for ages."

"I was looking this morning, and I couldn't find even one black dress — just when I need one. I ran to the shop and bought some material, but of course there wasn't time to make it up, only to cut it out. I'll have to make it up here."

"No time left today."

"Yes, there is. I sew quickly. I'll set the machine up here in the kitchen, when everybody's gone to bed."

"All right. I'll get it out and you can see."

Before going to bed they all looked into their mother's room, to see what news they would have to sleep on. Liusia felt for her pulse, and found it with difficulty — very feeble. Mikhail lost his patience and shook his mother by the shoulder, and then they all heard a distant sound from somewhere within, something between a groan and a snore. It didn't sound like their mother's voice at all. It was as if death, busy at its work inside, were snarling at them to keep their distance. Everybody hushed Mikhail, but that noise made them all feel uncomfortable. Even little Ninka pressed up against Nadia and grew quiet.

"Let's hope she lasts the night," said Varvara with a sob. Then she too fell silent.

They started getting ready for bed. The house was big enough, but in the fashion of the provinces divided into only two rooms. The old lady occupied one, and Mikhail and his family the other. Nadia made a bed for herself and Mikhail on the floor and gave up their bed to Liusia. A folding couch was found for Varvara, and set up in the old lady's room, so that Varvara could keep an eye on her. They were going to put Ilia on the floor in the same room, but he decided to sleep in the bath-house, which stood in the garden. It was clean, free of soot and stale air. They gave him a fur coat and some woolly jerseys to lie on, and a quilted blanket to cover himself with, and off he went, leaving instructions to wake him if anything happened.

They decided to switch off the electric light in the old lady's room, and leave an oil lamp on all night, with the wick turned low.

Nadia got out her sewing machine and stood it on the kitchen table. Liusia tried it on a piece of cloth. It worked well.

"Go to bed," said Liusia to Nadia. "Get some sleep while you can. There's no knowing what sort of night we're in for."

Nadia went out. Mikhail asked her something and she made some reply. Both spoke in a whisper.

The machine stuttered so loudly when Liusia began to sew that she started and let go the handle. It sounded like gunfire, and it brought out a frightened Varvara, her feet slapping against the floor. On seeing Liusia she calmed down somewhat: "Thanks be to God! I wondered who it was. You had me all shaking. What's all the hurry then?"

Liusia went on sewing without replying.

"Getting our black togs ready for the funeral, are we?"

"Is it really necessary to ask about it?"

"Did I say something?"

"Nothing really."

"You go on with your sewing, I won't say anything. I'll just sit beside you for a while, then go to bed. I won't get in your way."

Varvara pulled up a stool and sat down. She had not undressed yet, only unhooked her stockings, which now hung below her knees, looking like peeled-off skin.

From far away on the river came the muffled sound of a steamer's siren, then again and again.

Varvara raised her head to listen, knitting her brow in concentration. "What's all that about?"

"I don't know. Must be signalling to somebody."

"Fine time to do it. Gave me quite a turn."

She sat on for a little while, then reluctantly rose. "I'll be going. Will you be long?"

"Until I've finished."

"We shouldn't be going to bed tonight," said Varvara shaking her head. "We should have all sat up talking. It'd be cheerier. We're doing the wrong thing, I can feel it in my bones."

She went out, but soon came back, giving Liusia a start. She leaned against the wall.

"What is it?" asked Liusia.

"Either I'm imagining it, or she's gone. Come and see."

Liusia did not believe her, but since she could not

say so she went to her mother's room. She took her wrist, but her senses could detect nothing but Varvara's heavy, whistling breath behind her back. She had to chase Varvara away, and even then she could not immediately feel the faint beat of her mother's pulse. It seemed to emanate from a point many miles away, and didn't always reach her. It seemed even fainter than the last time, and often missed a beat.

"You lie down," said Liusia, feeling sorry for her sister. "As long as I'm sewing I'll keep an eye on her, and I'll wake you up when I've finished."

"I won't be able to sleep," said Varvara with a childish sob. "Our Ilia's a sly one. Off he goes out of the house — do as you please! How can I sleep at a time like this? I'd just keep turning things over and over in my mind. I'd rather sit here with you."

"All right, if you like."

"I'll be quiet."

She sat down again at the table, sighed, touched the material, and watched Liusia at her work.

"Will you take this dress home with you afterwards?" she asked.

"Why?"

"I was thinking that if you didn't, I might take it."

"What good would it be to you? You'd never get into it."

"Not for myself. My girl's shot up to about your height. It'd fit her perfectly."

"Is she that hard up for clothes?"

"She hasn't got much. All her dresses are worn. And you know how a girl likes to show a bit of style."

"What's so stylish about a black dress?"

"She's nice and easy to please. It'll be good for going out in the rain, when you can't wear flowery dresses."

"All right. When I leave I'll give it to you," Liusia promised.

"I'll tell her it's a present from her auntie," said Varvara gratefully.

"You can tell her that if you like."

They fell silent, and when Liusia stopped the machine the sound of snoring reached them from Mikhail's room. Varvara pricked up her ears: "Who could that be?" Then, when the snoring gathered strength, she became annoyed. "What a disgrace! And what a time to pick! Some people just have no shame and no conscience! Calls himself a son!" She stopped and suddenly appealed to Liusia in a piteous voice, "Can we go and take another look at her? I'm scared by myself."

As before the old lady was barely clinging to life. Everything in her seemed to have died, except her heart, which kept beating by force of inertia. But it was clear that it too had not much longer to run. Perhaps only until morning.

Varvara sat up as long as Liusia sewed. And then Liusia had to give up her bed to her, and take the folding couch herself. Otherwise Varvara would have given her no chance to get to sleep.

2

Morning came in due course, but before the sun was up such a dense, impenetrable fog rose from the river that everything was lost in it. The cows in the village lowed with hollow voices. The crowing of the cocks sounded short and muffled, like fish splashing in water. The sounds of human activity could be heard too, all in a dripping white haze which hid everything. These days the dawn came late enough as it was, and now this fog had closed in on top of it, so you really had to grope your way around.

Nadia was up first in the house. Until recently she had relied on her mother-in-law to get her up as soon as she heard their cow. Even if she was awake, Nadia would not start the day until the old lady called out from her bed. So now she did not get up at once, but waited, by force of habit, for her mother-in-law's call, although she knew it would not come. The unmilked cow, however, cried out anxiously for attention, and Nadia had to get up. Thinking constantly about the old lady, and fearful of the morning's news, she dressed noiselessly and stole out of the house, taking down the milking pail from a nail in the porch.

Varvara, who was used to rising early, got up next. Seeing that Nadia had gone and that the others were still asleep, she heaved four or five loud, deep sighs, ending each one with a prolonged groan, to wake Mikhail, who was asleep on the floor. But he didn't so much as stir. Varvara heaved another sigh, this time unconsciously. It was frightening to be in a house where all the living seemed to be under a spell of sleep. Trying not to disturb anybody, she crept to the door of the other room, where the old lady was lying, and stopped in the doorway. Apart from the front door, the house had no doors, only empty doorways. Varvara stood and peered apprehensively into the semi-darkness. She could not see the old lady's face as the foot of the bed was in her way, but something — whether alive or dead — was there under the covers, and Varvara hadn't the courage to go in and look. She turned back, thinking that she ought to go out to the privy now, so as not to have to later when she'd be too busy.

Varvara and Nadia came in from the yard together. Nadia set about pouring the milk through a cheesecloth strainer in the kitchen. Varvara hovered behind her, looking over her shoulder from one side, then the other. Liusia had left the sewing machine on the table from the night before, and Nadia asked in a whisper, "Did she finish her dress last night?"

"Yes," replied Varvara, also in a whisper. "Except for one or two odds and ends." Unable to restrain herself, she begged her sister-in-law, "Let's go and wake her. I can't bear it any longer."

"Just a moment. I'll take the milk out."

Like a shadow, Varvara followed Nadia into the porch, not once, but twice, because there were two churns and it didn't occur to her to take one, so she went out twice empty-handed. When Nadia had finished she wiped her hands on a rag and led the way into the old lady's room.

Liusia was asleep, that was clear, but nobody could undertake to say the same about the old lady. Nadia glanced at her and then averted her eyes. Varvara didn't dare look at all, but started shaking Liusia, who awoke and jumped up at once, sending the folding couch skidding away.

"Well?" asked Liusia. "How is she?"

Varvara got ready to cry: "I don't know. I don't know. You have a look."

Liusia collected her wits as she ran her hands over her hair and put on the dressing-gown which had been lying on a stool. Then she went over to her mother.

Knowing how to recognize the signs of life, she took her mother's wrist, but dropped it at once and started back when the old lady suddenly gave a thin, mournful groan and lapsed into silent immobility again. Varvara began to wail: "Ma-a-a! Ma-a-a! Open your eyes for us, please!"

Mikhail ran up in his underwear, still too sleepy to take in what was happening. "Is it over? Oh, Mother, Mother . . . I'll have to send Volodia a telegram."

"Don't," Nadia stopped him. "What's got into you?"

Liusia found her mother's pulse and said with relief, "She's alive."

"Alive?!" Mikhail rounded angrily on Varvara. "Then what the hell are you howling about, if she's not dead? Get outside, or you'll wake Ninka! Starting up your damned cats' chorus!"

"Quiet!" said Liusia. "Get out of here, all of you."

Before breakfast, while Nadia was frying some potatoes, Liusia set about making the buttonholes on her new dress, and sewing on the buttons she had brought with her.

Varvara went tearfully to the bath-house to wake Ilia. "Our mother's alive! She's alive!"

"Alive? Then why wake me?" grumbled Ilia.

"I wanted to tell you, and make you happy."

"You could have let me get my sleep, and then told me. No need to wake me this early."

"It isn't early. There's a fog."

The fog lasted until past ten, when some strange power came to lift it away, and the sun broke through, still with its summer brightness and strength. At once everything became more cheerful, and the village seemed to stretch joyfully. It was already September, yet there was no hint of autumn in the air, even the potato leaves were still green, and in the forest there were only a few patches of brown, as if the sun had scorched the leaves on a hot day.

In recent years summer and autumn seemed to have changed places: in June and July the rain poured down, and then the weather was as fine as could be right up to mid-October. Fine weather was all very well. The trouble was it came at the wrong time. How could the women know when to dig the potatoes? In the old days, this would have been the time, and yet, while the fine weather held, you wanted to give the potatoes a bit of time to fill out nicely. How could they fill out in summer if they were floating like fish in water? But if you waited it might rain again, and then just try picking your potato out of the mud. It was all a gamble. You just couldn't tell when was the time to catch them. It was the same with haymaking: one peasant would mow his hay at the usual time, only to see it rot in the rain. Another would drink the haymaking season away, not go out to mow till it ought to have ended, and get his hay in dry. The weather no longer knew what it was doing, it forgot when things had to be done, like a senile old woman. People put it down to the huge lakes which had been formed by damming most of the rivers.

For breakfast Nadia fried some potatoes, fresh out of the ground, and put out a deep bowl of salted milk-cap mushrooms to go with it. At the sight of the mushrooms Liusia let out a cry: "Milk-caps! The real thing! It's so long since I had any, I'd forgotten they even existed. I can hardly believe my eyes."

"I never say no to milk-caps," said Ilia, smacking his lips. "You don't see 'em every day. If we had something to wash 'em down with, I wouldn't say no to that either!"

"Why didn't you put them out last night," said Mikhail reproachfully to his wife. "They'd have gone down a treat with the booze. This way they're wasted."

Nadia, flushed with pleasure at having pleased her guests, explained: "I thought of getting them out last night, but then I thought they wouldn't be properly pickled yet. I only bottled them a short while back. But this morning I went and tried them and they didn't taste too bad. So I thought I'd get them out, in case anybody fancied them. Help yourselves if you like them."

"Are there any more where these came from?"

"A few. There's just no time to pick them. I see people coming back with some every day, but I just can't get round to it. Always something else that needs doing. I've only been out looking twice this summer, and then only in the closest spots."

"Our Tatiana used to like picking mushrooms," Liusia recalled. "She knew all the places. I went with her once when she was only a little girl, and before I knew it she'd got a whole bucketful. I asked her where she'd found them, and she said, 'Here.' I said, 'How come you can find them and I can't?' 'I don't know,' she said. I said, 'You must have been here before, and picked them and hidden them somewhere.' She got all hurt and walked away. We came home separately, she with a full bucket, and me with a sprinkling on the bottom of mine."

"She always used to leave a few," Mikhail explained. "She'd leave a little one, and pick it the next day, when it was bigger. She'd remember exactly where it was.

She used to take me along. Of course I just wanted to fill a bucket and get 'em home — never mind what they were like. But she'd see if I picked a little one, and go for me! Once we had a fight about it. For myself I preferred picking orange-caps. It's quicker. They usually grow in clusters."

"The real mushroom-picking artist was Ilia," Liusia remembered with a laugh. "He'd fill his bucket with grass, and cover it with a layer of mushrooms, to make it look as if the bucket was full of them."

"Yes, I won't deny it," Ilia admitted cheerfully.

"Remember how Mother used to send us to pick wild onions on the far side of the Upper Brook? It was marshy there, and the onions grew on the dry tussocks. We used to get soaked and plastered in mud — what a sight! We'd lay our sacks on a dry spot and go jumping from one tussock to the next. And we had competitions to see who could pick most. We even stole onions from each other. And we used to swim out to that island for garlic . . . What's its name . . .?"

"Fir-tree Island," Mikhail reminded her.

"That's it, Fir-tree Island. Where they used to mow hay for the *kolkhoz*. I remember raking hay there: it was hot, spiders stinging, hay getting into your hair, under your clothes . . ."

"Must have been clegs, not spiders," muttered Varvara. "Spiders don't sting, they just weave webs in corners."

"Maybe they were clegs. Except I don't think that's the proper word for them. But we used to cut our hay on another island . . . The name'll come to me in a moment. Some sort of tree again."

"Larch Island."

"Yes, Larch Island. The blackcurrants on it! Masses

of them! The bushes used to be weighed down to the ground. You could eat and eat till your teeth and tongue tingled from them. Big, fat currants, tasty as anything. You could fill a bucket in an hour. I expect there are still lots these days."

"You're joking. There aren't any," said Nadia with a flap of her hand. "No bushes left either, since the timber-works has been there. You can walk and walk and not find any . . ."

"Oh, what a shame!"

"There used to be lots of blueberries on the hill as well. Now they're gone too. The cattle trample them into the ground, and people take everything that's left. They tear them up as if there was no tomorrow, and take them away, leaves and all. I've even seen them with whole bushes."

"But there are milk-caps, you say."

"Yes, it's not a bad year for them. People are picking them."

"I must get out and pick some, even if I don't do anything else."

"You could have come mushrooming here without waiting for a telegram," said Varvara, needling.

At that Liusia lost her temper. "Varvara! It seems I can't say two words to you these days! Whatever I say, you don't like it. You can't jump on me every time I open my mouth, just because you're older. The rest of us are old enough to know what we're doing. You might remember that. What's wrong with you anyway?"

"I didn't say nothing, did I? I don't know why you flare up at me like this."

"So I'm the one who flares up!"

"Are you saying I do?"

"Eat up, won't you?" begged Nadia. "Or the potato will get cold. It's not nice when it's cold. You were saying how good the mushrooms are, and you're not taking any. Eat up, it's a long time till lunch."

"Tatiana ought to be here soon. Then we'll all be together."

"Should be here by lunchtime."

"Maybe sooner, if she's already in the district centre."

"Maybe she put up for the night in somebody else's house, rather than ours. Not good enough for her . . ." said Varvara, already finding cause for complaint.

"No, Tatiana will come to us," said Mikhail. "No airs about our Tatiana."

"Didn't used to have any, but we'll have to see what she's like now," Varvara insisted. "Been away so long."

"She's got furthest to come. It's not that easy to get here from where she lives."

"She didn't have to go off that far, did she? And if she absolutely had to marry a soldier, well, there are soldiers all over the place nowadays. She could have found one a bit closer to home. Running off like a homeless orphan!"

Liusia shook her head wearily. "Best not to argue with Varvara. She's always right."

"Don't you like it when you hear the truth?"

"What did I tell you?" Liusia stood up and said to Nadia, "Thank you Nadia. I enjoyed the mushrooms so much."

"No need to thank me, you hardly had any."

"It was a lot for me. My stomach's not used to these things now, and I'm afraid to eat too many at once."

"You won't get diarrhoea from milk-caps," said Varvara gently. "They don't upset you, I know from experience. My kids have never had no trouble from 'em either."

Liusia went out with a sigh of disgust. Varvara didn't understand, and asked her brothers, "What's got into her?"

"No idea."

"You can't talk to her at all."

"You ought to speak city language to her, speak proper, not like us," Ilia advised her with a chuckle.

"I don't speak city language. I've only been there once in my life. But she grew up in the village, didn't she? She ought to speak my language."

"Maybe she's forgotten it."

"She's forgotten my language, and I've never learnt hers — so now we can't say anything to each other. Is that it?"

After breakfast Mikhail and Ilia sat down on the porch to have a smoke. The weather was clearing. The last of the mist was receding higher and higher into the sky, forming wide, clear pools of blue, broken only on the horizon. Fearing this limitless beauty, unable to take it in, the eye sought something closer to rest on. The forest, caressed by the sun, turned a bright green and seemed to step back from the village, enclosing it on only three sides, leaving the fourth to the river. As the brothers watched, some hens in the yard clucked idly, aimlessly, and fluttered their wings. Some pullets cheeped, and a pig gave little squeals of pleasure as it lay comfortably slumped in the warm against the fence.

Ninka came out, and the sun dazzled her sleepy eyes. She shielded them with her hands and frowned, then, as soon as her eyes had adjusted to the light, she darted behind the woodpile and squatted down. A hen came up menacingly, contriving to stay behind her back.

Ninka shooed it away, turned round, and inadvertently showed her bare backside round the edge of the wood-pile. Mikhail shouted at her: "Ninka, how may times do I have to tell you to go further away from the house? I'll push your nose in it, like a kitten, if you don't!"

Ninka hid, and replied in a hurt voice with the excuse, "The hens'll eat it."

"I'll give you hens!"

Quiet had fallen over the village after the bustle of the early morning chores. Those who had to go to work had gone. The housewives had fed and milked their animals, and were now going quietly about their housework, out of sight. It was early yet for the children to be outside. Everything was still and peaceful, with only occasional, familiar sounds: a cow mooing, the creak of a gate, or the apparently unintentional sound of a human voice — none of this demanding an audience, nor any reply. It was simply to make sure that the world of the living should not seem empty and lifeless. This mid-morning lull stilled all voices and all movement, and combined with the bright, warm light that fell from the open sky to quietly, imperceptibly warm up the village, after the cool of the night.

"Our mother was a good soul, when all's said and done," said Mikhail, moved by the gentle charm of the silence. "She must have been. Look what a day it's turned out for her! It's not everybody gets a day like this to die on."

"Yes, the weather's turned out nice," replied Ilia.

"There's one thing we ought to do. Buy some of the clear stuff while it's still in the shop. If we don't, and the pay packets come in tomorrow, there'll be none left. Then we'll have to hunt high and low for some."

"You mean vodka?"

"Yeah. I don't go for that red wine. Don't care if we can get any or not. Bloody stuff gives you a hell of a head." Mikhail shuddered at the thought of the hangover. "You feel like the black death all day."

"We'll have to get some for the women though."

"We'll get a bit. No need for much. The women don't seem to go for it much either these days. Prefer the clear stuff."

"Equality all round, eh?"

"Yeah."

They exchanged knowing smiles, but this was not the time for a lively male discussion of the question of women's rights, so they let the matter drop.

"How much vodka shall we get?" asked Ilia.

"I don't know," said Mikhail with a shrug. "Better make it a crate. No use taking less. We'll have half the village here. Got to keep up appearances. Mother was never stingy."

"Right, a crate it is."

"Got any money on you?"

"Fifty roubles."

"I'll get some from Nadia. We'll have enough."

"Shall we ask Liusia and Varvara for some?"

"Varvara wouldn't have any anyway. We could ask Liusia though. She ought to have plenty, and she ought to contribute, being one of the family. She's not a found-ling, so it wouldn't do to make an exception for her. She'd be offended if we did."

"Shall we go straight away?"

"Yes, why hang about? I'll just find Nadia, then we'll be off. We must get it today, or it won't be there tomorrow if the wages come in, that's for dead certain. That's the way it is here. You're looking forward to it, tongue hanging out — and it's all gone. Drink some water instead. Of course, at any other time it wouldn't be so bad, but for us now, if it came to a dry funeral, we'd never live it down. We've got to see our mother off properly, sparing no expense." Mikhail stood up, but went on talking without pausing. "Listen: I'll go and see the wife. We should have a bit of cash left over. And you go and ask Liusia. I don't like to ask her for money in my own house. Then we'll go and get the stuff. We've made the right decision. We must get it. No good waiting."

They soon set off, fired with excitement at the thought that they were going to collect the liquor, a lot of it, more than one man could carry. The shop was close by, and before pay-day it was deserted, so they returned home without delay, the bottles clinking in the crate as they set it down in the larder.

"That's better," said Mikhail. "You feel easier in your mind when you've got it home. We'll leave it here, out of harm's way. We can pick up the port any time we like. There ain't much demand for it."

Suddenly Ninka gave a cry. Mikhail opened the door to shout at her to be quiet, but seeing that the three women had already set upon her he said nothing and listened.

"It was her," Ninka was protesting.

"What do you mean — her?" Liusia chivvied the girl.

"It wasn't me. It was her . . ."

"What did she do? Tell us. Or have you lost your tongue?"

"She opened her eyes and saw me and . . ."

"Yes? And?"

"Saw you, did she?" scoffed Nadia. "And how come

I saw you reaching into her suitcase? On whose invitation was that? Left something in it by mistake, had you?"

"She pointed to it herself!" exclaimed Ninka. "You weren't there, so what do you know about it?"

"Don't you dare talk to your mother like that! Wherever do you pick these things up?"

"Wait a minute, Nadia," Liusia stopped her and bent down to speak to Ninka. "Where did she point?"

"Where? Under her bed."

"She keeps sweets for Ninka in her suitcase," Nadia explained.

"How did she do it?" Liusia persisted. "Tell us all about it. How did it happen? Well?"

"I was looking at her. She wasn't looking at me, and then she opened her eyes and started looking back at me. And she pointed."

"Did she say anything to you?"

"No."

"Oh my goodness!" said Varvara with a deep sigh. "Where will it all end?"

"She's not usually a bad girl," Mikhail came in on his daughter's side. "Never has been. Maybe Mother really did have a few lucid moments before dying, and Ninka just happened to be beside her."

At the mention of death a watchful hush came over them, so that they thought twice before drawing breath, as if the air were tainted with corrosive vapours from beyond the grave, which the living must not breathe. Then they silently approached the old lady's bed, to see if there was any change in her. There was none. In fact, now that the light was stronger her face looked more dead than ever, but her heart was still beating, still holding her in the world of men.

Mikhail went back outside to Ilia, who had spent all this time crumbling bread for some chickens, and told him, "Ninka says our mother opened her eyes."

"Well I never!" exclaimed Ilia, putting out his foot to scare away a hen. "What made her do that?"

"I don't know."

"So she's still alive?"

"Yes. We went and looked."

There was some purpose after all in the day's turning out so fine. It could not be an accident, and the purpose might very well have something to do with the old lady. The weather seemed to be at its mildest and gentlest over the village, more so over the old lady's house than anywhere else. Lunchtime was drawing near, without the sounds which usually accompanied it. The day flowed quietly on, as if guarding somebody from unwanted disturbance. The sky seemed lower than it had been earlier, and almost lost in expectant thought. September days were not the year's youngest, having seen a lot since the spring, and this day gave every appearance of knowing everything that was going on, and perhaps even of wanting to help the old lady in some way, to move her from the exposed place of judgment where she now lay. An imperceptible nudge would be enough to dislodge her from the point where she had stuck.

Having brought the vodka safely home, Mikhail and Ilia did not know what to do. Everything else seemed trivial by comparison, and they felt that they were at a loose end. Time hung heavy on them. They exchanged a few words about the fact that Tatiana still hadn't come, although she could have been and gone ten times by now. Ilia asked Mikhail when he had to go back to work, and Mikhail replied that he'd got a bit of time off. But everything they said seemed somehow flat, unnecessary, and did not cling together as a conversation. The two brothers realized that the only thing they could do now was wait, but one could wait for something in a number of different ways, and they gradually began to wonder whether they were spending the waiting hours as they should, or simply wasting time. The thought of their dying mother would not leave them, but neither did it cause them undue anguish. Both had done what they had to do: one had spread the word, the other had come, and together they had collected the vodka. All the rest was up to their mother, or somebody else, but not up to them. You couldn't start digging a grave for a body that still had life in it. All their lives they had had work to do, and now, all of a sudden, they had none, because it wasn't done to get on with odd jobs in the circumstances, and the circumstances gave them nothing more to do.

Mikhail tried to strike up a conversation again: "When all's said and done, we knew she wouldn't live forever, we knew she hadn't long to go. We ought to have got used to the idea, but we haven't."

"Can't help it," said Ilia. "When it's your mother . . ."

"Yes, that's right enough. We've no father, and now Mother's passing on, and we'll all be left alone. We're not kids any more, but still we'll be alone. Well, she hasn't been normal for a long time, but still you used to reckon that as long as she was alive, her turn had to come before ours. She sort of shielded us, we didn't have to worry. Now we'll have it in mind all the time."

"Why keep it in mind? What difference does it make?"

"Maybe we shouldn't, but it's hard not to. It's like

coming out into an open space, where you can't hide." Mikhail shook his curly head and paused. "Then there's our own kids. As long as they've got a granny they're still little, and you feel young yourself, but now, with her gone, the kids will start pushing us along the way. You can't stop the buggers growing."

Before he could finish Nadia ran out and hurriedly called to them, her voice sounding strange and anxious: "Come quick, you men! Hurry!"

"What's up?"

"It's Mother . . ."

By the time they got there the old lady had lost consciousness again, but not without suddenly uttering a word. What it was they could not make out, and when Liusia and Varvara ran up she was still looking straight ahead, but her eyes were closing. Something was happening inside her, although she was no longer stirring. It was clear that some process had begun, and that she was about to move on from the point where she had stuck. Even in her face changes could be seen: there was more depth, more boldness in it, and the strength that was left in those depths caused it to twitch, as if winking with closed eyes.

They stood around their mother and looked fearfully on, not knowing what to think, or what to pin their hopes on. The fear that they now felt was quite unlike any fear they had ever known before, because it was more terrible, and its cause was death. It was as if death had seen and noticed all their faces, never to forget them again. And it was frightening to watch this happening: some day it would happen to them, and it would be just like this, and they did not want to look, so as not to have this scene constantly before them in the future, and yet they could neither leave nor turn away. And something else held them there — the thought that death, now busy with their mother, might be displeased if they left the room, and none of them wanted to attract its attention more often than necessary. So they stayed, and stood still.

Something began to stir behind the old lady's eyes, prodding them into motion, and after a moment, with difficulty, they opened, made an effort to cling onto the light of day, failed, and closed again. They remained motionless for several minutes, then came to life again and heaved themselves open. This time there was more strength in them, and in the uncertain light which they admitted the old lady saw something which was also uncertain and indistinct, like a vision. A look of despair and pain appeared on her face, and she blinked to try and banish the vision, but could not, and closed her eyes again, this time apparently by an act of her own will. But the vision she had seen would not leave her mind, it demanded to be checked. She felt as if memories had arisen of her former life, and she wanted to establish where she was now, and whether she was in her right mind. Slowly she raised her eyelids, over which she had now regained control, and looked out. Yes, they were still there. Now she saw them closer and recognized them. This was more than she could bear in silence, and a series of dry, feeble sounds broke from her chest, like a hen clucking.

Varvara gasped, clapped her hands and pressed them to her throat to stop herself crying out.

The old lady fell silent, as if she had spent her last ounce of life. Her eyes closed, but she was breathing so hard that her whole body shuddered. At length her breathing became more even, but the blanket could still be seen rising and falling.

They waited, feeling more acutely than ever that they were the sons and daughters of this old woman, feeling sorry for her, and even more sorry for themselves, because after her death they would be left with the enduring grief of bereavement. Besides this, each of them in his own way felt a new and unfamiliar kind of bitter self-satisfaction at being here, by their mother's bedside in her last hour, as a son or daughter should. In this way they felt they had earned her forgiveness, and some other forgiveness which had little to do with their mother, little to do with humans, but which was nevertheless vital to them. It was a mixture of fear and pain. What frightened them most was that, in watching their mother's slow death, they were witnessing something they felt nobody ought to see, and although they could not admit it to themselves, they wished it would end as soon as possible.

The old lady was still breathing.

Ilia could not contain himself and whispered something to Mikhail. As if in answer to him the old lady suddenly opened her eyes again and looked fixedly at him. She wanted to burst into tears, but could not — she had no tears. Varvara rushed to help her and started wailing in a loud voice. That voice was the support the old lady needed, and thanks to it she did not relapse into sleep again. The power of speech had left her, and yet the words dearest to her, the words which had always been on the tip of her tongue, came back to her.

"Liusia," she said with an effort. "Il-ia. Var-va-ra."

"We're here, Mummy. We're here," Liusia encouraged her. "You lie still. We're here."

"Ma-a-a!" wailed Varvara.

Now the old lady trusted her senses and the voices

around her, and lay quietly in her last moments of joy and suffering. But as she looked at them she seemed to be sinking further and further from them. Suddenly something stopped her, she surfaced again, and screwed up her face, looking for somebody. Varvara's crying bothered her. Somebody had the presence of mind to silence her.

"Tanchora," the old lady said imploringly.

On hearing her pet name for Tania, they exchanged glances and answered at once:

"She's not here yet."

"Any time now."

"She won't be long."

The old lady understood and gave a slight nod. A peaceful look came over her face and her eyes closed. Again she was far away.

They left her — all in need of rest. Only Varvara remained beside her mother, weeping softly, but nobody minded her tears. In fact they would have felt uncomfortable if she had stopped.

3

Whether it was a miracle or not nobody could say, but the fact was that the old lady began to revive when she saw her children. She lost consciousness two or three more times, as if slipping unnoticed into the dark depths beneath her, but each time she awoke again and cautiously raised here eyelids with a fearful moan. Were they really there, or had she seen them in a dream? One of them would unfailingly be at her bedside, and would call the others. She would recognize them and calm down, trying to weep. On the last occasion she had actually managed it, and she had heard her own feeble, worn-out voice, which came with such difficulty because it had apparently decided never to be heard again.

Little by little the old lady recovered, all her faculties and functions returned one by one to her control, and all seemed to be in working order. By evening she was so much better that she called Nadia and asked, "Could you make me a bit of *kasha* . . . the kind you used to give Ninka. Out of groats. Make it thin."

"You mean semolina?"

"That's the stuff. Just a drop. To ease my throat. Make it thin."

A flurry of activity began in the house. Luckily Nadia had some semolina, but now that lunch was over the stove had cooled right down. They decided to heat the semolina on the electric hot-plate, which they had to search long and hard for, and when they found it they discovered that the power hadn't come on yet. Mikhail was despatched to light the stove in the yard. Liusia and Varvara started arguing over what to heat the semolina in. Varvara favoured giving her mother a pailful, while Liusia insisted that it wouldn't be a good thing to give her a lot at once. If she wanted more, they could make it separately. Ilia went out with Mikhail and hung about at his elbow, repeating, "What a woman, eh? Ever seen anything like it?"

"It's in the family," said Mikhail. "We don't lie down and die that easy."

"Give us some *kasha*, she says. See that? To tell the truth I couldn't believe it. I thought it was all over. And up she pipes: Make us a bit of *kasha*. She's hungry.

Would you believe it!"

"Old women always do keep going a long time. The more decrepit they look, the longer they live. You mark my words. You think their time's up, they can't hold on any longer, but still they go on kicking. Don't know where they find the strength."

Ilia couldn't get over his surprise. "What a woman! What a woman! Whoever would have thought it! You and I get the vodka in for her funeral, and she pipes up: Wait a bit, children, she says. I want a bit of *kasha* first." He laughed, and repeated, "I want a bit of *kasha* first. Can't do nothing till I've had some *kasha*."

Mikhail was more restrained in his reply. "She's very weak. Bound to be, she hasn't taken a bite of anything for days. Who wouldn't be weak?"

The women ran up with tins and jars, and started fussing around the stove, as if their six hands were all needed to prepare some exotic, foreign dish, not a humble little bowl of semolina. Ninka was constantly under their feet, in spite of Nadia's efforts to chase her away. She understood that something out of the ordinary was happening, and was afraid she might miss something. Varvara kept running to and fro from the stove to the old lady's bedside, perspiring and clutching her stomach as she ran, as if she were pregnant, trying to keep her mother's spirits up: "Hold on, Ma. Hold on. We won't be long."

Liusia gave the old lady her semolina in a mug, not letting go of it in case her mother spilt it on herself. She sipped at it cautiously: two sips, and a rest, another sip, another rest. She took no more than a tiny baby, then fell back, exhausted, waving the mug away, and for a long time she could not get her breath back.

"Oh my! I'm all out of breath. It's like hard work.

My stomach's all knotted up like a handkerchief. No undoing it now . . ."

"Don't you worry, Mummy," said Liusia. "No harm done. You mustn't overload your stomach now. Let it digest what you've had first, then you can have a bit more."

"My stomach's all knotted up," the old lady repeated with wry pleasure. "It thought: Time we was off, Anna Stepanovna. Off to our new home! We're both ready. Let's go." While she got her breath back she looked straight up with unseeing eyes, appearing delirious. But she went on: "But I fooled it. I turned back, and now here I am laughing at it, stuffing *kasha* into it. It don't need no *kasha*, I should have realized that."

She ran out of breath and started coughing. Liusia said hurriedly, "You musn't talk so much, Mummy. You're still terribly weak."

"Expect me to keep quiet, do you?" replied the old lady spiritedly. "I see my children for the first time in years, and I can't say nothing to them?" She cast an uncertain, but nevertheless proud eye over them all, and went on in a calmer voice, saving her strength: "It was like somebody nudged me in the ribs and said: The kids have come. So I thought I'd have a look at 'em first, before I die. After that I won't need nothing else."

Speaking was a strain for her, and she could not keep it up. But the pleasure of seeing her children before her would allow her no rest. It shone in her face, kept her breast heaving and her hands in motion, and blocked her throat. They all stood watchfully by, saying nothing, so that she would not have to make the effort of answering. Several times she was on the verge of tears, and looked at her children with impatience and anxiety, unable to do more than make out which was which. Either because of her tears or her failing eyesight, she could not see them very well, and this made her angry with herself. Suddenly she decided that nothing she saw around her was real. It was all a dream, a delusion, or her last memory of a life now over — that explained the haze before her eyes.

She lapsed into peaceful immobility, while her mind groped to find its bearings.

The room was lit by that soft, pure light which comes before sunset on a clear day. The old lady was lying with her head under the window, so that the sunlight fell on her feet and cooled gently on the opposite wall, as if lighting it up from the other side. Only now did the old lady notice the sun, and enjoy the pleasure of recognition. After the prolonged darkness of unconsciousness she felt warmer at once at the sight of it, and on her sparing breath it entered her body and stimulated her circulation. So it was not a dream: in dreams the sun did not warm you, nor the frost chill you. She heard a faint, distant ringing in her ears, which stopped as suddenly as it had begun. She wondered where it could have come from, and decided that it must have been in her, never leaving her, from her youth. Then she had often heard it, and it had lodged in her memory for the rest of her life. There was no mistaking it. It was a living sound.

"Oh, Lord," she murmured. "Oh, Lord."

When she had got her breath back she raised her eyes. They were still there, they hadn't moved, but to the old lady they seemed closer. Now she could see them better.

Standing apart, right by the door, like a stranger in the family, was Nadia. Next to her was Ilia.

The old lady hadn't been able to get used to Ilia the last time he'd come home from the north. Under his naked pate his face didn't look like his own. It seemed to have been painted on in place of the one he'd gambled away at cards. Everything about him had changed. He was livelier, although at his age he ought to have been quietening down. It was plain that the place he had been living in did not suit him, and he could not get over it.

The old lady looked at Ilia until it was uncomfortable to do so any longer, searching for the Ilia she had brought into the world, raised, and kept in her memory, now finding him in the present Ilia, now losing him again. He was there, but far away. There was so much new flesh on him, and so many strange people had become his companions, without her, that she could not quite believe this was the same person. It was as if some bigger and brighter fish had swallowed her Ilia whole when he was still a tiddler, and now the two of them lived in one body. If you called out his name he might not answer at once, but turn his head to see whose voice it was, where it came from, and whether it was really calling him, Ilia, or somebody else. The old lady felt sure that life had not treated him any better in his new surroundings. He should never have left the village . . . That was something you certainly couldn't say about Liusia. She was a townswoman all over, from head to toe. It must have been a mistake that she hadn't been given some city lady as a mother, but she'd found her own kind in the end. Ilia hadn't. There wasn't much of the townsman or the countryman about him, not much of the stranger, not much of himself. He had a jolly face, but the old lady felt sorry for him as she looked at him, and why this was she herself had no idea.

Ilia's face was so jolly now because he could not get over his surprise at seeing his mother still alive, and he was laughing happily at himself, Mikhail, and his sisters: "She really fooled us, eh? Good for you, old girl!" As recently as lunchtime they had been quite sure she was in her death agony, when in fact it was the agony of the struggle for life. Ilia was laughing most of all at himself: yesterday, when he'd taken time off work at the garage, he'd told them he was going to his mother's funeral, and he had no doubt that he was telling the truth. What would he tell them now? That he'd been tricked? Ilia was ready to believe that his mother had deliberately pretended to be dying, so as to bring all her children hurrying to her, and although he knew that this was purely his own silly idea, he was in no hurry to dismiss it. He kept on turning it over, looking at it, teasing it, like a cat with a mouse. Her request for some *kasha*, so like a child's — except that she didn't want it in a bottle with a teat — and the way she had to learn to eat it all over again, was to Ilia a source of some amusement and considerable pride. He watched his mother with interest, wondering what she'd get up to next.

After resting her eyes a moment, the old lady located Varvara, who was sitting at the foot of her bed. Varvara thrust herself impatiently forward to meet her mother's eyes. Yesterday she'd been lamenting in a forlorn voice, "Ma! It's me! Your eldest! I've come to see you, and you won't even look at me!" But now Varvara's turn had come at last. The old lady did see her. Her head swayed, she gave a barely perceptible nod, and sighed. When she nodded she seemed to be wishing Varvara peace in her old age — the only happiness still within her reach; and she sighed because she knew that Varvara would not get it, and it was no use even thinking about it. As she looked at Varvara, it was all the old lady could do to hold back her tears. For herself she needed nothing more — her life, with all its successes and failures, was behind her. But Varvara still had some time to go, and how good it would be if she could live it out in peace!

She didn't overlook Mikhail, although she knew him better than she knew herself. But she wanted to know what he was like with the others, as distinct from when he was alone. She often recalled the old saying: Your first-born's for God, the second for the Tsar, and the third to look after you. She had given God and the Tsar more than their due. Counting them was enough to make you weep. But even those left alive had gone away one by one, as soon as they were old enough to work. It was as if someone had taken them away, like puppies from their mother, and put them in the care of strangers. Only Mikhail was left to her, and she had every right to say he had been born to look after her, so that she could live out her days in her ancestral home, because she could not imagine living anywhere else. She did not consider Mikhail in any way better than her other children. It was simply a matter of fate: it was her lot to live with him, and wait for the others every summer, and wait, and wait . . .

Except for his three years in the army, Mikhail had been here, close to his mother, all his life. Here he had grown to manhood, marriage, and fatherhood, developed a tough hide, like all men, and here he was inexorably approaching old age. She had grown so used to him and his ways that she noticed none of the changes in him. To her he was the same Mikhail today as he was yesterday. Ilia was a different matter: he'd gone off to the north with hair, and come back without any, and you had to be blind not to see that. The old lady could even see changes in Varvara, who came home almost every month: she had put on more weight, started snivelling and heaving old-maidenly sighs even when nothing seemed to call for them, and streaks of grey had appeared in her black hair. It seemed as if Ilia, Liusia, Varvara and Tanchora had left their mother so that she could see later how they had changed. They would come back to her as a thoughtful reminder of the passing years: she would reckon up the time that had elapsed since their last meeting, and at each visit add on that number of years at once. The result was that she aged not in her own good time, but by the number of years they brought with them. Without them she would have gone quietly about her business in the same place, until her time came. But how could she even think about that when she longed for them to come, ached to see them again, especially when she became bedridden? And of late their visits had become very infrequent. All of them had their own families and their own lives to lead. They weren't so young either. The years grated on them as they passed, no longer sliding smoothly by. The old lady understood that well.

She only glanced at Liusia and looked away at once. But then she started stealing furtive, sidelong glances at her again. In Liusia's presence she felt rather ashamed of herself, of being so old, feeble, and ugly. She thought that her daughter must also feel ashamed of her, being so fine and educated herself. She didn't even talk the way people here talked: the words she used weren't so

very different, but you really had to strain to understand them. Whatever you wanted to know, she knew
all about it: she'd been everywhere, and seen enough
for ten. And what had the old lady seen in her life?
What had she known but day and night, work and
sleep? She'd spent her life running on the spot, like a
squirrel in a treadmill, and everybody around her had
lived the same way, thinking there was no other. Liusia
led a different sort of life, which her mother neither
knew nor understood, in which many things were not
done in the old way. For all she knew, they might even
have a new way of dying. It was too late for her to
depart from her own ways: she would shed tears when
she felt like it, as she always had, and die as she knew
how. But still, when Liusia was there, the old lady took
care not to say or do anything which might annoy her.

She went on and on looking at them, greedily, hurriedly, awkwardly, and could not stop. She could not
see enough of them.

"You ought to take things easier, Mummy," said
Liusia. "Rest for a while."

"So you've come," said the old lady. She raised her
hands to cover her face, and began to cry.

"Yes, we've come, Mummy," replied Ilia cheerily
for them all. "And there's nothing to worry about."

Varvara shuddered and cut him dead with a re-
sounding whisper: "Don't shout so loud. Can't you see
you shouldn't?"

"So you've come," repeated the old lady in a calmer
voice, "and I've lived to see you again." She spoke in
the trustful, soothing tones in which elderly people of
many years' acquaintance talk to each other. After an
alert pause, she resumed in the same tone, still not
opening her eyes: "I woke up and couldn't understand

nothing, not even who I was. Couldn't feel me arms or legs. Couldn't feel meself at all. Nothing left but my living soul, and that had got lost somewhere. I thought I must have died, it was so dark all around. Praise be to God, I thought — no more suffering. But the moment I thought that, I saw it was as bright as day. My eyes had opened all by themselves, and I didn't know what was going on." She opened her eyes and let them get used to the sunlight, without looking at anyone. "It was as bright as this, even brighter. I wondered who was teasing me by making it look like day. Then I saw you, and I couldn't believe it. I never dared hope for that! All of you here, except Tanchora . . . And I'm lying here thinking, 'So that's how it is: your last joy in life comes after you're dead — to have one more look at what you've left behind you, and all your heart ached for.' "

"Good for you, Mum!" Ilia shook his head in cheerful amazement. "A moment ago you couldn't get a word out, and now look at you rattling away! Like you was reading a book!"

"That's true, Mummy. You shouldn't talk so much now," said Liusia, but without her former assurance, as if she was afraid of something.

"Oh no, let her speak if she can. All I meant was it didn't take her long to get going. Like in a story . . ."

"It's because of you," was the old lady's simple explanation. "All because of you. I was already there, you know. I was, I know it. And then you arrived, and I came back. Dead or not dead, back I came, back to you." Her voice was a thin, quavering thread, which rose and fell, at times disappearing altogether. "The Lord God helped me and gave me strength, made me look more like a living human being again, so you wouldn't be too scared to sit beside me."

"The things you say, Mum!"

"Show me the mother who doesn't feel stronger when she's got her children around her! Specially if she hasn't seen them for ages. Obvious isn't it? Well, me too. I wanted to have a few words with you before the end. I don't mind my arms and legs getting weaker, if it'll make my voice stronger. My voice goes on by itself. I just get it started, and on it goes till it gets tired. Getting started's a bit difficult, though. Like having to jump up high. And I run out of breath, like I have now. Wait a bit."

While she rested she kept looking at the wall, on which the sun was still shining. It was no longer the white glare of the afternoon sun, but a softer, clearer light. An expression of profound calm gradually settled on the old lady's face. This had to do with the approach of evening, to which old people are particularly sensitive. She looked unaware of everything, herself, her children, even her own breathing, which went on independent of her will. She seemed to see nothing but the patch of sunlight on the wall, which expanded and held her eyes to it as it entered them. And yet she was alive, more palpably and alertly alive than before, not straining to live, but under life's careful watch.

They waited. They could hardly go away. And it didn't seem right for them to talk among themselves. They waited for their mother to speak, as she had asked, and tried not to look at each other.

"It still feels like somebody was holding me up," she said, talking to herself as much as to them. "As if there wasn't nothing solid underneath me. It ain't frightening. It all seems right."

She lay for a while longer in silence and complete immobility, and then came to life again. She lowered her eyes, and her face took on an expression of long-suffering patience, which gave way, however, as soon as she saw her children, to one of warm, tranquil joy. And again the old lady could not believe it, and cautiously asked Liusia, "When did you get here?"

"Ilia and I arrived last night."

After a short pause her mother asked, "Didn't you bring any presents?"

"We were in such a hurry, Mummy, there was no time," replied Liusia, embarrassed. "We only just caught the boat. We had to run all the way to the jetty."

"I didn't mean for myself. I don't need nothing. I meant for Ninka, good little thing that she is." She stretched out her hands to Ninka, who was standing beside Varvara, but Ninka timidly stepped back. The old lady didn't mind. "I hide sweets for her in my suitcase, and take them out one by one. It makes me happy, and her too. She knows where I keep them. Comes to me and says, 'Come on, Granny, show me what you've got there.' And I says, 'I ain't got nothing,' but she keeps on. I pretend I don't understand, and play with her like I was little. She's my good little girl. Stays by her Granny. It makes me feel better talking to her. Old and young together."

"In the morning I'll run down to the shop and buy something," Liusia promised.

"She really doesn't need anything," said Nadia shyly. "You surely don't think she goes hungry. But she's so spoiled she goes begging for things."

"Get her something, do," said the old lady. "Only don't give it all to her at once. Just a bit at a time. Give the rest to me, and I'll hide it. Then she'll think it's from me. I'll feed her a bit more before I go."

"I sent you some grapes, Mummy," Liusia remembered. "Did you eat them?"

"You mean them green berries?"

"Yes. They're called grapes."

"Whatever you call them. I ain't got the patience to pick all them pips out. I fed 'em to Ninka. She ate 'em, pips and all, and made a lot of noise crunching on the pips. Let her eat 'em, I thought, if she likes 'em. What good are they to me? Waste of good food. There's really nothing I need, Liusia, now that God's granted me the pleasure of seeing you again before I die. I have to be thankful for that."

She started weeping again, finding relief in a short, soothing, tearless cry, and fell silent, wiping her dry eyes.

"There, there, Mummy, don't upset yourself," said Liusia. "You get better now, and everything will be all right."

The old lady made no reply. Again her eyes were fixed on the sunlit wall, on which the last flies of summer were basking, and everything about her suggested that she was frozen under a spell of almost impossible calm, as if it had been given to her alone to see and commit to memory things that nobody else could possibly understand. The house was now absolutely still, and no sound came from the street. It was just as well that the old lady's silence did not last long this time. Still gazing at the wall, she spoke in a bright, confidential voice, which seemed to come of its own accord, without her help. "I heard you crying over me yesterday, Varvara. I remember it was your voice. But I thought I was dead already, and you was wailing over my dead body. Yes. And before that, when I was still awake, I was lying here thinking: 'When I die Varvara will come and weep over me, and everything'll be all right.' That's how much I was counting on you. And suddenly I heard your voice, and I thought I was dead, and your voice was still getting through to me."

Varvara stood open-mouthed, unable to speak or even weep, and nodded to her mother. Ilia went up to Mikhail and said in an astonished whisper, "She's a bit funny, don't you reckon?"

"Who knows?" added the old lady. "Maybe they go on hearing things for a long time. Who knows? Nobody knows. You can pull their eyelids down, but their ears are still open."

"What are you on about, Mum?" asked Ilia in a loud voice. "What's all this?"

"Eh?" She found Ilia by his voice, and was too embarrassed to answer. "I'm just so glad to see you that I don't know what to say. Just chattering away. Don't mind me, silly old woman that I am. No brain left at all."

"Don't talk like that, Mum! Don't you think we're pleased to see you well? All you've got to do now is get well quick. We'll all go out visiting together. That's it! Why sit at home! We'll all go out together, and if you won't go we'll carry you. Plenty of hands here to carry you."

"Have a bit more of this," Liusia offered her mother the mug of semolina. "Your stomach can manage it now."

She tried to raise her head, but Liusia had to help her. This time she took more, and was surprised at herself when she recovered her breath: "How do you like that! Just like a bottomless pit. It's true what they say: Even a sick stomach keeps on eating."

"There you are, now you'll feel better. Later on we'll give you some more."

"Oh, I'll never manage any more."

"Yes, you will. Don't worry."

"If I could last out till Tanchora comes . . ." said the old lady plaintively. "Why's she taking so long? Maybe something's happened."

"She'll get here, Mummy. No need to worry. She's got a long way to come, but she'll make it."

"You won't leave me yet, will you? Stay with me a while. Once Tanchora gets here I won't keep you. I know you can't stay long."

"Nobody's planning to leave just yet."

"Stay with me. I won't bother anybody. I'll be quiet. I'll just lie here. I'm talking a lot now because it's so long since I saw you. I'm so glad I can't stop. But afterwards I'll keep quiet. You just get on and do what you want to do, and if I only see you once a day I'll be happy."

"Bother anybody? Keep quiet? — What do you mean?" protested Liusia. "What an idea, Mummy! You ought to be ashamed! There's no call for any apologies. You must understand that."

"Don't talk like that, Ma," said Varvara. "Don't talk like that, or I'll cry."

Ilia added his voice too: "There, there, Mum . . ."

The old lady cheerfully fell silent, but could not contain her joy for long: "I open my eyes, and you're all here around me. Now I could fly up and sail away on the wind, like a bird, and tell everybody . . . Oh, Lord . . ."

The day was dying fast, but the room was still

brightly lit. The clear evening sun shone straight through the window above the old lady's bed. Its rays now struck the ceiling and were reflected downwards. To her children everything here was dear and familiar, and everything seemed to repeat and reflect her words and gestures — speaking when she spoke, falling silent when she stopped, gazing at them with pride and tenderness, and listening with quiet, unobtrusive attention. It was hard to believe that the house could outlive the old lady, and remain standing when she was gone. They seemed to have reached exactly the same old age, the utmost limit of life, and each clung on only thanks to the other. You had to tread carefully on the floor, so as not to hurt Mother, and everything you said to her was trapped and held in the walls, the corners, everywhere.

Even the air here was the same as they had breathed as children: it lured them back, did its best to pull them back across the span of years. But, like their mother, it lacked the strength.

The windows and doorways seemed smaller. They had to bow their heads to pass through the doors. It was new to them to see the walls unplastered, the whitewashed timbers protruding. A ring for a child's cradle still hung from the tie-beam. There'd been a time when the cradle almost always had somebody in it: one child would grow out of it, and another would take its place.

Above the table on both sides of the window were two full cases of photographs. They were all here: Ilia and Mikhail in the army, with greetings from the places where they'd been stationed; Ilia in the north, at the wheel of a lorry; Varvara and her husband, both goggling at the camera, standing bolt upright, gripping the back of a chair as if they were afraid of falling down; Liusia on holiday somewhere, under some beautiful tall trees; Tatiana, still a little country girl with a thin, frightened face, as though only the direst threats had forced her to have her picture taken.

A lamp now stood on the icon case in the right-hand corner. Last night they'd needed it, but normally it wasn't taken down for months on end, and the old lady would cross herself without looking up. Further round towards her window hung a poster which somebody had brought home from the forestry office the year before last. It showed a small boy with a spade coming out of a wood, over the caption: "Plant more trees, and live longer!" At first the wood had been green, but the flies had soon turned it yellow, and the boy had also aged beyond his years, but the picture had become part of the furnishings, so they did not take it down.

The old lady was looking more calmly at her children, confident now that they would not suddenly take fright and run away. Her speech was easier, without strain, and she did not have to grope for words. Talking was still tiring, but now she was managing to husband her strength, pause when she knew she needed to, hold her reserves for what was to come, and not spend them all at once.

The fine evening was drawing to a close. In the house, and outside, it was turning cooler, and dusk was gathering.

Liusia started straightening her mother's blanket, turned it back, and suddenly stopped in her tracks. "Mikhail, come here a moment," she called out.

"What is it?"

Not knowing what was amiss, the old lady timidly shifted her legs.

"Mikhail, look at this," said Liusia, her voice like a coiled spring.

"Look at what?"

"This here, look."

"What about it?"

"What do you mean — 'What about it?' How can you ask? Can't you see what sheets your mother's got to lie on? They're black. Can't have been changed for a good year. How can you let your old, sick mother sleep on sheets like those? You ought to be ashamed!"

"Why turn on me? D'you think I'm the one in charge of the linen?"

"You could have had a look, couldn't you? And asked somebody to wash them? Is that so difficult? Or is it all the same to you what your mother has to put up with? You're master in this house, aren't you?"

Liusia did not look at Nadia, and didn't see that her face had turned bright red in acute embarrassment.

"Liusia, Liusia, please!" said the old lady several times before managing to silence her. Liusia then turned towards her mother, who gave a feeble flap of her hand: "I haven't the strength to keep calling out. Why didn't you ask me first? Of all the things to talk about! Why on earth should I need white sheets? I've managed all right without any all my life. It's one of these new-fangled ideas — white sheets to lie on! You wear your fingers to the bone washing 'em."

"I'm not talking to you, Mummy — I'm talking to Mikhail."

"Well you shouldn't be talking to Mikhail when I'm talking to you. You go on and won't stop, and I've no voice left to shout you down. Nadia's bored me silly with these sheets: Let me change them, let me change them. I'm sick and tired of telling her to leave off. Just let me lie here, and don't make me move. When I die you'll have to wash me down anyway, or they won't bury me."

"Why bring that up again?"

"You don't like it, eh? 'Why?' she says." The old lady lapsed into an irritable silence, but could not contain herself for long. "You had me worried. I still haven't got over it. I wondered what you'd seen under me, thought I must have done something. You can't expect me to have much control now. I'm worse than a little baby. Don't know what I'm doing."

"But your son must know what he's doing, and think of you," Liusia insisted. "It's his duty as a son. I can't understand how you, our mother, can be allowed to lie in sheets like those. And nobody seems to give it a thought, as if it was quite normal. It's a disgrace!"

Nadia, who had been standing silently by the wall all this time, suddenly stepped forward and slipped out of the room. In the awkward silence which followed, Mikhail muttered, "You've got those sheets on the brain."

"You shouldn't have said anything in front of her, Liusia," said the old lady, shaking her head. "It's not her fault. She's always on at me, and I never feel like moving. I'm afraid to."

"But I didn't say anything to her."

"Perhaps not, but who else could you have meant? She's the one who looks after me, not Mikhail."

Varvara heaved a sigh, "Oh dear, oh dear, oh dear! I don't know what to say."

"You'd better keep quiet then," snapped Ilia. "What a thing to happen!"

"I didn't say nothing to you."

"Did I say anything to you?"

To change the subject the old lady asked, "Did old Mironikha come and have a look at me while I was unconscious?"

"No, I don't think so," replied Mikhail.

"When she hears I've come round she'll come running over with a story to tell me. I don't know how I could have lived all this time without her. I always feel better after a chat with her. She'll come over for sure," she repeated, nodding her head. "She'll say, 'Well, old girl, how come death ain't taking you?' Always been a joker, she has. Look and see if her door's open, will you? You can see from the window."

Varvara stood up and leaned against the windowsill. "No, looks like it's shut."

"She's gone out somewhere. Can't sit still for a second, always running somewhere. Well, let her run, as long as her legs'll carry her. She'll have plenty of time to lie in bed when they give out. I'd go after her now, if I could . . . but my running days are over."

"Mum," Ilia interrupted with a wink at Mikhail. "Mum, would you mind if me and Mikhail drank a glass to your recovery?"

"Won't you men ever leave off drinking?" said Varvara agitatedly. "You just can't live without it."

"Too true we can't," agreed Ilia with a broad grin.

"Have your drink if you must," the old lady consented. "Only not here in my room. I don't want the smell of it in here."

"Sure, we'll go somewhere else, Mum, and drink to you. We don't want you being ill no more."

"Drink the Devil's own health if you want. He might like it better."

"Well of all things, Mum! The Devil's health . . ."

"I mean it. What pleasure do you find in it anyway?

I wouldn't touch the stuff if you paid me in gold, and you go wasting your money on it. As if you'd take any notice if I told you not to . . . Never the day. Have your drink if you must, but not too much . . . I don't know what you're like when you're drunk, Ilia, but our Mikhail's a bad one. Poor Nadia has an awful time keeping out of his way when he's drunk."

Mikhail, more cheerful now, appealed without taking offence, "You'd blame me for everything, wouldn't you, Mother?"

"I'm not one for wasting words."

"We'll only have a drop, Mother. To give us an appetite for supper."

When the men had gone the old lady went on, "Nadia's never given me cause to complain." She looked at Liusia, as if talking to her alone. He's my own son, and she's only my daughter-in-law, but I'll never say she ain't done right by me. It takes patience to look after me. She's never once raised her voice at me, and I'm not going to complain about anybody when I've no reason. She gives me something to drink when I'm thirsty, fills my hot-water bottle. It's only that bottle that keeps me alive when it gets cold. Quite cold-blooded I've become these days . . ."

"You need more blankets," said Varvara in the tone of an expert.

"How can I have any more blankets when Nadia piles so many rags on me I can't move a muscle. And my feet still shiver under all that weight. I call out to Nadia, or send Ninka for her. She comes, heats up some water for a bottle, and I feel better. Without Nadia I'd have been in the grave long ago — that I know. Mikhail's quiet enough when he's sober, but as soon as he gets drunk he's impossible. Plagues me, plagues her, and nothing'll shake him off."

"What do you mean — plagues you?" asked Liusia warily.

"I'll tell you. Starts demanding vodka from her, when he can hardly stand. Expects her to pour him some and stand it in front of him. And where's she to get it? How's she to pay for it? Drives her out to the shop: 'You work there, they'll give you some.' But she only sweeps up in the shop, never gets near the vodka. He might think of that himself, but no, he won't stop demanding his vodka. Stubborn as a mule. And if I try to talk him out of it he turns on me, wild as anything: 'You lie still, Mother, and be quiet.' So I keep quiet. I'm afraid of him now when he's drunk. I even bring Ninka in to sleep with me."

"I see," said Liusia quietly.

"The man's got no shame at all!" Varvara burst out angrily, looking round at the door. "What a way to treat his own mother! The nerve!"

"Or he'll come in and sit down and say, 'Let's have a bit of a talk, Mother.' Whatever can we talk about, when he's so drunk he can hardly hold his head up? 'Don't you want to talk to me?' he says. 'I feed you and keep you, and you won't even talk to me?' He doesn't see why I won't talk to him. Let him come when he's sober, and talk then. But not drunk. When I say that, he goes on and on at me — it's dreadful."

"I'll have a word with him," Liusia promised. "He won't like it, but I'll have a word with him. Whoever heard of anything like it! 'I feed you and keep you,' indeed! That's the last straw."

"Mind you don't try and tackle him when he's drunk, though. He won't understand, and he'll lose his temper. He's a menace when he's drunk. There's nobody'll tell you different. When he's slept it off he's right as rain. If it wasn't for the drink he'd be a different man. It'll be the ruin of him."

"Drinking's a bad thing," said Varvara.

The old lady nodded agreement and sighed. "Does anyone say it's a good thing? These days you can reckon you've found a good man if he drinks but keeps his head. And if you found a teetotaller, people would pay money to come and look at him, like some sort of freak. All our Mikhail needs is one little drop on his tongue, and he's like a leaky barrel: however much you pour down, it won't be enough for him."

"I'd no idea Mikhail had sunk as low as that," said Liusia, still shocked by the news.

"Well, if our Ma says so, you can believe it," said Varvara.

"Why should I tell lies?" said the old lady, offended. "Do you think I'd tell tales about my own son if they weren't true?"

"That's what I say: if Ma says so, it must be true."

"And yet our Ma goes on putting up with it," said Liusia, adopting Varvara's tone. "He abuses her for all he's worth, and she actually defends him. 'Right as rain when he's slept it off'," she mimicked her mother. "I suppose you'll wait for him to sleep it off this time, and wait for him to kick you out of the house."

"He's never kicked me out. What nonsense!"

"He hasn't yet, but he will if you let him off every time. It won't take long."

"Nobody in our family ever kicked his mother out."

"I'm sure nobody in our family ever treated his mother the way your son treats you."

"That's true. Nobody, as long as I can remember," Varvara agreed. "He's the only one."

After a pause the old lady began speaking softly: "Here you are getting angry, but you ought to live with me for a while. It's sheer misery for them. D'you think I can't see that? Bring me this, bring me that, bring me the other. Then these coughing fits take me and I'm helpless — coughing my lungs out. I can't go to the toilet without help. Never mind anywhere else. My time was up long ago. Why torment people any longer? Why torment myself? But I'm still here. You can't die till death takes you. When he's sober he puts up with me, doesn't say nothing, but when he's drunk of course he can't control himself. At first I feel hurt, but then I think to myself: why should I feel hurt? Once you've outlived your time, endure it. Our Lord bore his suffering, and told us to bear ours." When she had rested for a moment, speech came easier to her, as if the name of God was soothing to her. She heaved a relaxed sigh. "You mustn't say nothing to him. Leave him be. I'd rather die in peace, and have nobody think ill of me. Then I'll die easier. Whatever you think, I don't want you arguing among yourselves on my account. That makes things worse for me. I'm going to die, but you've got to go on living. You'll see one another, visit one another. You're brothers and sisters after all, all of the same father and mother. You should see each other more often, not forget one another. And visit the place as well. This is home to all our family. I'll still be here. I won't go nowhere. Sit by my grave, and I'll give you some sign, to say I know you're there. I'll send a little bird to tell you."

Nadia came softly into the room and stood by the door, afraid of being in the way. When the sisters saw her and turned towards her, she went to the table and sat down, her hands, weary from her work, resting in her lap. At once she was a different person: at work she was a dynamo, but the moment she sat down there was not a sound from her. It was as if she had fallen asleep with her eyes open, watchful, ready to get up and start bustling about again.

"Done all your chores?" asked the old lady, to draw Nadia into the conversation.

"Yes. When I've driven the cow out that'll be all."

"Not seen the men?"

"They're in the bath-house."

"As long as they don't get too drunk."

"With visitors here he might go easier."

"But he's not alone. He's got one of the visitors with him."

At last Nadia said why she'd come: "Shall we have supper here or in the kitchen? I've got everything ready."

"Have it here," said the old lady. "No need to leave me alone. Plenty of time later for me to lie here by myself."

"I'll put the light on then."

"Yes, why not? No fun eating in the dark."

"Should I call the men?"

"Think they can live on their evil brew alone?" replied the old lady without any trace of sarcasm. "There ain't much nourishment in vodka. Give 'em a shout, and let them say if they're coming or not."

"I thought I might give them theirs afterwards."

"No need to lay the table twice. You've done enough work for one day."

"Let me give you a hand, Nadia," Liusia volunteered. It was clear that she still felt uncomfortable with Nadia because of the business of the sheets, and she wanted to do something to set matters right.

"No, I'll see to it. You stay here. I must heat it up again, or it'll be cold. It won't take a moment."

Liusia stayed.

The brothers came in red in the face, as if they'd been in a steam-bath, and the likeness between them was now more apparent. Now anyone could see that they were brothers, with their prominent cheek-bones and thick, shaggy eyebrows that crept cheekily upwards. Both their necks were now crimson, and in Ilia the flush extended to his bald pate, making his head look red-hot.

They noisily took their places at the table, and Mikhail asked in a loud voice, "How's life with you then, Mother?"

Ilia answered for her — in the bath-house they had got into the habit of talking only to each other. "Not too bad, I should say. Our Mum's no weakling. Cheated death and got away with it."

"You can't cheat death," said the old lady after a pause, with a look of tolerant reproof.

"But you did it, Mum. You can't deny it. And so you should have done. Death can take plenty of others — there's no shortage — but not you. That's what I say. Plenty of kind souls in the world to die instead of you."

"He's right there," said Mikhail with a laugh.

"You'd better keep your shameless mouth shut," said Varvara to Mikhail suddenly, as if she'd been waiting for him to step out of line.

"What's the matter with you?"

Ilia, who did not sense what was afoot, tried to make

light of Varvara's words by turning them into a children's tongue-twister he remembered.

"You're disgusting!" Varvara shot back, and turned to Liusia for support. Liusia had to take up the matter she had broached:

"If I were you, Mikhail, I really would keep quiet," she said, looking him straight in the eye and enunciating each word sharply and distinctly. "The way you've been behaving towards Mummy just isn't good enough. Remember this: we're with her all the way, and we won't let you mistreat her."

"What's wrong with you? Gone off your heads? Who's mistreating her?"

"You are."

"Me?! And what, may I ask, do I do to her? Come on, tell me, now you've started."

"Liusia, Liusia," pleaded the old lady. "Why must you do this? Didn't I beg you not to, by all that's holy? Don't argue among yourselves. Have pity on me."

"No, let her tell me."

"All right, Mummy, we'll leave it for now," said Liusia reluctantly. "But remember, Mikhail, we've more to say to you yet."

Mikhail turned to Ilia and complained, "Just look at 'em. My own sisters turning on me. How do you like that?"

"We'll talk about it later," Liusia promised him.

"You don't scare anyone with your threats."

"Now, Mikhail, don't offend Mother," said Ilia. "You mustn't offend Mother."

Mikhail had no desire to argue with Ilia. "Yes, that's right enough. Mustn't offend Mother. That'd be wrong. I never offend Mother."

"She's the one who gave us life."

"Yes, that's very true. Couldn't have put it better."
Mikhail wiped away a drunken tear. "I understand
perfectly. I understand better than they do," he nodded
towards his sisters. "You know why they're mad at
me? Because I sent them telegrams, got 'em to come
here, and Mother decided not to die. As if I'd played a
joke and got 'em to come here for nothing. Oh, I understand perfectly."

"Do you realize what you're saying, or are you completely incapable of thinking?" Liusia flared up.
"Aren't you thoroughly ashamed of yourself?"

"You mustn't talk like that, Mikhail," said Ilia, putting his brother right again.

"All right, then I won't," agreed Mikhail. "You're
older than me, and I ought to respect what you say."

"That's not the point."

"I know: that's not the point."

Nadia came in and began ladling out the soup. In the
end they ate in two sittings after all, the men first, and
Varvara and Liusia after them. The old lady had a little
broth in her mug. They ate in silence.

The men went out, taking the lamp from the icon
case. Their mother gave a deep sigh as she saw them go:
"Surely they ain't got more out there! Heaven preserve
us! What are they doing?! What are they doing!"

4

Again the old lady saw the night through.

She lay for a long time with her eyes open, waiting
for the dawn. She had made up her mind that the mo-

ment it began to get light she would try and sit up. The thinly covered bones of her sides and back ached terribly from lying on them. But the dawn took its time, just as it did in December, and she was afraid to move in the dark. Seeing nothing, she might fall, and she didn't want to cry out. At last the window on the east began to brighten, she could see further through it, and then the other window began to stand out, and the first chill light of dawn entered the room from both sides.

She waited until the light had gathered, then, keeping an eye on Liusia to make sure she was asleep, she shifted her weight slightly towards the head of her bed, paused, then gingerly pushed herself up on her hands and swung her feet down onto the floor. Her head began to spin, and she gripped the bed with both hands so as not to topple head over heels, and to her surprise she could hold herself upright: who would have thought it? No flesh left on her bones, nothing to sit on, and yet there she was sitting up. She pulled a blanket over her legs so that nobody should see how wasted they were.

The fact that she had managed to sit up pleased her greatly. The almost complete numbness of months of lying on her back began to subside with an agreeable ache, through her back and her limbs. It was easier to see, as she could now look straight ahead of her, without rolling her eyes upwards. The day before she'd had to keep moving her eyes this way and that so much that she thought they'd fall out. Before long she felt that her feet were cold on the floor, and she pushed the edge of her blanket under them. At least that meant there was still some feeling in her feet, that the blood still reached them.

The morning sun did not fall into the house, but the

old lady could tell it had come up, even without the windows: the air around her stirred and sprang to life, as if something were blowing on it from the side. She raised her eyes and saw the first joyful rays of sunlight, which had not yet found the earth, like the rungs of a ladder flung across the sky, on which only bare feet could step. This made her feel warmer at once and she murmured, "Oh Lord . . ."

She heard the cow starting its morning lowing, but did not call out to Nadia: Nadia would have to get used to getting up by herself, since she, Anna, hadn't much longer to live. It would be easy enough to wake Liusia, but Liusia in her city life was in the habit of sleeping long into the morning, so let her sleep. She had no reason to get up early. The old lady sat and listened while Nadia dressed, then the door creaked as it swung open and shut again, and once again all was quiet. But she knew that the house was now like a pan on the stove, about to begin simmering and seething with activity.

And sure enough she soon heard the patter of feet — Ninka was up. Of course she wouldn't go out in the yard now, and the pot was under her granny's bed. The old lady leaned forward and called to Ninka in a loud whisper. She came pattering sleepily into the room, squatted on the pot with eyes closed, then climbed onto the old lady's bed, as she always used to do. Ninka always liked running to her granny in the morning, but this time the old lady was ready to cry, so thankful was she that another of life's pleasures had not been taken from her. Ninka obviously knew where she was even with her eyes shut, as she murmured sleepily: "When you die I'll always sleep here."

"I hope you will," whispered the old lady happily as

she tucked Ninka in. "You'll be nice and warm here by the stove, and winter's coming on. You couldn't be cosier in the good Lord's pocket. Safe and snug as you please. You're my good little girl! And you understand everything like a grown-up."Silence descended again in the house, but little by little there came more noise from outside, and the old lady listened hard, trying to tell whose cow was mooing and which of the housewives was slow in going out to milk it. She waited, expecting to hear Mironikha's cow give tongue, followed by Mironikha herself. Whenever she milked that cow of hers she strained her voice swearing at it. Some cow, if you had to ride your milking-stool all round the yard to milk it, and yell at it as well! It wouldn't be that difficult to change it for another, but maybe she actually enjoyed that daily performance.

But neither Mironikha nor her cow made any sound, as if they'd both died at once. What if that were true? How could she stay away all yesterday, and not call on old Anna? She lived alone. If anything happened it might never be noticed. The old lady craned her neck to look at Mironikha's door, but she couldn't see anything lower than the roof. As she didn't dare try and stand up, she settled down on the bed again with a sigh.

In her efforts to look out of the window she did not notice that Varvara had come into the room, and she started when she heard her voice: "Sitting up, eh?"

Her momentary fright passed, and she replied boastfully, "Yes, as you see."

"Are you sure you ought to?"

"I ain't going to ask nobody's permission. I can sit up when I feel like it." The old lady took umbrage, seeing that Varvara did not appreciate what it meant to her to sit up.

"Mind you don't fall."

"Don't fuss. Why should I fall? If I was going to fall I'd have done it by now, but I haven't."

"Did Ninka push you out of bed, or something?"

"Nobody pushed me out of bed. What nonsense! I sat up before she came in."

Varvara's eyes, still sleepy, peered uncertainly, and her hair looked as if some animal had slept in it. With a yawn she went on to say, "I dreamed about something, but now I can't remember what it was. It was a bad dream."

"How do you know it was bad if you can't remember it?"

"When I woke up I felt something was wrong, and I came straight here to see if you was all right."

"I'm all right so far." The old lady showed sudden signs of anxiety. "When you're dressed, go an' see Mironikha for me, will you? Maybe something's happened to her. She's all alone in that house. If she died she'd just lie there and nobody would know."

"Why should she suddenly die?"

"What? Why should she die? Why *do* people die? From joy, I suppose? She will go on running about, and she can't keep it up till she's a hundred. And her cow didn't moo this morning. I was listening hard, and it didn't moo. It normally wakes the whole village, but today there's not a peep out of it. If I could I'd go and take a look myself, but now . . ."

"I'll just get dressed, then I'll go over."

"Yes, do. She's like my own kin. We've lived all our lives side by side, always dropping in to see each other.

Makes my heart ache to think anything might have happened . . ."

Liusia awoke too, but if she did so while Varvara was in the room she didn't stir or open her eyes until Varvara had gone.

"Did our talking wake you up," asked the old lady apologetically. "If you want to go on sleeping, do, and I'll be quiet. And I'll tell the others to tread lightly."

"It's all right, I'll get up. I've had a good sleep." Even first thing in the morning Liusia's face was smooth, without puffiness or wrinkles.

"Did you have any dreams?"

"No."

"Varvara says she had a bad dream, but she can't remember what it was. I told her to go and see Mironikha. Maybe the dream was about her. And Tanchora still hasn't come. I don't dare to even think about her."

"She'll come, don't worry. She's sure to come to-day."

"That's what you all kept telling me yesterday, and where is she? I didn't sleep a wink all night. I thought: what if they're all asleep and Tanchora arrives and starts knocking at the door? I just kept lying there listening. At first there were people in the street, there were sounds to listen to. Then our Mikhail came clumping in. Grunting and groaning as he went to bed, like somebody was strangling him. Must have been the booze in him making all that noise. I could see they'd put a lot away. Well, they settled down, thank goodness, and then I was alone again, listening. Not a tap nor a tinkle anywhere, so I lay and listened to myself. The night seemed a whole year long. Whatever didn't I think about? I talked to my mother, told her I'd see her soon. And I prayed to God about Tanchora, asked him to get her here to me if he saw her anywhere. If only she can make it today. If not, I mightn't last long enough. I can see now, it's not my own life I'm living. This is an extension God's granted me, on account of my children, but the extension's got its limits too. Must have."

At this point Liusia started getting up. The old lady was glad that she didn't have to keep quiet any longer, having been forced to keep her thoughts to herself all night.

"I'd almost given up waiting for morning. Thought it'd never come. I wondered if night had started following night without any day in between, and nobody had told me about it. Everybody went on sleeping and sleeping, and I was worn out. Didn't feel like sleeping, but my eyes kept closing just the same. Once they've got used to closing at night, you can't stop 'em. But I wouldn't let 'em close: what if I fell asleep and didn't wake up again? Sleep's halfway to death, after all. But then I heard the cocks starting to crow, lifting the darkness. So it was over. When it started getting light I thought I'd sit up, otherwise I couldn't bear it any longer. I've been lying still so long my bones are coming through my skin."

"If you're sitting today you'll be standing tomorrow," said Liusia patiently as she cleared away her bedding. "You'll stand up, and walk, and you'll stop saying it's an extension you're living and not your own life."

"It *is* an extension," the old lady insisted.

Liusia did not argue. She folded her bed, went to the window and stood there, smoothing her clothes. A fine day was beginning: the sky above the village was cheerful and bright in the morning sun, and none of it was hidden in cloud. The river sparkled, and beyond it the forest, climbing away up the slope, seemed nearer than it was, but the sun dulled its unseasonable green. The peaceful sunshine lay everywhere. Only in the village could some lonely black shadows be seen, which even the dogs sidestepped, as if afraid of tripping over them.

Why there should have been mist the day before, and why this morning was so still and clear, was beyond all understanding. Liusia remembered yesterday's conversation about mushrooms, and decided that this was the perfect day to go looking for some, as long as all was well with her mother.

Varvara's excited voice tore her away from the window with the promise of astounding good news, or so it seemed when she called out as soon as she came into the room, "I've remembered, Ma, I've remembered!"

"Remembered what?"

"My dream, of course! It was a bad dream too. Didn't I say straight away it was a bad dream? Well, so it was. I knew it."

"Well? Let's have it."

"Well, we're all sitting down, all women, and they're all strangers — the women. Not one I know. We're all sitting making *pelmeni**, and what do you think we're stuffing them with?"

"Don't ask me. How should I know?"

"Mud."

"Eh?"

"Mud. Instead of meat we're taking the mud from under our feet. And we're all so happy at the thought

* *Pelmeni*: Dumplings stuffed with boiled meat.

of having *pelmeni* with mud, so happy we're laughing. And I say to the others, 'Why are you all using that bad mud? There's no fat on it. It's no good for *pelmeni*. I've got some good rich mud over here. Come and take some of this.' And they started taking my mud. Now I remember it, it makes me shiver."

"Did it go on after that?"

"No, I don't remember nothing else. But I can still see them *pelmeni* now: all in neat rows on the oven tray, all white. Didn't I say it was a bad dream?" She shook her head anxiously and asked, "What could it mean? It's so awful! If I'd known I was going to have that dream, I wouldn't have gone to bed. What do I do now?"

"You'd do better to keep your dreams to yourself," Liusia advised her.

"Am I supposed to say I haven't had a dream when I have?"

"Just eat your *pelmeni* by yourself. Can't you see that this is no time to tell Mummy about them? As it is she imagines she's living on borrowed time, and now you come along with your nightmares. For tact and timing that takes some beating."

Liusia went out angrily, without closing the door properly, and it started swinging back with a rasping creak.

"Push it to, would you?" asked the old lady, but Varvara wasn't listening and went on muttering, "Whatever I say she don't like it. I don't know! It's always Varvara's fault, everything that happens. Nobody else is to blame, only Varvara. Now I'm not even allowed to have dreams. And how am I supposed to stop them, if they come into my mind when I'm asleep. I don't invite them. Or aren't I allowed to sleep either?"

"Don't you listen to everything people say."

"How can I stop listening when she talks to me like that? I'm not deaf. She talks, and I listen."

"Oh, Varvara, Varvara! Why are you so simple? I don't know who you take after," said the old lady pityingly. Then she remembered something and interrupted her own thought: "Didn't I ask you to call on Mironikha? Have you done it?"

"Not yet."

"Why don't you go now."

"I'll go right away."

"Go on, Varvara. She's been on my mind since first thing this morning. I'm worried something might have happened. It won't take you a moment to run across the road. If she's all right, tell her old Anna wants to see her. I haven't seen her for ages." Varvara plodded off towards the door, and the old lady called after her, "And close the door. There's a draught, and I don't want no chill in me legs."

By now she was finding her sitting posture tiring, but Ninka was sprawled right across the middle of her bed, so she had to endure it. She didn't like to disturb the girl. Overcoming the ache in her back, she bent forward, bringing her arms up to fold them against her stomach. When her back was not erect it didn't ache quite so badly. She rested for a while, but then she thought that her new posture — bent double — might be dangerous: she could topple forwards. So she unbent again, straightened her back, and sat upright, swaying and sighing.

There was a tap on the window and Varvara called

out, "Ma, Mironikha's not in. Nadia says she saw her this morning, hurrying out to the lower fields."

The old lady took this in, paused, then said to herself, "Scurrying off somewhere again. Don't know where she gets the energy."

"You still sitting there?" asked Varvara.

"Yes, yes."

Mikhail began to stir in the other room. Groaning and tripping over things, he dragged himself into the porch, where a drinking scoop clattered. Naturally he didn't think to close the door, as if nobody lived in the house but him. The old lady moaned, but as she didn't want to call out to him she bent down gingerly and wrapped her feet in her blanket. But this was not enough to keep out the cold. Perhaps to others it wasn't very cold, but to her it was.

She huddled in her blanket and said nothing.

After a while she said to herself uncertainly, "A dream about the earth ain't a bad one though." And she looked around her.

The day was no longer in infancy. It had picked up speed and was making steady progress.

5

Mikhail drank a whole scoop of water, then paused to get his breath back. As long as the water was flowing down his throat he could feel its cool, refreshing power, but when he stopped drinking he felt his nausea mounting again. He shook himself, and the water slopped uselessly in his belly, like so much bilge-water. He wondered whether to drink a bit more, but did not. There didn't seem much point — it just meant extra weight, and extra running afterwards. He made his way to the front door, holding onto the wall as he went. Now the sun and the increasing warmth were repugnant to him. You felt better when there was a bit of wind or rain. Then at least there was something to distract you, but in this fine, dry weather you had no chance of a quick recovery. Barefoot, and shirtless in his singlet, he was past caring that he wasn't dressed for the street. Everything, in his house and beyond it, seemed equally flat and wearisome.

So as to take the weight off his feet, Mikhail sat down on the doorstep, but got up again at once. Faint, vaporous memories of the day before reminded him that there was still some vodka in the pantry. It was surprising that he hadn't thought of it before. Doubtless old habit was the explanation for that: he'd never had so much liquor in the house before, and in the ordinary way there wouldn't be a single drop left in the morning. He stood for a moment hesitating. He knew one thing: he and Ilia had brought home a full case of vodka, and with the best will in the world they hadn't been able to finish it at one sitting. But he still couldn't believe it: "Pull the other leg . . ." he thought. In the larder, which was just off the porch, he carefully lifted some of the junk in the corner, and his face broke into a cheerful grin: from the gloom the untouched bottles reflected the light with a special, lively glint. Only three compartments in the crate were empty, the others were in their virgin state, looking no worse than they did in the shop. Fancy that now! They'd been there all night, and nothing had happened to them. Mikhail took out another bottle and hastily pushed it into his trouser pocket.

He sat down again to rest on the step he'd just got up from. The nausea was still there and showed no sign of leaving him, but that familiar and most welcome promise of hope cheered his body immensely. It had an unerring sense of what was ahead. Now Mikhail felt he could cheat his hangover, pretend it had him beaten, that he couldn't go on living with it, while knowing all the time that it wouldn't last much longer. Once you knew that relief was near you weren't afraid to look and see what sort of beast you were dealing with. That was only human nature. Just like feeling dog tired the moment before you went to bed, when you didn't need to worry about it. Since the cupboard wasn't bare, Mikhail was now equipped for the same kind of simple ploy.

He would have sat longer on the doorstep, teasing his hangover, but he heard Nadia's voice from the vegetable plot, and thought it would be better if he didn't meet her now. That could wait till later. He knew perfectly well what she would have to say to him now. He wanted to go back into the house to put his shoes on, but thought to himself how awkward it would be trying to do that with a bottle in his pocket. Moreover he could all too easily bump into Nadia or one of his sisters, so he didn't go into the house. Instead he set off barefoot in the direction he had first intended to take — to the bath-house, to see Ilia.

Ilia was dead to the world, sleeping as soundly as if he'd been threshing till late at night and had no cares or worries on his mind. Mikhail squatted down in front of him on the log he'd dragged in the day before, and hid the bottle behind the chicken-coop. This chicken-coop, in which the hens lived in winter, did duty when necessary as a table in the bath-house. Yesterday it had served this purpose admirably for Ilia and Mikhail. Two bottles were still standing on it, the third had miraculously found its way into the coop, where it was lying on its side, although the hatch was closed. It wouldn't do to leave that bottle there. If anyone came in he might get the wrong idea. You couldn't, after all, say the hens had drunk it. Mikhail thought he'd get it out, but to do that he would have to stand up and step across Ilia, so he dismissed the idea — let it lie there, if it was empty. He'd take it out later on.

"Ilia!" he called. This was his first word of the day, and it sounded hoarse and grating. Everything inside him was so parched that he could hardly get a word out. He coughed and tried his voice again, "Ilia, d'you hear me?"

Ilia's even breathing changed, as if he'd heard something in his sleep, and was on the alert.

"Get up. You've slept long enough."

"Too early yet," mumbled Ilia, without moving or opening his eyes. If Mikhail had paused or fumbled for words Ilia would have gone off to sleep again, because he still wasn't properly awake and didn't want to wake up. He was clutching at sleep, like a small boy who refuses to go to bed at night or get up in the morning.

"Early? Nonsense! Morning's here."

"Why can't any of you sleep here? Varvara got me up yesterday, you today. Went to bed late enough, didn't we?"

"How do you feel?" asked Mikhail, not listening to him.

"Don't know yet. Seem to be all right." Ilia finally opened his eyes.

"I feel as if I'd been through a mincer. Can't feel my arms and legs. I don't know how I made it this far. Had to rest on the way."

"I suppose we overdid it a bit yesterday."

"Before I even woke up properly I thought: This is it, I'm dying. And I couldn't go on lying there. But when I got up I felt like dropping. It's okay for you. You just sleep and sleep. Wish I could."

"I always have to lie in the morning after. I can sleep it all off and wake up as fit as a fiddle. But you've got to let me sleep."

"Your system works different, eh?" said Mikhail enviously. "Shouldn't do, with us being brothers."

"Brothers or not, what's the difference?"

"Yeah. Lucky we was on the clear stuff. That red wine would've made a real mess of me. I'd never have got up today, that's for sure. I'd have been laid out. I know what it does to me."

"It don't do me no good either."

"Like buying a disease. Bloody muck."

"Eh?"

"Like buying a disease, I said," Mikhail indicated his aching head. "You pay money for it."

"That's right enough."

"Only five years ago I didn't know nothing about it. I could drink or not drink, and get up just the same in the morning. But these days, when I go to bed conscious I'm already worrying about getting up in the morning. Will I be able to? You can drink that red muck by the cupful, and it only comes out in drops, and you don't feel human again till you've wrung every last drop out of your system. You spit, and think you've got less left inside you, even though you only spat out a tiny bit. There's no end to it."

"Reminds me of a joke," said Ilia. "Mum sends her daughter out to find Dad. 'Look in the boozer,' she says. 'That's where he'll be, the old so-and-so.' Sure enough, he's there, and the girl says to him, 'Daddy, Mummy says you've got to come home.' He hands her his glass of vodka and says, 'Drink that!' She refuses, says she doesn't drink and doesn't want to. 'Drink it, I tell you!' he says. She takes a sip, coughs like fury, waves her arms, turns blue in the face, and says, 'Ooh, it's so bitter!' And he says to her, 'I suppose you and your mother think I'm sitting here drinking nectar.' "

Mikhail laughed. "They think we're drinking nectar here, and it's pleasure all the way."

"Never heard that one before?"

"No. Lot of truth in it too. True to life." He was silent for a moment, nodding thoughtfully at the wisdom of the story, and decided there was no point waiting. "Well then, Ilia," he said, pulling the bottle out from behind the hen-coop. "Time for the hair of the dog."

"You got some already?" Ilia's voice quavered so much that you couldn't tell whether he was pleased or frightened.

"I was passing by, and I thought I'd call in. So as not to have to go for it specially."

"Maybe we'd better wait a while though . . . hadn't we?"

"Do as you like, but I'm having some. I won't last till evening. This hangover'll kill me. As it is I can hardly breathe. You'll have to bury me instead of Mother."

"How is she today?"

"I don't know, I haven't been in. All right, I suppose, or the women would have come running to tell us."

"Yes, they would."

"Well then, shall I pour you some?" Mikhail unstopped the bottle.

"All right. Just enough to keep you company."

"That's the way."

"Nothing to eat with it?"

"No. Go and get something if you want, but I'm not going there now. To hell with them! They think we're drinking nectar."

"I don't like to go rummaging about there."

"Why not? Not a stranger here, are you? Just take what you want and bring it here."

"All right, we'll manage without."

"Right. Death if you drink, and death if you don't, so let's die drinking," said Mikhail as if reciting a prayer, and drained his glass. He waited attentively, following the progress of the vodka to its resting place inside him, and only then set down his glass on the hen-coop. "They think we're drinking nectar," he said in an unsteady voice, repeating once again the words which he found so appealing.

Ilia sat on his bed, frowning as he watched Mikhail. "How does it taste?" he enquired.

"Gone down all right. Only one way for it to go. Drink up, or it'll stick in your gullet later. With the first one you always have to steel yourself and push it down."

At last Ilia drank his glass, and waved his hand in front of his mouth, as if to wave the drink goodbye. This had become a habit with him. Yesterday Mikhail had found it amusing, and once or twice he'd done the same himself, to keep his brother company, but not derived much pleasure from it. In any case his own habit of drinking first was stronger, and then he didn't feel much like seeing anything off, although to Ilia the gesture probably meant something quite different. Mikhail did not ask. It wasn't the sort of thing you could ask about.

The bath-house, when you looked at it, was really more like a kitchen, and not only because of the hen-coop. In fact it was not a real bath-house at all. The real one had burnt down three years earlier. Mikhail had temporarily converted one of the sheds into a bath-house. It had no ledge on which to sit and steam, and an ordinary iron stove heated the water instead of a stone furnace. In short, it was a bath-house in name only, but they got by, and whenever Mikhail wanted a steam-bath he went to his neighbour Ivan. He hadn't got round to erecting a new bath-house, and besides, a job like that was no joke for one man alone. In any case the site of the old one had produced splendid potatoes three years running. When the other villagers had potatoes no bigger than peas, Nadia was already digging up fat ones ready to eat. Which all went to show that you couldn't be unlucky without being lucky, and vice versa.

Mikhail was sitting by the window, and looking out of it he saw Varvara bearing straight down on the bath-house like a tank. With an oath he hid the bottle. Varvara came lumbering through the door and stopped, narrowing her eyes. After the light of day the bath-house seemed pitch-dark.

"That you?" she asked, peering at Mikhail.

"No, it's Jesus Christ."

"Cut your joking! How am I to know where you've

got to? I thought Ilia was alone, and came to tell him Ma's sitting up."

"Sitting up?"

"Yes. I looked in and couldn't believe my eyes. There she was sitting on her bed, looking round, her feet on the floor . . ."

"Head in the air?"

"Don't make fun of me, Ilia," Varvara rebuked him. "You mustn't talk like that about our Ma. She's somebody special."

"What makes you think I'm making fun of anybody?"

"Go and see for yourselves. She's sitting up. I'd never have believed it." Varvara very much wanted her brothers to see it and come away as pleased as she was. "Go on, go and look, see her sitting there. Or you'll say I made it all up."

"No need to look. Let her sit in peace," replied Mikhail to get out of it. "We mustn't tire her. You just make sure she don't fall."

"Oh, she won't. She's sitting well."

"We'll come along later," promised Ilia.

Varvara looked carefully around, but finding nothing else to say she turned to go.

Mikhail detained her: "Is Nadia in the house?"

"Yes, everybody's there. Liusia and Ma too."

"Ma too, eh?"

"Oh, leave off!" retorted Varvara, realizing she'd said something silly. "I'm not going to talk to you. I'm going."

"Off you go. Keep an eye on Mother, or she'll run off somewhere and we'll have to go looking for her."

Varvara lowered herself gingerly from the high step — it hadn't occurred to anybody to put a log under it

— and paused, wondering where to go next. After the conversation with her brothers her joy had subsided a little, and she felt restless and uneasy. It would have been different if the brothers had gone to see their mother. Then she would have gone with them to witness their surprise at somebody who yesterday could only lie on her back, and had now managed to sit up, as if she was in perfect health. But Ilia and Mikhail had stayed behind. That bath-house seemed to mean more to them than their own mother, and now Varvara didn't know what to do. She remembered her dream about the *pelmeni*, and her uneasiness grew into anxiety. That had been a very bad dream. Whom could she turn to to ask what it might mean? It was no good asking Liusia, not after the way she'd snapped at her, and Nadia was so busy she never had a moment. Varvara took a step, hesitated, looked about her, and only then decided to go out of the yard and find other people.

No sooner was Varvara out of the door than Mikhail drew out the bottle and stood it on the hen-coop again, with an emphatic tap to savour the moment. He had cheered up considerably since coming out to the bath-house. His face had taken on more colour and his eyes were brighter.

"Well then, Ilia, things seem to be looking up. Now's the time for a drop more. Can't leave it too long after the first one, or it won't catch up with it."

"I can't take no more without a bite to eat," replied Ilia. "Even an old crust would do, but it's no good with nothing. It'll be the death of me, and that's no joke."

"What if I take an onion from the garden?"

"Onion's no good by itself. We ain't even got no salt."

"Yes, it's better when you have something to chew on," Mikhail agreed, and he paused dejectedly. "We'll wait a bit, there ain't nothing else we can do. I'm not going in now. They'll be at me again. I'll nip over as soon as Nadia goes out."

"You have a glass if you feel like it."

"I'll wait. There's no hurry. I don't care for drinking by myself. The bloody stuff has more bite. Better not to tangle with it alone. I know. I've studied it."

"They say it's better not to tangle with it at all."

"Yes, I've heard that said. People say all sorts of things. You can't listen to everything. Sure, anyone who doesn't drink should stay off it, live without it, but anyone who's got a taste for it . . . I don't know." He sat shaking his head for a moment. "I really don't know. I reckon it pulls you back. There's a hell of a power in it. It don't let go easy, whatever you do. I don't even hope for anything now. When I was young I gave it up lots of times, but I've stopped trying now. No use trying to fool yourself, or anybody else. As I see things now, good or bad, I'm stuck with it. And there's no point trying to give it up. That'd only make people laugh. Of course, drinking's an art, like lots of other things. You and I drink the stuff like it was water, till we get drunk."

"Right enough, drinking's an art."

"You often drink?"

"Not too often when I'm driving the truck. I can't. They're pretty strict about that in town. And the wife's dead against it. But any time I can get away from the wife and the truck I get plastered all right. Right up to the gills."

Mikhail cast a glance at the bottle — it was still

there — and asked, "How about a glass then, eh? You can have a bit more to eat later."

"No, I can't. You go ahead, never mind me."

"I think I will have a drop. I'm not feeling so good." True to his word he poured only a little into his tumbler, and almost in the same movement tipped the contents down his throat, as if hurrying to wash away some nasty taste. "There we are," he said, exhaling noisily. "That's better. As they say: one before your soup, one after, and one in its memory. Got to drink it down like a man."

"Wouldn't mind some soup now. That's for sure."

"Why do we drink?" asked Mikhail, ignoring this remark, and pausing, nodding to himself while waiting to see if Ilia could answer his question. Ilia said nothing. "Some say, from misery, or one thing or another, but that's not it. Nothing to do with it. Others say it's habit, and habit's second nature. And it's true it is a habit, like having bread at table, but that still isn't an answer. There has to be a reason for the habit. I reckon we drink because these days we have a need for it. What did we need in the old days? Bread, water, salt. Well, now this stuff has added itself to the list," he nodded towards the bottle. "Life ain't what it used to be. Everything in it's changed, and all the changes have added to our needs. We get tired as hell . . . not so much from work, Christ knows what does it. But at the end of a week I can hardly pick my feet up, I'm all in. Then I have a bit to drink, and I feel like I've just had a good steam-bath, taken a load off my shoulders. I know I'm to blame for a score of things: quarrelling with the wife, spending our last kopecks, not showing up at work, cadging money in the village. I'm ashamed to look anybody in the eye. But on the other hand I feel better. In one way worse, in another — better. You can go to work again, redeem yourself. Do the work of three men for two, three, even five days, you've got the strength. Then everything seems normal again, the shame passes gradually, you can live normally. Just stay off the booze. In one way you feel better, in another — it gets harder and harder. You need it more and more." Mikhail gave a flap of his hand. "And you get pissed again. Can't hold out. And it starts all over again. You get tired, your system needs a break, and it's your system that does the drinking. And the system needs it, like bread. It's just a need. What do you think?"

"Sure, it's a need," agreed Ilia. "Each drinks according to his ability and according to his needs. As much as he can."

"How can anyone not drink," Mikhail went on. "You can cut it out for a day or two, even a week. But imagine cutting it out altogether, for the rest of your life. Nothing to look forward to. Every day the same as the last. You have so many ropes binding you at home and at work that you can't breathe. So many things you ought to have done, and haven't done, and more and more obligations stretching into the future — to hell with them. But when you've had a drink, you're let out, you're free, and you don't have to do a damned thing. You've done everything you had to do. And what you haven't done you shouldn't have done, and you've done right not doing it. And you feel so good. Is anyone fool enough not to want to feel good? The day you have a drink's always like a holiday. If you only know when to stop."

"If we knew when to stop, the stuff wouldn't do us half the damage it does."

"No, of course it wouldn't. On the other hand, if

you told me to stop now, do you think I would? Even if I'd had enough and felt better, and would get drunk if I had any more. I'd still need more. That's just the way I am. There's something inside me that won't be restrained until it's had all it wants. It doesn't like doing things by halves, cutting corners. It must go the whole hog, working or drinking. You know how it is."

"How much do you get in a month?"

"How much what? You mean booze?"

Ilia laughed, "I know you don't keep count when you're drinking. I meant, how much do you earn? What do they pay you a month?"

"Pay? . . . All depends, Ilia. The pay ain't what it used to be. The machine-operators are raking it in, but they're holding us footsloggers back. I only get about half of what I used to get in the old days. In the old days a man could load two or three barges, and sit back, take it easy for a while. You worked hard, though. Not like now. Rolled the logs by hand. These days you have cranes. You just hook 'em up, unhook 'em, and see you don't get underneath 'em. It's the same every-where. More machinery, less people."

"It's easier that way, with machinery."

"Yeah, you can't argue about that. Much easier. We don't strain ourselves." After a moment's thought Mikhail said with feeling, "All the same it used to be more fun then, loading them barges. I used to like it, and not because of the money, although the pay was good. I liked the work itself. We wouldn't leave the wharf for two days on end. We'd stay until the barge was loaded. The kids would bring us our meals in mess-tins. We'd eat, and get straight back to work. There was some spirit in it. You put your back into it. I don't know why. You sort of had a feeling for the job, like it was alive. You weren't just sweating out another day."

"You were younger and fitter then."

"Yes, I was younger . . . But that's not the point. Remember how life was on the *kolkhoz*. I don't mean the money — there were times when we got bugger-all. But we got on well together, pulled through every-thing together, thick and thin. Now it's every man for himself. Can't be helped: our people have all gone, new people have come. Now there's lots I don't know in my own village. As if I was a stranger myself, as if I'd moved to a new place."

The door of the house creaked, and Mikhail looked up. Ninka, not Nadia came out. She looked about her, saw nobody, hovered by the woodpile, and darted behind it. Mikhail waited for her to finish, then put his head out of the door: "Ninka, come here."

"What for?" she asked, scared. She never expected anyone to watch her from the bath-house.

"Come here, my sweet, and you'll find out."

"I won't do it again."

"Come here, and get a move on, before I give you one."

Looking about her, Ninka sidled into the bath-house, already breathing hard with excitement.

"How many times do I have to tell you where to go? D'you think your legs'll drop off if you run to the right place."

"I won't do it again."

"I've heard that song before, and I'm tired of telling you. I ought to give you a good thrashing now, so you don't forget. And Uncle Ilia will be here to see how you like it. Your bottom's been itching for a spanking for quite a while, and I think it's time I gave it one."

Ninka's breath came harder than ever.

"Well? Say something."

"I'll tell Mummy you're here drinking vodka," she countered with a rapid-fire threat, and made for the door, ready to bolt for her life.

"You what?" Mikhail nearly hit the roof. "You won't even recognize your Mummy when I've had a talk with you! D'you think we taught you to speak so you could sell your own father?" He lamented to Ilia, "Tell Mummy! What a louse! Knee high to a fly, and at it already! Just look at her."

"Then don't hit her."

"Nobody's hitting you, so you keep quiet. I really ought to give her something to think about though for pulling stunts like that."

Ilia felt sorry for Ninka. "Let the girl go. She won't do it again."

"Will you, eh?"

"No," replied Ninka with alacrity, and raised her head. Her eyes darted round the bath-house, taking in all the details she had not managed to notice so far.

"You're a sly one, aren't you. Think you've got out of it because you've said, 'I won't do it again.' Like the cock who crowed once and went to sleep again, didn't care if it got light or not. Wait, no need to hurry, nothing's burning. You've plenty of time. I'd give you a good spanking, but Uncle Ilia doesn't want me to. So in return you can bring me and Uncle Ilia something to eat. Got that?"

"Yes."

"Like hell you have."

"I'll tell Mummy, and she'll give me something."

"Here we go again! Telling Mummy again. Can't you do it without telling Mummy? Forget about

Mummy, put her right out of your mind. Bring us something without Mummy seeing or hearing you. Got that now?"

"Yes."

"Look on the table or in the larder, find something, and bring it here. Quietly now. And afterwards I'll give you a bottle." Mikhail set aside one of yesterday's empties.

"You'll give it to me, then take it away again," said Ninka mistrustfully.

"No, I won't take it away. Off you go now."

"You took the other one away."

"But I won't take this one away. This time I've got my own. I won't take it. Uncle Ilia's my witness."

"I'm your witness", said Ilia, slapping his chest.

Ninka didn't move.

"Well? What's the matter? Get a move on!"

"I want two," Ninka cast a fleeting glance at the second empty bottle.

"All right, I'll give you two, but get moving for God's sake." He stood the second bottle beside the first.

Ninka brought them a bread roll under her dress. That was all, because her mother had shooed her away from the table. Taking the roll had been less difficult, as it was lying in the porch, where Nadia had left it before breakfast. Naturally a bread roll was better than nothing at all, but by itself it wasn't quite enough for the morning drink. But then Mikhail suddenly remembered that two or three hens were in the habit of laying in the bath-house roof, just above their heads. Ninka climbed up and fetched down five eggs in the hem of her dress, together with a nest-egg which had probably been there since the spring. After a glass of vodka Mikhail managed to swallow even this, thanks to his habit of gulping things down without looking. Even though he had some liquor inside him, his eyes rolled up and he amost retched, so that he had to wash the rotten egg down with another glass of vodka, to ease his throat. After this he went on spitting and swearing for a long time, and stuck to bread, not sucking any more eggs.

As thanks to Ninka for the eggs they gave her the third bottle, which was lying in the hen-coop, and in return for fetching some salt they had to promise her the fourth, still unfinished bottle. She insisted on staying in the bath-house to keep an eye on it. Besides, she had no inclination to go into the house because even at this distance she could hear her mother looking for the roll, which seemed to have vanished into thin air. Ninka maintained a calm silence. She felt perfectly safe with the men and watched them with clear, innocent eyes. Now that events had bound them together, Mikhail could rest assured that Ninka would not give him away. Soon they finished the fourth bottle, and she carried it off and hid it behind the woodpile. Then she wandered about the yard, as usual, gradually going towards the house. It was clear that she was hungry.

After the vodka the men's talk became livelier, flagging only once, when Ilia seemed to feel a need to make excuses to somebody for this untimely drinking session: "What can we do? I don't see no point sitting beside Mother all the time. She's already sitting up. She'll be running about before we know it."

"That she will," nodded Mikhail.

"Who'd have thought, though, eh? I'd never have believed it. Laid out all ready for the grave, no life left in her, and then something happens, brings her round.

What a woman!"

"Still up to her old tricks."

"Gave death the slip all right."

"I'll tell you something, Ilia: she shouldn't have done it. Better to die now. Better for us, and for her. I wouldn't say this to anyone else, but why should you and I keep anything from each other? One way or another she's going to die. And now's the time to do it, while we're all here and ready for it. She was ready, and she should have got it over with then and there, and not string us along like this. I believed her, and you believed me when I sent word."

"Don't take it like that," Ilia objected. "Let her die when her time's up. That's not up to her."

"I'm only saying it would be better that way. Of course nobody's going to say to her, 'We want you dead and out of here by tonight, and don't talk back.' But you'll go home, she'll live a little bit longer, and then die all the same. You mark my words. She's had her warning. And I'll have to send you all telegrams again, and you won't be so eager to come next time. Some'll come, and some won't bother, and that'll be ten times worse. It'll be too late."

"How could anyone not come?"

"All sorts of reasons. Tatiana doesn't look like coming now."

"No. It's as if she knew, and she's not hurrying."

"She doesn't know, that's the point. And she's not hurrying. If she doesn't get here today Mother will go crazy. As it is she's bored us silly with her 'Tanchora, Tanchora', dreaming about her, and I don't know what else. You don't live here, you don't know."

"She'll come. Nobody could get a telegram like that and not come. That'd be awful."

"Well, if she comes we'll all have a drink. Have to celebrate it properly, she's our sister, after all."

"Yes, we'll have a drink, naturally."

"And if she don't come, we'll have a drink all the same," said Mikhail. "You and I have no choice left."

"No, what else could we do?" Ilia concurred with a wistfully merry air. "We're not going to pour the stuff away."

"Who'd give you permission to pour it away? That's a criminal offence. It's a serious matter."

"Yeah, we have to drink, like it or not."

"Funny way you have of putting things, Ilia. 'Like it or not.' You can't put it in those terms. Our wishes don't even come into it. If we have to, we'll drink," Mikhail insisted. "We don't see each other every day. Why shouldn't we take that obligation upon ourselves?"

"Sure, why not?"

"That's okay then."

Their talk again took a familiar, inviting, harmonious track. Fired by it, the men wanted more to drink — particularly as the vodka was close at hand and all paid for. Enough to drink themselves stupid. On the pretext of wanting to put his shoes on, Mikhail decided to make another sortie to the pantry. He set off, his bare heels showing white as he went, and in the meantime Ilia rolled up the bedding on which he'd been reclining all this time, and stepped outside to stretch his legs.

Mikhail did not get as far as his shoes. He went into the pantry first, looked, and at once his vision became clouded: virtually half the crate had been shamelessly looted. What did his shoes matter now? He snatched up the crate, lighter by half, and rushed back to the bath-house: while there was still something to save, save it! In another minute that too might be gone.

In the bath-house he gave vent to his feelings with a long stream of oaths. It was plain that the family had hidden the bottles, but that didn't make it any easier to get them back. This wasn't the sort of time to hold a knife to anybody's throat and tell him to hand over the bottles, because they'd bought the vodka for a definite occasion, with money from a common fund. Certainly the men had most right to it, but only sober men had rights at all — the rights of drunkards always seemed to be in doubt. So they would have to pretend nothing had happened, everything was fine, while keeping their eyes open, ready to seize the chance when it came.

They had only just taken the seal off a new bottle when Ninka announced from the door, "Mummy's horrid."

"Hanging's too good for that Mummy of yours," replied Mikhail, whose anger still had not cooled.

"Ooh, let's hang her, Daddy, and see what happens."

"I wouldn't think twice about it, but she doesn't deserve the honour."

"What's she done to you?" Ilia asked Ninka.

"She says I stole the bread. She didn't see nothing, but she says she did."

"She's trying to trick you. Don't you let her," warned Mikhail.

"I didn't. I said: You can ask Daddy, or Uncle Ilia."

"You shouldn't have said that. No need to bring us into it. At the moment we have no power there at all, you should know that. None. You should have thought of that."

"She's horrid," said Ninka stubbornly.

"No good saying that. I might have even more bones to pick with her than you have."

"They're saying you're off on another binge, and a long one," Ninka reported. "And that you're no better than a drunken sot, Daddy, and that it's all your fault."

"What a way to talk in front of a little girl!" Mikhail shook his head bitterly. "Have they no idea when to stop? Don't you listen to them," he ordered Ninka. "They'll say all kinds of things. Who do you believe: us or them?"

"You."

"That's the way. Stick with us, and you'll be all right. Don't listen to them."

The men set to again. Emboldened by her father's words, Ninka stayed beside him, taking his glass of vodka, sniffing at it, and snorting, then sniffing at it when he'd drained it, and snorting again. She butted into their conversation as an equal, while keeping a close eye on the level in the bottle and urging the men to drink up. Mikhail felt sorry for her and did not chase her away. As it turned out, this was just as well.

"Daddy, do they take unemptied bottles back in the shop?" She had to repeat the question three or four times because Mikhail was deep in conversation with Ilia and had no time for her silly questions.

"What unemptied ones?" he turned to her at last.

"The ones you can't pour away. I was trying to empty them, and I couldn't."

"And what, may I ask, were you trying to pour out of them?" asked Mikhail, still not unduly worried.

"The vodka."

"What vodka?"

"She shouldn't say I stole the bread. She didn't see me, so she shouldn't say I did."

"What were you trying to pour out?" Mikhail bent over her and held her carefully, gently, so as not to alarm her.

"The stuff in the bottles, of course. But the bottles won't open."

"Where did you find them?" asked Mikhail, exchanging glances with Ilia.

Ninka felt well disposed to her father today, and had no intention of keeping anything from him. "You gave me some yourself, and I took some more from her. She shouldn't say I did it. She didn't see."

"Quite right. And where are those bottles that you took from her?"

"In the flour."

"Where?"

"In the flour. They were in the larder, where she'd hidden them. She thought I wouldn't find them, but I did. They were in a sort of cage. There are still some left."

"I see. So you can't empty them, you say. But you would have emptied them," he said with a groan. "Where were you trying to empty them? Onto the floor?" He almost winced with pain as he pictured to himself the vodka splashing onto the floor like so much pig-swill, and soaking into the floorboards.

"No, I wanted to pour it into the flour, so she wouldn't see any wet patches."

Mikhail hadn't the patience to keep up the game any longer. Wagging a threatening finger at Ninka, he ordered her, "Not a word to anybody about those bottles! Do you hear?"

"Yes."

"Not a word to a soul. You hear?"

"Yes."

"It'll be too bad for you if you tell anyone, so watch out!"

"Anyway they don't take 'em back unemptied," added Ilia, trying to soften the severity of Mikhail's words.

"And they don't take them back with the stuff poured out. Only when it's been drunk. Understand?"

"Yes."

"You do catch on fast! I wish I was as quick. What a clever girl! But you can run along and go for a walk now," said Mikhail, hurrying her on her way. "Off you go. This is no place for you. And don't forget what I told you. Not a soul. Play with your dolls, not with bottles. We don't need no bottle-collector."

He shut the door behind her and paused to get his breath back. "She really would have done it too. She'd have taken them back. 'Unemptied' — there's a child's mind for you. And they'd have been only too glad to give her twelve kopecks for them, same as for the empties. Twelve kopecks for the goods intact. That'd suit 'em down to the ground. Little beggar. She found 'em though. She's got brains. Cut her head off and she'd grow a new one."

In the meantime Ninka had reached the middle of the yard, looking round as she went. From this safe distance she made a threatening gesture in the direction of the bath-house, said, "Daddy's horrid," and went to look for her mother.

6

Liusia had looked in again on her mother that morning, to see how she was, and then got ready to go out to the forest. After Ninka had gone the old lady had lain down again and dozed off, but she slept lightly, opening her eyes at the slightest murmur. It was clear that she was much better today and could safely be left alone.

Liusia was not particularly eager to go out, but could think of nothing else to do. She didn't want to stay at home all day. At first, without thinking, she had invited Nadia to go with her, and Nadia had agreed, but then she herself had dissuaded her, because, in the first place, she would have had to talk to Nadia, and she didn't feel much like talking, and secondly it seemed dangerous to leave Mother alone with Varvara, who was quite helpless and wouldn't be able to do anything. Nor could anyone rely on the men. They needed watching themselves, in case they became unruly and started bothering their mother. The old lady couldn't abide drunkards, and she might take a turn for the worse if her sons came in.

It took Liusia a long time to get ready. She wanted to wear something that was comfortable in the forest, and she wanted to look presentable, avoiding that sloppiness which bespoke bad taste. Not for other people — she might not see anybody in the forest — but for herself. Dressing well was an unbreakable rule with her. Her mood depended on it, and it even affected her actions. Liusia believed that misfortune had eyes, and that before descending on somebody it studied his demeanour, his worth, and even his appearance. It didn't often dare to strike at a strong, happy person.

Nadia had given her a suitable dark cardigan, but Liusia could not make up her mind what else to put on. Nadia had also brought her some baggy trousers and a pair of boots, but Liusia laid them aside — they didn't suit her. How she wished she had her slacks and those walking shoes she had bought specially for such excursions into the country, but who could have told her she would be going mushrooming this time? She'd had other things in mind when she packed her bags. She was on the point of changing her mind and staying at home, as she had nothing to wear, when she heard Varvara's voice outside, on her way home. At the thought of Varvara mooning about all day, getting on her nerves with her snivelling, she asked Nadia for her canvas shoes and took them straight off Nadia's feet. Anything would do, as long as she could get out. She could hardly bear the thought of staying in, she wanted to see no one and talk to no one, and give neither sympathy nor encouragement. This was her closest family: with them she could not behave quite as she behaved towards other people, but nor could she feel any special bond of intimacy linking her to them. Only her mind told her that such a bond existed, and because of this she was annoyed with herself and her inability to feel at one with them and share their unaffected joy at meeting again. And she felt annoyed with them, and even with her mother, on whose account she had made this unnecessary journey — annoyed because the journey was unnecessary. Nobody could say how long she would have to stay. Another day, or two, or three? Perhaps even longer.

So as to avoid meeting any of the village people,

Liusia took the back way out of the garden and climbed the nearest hill. She had made up her mind not to hurry, she would simply stroll in the forest and breathe the fresh air. She was used to travelling long distances into the country at weekends to do precisely this, and here the forest was right beside her. It would be unforgivable to miss this lucky chance to stroll in it without any of the preliminary fuss — arranging transport, preparing food. Here she could simply walk out of the house into it. And collecting mushrooms now seemed like hard work, as the villagers were not in the habit of walking in the forest without a reason. If any mushrooms happened to catch her eye she would pick them, and if not it didn't matter.

At the top of the hill she stopped to rest. The hill seemed lower than when she was last here, and not so steep. At first she presumed this was because she had grown up and her perception of size had changed: things which had once seemed big and substantial had now assumed normal proportions. But no, the hill really was lower. She remembered how as children they had rolled down it with ease to their gate. She looked down at the two slanting posts, which were all that was left of the gate, and thought that nobody could roll that far now. And why was there no gate? Where had it gone? But of course, if they didn't plough and sow, there was nothing to protect from the cattle, no need to enclose anything. Beyond the Upper and Lower Brooks the gates had also gone and the pastures were unfenced.

Suddenly Liusia realized why the hill seemed lower: the crest had been shaved off. Before it hadn't been very high, but steep, and difficult for vehicles to negotiate. That must have been why they'd brought in a bulldozer. Now you hardly noticed the ditch on the left, and it used to be a veritable ravine, twice the height of a man. In spring a torrent of water, red from the clay, would thunder through it and flood the vegetable patches. The eroded banks of the ditch rumbled so loudly that they echoed. Mothers seeing their children off to school first instructed them not to go near the ditch. Everything else, like orders not to poke each other's eyes out, took second place. And in fact the ditch did hold for the children some disturbing, unknown menace, hidden from the sight of human eyes. There were few forbidden places in the vicinity which they did not explore thoroughly, but they always avoided the ditch, although it was easy enough to get at. Someone had once spread the word that the bottom was false, that it concealed a void that reached almost all the way to Hell, and they had not forgotten this. Even if they didn't really believe it, they did not forget it.

Now the ditch had been filled in, the earth packed down, and all its terrors buried. Yet another mysterious place, which had once inspired respectful awe, had vanished. Such places were becoming steadily fewer in the world.

Further away to the left, beyond the ditch, where a dark patch of nettles stood, had been the *kolkhoz* silage pit. On spring evenings, when a breeze was ruffling the river, a pleasant, musty smell wafted right across the village from the open pit.

The pit was usually filled by volunteers on Sundays. It was a merry, noisy job — cutting and carting grass and nettles and dropping them in. A horse, with one of the children on it, trampled it all down while the level rose higher and higher, and a large crowd of excited children clustered round the pit, getting in everybody's way. When chased away they would retreat, but in no time they would somehow be back at the edge. On these days the children knew countless joys and sorrows. Angry peasants would clip them on the ear without thinking about it, and the nettles with which they whipped each other, and into which they pushed the unwary, gave them itchy swellings. Liusia recalled how they used to rub these with earth and spittle, and then whitish spots would appear on the skin under the muddy plaster. Another memory made her smile: among her contemporaries it was thought that Kolia Komarov had the most effective saliva for this purpose. He even charged for it, and had a good half of the school-age population in his debt. They chose Kolia, she supposed, not because his saliva really had any more healing properties than her own or anybody else's, but because in some strange way somebody else's touch held excitement and magic, like all sorcery, and Kolia was the only one who would lick other people's nettle-stings.

She wondered what had become of Kolia Komarov, and decided to ask about him at home. At one time he had payed court to her, and it was possible that if she hadn't gone away their lives would have been joined.

And this memory was followed at once by another. Liusia walked on towards the place which was linked with it. On the hill on the right of the road there used to be a tiny little field, less than a hectare in area. For as long as she could remember it had never been ploughed. It wouldn't have been worth the trouble. Here they carted the straw in autumn, and from then until winter the strawstack teemed with children. They would get lost in it for days on end, digging tunnels, burrows, and secret dens, and at night the older lads would brings their girls here. Not that the darkness helped them much, because in the overhanging birches the smaller boys kept watch till dawn to see who was with whom. The boldest spirits among them, on finding where a couple had made themselves comfortable, were even in the habit of jumping on them. But to take part in this jolly country sport you really did need daring, and long legs, or the disturbed lover might do you an injury.

These memories aroused Liusia's curiosity more than any other feeling. How strange and how remote it all was, as if none of it had happened to her, not even in her time, but in some earlier time, before she had been here. The memories came by themselves, uninvited, in response to things her eyes lighted on.

At the next long uphill slope the road made a detour to the left. This hill could not so easily be trimmed down. But Liusia went straight ahead, along the old road, now little more than a deep-cut path, its fringes overgrown with tall, over-ripe grass. She ran her hand over it, and the seeds fell with a soft rustle, tickling her palm. On the hill the trees grew thinner and the open fields could be seen through them. Tree stumps jutted out at every step, and near the road lay blackened, cracked stakes, cut for fencing, but forgotten. Thick, tangled grass had grown up, as usual at the scene of such wanton vandalism, and out of it stuck dead fallen boughs, like skeletons. In the old days these would have been collected for fuel, at least close to the village, but now nobody needed them. Liusia had seen the river bank yesterday, all covered in logs left behind after loading, and each house had its pile of logs. These days they used chain saws — in a couple of minutes you'd have all the fuel you used to collect in a day. On those Sundays they'd all gone out together, with all the village children, to do jobs that would have been too much for one family alone. The children were given work within their strength. Liusia remembered how she used to like stacking logs, finding a sort of primitive pleasure in arranging the pleasing, yellow pine logs, with that fine silky bark from near the crown of the tree. Then there was only one logging season, the spring, so that the felled trees could dry out over the summer, but now they picked up and sawed timber at any time of year, timber which had already been felled.

"Yes, there really was something about those Sundays," thought Liusia, with unexpected nostalgia. "People went along willingly. And if somebody wasn't invited to come along, he realized that he wasn't one of the family, and wasn't regarded as a trusted friend."

They all went at it heartily, lustily, to the ring of axes and saws, and their hearts thrilled to the thud of falling tree-trunks. They kept up a constant, lively banter in the eager anticipation of a good meal, for which purpose the mistress of the house was allowed to go home early. With the onset of spring, this was their first task in the forest, not a very difficult one, and one they all enjoyed. The sun, the forest, and the intoxicating scents of the awakening earth produced in young and old alike a state of childish excitement, which did not subside until they were dropping from weariness. As the soil was renewed, so one's feelings seemed to change, uniting in some inexplicable way with a distant age when the eyes and ears of men were more alert to sights, sounds, and fine distinctions. With a strange insistence the timeless instincts compelled you to look more closely at some things, sniff at others, and look for something in the air and under foot, something lost and forgotten, but not gone forever.

Instead of water they drank birch sap, which the body accepted like a drug, in sparing, attentive sips, confident that its effects would soon be felt. The birch sap was collected by the children, who also dug up the first yellow bulbs of the forest lily and melted them in their mouths like sweets. They sucked on spruce needles, their faces drawn, not to slake any peculiar inner thirst, but so as not to be outdone by their friends. And of course there was larch resin, without which the day would have been as incomplete as Easter without eggs. Even the men chewed it, and usually tore their gums on it, then swore and reached for their tobacco.

As soon as she had climbed the steepest part of the slope the fields spread out before her. Liusia came out into the open, and looked about her, puzzled. Could she have lost her way? Surely she couldn't have got lost a stone's throw from home. No, of course she hadn't. Those fields to the left, running down to the Lower Brook, were known as Kasalovka, and that one in front, with the hedge of the old threshing ground to one side, was the Home Meadow. Beyond it was the Knoll, and the track to the right led to the Far Meadow. These names came to her as easily as if she used them every day, although not so long ago she hadn't been able to recall the names of the islands opposite the village. Liusia was surprised at herself: how could this be? It was as if some voice — in the grass or the wind — were telling her the words which lived here, and her ear caught them and repeated them.

Liusia walked on slowly along the road, recognizing with difficulty the places that she saw. If you looked up and into the distance it was easy to distinguish

Kasalovka, Home Meadow, and the Knoll, but if you only looked at the foreground you saw nothing but a wasteland of neglect, alien and shocking to the eye. The narrow track made its way up the hill to rejoin the wide new road, which ran sprawling on, devouring land on both sides. The fields were overgrown. A dense thicket of aspen was spreading up from the lower edge, a clump of young pines was rising nearer to the middle, and tall weeds were poking up here and there. It was already difficult to distinguish the fields from the boundary strips between them: the wild vegetation had claimed both as one. The scent of crops, which ought to be in the air at this time of year, had long gone from this place. Instead there were the mingled smells of over-ripe woodland plants, and the sweetish, dry smell of the neglected soil.

Liusia succumbed to the temptation to turn left and strike out across the field. Nature had not yet reclaimed everything, and the ground was uneven and grey. Being in the habit of pushing up cereal crops, it seemed to be waiting for a miracle, hanging on to the last in the hope of being sown again, but beside the young pine grove the ants, scenting resin, were busy, and that meant they were sure nobody would bother them here.

How long was it since the *kolkhoz* had gone? Seven years? Eight? Nine? Liusia did not know exactly, but it was about that. You could say it hadn't so much gone as disintegrated. They'd taken away the machinery, what little there was, and some of the tools. They couldn't take the fields, and the people had also stayed. It wasn't that easy to leave your established home, the place made sacred by the graves of your parents, and move on to who knew where. Only three families, who had been resettled here from the west, moved on, and one of them came back later.

The *kolkhoz* was called "Memory or Chapaev"*, and again Liusia was surprised at the ease with which this useless name came to her, without her searching for it, and flew off over the fields like an orphan seeking a home. If she had not been here among the things that were bound up with that name, she would never have remembered it. Later, however, after Liusia had left, it had been renamed, renamed more than once, she thought, but she didn't know any of the other names.

"Memory of Chapaev", which had always had to struggle to survive, had met with bad luck on two fronts at once. First a timber-works had been set up right next door, in the same village. It had plenty of money, it paid its workers without fail every two weeks, and the young people resorted to every ruse they could think of to get out of the *kolkhoz*. They didn't need to move or change their way of life, because the timber-works was as near home as the *kolkhoz*. How could the *kolkhoz* hope to keep a good machine-operator when he could get at the very least three times as much at the timber-works? The *kolkhoz* did all it could to keep its workers, using threats, and the law, but to no avail.

While the *kolkhoz* was fighting this battle, another misfortune struck: the amalgamation of *kolkhozy*. "Memory of Chapaev" found itself merged with an equally unprofitable *kolkhoz*, separated from it by almost fifty kilometres of forest. At this, virtually the whole village, not only the young, flocked to the tim-

---

* Chapaev, Vasily (1887-1919): hero of the Red Army, killed in action during the Civil War.

ber-works. The point was reached where there was nobody to feed the cattle. The cattle and sheep were driven across to the new *kolkhoz*, which worked the fields for a year or two, sending its own hands over, although it was short-handed itself. After doing this half-heartedly for a while it transferred the remaining equipment to its own base. The fields were abandoned, and here they still lay — what was left of them.

Liusia looked about her again and felt a sudden twinge of guilt, as if she ought to have done something to help, and had not. But she dismissed the thought as soon as it occurred to her: "What nonsense! It's nothing to do with me. I left long before any of these changes. It's not my business." She reflected that the village people who had deserted the land for the tim-ber-works ought to feel this guilt more strongly than she did. Well then, let them suffer its pangs, if they were capable of feeling them. She herself was only a casual visitor, and it was most unlikely that she would ever come here again. But nevertheless the confidence with which she had set out had evaporated, the relaxed mood of her stroll in the country was spoiled, although she did not know why. She wished she had stayed in the house, but now she could not have turned back even if she had wanted to: something stronger than her own wishes was leading her on, and she obediently submitted to it. On a boundary strip she saw from afar a white log, polished by the rain and the sun, and thought she would sit down on it to rest and calm her feelings, but without even realizing it she walked past the log and went on. She looked back and wondered whether to return to it, but she knew that she would not, that she could not, that she was not free to act as she pleased.

A thought took her by surprise. She thought that she ought to feel far more upset than she did, as she was seeing this abandoned, desolate land for the first time since its decay had begun. But she felt no bitterness, no pain. She had a confused feeling which gradually developed into a sense of alarm. This seemed to stem from the soil, because it remembered Liusia and was awaiting her decision as judge. After all, she had been here many times before and had even worked here. "Even worked here," she repeated the words to herself as a sort of self-justification, and only now realized, with a sense of surprise, what they meant.

The words had forced her to stop and look about her again. Slowly she cast her eyes over everything she could see, and scanned the sky as well, not quite certain what she was looking for. Then she turned down the slope, towards a thin copse. Beyond it lay a small field which ran down to the Lower Brook. This field occupied a special place in her memory. Liusia hurried on, fearful that the field would be so overgrown that she would not be able to find it — as if a few minutes could make any difference. She remembered that somewhere down there there ought to be a path leading to the field, but it seemed too far to walk, and Liusia went straight through the copse. She wanted to steal a glance at it first, from cover, to make sure it was the one, that her memory hadn't failed her, and that nothing had happened to it, and approaching it along the path would mean giving herself away. She could not free herself of the uncomfortable feeling that somebody had been watching her every move since she had set out, and so she tried to keep out of sight and avoid open spaces.

At last she emerged into the light and saw before her

the field she expected to see. She looked at it from the edge of the copse. The broad boundary strip was still distinct, but now it resembled a cutting in a forest: its hard-packed, grass-covered soil did not allow the seeds of trees to take, whereas on the former ploughland beyond it a thin growth of aspen was creeping down the slope. At its lower edge, wildly improbable though it seemed, lay a vegetable patch. Somebody evidently liked the soil here, and had planted potatoes. Unprotected from the sun, the leaves had withered more than they would in the village, and were shorter, though still standing. They looked more like pumpkins, with nothing underneath them, but that was because it was so unusual to see potatoes growing here.

The memory which drew Liusia to this spot went back to the hungry years just after the war, about 1946 or '47. In the spring, before the sowing, Liusia had been sent out to harrow this field. Rain had fallen the day before, so the soil was damp and clung to the harrow, which dragged like a heavy bearskin rug. It would have been more sensible, of course, to wait and let the ground dry out a bit, but they either couldn't wait or didn't want to. What was worse, the field had lain fallow for some time and was thickly overgrown. Last year's grass kept getting entangled in the teeth, making the harrow ride up. Liusia constantly had to turn it over and clean it. She had been given an old, feeble horse. That spring none of the horses could do much more than drag themselves along, but this one was no more than a shadow.

And yet again Liusia heard the name she was looking for sounding within her. The horse was called Igrenka,* and with this name ringing in her ears the memory at once became much fuller and sharper. She

* From *Igrenevy* — "skewbald"

could clearly see that chestnut horse with its silver mane and that silver spot on its forehead. It was so skinny that even its hooves looked dried out and wasted. And she could see herself behind it, a thin little girl dressed any old how, flicking the reins and hopping on one foot as she tried to drive the harrow into the ground. Behind them lay a waving, irregular track.

Igrenka's shoulders went to and fro in time to his feet. He could pull the harrow downhill all right, but when he turned round and went uphill he had to stop ten times or more. He strained and wheezed as he picked his feet up. Liusia gave up trying to urge him on, and she cleaned the harrow only when his strength failed. After cleaning it she would urge him on again. Igrenka was too weak to make a standing start. He had to swing into his tottering step. Often he was dragged to one side, and he pulled uphill with his eyes shut, probably so as not to see the distance remaining to the edge. Before long she was exhausted with him, the grass and the mud, and like Igrenka was ready to drop. The exhaustion she had felt then, as a young girl, came back to her now, as she looked out at the field again, and she felt such overpowering weariness and helplessness that she sat down on the grass.

Finally Igrenka stumbled and fell. Frightened, Liusia started tugging at the reins, and when this had no effect she seized the bridle and pulled his head up. He shook it and lowered it to the ground. She started shouting at him, not so much in anger as in fear, and she kicked his sunken flank. Her kicks sent convulsive shudders through his body, but he made no attempt to get up. Liusia stepped back and looked about her, then flung herself at the horse and tried to lift him in her arms, scratching at the flank he was lying on, but succeeding only in stretching his loose, pliant skin. Then she fled back to the village.

Mother was at home, thank goodness. Together they ran back to Igrenka. He was lying on his belly with his legs drawn up under him. The ground near him was churned up, as if he had been trying to get up, frightened by a sense of foreboding. Having failed, he was now quietening down, soothed by a calm that was rising through the ground, and accepting what had to be. Mother knelt down in front of him and stroked his thin, badly chafed neck.

"Igrenka," she said softly. "What do you think you're doing? Bad horse, bad horse. The grass is springing up, and you think you're a goner. If you only hang on a week, you'll live, you'll have grass to eat everywhere. Hold on, Igrenka, don't give in. If you've lasted out the winter you've only got to keep going a little bit longer. You must, God wills it. Not long to go now, no time at all. We made it through the winter, not just the winter, we pulled through the war together, you and me. You slaved away right through the war in the logging camps, hauling tree-trunks. You pulled through. And this job's nothing compared to that. All you need is a bit of determination, that's what keeps me going."

The horse turned his long, beak-like head and stretched towards her hands.

"Oh, I ain't got a thing," said Mother, alarmed. "Igrenka, I didn't bring nothing with me. How stupid of me! He understands everything, this horse. Ain't nothing Igrenka don't understand." She stroked his nose and tugged at his forelock. "Understands plenty that a lot of humans wouldn't understand. The year before last, when a log broke his leg and they wanted to write him off as horse-meat, who do you think galloped off into the forest on three legs? Igrenka did. And he lay up there and didn't come out till the bone had mended. After that he was lame for a long time. But I didn't let anyone else have you as long as you were lame, and when I took you to carry water, I never filled the barrel, so's you wouldn't hurt your leg."

Igrenka tossed his head and gave a thin, guilty neigh. Mother rubbed his neck and he replied by neighing again and thrashing feebly with his feet underneath him.

"Hold on, Igrenka, hold on," Mother hastened to free him from the traces. "Now we'll get up. Been lying down long enough." The horse watched her, trembling with impatience and fear at his own weakness. When Mother took him by the bridle he threw out his forelegs firmly, but too far, so that he had to pull them up closer. He strained and heaved, trying to lift his hind quarters, but failed and sank down again. Turning away from Mother, he gave another neigh, and his voice was despairing: I can't, look for yourselves, I can't. Mother spoke to him in a soothing voice: "Hold on, Igrenka, have a rest. Not too much at once. You shouldn't have tried so soon. You just sit quiet and rest, and then you can get up. Never mind, Igrenka, silly Igrenka."

She looked round at Liusia's work and said to her reproachfully, "You should have gone across the slope, not up and down it. Not even a healthy horse could pull up that hill, let alone a horse like this . . ."

"Yes, but he can go faster downhill . . ."

"So what? No need to hurry. You should have gone nice and slow. It's the same field, whichever way you go, and it won't get no bigger if you go slowly."

She handed the reins to Liusia, went to Igrenka's side, slapped him on the back and got hold of him by his lower flank. Igrenka put out his front feet, as if to get away from the spot which had let him down. Pulling up his hind legs he made a last, desperate effort, straightened them, and rose to his full height. He swayed on his feet, but Mother supported him with an arm across his back and she kept joyfully repeating, "There you are, there you are. What did I tell you? And you was all ready to die, and that's a sin. If I told anybody, they'd laugh at you and say you was one of them disserters, like in the army. But you're not, are you, Igrenka? Lord above! You're no disserter. You'd collapse if I swatted a fly on your back. Some disserter! You shouldn't have been sent out to work in your state. Come on, disserter, let's go home."

She took the reins and led him away. He lurched off to a wobbly start and stopped almost at once, as if afraid of falling down again. But he hobbled on.

Liusia stood up, shook the grass off her clothes, and looked again at the vegetable patch in the middle of the field, as if to assure herself that all this had happened not just now, but long ago, over twenty years ago. Shaking off that scene from the past she made her slow way back up the slope, but the memory would not let go completely. It was as if she had not understood something in it, and the memory had returned not simply in order to remind her how hard life had been, but with some secret, nagging thought of its own, which she had failed to recognize. She was annoyed with herself for falling prey to an unfamiliar feeling which so disturbed her by its probing, and she decided to go faster in order to throw it off.

"Even worked here" — again she recalled the words

which half an hour before had compelled her to look for this field. Yes, she had worked here, like everybody else. She had mown, raked, harrowed, weeded, harvested when it was undermanned. "And ploughed," added a voice within her. Indeed she had ploughed. How had she forgotten that? Only two days, it was true, because although she could walk behind the plough she wasn't strong enough to lift it from one furrow to another. She had not been very strong as a girl, and had gone out to work later than her friends — only at the end of the war. Until then her mother had felt sorry for her and left her at home with Tania, the same Tania who was now expected from Kiev.

"If only Tanchora would come today," thought Liusia, delighted at the opportunity to think about something else. Mother wouldn't give anybody a moment's peace if her Tanchora didn't come, and as long as she was still waiting the situation couldn't resolve itself.

Liusia came to the edge of the trees and emerged again into the fields which rose away from it. Here in the open the day was bright and warm, and the sunlit air clear and sharp, so that there seemed to be faint ringing sound in it, and this sound from above was the only sound to be heard. On earth everything fell watchfully silent at the sound of Liusia's steps. The hard ground seemed deaf to her footsteps. The trees on the hill shimmered like ghosts, and a whitish haze, hardly visible in the air, rose from the autumn birches, sated and warm. The sky came evenly, calmly down behind them, behind the earth — a high, open sky, but its blue had already faded, there was less feeling, and a hint of weariness, in its impenetrable depths.

In the field Liusia turned further left, towards the

brook. She trod carefully, as if stealing up on something, although she was exposed to view from all sides.
The track must lie somewhere near, and she thought it
would really be safer to follow it, even if that meant
making a detour. She knew perfectly well that she had
nothing to fear, but she could not shake off the inexplicable feeling, even certainty, that somebody was
watching her. This was no ordinary presentiment of
what was to come: it was in some strange way connected with the past, with some lost memory for which
she was about to be called to account. She felt as if she
had been lured out of the village, unthinkingly rising to
somebody's bait, and now it was impossible to turn
back. If she did, the event for which she had been lured
out of the house would take place at once, and she was
fending it off, afraid of it, and kept walking so that it
should not catch her.

She found the track in the end, but this did not make
her feel any better. She resisted the temptation to rush
back along it to the village as fast as her legs would carry her, and went on up the hill, slowly, as if testing the
ground to make sure it was safe. No, she wouldn't run
there. She had forgotten how to run. The track was in
disuse, and its ruts and tussocks were baked hard. The
air over the track also seemed to have been baked dry,
and Liusia soon felt hot. She thought that it would be
better to go across the field, but she stayed on the track,
unable to take a step away from it, in the grip of some
alien will which had to be obeyed. Liusia realized that
she should never have set foot on this track at all, that
it had become for her a long, narrow corridor with
high, invisible walls which could not be scaled. And
this corridor would lead her to something unexpected,

and perhaps terrifying. The sharp, dried sods cut her feet through her shoes, but she ignored the pain, concerned only lest some other more insidious danger catch her unawares.

On and on she went until an obstacle made her pause: right in the middle of the track, like a hedgehog, lay an anthill. She stared mistrustfully at the living, seething mound: why should this anthill be here, instead of somewhere else? How would she get past it? What should she do? Was this the time to turn round and go home? She turned, but could see nothing behind her, as she was looking into the blinding sun. Cautiously, her arms outstretched so as not to bump into the invisible walls, she stepped across the edge of the anthill to the other side, and was glad that nothing had happened. She was so pleased that she was actually able to smile.

"What's the matter with me?" she asked herself reproachfully. "How can I have lost my grip so badly? How can anything happen to me here, where I know every bush for miles around? How stupid! To go out for a walk, to get some fresh air, and give in to these silly, childish fears. It's my nerves — I must do something about them. In a minute I'll reach the place where the mushrooms grow, and I'll pick some, then go home. How can there be anything to fear when I know this place so well? How silly of me!"

She went on with a surer, sprightlier step. She had not far to go.

All of a sudden her confidence was shattered by a thin, piercing cry, distant, dying in the air, but clearly audible, unending, and filled with terror: "Mi-i-sh-a!"

Liusia shuddered and froze in her tracks. She recognized that cry: it was her own voice. Very slowly, as if she had a huge weight on her back, she turned to her left. The bird-cherry bush was still there, in the middle of the field. Long long ago a ploughman had spared it and ploughed round it, and the bush had seized its chance and spread out in its hollow and upwards, claiming more ploughland for itself and eventually giving a harvest of berries. Submitting to her first impulse, Liusia took a step towards it, unexpectedly leaving the track, and the track let her go. Liusia was not surprised. She realized that she could not decide where she was to go, that she was under the control of some strange power which lived in these parts and was now calling her to confession.

At closer quarters she saw that little was left of the bird-cherry. Its mutilated, withered branches lay on the ground. Not yet completely dead, with some leaves still left, but draped in cobwebs, they looked wretched. The strongest branches had been torn off. Only a thin, peripheral growth remained, no taller than she could reach, round naked stumps chest-high. The surviving bent bushes were offshoots of these. Here and there hung clusters of berries. Liusia picked some. They were soft, cool and sweet, just as before, with a minty taste. And again that cry sounded suddenly, reaching Liusia across the years and clutching at her heart. Frightened, she looked about her. There was nobody to be seen, but to make quite sure she went behind the bush, so that she could not be seen from the Lower Brook.

Like the other incident, it had happened soon after the war. Life had not yet settled down after those four accursed years. It continued to deal out cruel, random blows: famine, violence, trials, and tears. This was the second summer that fleeing *Vlasovtsy** had come southward along the river, sowing terror in the villages in their path. In one village they would kill a cow, in another rape and kill a woman, loot a shop in a third, and knock a whole family out in a fourth to rob them of everything they had. At one time the men mounted guard at night, but the convicts always struck when they were least expected. Nevertheless two of them had been recaptured. Liusia remembered seeing the two being taken to town. They were seated in a cart, back to back, with their hands tied; tattered, unshaven, and malevolent, glowering at the onlookers with weary defiance.

The convicts generally made their breaks in early summer, and by autumn talk of them would die down and life in the village would be peaceful again. The women would go into the forest without fear, and cross the river to the *kolkhoz* fields. They would go anywhere, as if there were a convict season, like a tick season, after which there was nothing to fear.

About the middle of August Liusia and Mikhail had been sent by their mother to the hollow where the bird-cherry grew. She must have noticed it earlier with its thick, bright blossom, and gone to check up later. Although it was a bad year for bird-cherry, this bush

---

* *Vlasovtsy* (sing. *Vlasovets*): members of the anti-Soviet "Russian Liberation Army" formed in 1943 from Soviet P.O.W.s, mostly recruited in German concentration camps, to fight the Soviets and the Allies under the command of the captured Soviet general, Andrei Vlasov. The name was also loosely applied to members of other anti-Soviet formations under German command. On their recapture or repatriation, those not executed for treason were sentenced to twenty-five years in Soviet labour camps.

was weighed down with fruit. It could not be seen from the track because of the high corn, and the branches under the weight were almost on the ground. That was why nobody had noticed it, and the fruit had had a chance to ripen properly.

Picking the berries was a joy. Mikhail did not usually enjoy it much, lacking the patience to repeat the same movements hundreds upon hundreds of times, but this time even he was fired with enthusiasm. The cherries were big, and grew in long, heavy clusters, bare of leaves. All you had to do was put out your hands. Mikhail dragged his bucket round the bush after him, and Liusia hitched up the hem of her skirt to hold the fruit, emptying it only when the weight became inconvenient. Every time she tipped them out the level in her bucket rose several inches. It was fun to let them roll over your hands, like a cool, gentle stream. Although soft and ripe they did not crush, but settled neatly in the buckets. In a matter of two hours Mikhail and Liusia had filled two buckets to the brim, and they had hardly picked half of what there was.

They carried their buckets home and decided to come back, not wanting to wait till the next day. Now that they knew the way, they felt that if they waited other people might come across the bush. By afternoon the heat had built up. Mikhail made his lethargic way up the slope, and Liusia left him far behind. She didn't feel like waiting for him and went ahead. She was approaching the boundary strip, hardly visible in the corn, with the little bush on it, and had only about twenty paces to go when the bush suddenly came to life and out jumped a man — a terrible-looking, strange man in a fur cap with the ear-flaps tied on top. That cap alone gave him a terrifying appearance on this stifling summer afternoon. Liusia was so stunned that she could not move, and instead of running away she stood rooted to the spot. The man gave a short, impatient laugh of triumph, and beckoned her to him. She noticed his appearance: he was short, robust, with a swarthy, unshaven face concealing his age, and his pale eyes blazed with the white fire of madness.

This was the spot where he had stood, his booted feet firmly planted, so confident that she could not escape that he allowed himself the pleasure of playing cat-and-mouse with her, of having a bit of fun first, so as to savour the full sweetness of the conquest, working up an appetite for it. And again Liusia felt the full measure of the horror and danger which that encounter held for her, and she shuddered. She looked round and took a step away from the bush into the field, but remembered that she would not be able to leave this place yet. She would not be permitted to.

When the man laughed and beckoned to her she backed away. He looked offended and spread his hands, as if to say, "Come on, now. None of your funny business." She backed further and further away. Unable to restrain himself, he started towards her, softly, as if anxious not to scare her. His face was twisted to one side from cold excitement, and a cruel smirk played on it. At this point Liusia turned and fled.

She sprang onto the track and rushed down it towards the village. The convict, who had lost ground in the field because his boots sank in the soft soil and the corn tripped him, now gained on her. She could hear his loud, rasping breath behind her. She was wild with fear, still clutching her bucket, which tore at the air. His hands were already swiping at her back, but at the last moment she sprang clear of them, let go of the bucket, which bumped along the track behind her, and screamed: "Mi-i-sh-a!"

No sooner had she uttered this cry than she saw her brother before her. He was ambling along unhurriedly, and on hearing her scream he stopped in his tracks. But the next moment he dashed towards her. The convict also noticed Mikhail and pulled up sharply, he had not expected to meet anybody here, and for a moment he did not know what to do. Liusia ran past Mikhail, but at a safe distance she stopped, fearing for her brother. She screamed again. The convict had sized him up and realized that he was little more than a boy, and now he was coming towards him with stealthy, mocking steps.

"Misha! Run! Run away! Mikhail!" yelled Liusia at the top of her voice.

Mikhail picked up a stone and tensed to defend himself. The convict dropped swifty into a crouch as if to spring, and Mikhail jumped back. The man gave a vicious, staccato laugh. Again he tried to scare Mikhail, but Mikhail held his ground, holding the stone in his hand, and waiting. Then the man made a rush at him, but immediately veered off to one side and set off at an easy trot, with a contrived limp, and the air of a strong man who has no time for trifles, across the field towards the Lower Brook. Liusia had screamed too loudly for his liking, and he had decided to take cover while there was still time.

The cry ceased as suddenly as it had begun, and everything far and wide was bathed in silence as gay and bright as the sun. Liusia realized that she could now go on her way, the memory was over. Wearily, with a sense of helplessness, she set off again for the place where the mushrooms grew. She now saw in the mushrooms a faint hope of salvation: if she could pick even one, even a tiny one, there would still be hope that all would turn out well. But what exactly was it that had to turn out well? What was she afraid of? She did not know. She knew nothing. She was afraid even to wonder whether she ought to be afraid of something, because she felt that even her thoughts might be overheard here and misconstrued. She was tired, stumbling at times, but she was not tired from walking — she hadn't walked far at all, no more than three or four kilometres. Something else, something bigger and more important had made her tired, perhaps these memories, all too real and too vivid, which seemed to have conspired today to ambush her at every step and force her to experience them anew, for some secret purpose of their own. Life seemed to have sent her back because she had left something behind here, forgotten something very precious, without which life could not go on. But these events long past, having returned, did not vanish altogether, they simply stepped aside to see what would happen to Liusia after their return visit, to see what she had gained or lost, what had awoken, and what had perished. Now they had surrounded her and were accompanying her on her way: on her right Igrenka was plodding along, swaying from hunger, hauling the harrow with the last of his strength through the mud of spring. On her left that terrible figure in a fur cap was dancing on the bird-cherry. More and more memories ringed her round.

Liusia stopped. There was nothing to fear. There was nobody here, not a soul of whom she need feel afraid. She was alone. Her fears were as ridiculous as the convict's fur cap on that hot summer's day. She was worrying about nothing. After the telegram her nervous system had prepared itself for the worst, and now it demanded retribution for being needlessly troubled.

She looked about her again and again. There was nobody to be seen: nothing but sunshine, peace, and silence. It was too sunny, too peaceful, and too quiet for her to feel completely safe. She was alone, but alone in an alien silence of secrecy, in which all the sunshine and all attention was focussed on her. She had nowhere to hide, everyone could see right through her. No, she had to run away from this place. "Run away, run away," she repeated. Why had she come out for this walk? What had brought her here, as if she had forgotten something and come back for it?

"Forgotten?" Her train of thought halted at this word and brought it closer to Liusia. Forgotten . . . That was what had been gnawing at her secretly since morning, a kind of wordless sense of dormant guilt, for which she would now have to answer. In her new life in the city Liusia had forgotten everything: those spring Sundays spent working in the forest, and the fields where she had worked, and Igrenka's collapse, and the incident by the bird-cherry, and much more that had happened even earlier. It had all gone from her mind, leaving a vacuum. She had forgotten that she had harrowed and ploughed . . . Yes, imagine it! She had actually harrowed and ploughed. How strange it was that she had indiscriminately dismissed even this from her memory, something she had every right to be proud of. How many of her friends had actually ploughed the fields? Her memories of the village had lain so long untouched that they had petrified, formed into a solid, rejected lump which had been pushed into a remote, dusty corner like a bundle of cast-off clothes.

And today they had suddenly come to life.

7

At last Mironikha paid her long-awaited visit.

The old lady was lying on her bed, apparently weightless, as the springs did not give under her. Only her eyes were watchful. Her body, which seemed to have frozen in numb immobility, lay motionless and untroubled, as if it were a separate entity. There was no need to disturb it: she had been lying here so long that her body seemed to have got left behind, and could not catch up. Towards lunchtime the sun's rays shone in through the window, and the old lady, thoroughly sick of her own company, could warm herself in its untiring, merry beams.

Mironikha, wary in the silence of a house which she knew to be full of visitors, peeped timidly round the partition, saw that old Anna was alone, and leapt forward, throwing up her hands.

"Well I never did! Still alive, eh, old girl?"

The old lady was so pleased to see Mironikha that tears came to her eyes and she started trying to sit up, but she remembered that sitting up was a long business, and instead stretched out one serviceable hand to her.

"Yes, still here. Nearly two days since I woke up. Didn't nobody tell you?"

Mironikha held her hand for a moment, then let go, but the hand found the strength to lie down beside the other hand, the left, and snuggle up against it.

"How come death ain't taking you, then?" asked Mironikha, sitting down on the edge of the bed and bending towards her." I was coming for a wake, thought to meself: she'll have hobbled off to the other world by now. And she's still here! Same old trouble-maker as ever you was. You've been here long enough for me."

The old lady was only too pleased to join in the game: "I'm waiting for you, my lass. Didn't you know? I'd get bored in a grave by myself, so I'm waiting for you. So's we can share a coffin."

"That's no good, old girl. I'd be kicking you, and I've got sharp feet. Been running all me life and sharpening 'em on the ground."

"You would too, I know you."

"Don't you wait for me, just get yourself ready to go. Don't warm a place for me. I'm going to stay here and run about a bit longer. Instead of you I'll find meself some old boy to lie with, and we'll makes ourselves a baby before you know it."

"Didn't you hang up your baby-tubes even before I did?"

"Ah, I've got a new set now, better than the old lot. Got 'em from a city lass last summer. Swapped 'em for some berries. Fine young girl she was, and I persuaded her to swap. You can't equal that, can you, old girl?"

"Come off it! I've had enough of you and your fibs."

"Think I haven't had enough of you? Time you turned your toes up, I reckon, and left me in peace."

"You'll weep when I die, old girl."

"If I do, it won't be from sorrow."

"I dare say it won't," the old lady agreed, not wishing to provoke Mironikha into saying unpardonable things. It was all too easy to go too far with Mironikha, who wasn't in the habit of keeping watch on her tongue. When she was younger it was safer not to argue with her. She always had to have the last word, and even now her tongue hadn't lost its edge. She could still spit out some coarse expression with the greatest of ease.

Only in recent years had Mironikha quietened down a little. Now when she sat down she could keep still for a while, whereas before she'd been almost too boisterous and could raise Cain without even noticing. She said her legs weren't what they used to be, but when she got going, younger people had to run to catch up with her, or not catch up with her at all. All her life she'd been a glutton for work, and she'd never let it wear her down. Between her and old Anna there was no comparison: Mironikha was rounder, livelier and above all, she could run about wherever she pleased on her own two feet, her short dark arms out in front of her like pot-hooks at the ready. Her broad face was dark too. She had a hoarse voice, but after a talk with her anybody else would have no voice left at all, while hers would have only a slight rasp. She was only four years younger than old Anna, but she looked fit for a lot longer than four years.

The old lady cheered up when Mironikha arrived. Her eyes, with faded brown irises, brightened, and her face took on an expectant look. What would Mironikha have to tell her? She hadn't seen her for days, and in the meantime life had flowed unceasingly on, life in all its breadth, life in plenty for everybody in every town and every village, in well measured portions. Up till last year the old lady had had a radio on her bedside table, and she used to twiddle the black knob herself: here she'd find singing, there — weeping, further on — somebody gabbling away in some foreign language, further still — something that wasn't Russian and wasn't foreign either. You'd tie your tongue in knots trying to talk like that. The old lady liked listening to traditional songs, and she would send Ninka to fetch Mironikha so that they could listen together, but it wasn't often they played those songs. Mostly they played some jangling sound. But when she heard those old, lingering songs she felt as if she was soaring up above the earth and wheeling in big, sweeping circles, secretly weeping for herself and all those souls who had not yet found peace. At such times she did not mind the thought of death, and she imagined that these songs were being sung at a wake, after the coffin had been laid in the ground. And she hummed the songs to herself, seeing the newly released soul on its way, certain that in the next world it would be greeted by singing just like that.

Last year the radio had stopped working, so the old lady's chats with Mironikha were her only remaining pleasure.

"Why didn't you come and see me all this time?" asked the old lady reproachfully. "I sent my Varvara over this morning to see where you was. But you're always out, you vagabond. Whenever are you at home? About time your legs packed up, I reckon."

"They're packing up already, old girl," replied Mironikha, bending close to the old lady's face and rocking the bed. "At the moment they ache all over. I've given 'em too much to do, I've been running about for days looking for that cow of mine. She's gone missing, hasn't been home."

"Oh! That's why I didn't hear her this morning, when I was listening for her. Where's she got to then?"

"If I knew that I'd tell you, old girl. But I don't. I've searched all the meadows, but I can't go chasing all over the place after her, confound it! This ain't the first time she's strayed, but this time I'm more worried than usual. Have you heard that Golubiov's heifer's been mauled to death by a bear?"

"I ain't heard nothing," said the old lady, so startled that she began to stir, and her flagging voice rose. "Don't ask me if I've heard. Where would I hear anything? Who'd tell me? So a bear's killed Golubiov's heifer, you say?"

That was the great thing about Mironikha: who else could bring news that so chilled your heart? So the old lady hadn't waited in vain — she was sure Mironikha wouldn't come empty-handed. Now she looked at her in rapt attention, as if Mironikha herself had set the bear on the heifer and was about to tell how she'd done it.

"Yes," said Mironikha. "And Golubiov was planning to keep the heifer instead of his cow. His cow's old, don't give no milk. And look what he's got now. The day before yesterday Genka the foreman was coming out of the wood, and he looks round and sees the grass is all red and crushed down. So he takes a closer look, and there's the heifer lying in the bushes, hardly covered at all. The bear had sucked all the blood out of it, and left it for later. Prefers its meat a bit high. When Genka saw that he was off like a bullet. Flew home, he did." Mironikha leaned towards the old lady again and changed her voice. "I hear Genka's wife spent all day yesterday scrubbing his pants in the river, and she's still at it today, and when the women downstream need clean water they have to come up here for it."

"Don't you laugh at him," said the old lady reproachfully. "If you haven't just made it up, don't you laugh. Should have been there yourself."

"If I had been I'd have stayed there. I'd have sat down and waited for the bear to come back to get the heifer. And then I'd have stamped my feet and screamed and swore at him: 'What do you mean by ruining Golubiov? Damn your eyes!' He wouldn't have gone for me, he'd have thought I was death coming to take him away. I'd have given him such a fright that no she-bear would have been able to kiss him better."

"I ain't got the patience to listen to all your tales. Why can't you just tell me the facts, straight out, like anybody else? Where exactly did the bear kill the heifer?"

"You don't let me get a word out, or I'd have told you ten times over. You remember where the path turns up from the Lower Brook?"

"Course I remember. I've still got some brain left in me head."

"Well, that's where he got her, just outside the village. There'll be bears coming into the village next. There's no food left for them in the forest, and they're not going to go to their dens hungry. So they'll come roaming round the village."

"That they will," nodded the old lady. "That they will, for sure."

"I don't know where to start looking for that critter of mine. Does she think I'm going to run after her for a whole month? I've walked miles already. Don't even know if she's still alive . . . Some of the men say there's a couple of cows roaming on the far side of the ridge, but I can't go haring up there on my old legs. If I had my young legs under me I would, but on these old pins I'd be dropping before I got anywhere near."

"Don't you go running up to that ridge. You'll get stuck there, and what'll I do without you?"

"How come we can't stop talking about you?" asked Mironikha stubbornly. "I'm trying to tell you about my cow, and you can't stop talking about yourself."

"That cow of yours ain't got no milk now anyway."

"It ain't the milk I'm thinking about, dear. I just want to see my cow again, to be sure no bear's eaten her. Otherwise she can roam wherever she likes."

"Oh, you've got that cow on the brain, old girl. If I was you I wouldn't keep her and have to worry and waste the last of my strength on her. Did she ever bring you anything but bother? You have to pay people to mow hay for her, pay people to get it home, and if you haven't got enough for winter you have to buy more. Isn't that a lot of trouble? That's what keeps you running from dawn till dusk. It's not as if you had seven starving kids begging for food, is it? Goodness! If you want a bit of milk you've only got to talk to Nadia. She'll give you a jar of milk every day, and you won't drink more than that. You should sell your crock of a cow and put your feet up. You'd have an easier time, and you'd have the money as well. If she was mine I'd give her away to be rid of the trouble."

"Oho!" said Mironikha in a mocking, sing-song voice. "So she'd sell the cow and not take no money for it! How about that? You're a funny old dear, you know. How will I live without a cow when I've had one all me life. That'd be living death for me. It ain't the milk I want. I just want to have a cow mooing in the cowshed. I'd never want to stop keeping one."

"Well, the devil take the pair of you. What do I care?"

This wasn't the first time they'd talked about this, and the old lady privately agreed with Mironikha: once you'd got used to the trouble of having a cow you couldn't live without that trouble. And besides, could you call yourself a woman if you hadn't got a cow? The old lady herself had looked after cattle to the bitter end. Even when she could hardly walk she would still pick up her pail and set off, until she was forbidden to do so. And now she was arguing with Mironikha chiefly out of a sense of injustice, almost jealousy, because Mironikha was fit enough to keep a cow, and she was not. If Mironikha got rid of her cow they would both be in the same position, like it or not, and the old lady would be happier. She had resigned herself to her impotence, but she still needed to share it with a friend, and not any friend, but Mironikha, who had been her friend all her life.

Without a word to Mironikha, the old lady began to heave herself into a sitting position and found that she could do this with greater ease than in the morning. This time she felt more sure of herself. Mironikha made no move to help her, knowing that the old lady might snap at her if she did. They sat side by side, the old lady looking even feebler than before. Her shoulder-blades protruded like wings, and she looked as if she might flap them and fly away. Mironikha glanced sidelong at her and remarked, unable to restrain herself, "You're wasting away, old girl."

"Yes," nodded the old lady, knowing that this was so and feeling no need to look at herself.

"So your kids have come back. What have they got to say to you?"

"Say? They've come to have a look at me."

"They've come to bury you, old girl."

"Bury me as well. That's their duty — to bury their mother," the old lady agreed quietly, without taking her eyes from the window, as if talking to somebody outside.

"Don't be afraid to die, then. You don't think they're going to hang around, do you, waiting for God to take you?"

"There's no need for them to wait," said the old lady with the firmness of resignation, and turned towards Mironikha. She was still gripping the edge of the bed, afraid of falling. "I won't keep them. They want to go home. They've got their own families. I know that. But I want to see my Tanchora when she gets here, and then I'll get ready to go. I'll have any easy death, I can feel it. I'll just say my goodbyes, close my eyes and die. Varvara will come up to me to have a look, and she'll see I've breathed my last, and she'll tell the others. All I want is to see Tanchora again. She's a long time coming. I hope nothing's happened to her. They said she'd get here yesterday, and she didn't. Yesterday they said she'd be here today, and she still isn't. I'm so worried I don't know what to think."

"Don't you fret, old girl. Give her time and she'll come. No good worrying about nothing. Maybe there's no aeroplanes where she lives. These days everybody goes by aeroplane. They tell me you can fly round here, but maybe where she lives the sky ain't right for it, or there wasn't no plane for her. It's one thing for you and me — all we have to do is cross the road. We don't have to wait for nobody. But from her place it ain't so easy."

"They won't have to wait for me," repeated the old lady, shaking her head. "No, they won't need to. I can't stay here any longer. It ain't right. As it is I'm living my second life. When the children got here, God heard about it and gave me a bit of somebody else's life, so's I could see 'em and have a last chat with you. Time to return that bit now. I might last one more day, but that'll be all. Then it'll be time to go. Then they can see me off properly and weep over my grave, so they won't have made the trip for nothing. You can't help feeling your mother's death. I remember my mother's funeral. I cried my eyes out, and I wasn't that young. It's only natural. None of us can live forever. Our time comes in the end. And will you, Mironikha, give 'em a hand laying me out? I know you say I'm a trouble-maker, but that ain't so. Never was."

"I shouldn't have said it."

"Oh, it's all right. I don't mind," said the old lady more warmly. "Don't think I'm angry with you. We've said worse things to each other in the past, you and me, and forgotten them. I'm not going to get cross with you. What would I do without you? I've been waiting for you since yesterday. Come again tomorrow and sit with me. Funny, we've lived a long time, but we've still got plenty to say to each other. It'll be dull without you in the other world."

"I might yet die before you, old girl."

"Die before me? Rubbish! Talk sense, if you're going to talk at all. Didn't you hear what I said? I wasn't pre-tending, I was telling you straight. Don't get me wrong."

"I wasn't."

"Then don't argue."

Mironikha raised herself and leaned across the old lady towards the window. "I think I'll run over and see if that critter of mine's come home. I'll just have a quick look, then run back and sit a while longer. You wait here for me."

"Run along if you have to. I'll not keep you."

"I'm not leaving you. I'll be back in a minute."

"It's all right, off you go."

Left to herself the old lady felt a kind of mild sad-ness coming gradually over her from nowhere, bringing tears to her eyes. But this passed quickly, and she stopped crying, without wiping her eyes, as if she had said a short, purifying prayer. The sunlight was playing on the floor beside her, and she moved her feet into it. The sun showed no fear of her wasted limbs and caressed and warmed her bones, so that she felt almost blissful and ready to weep again, as if she had begun to thaw out and melt from her feet up. She actually dared to let go of the edge of the bed and take the weight off her arms, thinking that if she did fall, she would fall in the sunlit patch and lie there in the warm, and then Mironikha would come and pick her up. But she did not fall, in fact she forgot all about falling and looked out of the window at the day, which was nearing its watershed, and the fading blue of the high arch of heaven. The sun held her in a kind of spell — not the fiery globe up there in the sky, but the light and warmth that fell to earth from it, and warmed her. For the second day she strained her senses, looking for something in it besides warmth and light, but not knowing what. She didn't worry. No doubt everything she needed to know would be revealed to her in good time, and the time had evidently not come yet. She was certain that when she died she would learn not only this, but many other secrets which had not been hers to know in life, and which would finally explain the age-old mystery of all that had happened to her in the past, and all that would be in the future. She was afraid to speculate about this, but in recent years she had nevertheless thought more and more about the sun, the earth, the grass, the birds, the trees, the rain, the snow — about everything that lived side by side with man, sharing its joy with him, preparing him for his end by holding out to him the promise of help and consolation. And the thought that all this would remain when she was gone was a comfort to her: you didn't have to actually be here to hear that voice repeating its call, repeating it so as not to lose its beauty and its faith, and calling out to life and death alike.

Mironikha came running in and flopped down on the bed beside the old lady, who started, jumped back from the window, remembered where she was, and recognized Mironikha. Mironikha gave a flap of her hand, and the old lady remembered that she'd been to look for her cow, and understood that it still hadn't come home. Wherever could that cow have got to? The old lady began thinking about this question, so as to be prepared for the conversation, whose thread she had lost. Mironikha was bound to continue it, and she would have to make some answer. She couldn't just sit there like a dummy.

"That bath-house of yours is jumping up and down," said Mironikha.

"Bath-house?" In her thoughts the old lady could immediately place the bath-house, but she couldn't immediately see why it should be jumping up and down.

"I was going past, and it was hopping this way and that, this way and that," said Mironikha slyly. "Got somebody staying in it? Some men on some expotition?"

"Expotition? What are you talking about? My kids are in there."

"What, all of them?"

"No, why should they all be there? Liusia went out for a walk early this morning, and Varvara's gone somewhere in the village. The boys are in there — Ilia and Mikhail."

"Why do they need to wash at this time of day?" asked Mironikha, pulling the rope tighter.

"Wash? You're like a child, dearie. I never did!" replied the old lady crossly. "Washing! This is the second day they've spent there, enjoying their little treat, and I don't know if they washed first or not. It's their throats they're washing now — they was all clogged up, so they couldn't get no food down."

"Are they drinking vodka?"

"No. Nadia heated a basin of water for them and they're clinking glasses and knocking it back to their hearts' content. Tastes so good they can't stop. Ain't you heard the old saying: 'Money comes from God, and the Devil collects it'? Well, the Devil's collecting his share now."

"But they ain't alone in there. I thought I heard Stepan Kharchevnikov's voice."

"Stepan Kharchevnikov?"

"Sounded like him."

"And why's that so surprising? Do you think he'd be too shy to come? He ain't no teetotaller either."

"No, there ain't many of those nowadays."

"No, not many. Every time I look out I see people bumping into each other. I don't know what the world's coming to. Why do they drink so much? Why do they need it? They're drinking themselves into the ground. And the woman do their best to keep up with the men, tippling for all they're worth. It wasn't like that in the olden days, was it?"

"Don't you think about it. No good talking about the olden days."

"You remember Daniel the miller? He drank, and he wasn't considered human. No better than a drunkard. That was his nickname: Daniel the drunkard, because he was the only drunkard around. And now Golubiov's the only one who don't drink, and nobody thinks him a man. They laugh at him for not drinking."

"That's true enough. What they need is a good scare, to take away their appetite for the stuff, but nobody says nothing to 'em, nobody does nothing, so they do what they like. Some of 'em ain't even got a bone to give a dog, but they drink and make merry like lords. They go round the village, having a glass here and a glass there till they're full. They want more and more, even when they can't stand up. Can't get enough."

"No, old girl, they do tell 'em off. When I used to listen to the radio," said the old lady, pointing to the bedside table where the radio stood, "they used to talk about all this drinking, and they said it was disgraceful. Didn't say nothing good about it."

"So what? You know what the men would do with that sort of talk? Shit on it and rub it in. You think they listen? You have to punish 'em, not talk to 'em, then maybe you'll do some good. Whoever they are, however sorry you feel for 'em, they've got to be punished, to give 'em some respect for decent folk."

"You're right there, dearie. You get nowhere if you don't do nothing."

"Didn't I tell you so?"

"In the olden days at least they knew when to stop. Now they don't any more."

"In the olden days they had some shame as well."

"Yes, now they ain't got no shame either," said the old lady with a sigh of distaste, and paused for a moment. "Take my Mikhail: he gets so pickled I can't bear to look at him, then next morning he gets up, rounds up his drunken pals, and they all set to again, laughing and joking like nothing had happened, going over all the funny things they got up to the night before. They think it's funny. If I was one of them I'd burn up with shame."

"They'll burn up with booze, old girl, not shame."

"That's right. There's something I wanted to tell you. You reminded me, talking about shame." The old lady paused to give her memory time to carry her back to the distant days in which that familiar, muffled echo originated. "It was during the famine, the one before last," she began. "My Varvara was already a big girl, helping me about the house, and Ilia was growing. He was full of beans, picking things up left and right. But Liusia was ever so sickly — arms and legs like matchsticks, and so pale it was pitiful. I thought the life could go out of her just like that. I wanted to fatten her up a bit, but didn't know how. By then Misha was already running about, but Tanchora was still crawling. Or had she started walking? I'm not sure now. They was all crying and pleading for something to eat, and they needed a lot. It broke my heart to hear them. But I don't need to tell you about that — you had two kids yourself then." She stopped and asked Mironikha, in case she forgot later, "Are they thinking of coming to see you?"

"They don't write."

"Maybe they'll come without writing."

"I don't know, dearie. I expect they'll come when I die."

"Well then, I'd had about as much as I could take with 'em, I can tell you. My husband was away carting something for the *kolkhoz*. He was hardly ever at home. And Vitia — the one who was killed in the war — was on a course in town, so he couldn't help. I was all alone with 'em. Put one down, and the next starts yelling. And that year, to make matters worse, our cow had no milk. But we didn't want to kill her, because then we'd have had nothing. I thought, if we could keep going and keep the cow, then at least we'd have milk next year. And Zorka, our other cow, was in the *kolkhoz* by then. You remember Zorka, the polled one? Such a good cow she was. I'm still sorry we lost her. When they were gathering the stock into the *kolkhoz*, my husband handed her over voluntarily. I cried and cried, I can tell you. And Zorka remembered our yard, she kept coming back, and until the famine I used to take out the scraps to give to her, or a slice of bread sprinkled with salt. Of course they didn't get the same care in the *kolkhoz*, there were so many animals there. So during the famine she kept coming back to us. In the evening they'd milk 'em and drive 'em out straight away, and the flies were something terrible. The cattle would struggle and bellow and rush about. Zorka would come to our gate and moo and moo. I'd feel so sorry for her I'd open the gate and let her in. I'd get the flies off her with tobacco smoke and wash her udder — she didn't like it when her udder was dirty. One day I'd just washed her udder in warm water and I thought I'd see if she had any milk left. I gave a squeeze, and she had. So I started milking her. On the *kolkhoz* they weren't milking 'em dry. After the evening milking she could still give me a jamjar full, and that was something. I was glad to be able to share it out among my kids. A few drops was better than nothing.

"Well, one day I was sitting under our Zorka — although she wasn't really ours any more — milking her, when I heard the door creak. I always milked her in the cowshed and closed the door behind me. I looked round, and there was Liusia standing there staring at me wide-eyed. Those eyes reached right into me.

She was big enough to know that Zorka wasn't ours. I sat there struck dumb, too scared to get up. God above, I thought, what were you thinking of? Why didn't you strike me dead the first time? And I was so ashamed I couldn't go on. And after that I felt so guilty I couldn't look Liusia in the face for a long time. Even now I wonder if she remembers that or not. I think she does, and thinks worse of me because of it. Maybe that's why she wouldn't live with me and went away."

"Don't even think about it, dearie. How could she remember? She was a tiny little thing."

"Yes, but she's always had a good memory. And that might have stuck in it."

"What if she does remember? It would have been worse if she'd starved to death while you just washed your cow's udder. Plenty of people did die then, but you pulled your kids through."

"Yes, that would have been worse, but I still don't like it. You can't wash away shame. I'd never stolen anything in my life, and suddenly I was doing worse than stealing."

"You can't go through life without a bit of shame, old girl. But that's enough now. What a thing to go on about!"

The old lady obediently fell silent, letting her agitation subside, and she flopped wearily back onto her bed. When her head was already on the pillow she pulled up her legs onto the bed. Mironikha moved closer to her and glanced out of the window again.

"See anything?" asked the old lady.

"No. When that shameless critter gets home I'll break every bone in her body. Does she think there's no limit to my patience?"

"If I was you I wouldn't threaten her till she gets

home. Maybe she ain't coming because she's scared of you."

"I'll give her 'scared', damn her! Not scared of a bear in the forest, but she's scared of me. If that bear don't eat her I'll make her wish he had. She's got me half dead from worry."

The old lady picked up Mironikha's words: "*You* half dead? I thought I was the one who smelt of the grave."

"Don't you fret, dearie."

"As soon as you sit down I can tell you've come from outside. I ain't been outside for ages. I spend all my time here, in the same spot." Without looking at Mironikha she said of them both, "We've been too long in the world, you and me."

"How's that?"

"Why did we have to live this long? It would have been much better if we'd died long ago. Then you wouldn't be looking for your cow today, and I wouldn't be lying here hoping you won't go away and leave me to get sick of my own company again. You've been a gift from God to me, Mironikha. That you have. How could I have lived without you?"

She closed her eyes and nodded agreement to herself, her own words, and Mironikha. Her eyes did not open, and she remained in a world of her own, having forgotten everything around her, lost either in dreams or in peaceful repose. Mironikha sat watchfully beside her and thought how good it would be if they both died at the same time, so that neither of them should be left alone. She sat on for a long time, until Varvara arrived.

8

"Come on, Stepan, tell us how you put one over your mother-in-law," said Mikhail to Stepan Kharchevnikov, the tall, red-haired peasant who had joined him and Ilia at their bittersweet pastime. "Tell Ilia, he hasn't heard." Mikhail lowered his head and his face creased into a grin. "Come on, Stepan. Let's hear it."

They'd opened a new bottle in Stepan's honour, and the food supply problem had eased. By now Mikhail had no fear of the Devil or his wife. He'd made two forays into the house and even managed to bring back some soup, which they had to sip without spoons from the edge of the saucepan. He had also brought back the bottles Ninka had hidden in the flour, and laid them like logs in the stove, where nobody would ever think of looking for them. He was using the crate as a seat. As before he was barefoot, having forgotten about his shoes under the pressure of more important matters, and had pushed his feet under Ilia's bedding. Ilia was now on duty with the bottle on the other side of the hen-coop, reviewing the parade of glasses.

"Come on, Stepan. Tell us about it," Mikhail persisted.

"Well, I heard Ilia had arrived," said Stepan, explaining his presence, although he'd already shared a drink with the brothers. "I thought, whatever I do, I ought to see old Ilia. He and I are exactly the same age, we used to run about the village together, get up to all sorts of monkey business." Stepan spread his hands the breadth of the bath-house, to show that he couldn't possibly fail to see Ilia. His voice was harsh and unemphatic, which was why he needed his hands to help it. "So off I went. And I almost went to the wrong place. I was heading straight for the house, not even looking at the bath-house. I'm a bit slow. Just at the last moment I twigged and wondered what sort of conference was going on here."

"You did right to come, Stepan," said Ilia approvingly. "Our mother's laid up, as you know. We can't leave her. That's why we've moved in here, to be on call if she needs us."

"Yes, you couldn't have done better, Stepan," said Mikhail. "We've had a drop to drink, and we'll have a drop more. We've got plenty, don't worry. There, a whole stove-full. And all the same. Good, clear, strong stuff."

"You couldn't have done much better than that," replied Stepan, mocking Mikhail's favourite turn of phrase. "And you couldn't do much better than get pretty plastered on it, if you wasn't careful."

"Now, Stepan, no need to talk like that. You come here and I greet you as a guest. You're a mate of my brother Ilia, and a mate of mine, as we live in the same village. We've never said a cross word to each other, you and me. On the contrary, we've shared a few bottles together. And you start saying things like that, like I was drunk already. I can drink some more yet, Stepan. I know my quota. But I'll go beyond it if need be. Why shouldn't I? You two have met, and if I want to stay and talk I will. You seem to be packing me off to bed, as if I wasn't allowed to stay."

"No, you stay here. It's your house, and I've no right to tell you what to do."

"Tell us about your mother-in-law, then." Mikhail remembered the story he wanted to hear. "Tell us how you put one over old Auntie Liza."

"Is there any point? The whole village knows all about it by now."

"The village might, but my brother Ilia doesn't. He's come from the town, so you'll have to tell him."

"Well, no harm in telling him," agreed Stepan, with an air of assumed reluctance. He suddenly gave Ilia a merry wink and said, "Here we go then, Ilia. You listening?"

"Yeah, sure I'm listening."

"There ain't much to tell really. I don't know what everybody sees in it. No different from lots of other stories. The sort of thing that happens all the time here. It happened in the summer. Me and Genka Suslov had had a bit to drink, but not in a bath-house, in his vegetable patch. His wife had sent him out to dig potatoes. Well, we got down to it, and I'd brought along the bottles I'd owed him since last winter for some hay. I reckoned that if I offered him cash he wouldn't take it, so I'd do better to take him a couple of bottles. When I got there they told me Genka was in the garden. Well, all the same to me, off I went into the garden. Genka took one look at my bottles and drove his trowel into the ground and left it there. He knew what I'd brought 'em for. Some choice, eh? — dig potatoes or have a drink." Stepan spread his hands and gave them a disdainful shake, as if to show that the question of choice had never really arisen. By now he was carried away with his story, and was obviously enjoying telling it. "Well, there we was, sitting in the furrow. The neighbour's boy had run and fetched us a glass, Genka had picked a pocketful of young cucumbers, then gone back for another pocketful — and we had all we needed. So there we was sitting there, tossing this glass to and fro like a ball. Not very civilized maybe, but we enjoyed it. I could give it all my attention, as I'd gone there to drink, although Genka had gone out with something else in mind — digging potatoes. Still, the potatoes could wait. We finished off the bottles and Genka said, 'I'll just dig a few more, so the wife won't notice nothing tomorrow, and then we'll go into the village.' Okay, I thought. Do your digging, and I'll watch. But he says to me, 'Why don't you scoop some of them weeds into the furrow instead of just sitting there. It'll be quicker that way.' I stood up and looked, and saw he was past tellings spuds from weeds. He was chucking 'em all into one heap. I said, 'If you can't do a better job than that your wife'll take a hoe to your hair tomorrow.' He took some notice of that. 'Let's go to the village,' he said. 'I'll finish the job this evening, when the sun's not so hot.' So off we went. I had some money in my pocket." Here Stepan seemed to stumble and slow down slightly, and he added fondly, "Whatever happened after that, I can't remember it."

Mikhail gave a delighted chuckle and tossed his head, adding his confirmation, "It gets you that way sometimes. Go on, go on. And you keep listening, Ilia."

"Well, you know what comes next. I come round like after an atom bomb, and before I open my eyes I'm trying to work out what day it is — still the same day as when me and Genka was digging potatoes, or the next day. And I didn't know if I was at home, or where. Right, so I opens me eyes gradually, and there's the wife lying beside me. Recognized her straight away. And there are the kids — my kids — on the next bed. And there's me mother-in-law with her eyes fixed on me from her corner. I take a look around and reckon I ought to get up. As soon as I make a move me mother-in-law jumps up from her couch like a cat. I don't take no notice of her. I get up, and only then I figured out what she might be up to. Everything that old bag does is to spite me. We've had this guerilla war going ever since we met. If she'd had her way she'd have chopped my head off long ago, for her own low-down ends. And she wouldn't even have crossed herself afterwards. She ain't very civilized.

"Anyhow I gets up and goes over to see how Genka's feeling, but Genka's woman meets me at the gate and tells me he's out. I knew she was lying and just waiting for me to go away. Well, let her have her Genka and choke on him! What do I care? Worse luck for him, though. If she had any sense she'd realize she wouldn't be the thing he wanted for his hangover."

"Yes, you couldn't have put it better, Stepan," said Mikhail admiringly. "Couldn't have put it better. Good lad."

"Then I went to call on Petia Sorokin. He pretended he didn't drink and never had done: 'None here,' he says, 'and no money neither.' As if I owed him some. Nothing for it, I had to head for home. But I knew that somewhere in our cellar there ought to be some of our home-brewed stuff. The wife had gone to work. That only left me mother-in-law. I got home and found she'd put this stool on the trap-door, stood her spinning-wheel on the stool, brought up her kneading-trough to put more weight on the trap, and there she was sitting, spinning. She'd worked out where I'd want to go before I'd even decided myself. That's her one and only reason for living — to spite me. She's got nothing better to do. All right, I thought, we'll wait. You can't sit there forever. If I could only get into that cellar there'd be no getting me out, not even with a crane. But I didn't give any sign of being at all interested. We was both playing it crafty. I went outside and waited there for a bit, but I couldn't wait forever either. My head was ready to split in two. I was thinking, 'How much longer do I have to put up with you?' I went back to scout out the situation, and she was still sitting there, like she was bolted to the floor. I says to her politely, 'You must be tired, Mother, from all that spinning. You ought to take a break, go out for a stroll somewhere.' And she says, in the same rude, uncivilized voice as ever, 'I'm all right here.' I thought, you'd be even better if I gave you one over the head. Well, what could I do with her? She looked all set to stay there to the death. And if I just picked her up and moved her, spinning-wheel and all, she'd start creating, like I was going to cut her throat. And if I lost my temper and hurt her just a little, there'd be hell to pay. Okay, I thought, stay there. Sit there and don't budge, you old cow." Stepan wagged an angry, mottled finger at the floor. "And just when it looked as if the position was hopeless I decided I wasn't going to give in that easy. I could do without one of her sermons. I took a spade from the shed and went to see Ivan. You remember our house. It's like a barrack hut. I have one end of it, Ivan has the other, and the cellar's divided by this flimsy little partition. Last year I patched it up a bit with two new boards, or it wouldn't have been no use at all. I went to see Ivan on the pretext of wanting to have a look at the partition from his side, and went down into the cellar. All it took was a couple of kicks. And I crawled through to our side. Nothing to it. I shook myself down, looked around, and there it was — the medicine bottle. And food too. What more could a man want? I could hear my mother-in-law up above, huffing and puffing. I thought, just sit still and don't move. I need you there to keep other people away. And I took my time." Stepan paused, and his eyes narrowed merrily. "And when I started singing 'Over the hills and over the dales' she nearly had a fit. I thought she'd blown away. All I could hear was the spinning wheel."

Ilia gave a burst of laughter, looked with interest at Stepan, and asked, "You mean you drank the stuff there?" He asked this not so much because it was hard to believe, as in order to please Stepan and relish the picture of Stepan breaking into his cellar.

"Yes, of course," Mikhail repeated merrily after Stepan, delighted that Ilia liked the story. "She's on watch up above, and he attacks from below, crawls from one cellar to the other, like a worm, and goes to work on the good stuff. That's the way. Couldn't have done better. That's what I like about Stepan."

"Why the song though?"

"For the hell of it." The roguish grin on Stepan's face widened. "And 'cause otherwise she'd have gone through life without ever hearing no singing coming up from the cellar. Uncivilized old bag."

"Well, you have some high old times here, I must say." Ilia shook his head in surprise and envy, and laughed again. "High old times."

"Got to liven things up, haven't you. Well, we do our best. Makes life more interesting."

"What did your mother-in-law say when you climbed out of the cellar?" enquired Ilia.

"Not much good saying anything. I was past caring by then."

"Didn't your wife say nothing either?"

"You know, Ilia, I never let the wife upset me. I

don't give her a lot of scope. She's well trained, and she never forgets who wears the trousers, not even in her sleep. And it's up to the man to keep the upper hand." Now that Stepan had warmed up with his story it was hard to stop him. "Of course I can't say she hasn't no grounds for complaint. She has, specially when it comes to the booze, as you can probably guess. And in the morning she sometimes flings her complaints straight in my face, or down my ears if I'm not looking. At the top of her voice, like she was saying, 'Hands up!' Well, of course, I have a few things to say in return, from the male point of view. And I let her hear them in a voice she can understand, so we don't need to waste no words. After that there's no more trouble."

"No, Stepan," Mikhail disagreed, struggling with his words. "A woman, besides being a woman, is a human being. You can't beat her. Whether she's your woman or my woman, besides being your woman or my woman, she's human and she's got rights as a citizen of the state. She can take you to court."

"Who said anything about beating?" Stepan objected. "You ain't hearing me right, Mikhail. Why beat 'em? That's the highest penalty. Like shooting. If a woman's prepared to listen to me, I'm prepared to listen to her. Besides, I've got my rights as a citizen too. I'm not a cave-man. Me and the wife are both registered as members of the population of the country."

"I couldn't agree with you more. Couldn't have put it better myself."

"I know our wives are human, Mikhail, from the official point of view, with rights. You've no need to tell me that. I know a few things myself. I read the papers."

"I know you do, Stepan. I know."

"I take three papers," said Stepan, turning to Ilia, who nodded, losing interest. "The local one, one provincial paper, and one national paper — *Pravda*. And I read 'em all. Some people only buy 'em 'cause they need paper around the house, but nobody dares lay a finger on *my* papers till I've read 'em from cover to cover. *Pravda* comes out seven days a week, and I read it every day, so's to keep up with the international situation and the domestic situation. Whenever there's a coo de tat anywhere, or the workers go on strike, I know all about it."

It was all Mikhail could do to keep up with the conversation. "You couldn't have put it better there. They have all them strikes and coo de tats. I know about them too. But in this country a woman, besides being a woman, is still a human being, and you can't call her any of them rude names. It's dis-res-pect-ful." Mikhail separated the syllables of any word he found difficult, so as not to trip over them, saying them only when he was quite sure what had gone before and what remained to be said. "Don't get them other countries mixed up with our country, Stepan. You and me live in this country."

"Oh? I didn't think we did."

"We do, Stepan. Don't get 'em mixed up."

Stepan winked at Ilia, looking sidelong at Mikhail, as if to say, "He's had it, this one. Burbling on without knowing what he's saying, and preventing us from talking." Mikhail's head was sinking further and further towards his knees. Stepan no longer answered him, perhaps hoping that if Mikhail heard no more voices for a minute he would fall asleep completely, and then they could lay him on the bed like a sack and go on talking in peace. Stepan bent down and fixed his eyes on the level of vodka in the bottle, as if to make sure it wasn't falling as he watched. You never knew — while the bottle was standing open all sorts of things might fly in and lap up the contents. His conscience would not allow him to look without pain at a bottle which had been opened but not emptied. To him it was just as bad as dragging out the agony of a mortally wounded animal. If you're going to kill it, be quick about it. Stepan tried to catch Ilia's eye to hint that they'd kept this poor bottle in agony long enough, but Ilia was not looking.

The strain of the vodka and the conversation was also telling on Ilia, but unlike Mikhail he was not beaten yet. That brief, happy moment when he should have stopped had long past, and there was no point regretting it. What could he do now? What was there left to do? If only someone could tell him. Before Stepan's arrival Ilia had looked in to see how his mother was. She was dozing and did not hear him, or at least gave no sign of hearing him. Could she perhaps have been silently observing him? But he was glad there was no need to talk to her, because he didn't know what to say. He was not so drunk as to be able to talk non-stop. The vodka did not seem to affect him, it only added to that burden which would make itself known again later, tomorrow or the day after. On Stepan's appearance Ilia had brightened and come to life, but now that they had said all the things one says at first meeting, asked each other all the usual questions, without starting to share reminiscences, Ilia had flagged again and now had to force himself to follow what was going on. He felt as if he had been with these people so long, even with Stepan, that they had all grown thoroughly tired of each other's company. He would have loved to be able to close his eyes and go to sleep, but Mikhail's example was a deterrent. Not wanting to look as silly in front of Stepan as his brother did, he did his best to put a brave face on things.

After lunch the sun had turned the corner and found a little window in the bath-house wall. It soon became uncomfortably stuffy, but they didn't want to open the door in case anybody came in, whether hens, dogs or humans. So they had to put up with the heat. Stepan was sweating, and Ilia's bald pate was also covered in little beads of sweat. Only Mikhail did not mind whether it was hot or freezing cold.

Stepan recalled his recent conversation with Mikhail, and said in a plaintive, injured tone, "As a matter of fact she's got a bit too ladylike these days. And I need someone to live with, not just someone to take to the pictures. What I want is a bit less of the lady. A woman. A real woman. One who can do any job, and not wait for her man to come to fetch her a bucket of water, 'cause she can do all that herself. Someone who's patient, won't make a fuss over nothing. Why should the whole village, or the whole town, know about all the little differences you might have in your own house? 'I'm a woman, I'm a woman,' " he scoffed. "Well, you're not a man — anyone can see that. But don't expect anybody to applaud or pat you on the head for that. You've got to do something to deserve that. You're a person, like anybody else, only of the opposite sex. It's plain enough to everybody what the physical differences are, but you can't claim no special privileges because of them. Sure, we can't live without 'em. I won't argue about that. That's the way life is. But can they live without us? They're even worse off without us. It's in their nature. And secondly, when a man's not at work he has other interests, besides women. But they haven't."

"That's true," agreed Ilia. The thought that a woman needs a man more than a man needs a woman pleased him and cheered him. His face assumed a sly, roguish expression, as if some clever practical joke of his had worked, but nobody yet knew it.

Stepan threw a sidelong glance at the bottle, indicating, perhaps involuntarily, that one of those male pastimes he was alluding to was drinking.

"I was up in town last year," he went on. "Had a good look at the women there, and it was all I could do to find one who was what I'd call a woman. Made of flesh and blood, not springs and a motor. When I did see one it warmed my heart to know they weren't extinct yet, because soon we'll have to dig for 'em, like them prehistoric mammoths. But when one came along, you could see she'd had a mother and a grandmother, and that she'd got her place in life, because those city women these days, specially the younger ones, they're like clockwork dolls. All look alike, so you can't tell 'em apart. They're not born, they come off assembly lines . . ."

"All to the N.S.," interjected Ilia.

"Eh?"

"All to the N.S., the national standard measurements."

"Yeah, that's right. But some are better finished than others. That's the only difference. And they go around flaunting 'emselves: Here I am. Look at me. See what legs I've got, here's my right leg, here's my left. As if they was the only ones with legs, and the rest of us had crutches. And here's my fanny — I can wiggle it this way and that. How do you like that? As if nobody else had one or knew what it was for. They ought to keep it covered up, but no — they have to show it off. And look at all my hair, and look what eyes I've got: I can't see you at three feet, but you can look at me and admire me. That's their whole aim in life: to show themselves off. I don't know how they live when there's nobody to admire them. And at the slightest excuse it's 'Oh, my poor nerves!' Their arms are all nerves, and their legs, and the spot their legs sprout from. Nothing but nerves. You can't say a word to 'em. I stayed four nights with a friend of mine, and his wife's that type as well. As soon as she's a little bit displeased with him, off she goes to hospital. When I was there she was running to the hospital every morning. I used to ask her, 'Where does it hurt?' 'It's my nerves,' she says. 'But where exactly do they hurt, what place?' I says, and she says, 'Just weakness all over, you wouldn't understand.' That's what she thinks. I can see the sort of weakness she's got. Still, off she trots to have her fun. That's what they're like, these women. It don't matter what you call 'em, the fact is they can't do nothing. They ain't adapted for work. They'll even forget how to have children soon. I don't know . . ." Stepan gave a worried shake of his head. "What if there's a war? What could you expect these women to do? Shed tears and die? The last war was half won by women, but real women, the kind you don't see nowadays. What do you reckon, Ilia?"

"I reckon you're right."

Stepan nodded towards Mikhail, who had folded into a huddled position, "He was talking about women and disrespectful names for 'em, but I don't see nothing bad about our word *baba* for a peasant woman, and I don't mind when people call me a *muzhik*. On the contrary, I mind when they try to give me fancy titles, as if I hadn't no right to be a *muzhik*, wasn't suited for the work, or something. I am a *muzhik*, and I don't want to be nothing else. Same with our women. Why call 'em anything but *baba*? Why should it offend them? Take your mother, Aunt Annie. Was she ever anything else in all her life? Did she mind? Let other women follow her example. Nobody's got no right to say nothing bad about her. Nobody could." Stepan fell silent abruptly, as if something had stuck in his throat. A thought occurred to him. "Come on, Ilia. Let's drink to your mother," he said slowly and with obvious pleasure, the pleasure of a hunter watching his quarry tumbling from the sky, knowing that his aim has been truer than ever, and justly pleased with himself. "Come on, Ilia. No harm in drinking a glass to Aunt Annie."

"You couldn't have put it better," came Mikhail's voice unexpectedly. Mikhail raised his head from his knees and fixed his gaze firmly on the bottle, waiting for one of the others to make it do what bottles are supposed to do. "We can't refuse to drink to Mother. Come on, Ilia. Fill 'em up."

"Thought you was asleep," said Stepan, looking askance at him.

"Maybe I am, but I can drink to Mother even in my sleep. We bought this booze to drink to Mother, nobody else. Ain't that right, Ilia?" Mikhail lurched and gave a hoarse laugh. "And we forgot about her. Just as well you reminded us, Stepan. You couldn't have done better, or we wouldn't have thought of it. We couldn't help it, we'd just forgotten. We was just drinking normally, as if we hadn't got nobody to drink to. We slipped up, of course. We didn't think we'd be drinking to her while she was still alive. Ain't that right, Ilia?"

"No need to talk about that," Ilia cut him off.

Mikhail fell silent and looked at Ilia with unhealthy, narrowed eyes, then said slowly, "All right, if there's no need, there's no need. If you don't like it . . ."

"You've got a good mother," said Stepan.

"She hasn't died," said Mikhail mournfully, and it was impossible to tell whether he was lamenting the fact or boasting about it. "She hasn't died after all. She's still alive. If you don't believe me you can go and look for yourselves." He reached for his glass and Stepan, fearing that he would fall, hurriedly handed him his own and took another from the top of the hen-coop. "To Mother! Bottoms up!" Mikhail commanded them, and as usual drained his glass first, then rolled it across the floor to Ilia. Ilia picked it up, and he and Stepan clinked glasses in silence.

"Do you remember, when you was little . . .? Although you might easily have forgotten . . ." Stepan was talking to Mikhail, but Mikhail did not hear him. His head was sagging again and he was making himself comfortable on his box. Stepan turned to Ilia. "Remember, Ilia, what your mother did to settle a score for him? You must remember that, don't you? Denis Agapovsky, may he rot in hell, caught your Misha at the *kolkhoz* peas and let him have a charge of salt from his shotgun in the back. Remember that brute Denis and the way he used to guard those peas? A real hero, he was. Well, he caught Misha. Took all the skin off his back. It was a terrible sight. Your mother didn't take that lying down. She filled two cartridges with salt, went to Denis, and gave him both barrels in the backside, point black. Salted him so well he couldn't sit down for a long time after that, nor lie down. He had to crawl on all fours. Remember?"

"Yes, I remember," said Ilia with a smile. "They wanted to sue her, but they forgot about it after a while."

"Sue her indeed! I'd have shown 'em! On Denis's account! Might have been different if he'd been human."

"What's that you're mumbling about?" asked Mikhail, hearing them. "A song. Let's have a song," he demanded.

"You don't die easy, do you, Misha?" exclaimed Stepan. "What song would you like? How about the one about the bears who scratched their backsides on the earth's axis, or was it something else? That's a fine song. That's the song for us."

"No," said Mikhail. "Another one. My favourite. A Russian folk song." He raised his head slightly and kept it up while he sang,

    "If they gave us some
    We'd be drinking some . . ."

His head toppled and fell back into his knees. He sobbed out the last two lines:

    "But they don't give us none,
    So we ain't drinking none."

"What can he be hinting at?" asked Stepan with a grin.

Mikhail sang the same verse again, that being all he knew of the song. Then he curled up easily and without a sound, and rolled off his crate onto the bed. Ilia and Stepan looked on admiringly. "Shall we have a song, then?" Stepan suggested.

"Might as well. A binge with no music ain't no binge at all." The last glass of vodka had made Ilia more decisive, and little lights were playing crazily in his eyes.

"But not those songs they play on the radio these days. I don't like 'em. They're sort of . . . They might make you laugh while they're singing 'em, or tickle you a bit, like you was a child and somebody was teasing you. But when they get to the end . . . You remember that game the kids play, telling you something, then saying, 'He believes it — silly fool'? It's like that. As if you was a silly fool for taking any notice. Let's have one of our songs, the kind that get you here, with no fooling."

"How about your favourite, then?"

"My favourite? What's that?"

"The one you sang for your mother-in-law from the cellar."

Stepan laughed. "Why not? It'll do to start with."

In unison they struck up the rousing, time-honoured "Over the hills and over the dales." Mikhail added his mooing voice to theirs.

9

Except for the old lady, nobody now expected Tanchora to come. If she were going to come she would be here by now. It wasn't as if she lived in America, and even if she did she could have got here from America in three days. A letter would probably come later, saying "Sorry, I couldn't come, I was away," or something like that. They wondered what she would say about her mother, as she didn't know whether she was still alive. In the end she'd have to write and say something. She couldn't just keep quiet, nor get by with greetings to all her friends and relations without mentioning her mother. But that was her own lookout, let her wriggle out of it as best she could if she didn't think it necessary to come. But what could have kept her? Of course nobody knew, and it was hard to pass judgment. Only one thing was clear: she wasn't there, and there was nothing to raise hopes of her coming.

Only her mother went on and on waiting. She trembled at the slightest sound outside her window, and froze at every rustle at her door. Although she didn't remember Tanchora having such habits, she thought that her daughter might steal in and peep at her before revealing herself, and for this reason she kept the door constantly ajar, so as not to miss Tanchora when she peeped round it. The old lady's sight was good. At her age she could hadly complain, but her eyes got tired when she had to stare endlessly at one spot, as if they had to hold the wall up by themselves. The old lady gave her eyes no rest, she forced them to stare. What was the good of taking care of them now? They had enough strength left in them to have a good look at Tanchora, and that was all she needed. And only when her tired, aching eyes actually began to stream with tears did the old lady close them, to let them rest, leaving a narrow chink, however, in one eye, then the other, so that she could still watch the door.

The more time she spent in this fruitless, wearisome anticipation, the less time there was left to wait. The old lady realized that if Tanchora was going to come at all, it had to be today, that this was the end of her borrowed time. Tomorrow there would be none left. She did not know what tomorrow would bring, nor was she anxious to find out: as long as any hope remained she hoped and clung to the belief that Tanchora would get here in time, and not deny her mother a last look at her. If she had not come one minute, she would get here the next, there was still time, and there was no point wearing oneself out with worry. She would come, she wouldn't get lost. Some time after lunch there was one moment when the old lady's heart started pounding, and she took this to mean that her heart had sensed the presence of Tanchora, who was now drawing near. The old lady sprang to life as hurriedly as a young girl. She wanted to be sitting up to meet her daughter, so as not to appear utterly helpless at first glance. In her haste she forgot to take care, and very nearly fell. Only a miracle kept her from falling off her bed and breaking something. Not even allowing herself time to rebuke herself for her clumsiness, and before she was firmly seated, she turned her face towards the door in readiness. And she did hear footsteps, the curtain twitched — and in came Varvara. Her feverish mind unable to accept this, the old lady thought that Varvara must have come to announce Tanchora's arrival, but Varvara started telling her what the village people were saying about her dream, as if she wanted to keep her mother on tenterhooks. But you couldn't blame Varvara for being Varvara. Taking no notice of her, the old lady strained towards the door, certain that in a moment she would hear other footsteps and another voice . . . But something was keeping them, they did not come.

She sat like this for a long while, at times lost in concentration, when it seemed as if her place had been taken by somebody else who heard nothing because he didn't care whether Tanchora got there or not. After such moments she forced herself to listen harder. Ninka scuttled back and forth muttering as she ran, her lips smeared with sweets. Varvara tramped heavily about the house, tormenting the squeaky floorboards, which annoyed the old lady by preventing her listening for the sound she wanted to hear. Then Liusia came in and started asking whether she was all right. She nodded, wishing Liusia would go away. Liusia did leave the room. She went into the other room and lay down on Mikhail's bed, evidently having decided to rest her legs, which were not used to walking.

At length the old lady felt too tired to sit up any longer, and her head was beginning to hum from the effort of constant listening. She reminded herself that joy and sorrow preferred to come unannounced, out of the blue, and she reproached herself for waiting too eagerly, and thereby keeping Tanchora away. There was truth in what they used to say: Tell a fool to prostrate himself, and he'd split his skull on the ground. What did it matter if Tanchora peeped in and saw her lying down before she showed herself? How could that make any difference? At least she would be here and the old lady would see her daughter before her, and would shed her last tears of blessing for her. There was no need to hurry, because whatever happened she would not be able to jump off her bed, run to meet her, and fold her in her arms . . . How could she? She was in bed, and she would have to go on lying there, as that was all she could do.

She obeyed her own instructions and lay down. Now she wanted only to stop thinking about anything, to recover from the strain of waiting, as from pain, to let her whole body relax into oblivion, resting before the pleasure which would soon be hers. She made herself comfortable in bed, so as not to feel her own weight, and tried to let the silence engulf her — the gentle, alluring silence, which would silently draw her weightless from her bed and cast over her the spell of a far-off purling of water.

The sun had not yet sunk out of sight. Its golden light had lost its brilliance, but was still warm. Having warmed herself in it, the old lady gradually calmed down, until she hardly felt conscious of herself and hardly knew what she wanted in the last hours of this bright, calm day. Once again, as so many times today, she dozed off, but she slept lightly, watchfully, more than ever aware that she was asleep, and ready to wake up at any moment. Having lulled her body to sleep, her heart remained on watch, and its attentive beats did not let her sink into too deep a sleep. And so, when Tanchora appeared before her, the old lady could not believe it: her memory told her that her eyes were closed and she could not really see Tanchora. But this was not a dream either, because she was not properly asleep. She was all this time holding herself halfway between sleeping and waking. No, the faint, tormented vision before her was the work of that state of unfulfilled expectation from which her tired mind was now freeing itself. Realizing this, the old lady could relax. In her drowsy state she thought again about Tanchora, and realized that her limpid, crystal-sharp and agreeable thoughts were coming to her of themselves, already fully formed. And they brought her comfort. In them she sought an answer to the same question: What could be keeping Tanchora? And she found one. Tanchora must have started out on the journey with her husband, and she should have left him at home. He was a military man, and God, who never smiled on soldiers, had seen them together and stopped them, not realizing that this soldier was different — he was Tanchora's, and that they were in haste to reach the old lady. No doubt he'd soon noticed his mistake and let them go on their way, but they'd been held up, and nothing could change that now. It wasn't Tanchora's fault. It was all because of her husband. But now they were drawing near. They'd be here any minute.

The old lady felt easier in her mind and more relaxed, and in her weightless state she soared up higher and higher, where the unwanted sounds of life around her could hardly reach.

She had not seen Tanchora for a long time. Exactly how long she didn't know. She kept count of time not in years, but in terms of her maternal instinct: there was no difference to her between three, five, and ten years. They all amounted to the same thing. Tanchora had not been home for a long time, longer than any of the others. Liusia had been here more recently, and Ilia had come back from the north, and of course Varvara visited her once a month. But Tanchora did not come. Once she wrote to say that her husband was being transferred to a new posting, that they would be passing near home on the way there and would definitely call in. In those days the old lady was still mobile, and she set to work to be ready to welcome her daughter and make the best impression on her son-in-law, whom she had never seen in the flesh. She scrubbed the floor every day, so as not to be caught unawares, prepared all sorts of delicacies and even made Nadia buy two bottles of wine at the village shop. These she kept hidden from Mikhail under her pillow, but in the end she had to give them to him anyway, because Tanchora did not come. Her husband had in fact been posted, not to the place they had first ~~expected to go to~~, but to Kiev, where they had lived ever since. Later there'd been talk of a tour of duty somewhere abroad, and again Tanchora had written to say that they would have some home leave first to say their farewells, but in fact her husband was not sent anywhere, and was given no leave. The old lady was sorry not to see Tanchora, but relieved that her daughter was not going to live even further away, among strange people who didn't even speak the same language, and among whom life would certainly not be easy. That had been the situation ever since.

Tanchora didn't write often, but more often than the others nonetheless, and her letters came straight to the old lady. She was the only one who addressed her letters to her mother, and when the old lady was handed one of those pretty envelopes with a red and blue border her heart stopped with pride and anticipation: in a moment she would learn all that Tanchora had to tell her. She did not hurry, and usually studied the envelope carefully in a good light, examining the picture and the postmark, and only then opening it with great care, trying not to damage the envelope, and drawing out the closely written sheet of paper. Unable to read, she could keep a letter with her from morning till evening, in wonder at the secrets within it, and trying to penetrate them. Then came the time for reading: she made Nadia read her letters, and Mikhail, and anybody else who called in, fearing that different people might read different things in the same letter. Only when she was sure that all readings concurred in every detail was she satisfied. Then she would hide the letter under her pillow in order to preserve her happiness and see Tanchora in her dreams.

The old lady had less authority over Liusia's and Ilia's letters. These were read to her once only, if that. Often she got no more than a summary of the contents in two or three words, and she had no choice but to make do with this. She guessed that they didn't always even tell her when they received letters from Liusia and Ilia, not because they didn't want her to know, but because they forgot about them, or didn't know what to tell her, because there didn't seem to be anything in them that absolutely had to be passed on, or anything to make them worth the trouble of writing. Liusia always instructed the family to look after Mother. Ilia would ask facetiously in passing, "How's tricks with Mum?" and more often than not that was the limit of his curiosity about her, so that it really wasn't easy to summarize his letters. Sometimes Liusia sent long, detailed letters, especially when she had not written for some time. In these she would devote more space to her mother, saying things like this: "Tell Mummy that medicine helps you whatever your age." That was when the old lady was refusing to take any pills, saying that no pills would save you from old age. Or else she would write: "See that Mummy dresses warmly in winter," as if she didn't know that you couldn't go about in summer dresses in the middle of winter. Ilia, thank heavens, at least spared her the advice. That was not at all what the old lady wanted. She wanted to know how they lived, what they wore against the frost so as not to freeze, what they ate, if they didn't keep any cows, hens, or pigs. In the end she just had to force herself to believe that people didn't starve in the cities, but she couldn't understand how they managed it without animals. She couldn't see how they could possibly live at all. Liusia and Ilia wrote so little about themselves that the old lady pestered Nadia, who read their letters, with niggling, caustic questions, as if Nadia had either kept something from her or overlooked something, and Nadia was at a loss for an answer. Where was she to find more information than there was in the letters? She couldn't start making things up on behalf of Ilia, who sent terse little missives once a year. Reading his and Liusia's letters to the old lady was a form of torture, and it usually fell to Nadia to do it. When Mikhail was asked by his mother what they had to say, he could brush off the question with, "Nothing much," and walk away. The task was left to Nadia.

Tanchora's letters were not fully to the old lady's liking either, but here she was prepared to overlook many things, as she took a special view of them. These letters were written especially for her. Tanchora wrote them specially, the post office conveyed them specially, and to make sure they didn't get lost, the envelopes on which Tanchora wrote her mother's name were specially stamped with important-looking postmarks. Everything that Tanchora had to say she said to her mother directly, as if she could see her in front of her. She didn't say, "Tell Mummy . . ." She said, "My dear Mother . . ." and this affectionate, lonely cry always stopped her heart with joy and fear. She felt as if cold needles were running over her body at these words. She did not remember Tanchora using them at home, or rather, she knew that Tanchora had not used them. It wasn't a matter of forgetting. Not even the most forgetful of mothers would forget those words. That meant her daughter had found them there, far from home. She whispered the word again, moving only her lips, and heard in them such a cry of loneliness and pain that she was filled with terror and began to cry, while trying to pretend to herself that she was not crying, and telling herself that she had started crying for some quite different reason. To cry for the real reason would be to succumb to her fears, and that would be worse. Then it would be all the harder to find hope. All hope came from God, the old lady thought, because it was timid, shy, and kind. And all fear came from the Devil, which was why it was so rude and importunate. So why should she succumb to it? As if she didn't know where it came from!

Suddenly she cheered up and said the words again, with only the very corners of her narrow lips, and this time she heard in them only a soft caress, uttered in Tanchora's gentle voice. Then the words came again without her moving her lips, in Tanchora's voice alone, sounding clear and close by, as if she were really there, but fainter and fainter. Finally they faded away altogether, but even then the old lady still felt completely happy at their welcoming warmth and power. After that she cursed herself roundly and at length for first hearing in those words something which was not there at all, and like the basest of sinners she begged her daughter's forgiveness for being so deaf.

She knew better than anybody that her Tanchora had grown up more affectionate than her sisters. Not that the old lady had any complaints against Liusia or Varvara. There was nothing to complain of. But in her eyes Tanchora stood out. After all, she was the last of the line. As no other child had come after her, her mother had noticed her more than the others, and as she couldn't get used to living without tiny babies she'd been slower to let her go. Before Tanchora, she'd had one child after another, each appearing before the last was even walking. The newest claimed all her attention, and the one before was set aside to crawl or walk wherever he liked, as long as he didn't kill himself and didn't yell. Now there was somebody else to do the yelling. No one came after Tanchora to chase her away, and she stayed at her mother's side, always there, as if on a leash, running up with her babbling cry of "Mamma, Mamma." Wherever had she got that word? As far as she knew, nobody in the village said that, and it didn't seem likely she'd picked it up from strangers, or heard a voice saying it to her in her sleep. Later, when she was bigger, she said "Mummy", like all the other children, but often she would remember the word she used to use and say, laughing, as she tugged at her mother's skirts, "Mamma, Mamma." Her mother liked this silliness, although she discouraged it. And now she was calling her "my dear Mother". Why, after "Mamma", should it cause the old lady such anguish? It didn't make sense to worry so much about it.

But the fact that Tanchora had come last was not the whole story. Being last, she might have turned out worst, repaying the greater care and affection lavished upon her with less love. That happened often enough. But not with Tanchora, who in character was like her mother. As far as character went, Liusia was the one who had most clearly inherited her mother's temperament. Like her she was proud and determined, and did not give way to anyone. She had enough pride and determination for three. When she was only a little girl she would sulk for three days on end, not looking at anybody, and nothing would shake her. What Liusia was like these days the old lady did not know. Most likely she'd had the sharp edges rubbed off her among others who also had sharp edges, and found her place. If you had a difficult nature life was more difficult for you. Liusia must have learnt that. She was educated, and she certainly didn't look as if she was finding life hard. The old lady didn't like to ask. If she did, she'd get the answer, "Fine," and you could interpret that any way you liked. That was what they all said, so as to ward off further questions. Varvara was the only one who would find cause for complaint even if she lived in the lap of luxury, without a care in the world. Although they were sisters the two were poles apart. Even when Varvara was a big girl, little Liusia would make her cry, so would the boys, so, it seemed, would a fly. She'd been a booby and remained one. If a hail of blows was coming at her, she had to put her head under every one.

Tanchora was not like either of her sisters. She stood halfway between them, with her own distinct nature, which was gentle, gay, and sociable. If she got cross, her anger passed at once. If she was hurt, she could forget it in a moment, and if she cried, the old saying might have been made to order: "Shed one tear and call it back." Wherever people were gathered she was always drawn to them, afraid of neither old people nor children, and she liked to talk and laugh, which she did with natural timing, to everybody's delight, not just for her own merriment. No gathering of the young people of the village was complete without her. If she was late the girls would come running to her house to fetch her, not because they needed her leadership, not at all, but because without her a party was dull and lifeless, and when the boys started making passes there was nobody to give them the sort of answer you could re-tell endlessly to your friends afterwards. There was nobody to start laughing softly when a couple who couldn't wait decided to slip away from the log-pile where they met, by the village soviet. Nobody else could laugh the way she did, in a low voice, as if to herself, while looking into the darkness after the vanishing couple. And that laugh, like a signal, quickly infected everybody, and soon the sleepy village would be rocking with it. Without her there would be nobody to strike up a song that would rise on strong voices and embrace the whole village in its joy or sorrow, instead of fading away at its birth in the grass.

"Come on, Mummy. Give me your head," she would say, knowing how her mother like having her scalp scratched with a knife-point, and nobody, not even among the old women, had Tanchora's skill, nor her gift for finding the very place that most needed scratching, without harming a single one of her greying hairs. Tanchora was the only one of the old lady's daughters who did this for her mother. She would work the knife to and fro ever so quickly murmuring as she did so, "There's nobody like you, Mummy."

"What are you on about now?"

"You brought me into the world, and I'm alive, and nobody else would have done it if you hadn't, so I wouldn't have seen the world at all." Tanchora would laugh and tuck up her mother's hair as she stroked it.

"Get on with you!" replied the old lady, pretending to be angry. "You go on muttering away, and you don't even know what you're talking about."

"I do. There's nobody like you, really, Mummy. You're better than everybody. Haven't you got good children?"

"I don't say you're a bad lot."

"That means we're good children. Remember that.

We've been really lucky to have you. Nobody else has got a mother like ours. That's the truth."

The old lady was taken aback by these words. She didn't know it was possible to say them aloud. In a village where people were not used to displays of affection, nobody else would be likely to say them. It was so obvious that nobody but her could have borne her children, but you didn't talk about things like that. There was no need. She felt afraid, and pushed her head deeper into Tanchora's skirts.

"You'll go on living a long, long time, longer than anybody else, because you're better than everybody else, and we won't let you go, not to anyone, and not to old age."

"Don't make such a fuss," said her mother, interrupting her.

"I'm not. I can't even begin to imagine that some day we'll have to live without you."

The unconcealed love in these words brought a film of tears to the old lady's eyes, and she would get up hurriedly. "That's enough for today. We've got things to do."

These conversations occurred only infrequently, but the old lady feared them, with the agreeable, fearful flutter of a bride before her wedding night. Long afterwards she would go over them in her mind, pretending to herself that odd words accidentally retained were now accidentally recurring, whereas in fact she had carefully stored them all in her memory, so that she could use them to warm her heart later, whenever she liked. How could a mother be indifferent to such talk? How could she disbelieve Tanchora if Tanchora treated her with such warmth and affection, sharing secrets that few mothers were privileged to learn? Even when she was getting married she wrote and asked her mother's blessing. The old lady gave it, not daring to refuse, although she was sorry she didn't know the future husband.

And when her Tanchora left home she went for good.

Latterly the old lady had been inclined to blame herself, rather than her daughter for this. Where her fault lay she wasn't sure. She would never be able to go and see Tanchora, who lived so far away that her mother couldn't transport herself there even mentally. But she was sure of something else: a mother should not be separated from her daughter for so long. She felt awkward about it before others, ashamed for her daughter, and it was hard for her. People might wonder what sort of mother she was if she could endure it so long. And what effort had she made to see Tanchora again? She had done nothing but wait. But what else was there that she could usefully do? If only somebody would suggest something! On Liusia's account she had nothing to fear. She knew Liusia could look after herself, she was that type. Varvara, on the other hand, was easily hurt, but Varvara lived close by, almost next door. Ilia was a man, he ought to be able to stand up for himself. Tanchora was the only one whose absence the old lady felt in her heart, as if she had wilfully tossed a piece of her heart away. It troubled her endlessly, day and night. If she could only steal one little peep at her, just once, to see what had become of her, and what sort of life she led, far from her mother, among strangers. One look at her face would tell her a lot, and then she would know whether to pray for Tanchora, or rejoice for her. And she also had to see her, if only for a moment before she died, to lift from her own soul the sin of not seeing her for so long, to cleanse herself in the sight of God and calmly, joyfully, stand up for him to judge her: "Here I stand, Anna, servant of God, and I bring no uncleanliness with me."

But today was the last day: if Tanchora did not come by nightfall all hope would be gone.

Reassuring himself that Tanchora was bound to come, if only she had patience and did nothing to impede her progress, the old lady felt relieved and fell into a doze. At first she slept very lightly, still alert to every sound, not forgetting for a moment that she was dozing, but soon, as usual, she could not help letting herself go, and she slipped away, leaving her body like an empty sack behind her. And nobody knew where she had gone or what she was doing.

The sound of voices brought her back. She first heard them from afar and could not make out what they were talking about. Her hearing was the first thing to return to her, but it was still weak and could pick up only indistinct, muttered snatches, like the splash of somebody throwing stones into a pool. The old lady was no longer what she used to be, and she could not wake up instantly now. She required time and strength to collect all the senses a person needs: hearing, sight, and memory. It was as if she had fallen to pieces in her sleep, and each of her component parts had managed to forget what it was supposed to do.

When she opened her eyes she could make out nothing at first: the twilight of evening was already becoming the darkness of night. Some light entered only from the windows on the street, but not much could get through the panes. Liusia's clipped, insistent voice was saying to somebody, "You ought to be ashamed! Getting yourselves into this state, with Mother lying here half dead!"

The old lady did not even take fright immediately. She managed to make out Mikhail's head, bent over the table, and Ilia sitting across from him. Ilia stirred, trying to say something in answer to Liusia, and the old lady sensed, rather than saw, that the men were still wallowing in a haze of drink, struggling in it, like flies in a pool of fly-poison baited with cream. At the old lady's feet Varvara heaved a deep, groaning sigh. She could not see Liusia, but her voice came from the right, where the bedside table stood under the icon case.

At this point the old lady was suddenly seized by fear. Curling up in her bed she cried out, not enquiring, but calling, and demanding an answer: "Tanchora!"

Before bending over her, Varvara announced to everybody, "Ma's woken up."

"Tanchora!" she called again, after listening with all her strength and all her remaining breath for Tanchora's reply.

"She isn't here yet, Mummy." At the click of a switch the room seemed to have been turned inside out, like a glove with white lining. Liusia was standing by the switch. "Tanchora isn't here yet," she repeated, seeing that the old lady did not understand.

They shielded their faces from the light, and narrowed their eyes. She thought that they were hiding from her, not wanting to tell the truth, and she did not believe them. Her head swaying, she swept her eyes over them, with an intense, pleading look which only Liusia managed to face, and gasped for breath, as if she'd climbed a steep hill and hadn't the strength to take another step. Tanchora was not here. The fact had to be accepted from the start. If she were here, they'd be talking about other things. She must have been and gone already. The old lady went on shaking her head, not believing herself, nor her children, and unable to utter a word. With a desperate look of beggarly entreaty, her head shivered on the pillow, and her throat remained in the grip of the sudden pain which had seized her as she endured her inability to bring back any spark of light to show Tanchora the way. Like a mirror with its back painted black, the window reflected only the room, lit by the electric light. From outside there came no light at all. The old lady raised herself on her elbow and strained forward, so that she almost fell out of bed, and asked impatiently and plaintively, "Where is she? Where?"

She froze into tense immobility in this position, waiting for an answer. Her eyes, though not looking at any one of them, were wide open, so as not to miss the one who answered her.

"If we knew where she was we wouldn't keep it from you," said Liusia calmly. "You must see, we just don't know."

"We ain't seen her, Ma, really we ain't." Varvara pressed her hands to her breast for added conviction. "I wouldn't lie to you. We ain't seen her."

"She'll come," added Ilia cheerily, even happily. Perhaps he really was happy, now that he and Mikhail were no longer the subject of the conversation. "If she hasn't made it today, she'll make it tomorrow. That's for sure."

"That's what you kept saying yesterday, but where is she?"

"Well, we can't tell you that. When she gets here she'll explain everything."

"That's what you said yesterday, but where is she?"

repeated the old lady in a lost voice, as though she were delirious, not hearing her own words, because, having received no answer the first time, they had returned and echoed guiltily in her as they came back. Why should she ask again? What was the point? Now she knew that Tanchora would not come. Her borrowed time had expired. It was no use waiting any longer. Tanchora had not come, and the old lady had not seen her.

She let her head fall back onto the pillow and began to cry.

"This is it," muttered Ilia. "Here we go."

"Ma-a-a!" Varvara went into a flap.

Suddenly something within the old lady snapped, with a short moan, which before dying away turned unexpectedly into the ringing sound she had heard yesterday — those soft chimes from her youth, uninterrupted, each one flowing into the next. This tolling drew her to itself so powerfully that she could not even think of resisting. She was forced to go with it for a while, but then the sound began to draw away, pulling her along behind it, but still sounding just as pure and clear as before, so that she should not lose faith in it and should know which way to go. She almost forgot that only a moment earlier she had been in pain, weeping over something — whatever was it? Now the pain was muted, and she could follow the bell with relief and joy. Now she was weeping with joy, in the knowledge that everything could end so well.

She wept without covering her face, without raising her hands from her sides. Her eyes were open, and occasional dark tears trickled slowly down her cheeks. She wept without moving, and without a sound. Only her tears showed that she was crying. Her expression was almost peaceful, and this gave her face a mocking look. The combination seemed so bizarre, improbable, and frightening, that Varvara sat dumbfounded beside her mother, and when she emerged from her daze she screamed and threw herself upon the old lady, shaking her with all her might. Liusia leapt forward and Ilia stepped up to the bedside, peering over his sisters' backs. Mikhail made to get up, but sank down again onto his chair.

The old lady let out a groan. At last Liusia managed to break Varvara's grip, and the old lady turned her head away, as if begging them not to touch her. In order to pull her crazed sister away, Liusia sat down on the edge of her mother's bed. The old lady stirred and, with an effort, moved away from her daughters towards the wall, wiping her silent tears from her face.

"Why did you have to give us a scare like that, Mum?" asked Ilia, returning to the table. "I told you: if she hasn't come today she'll come tomorrow. That's for sure. We've only got to wait."

"All sorts of things might have held her up," Liusia supported him, frowning because she herself didn't believe what she was saying. Nevertheless she went on, "We'll wait, there's no hurry."

The old lady only half heard them. She heard the words they were saying to try and give her heart, she could tell who was saying what, but the actual words and their meaning did not impinge on her conscious-ness. She let them flow over her. She lay looking straight in front of her with unseeing eyes, feeling a warm vacuum within herself, aware that she was lying here only because she had not yet managed to die. There was nothing else to keep her, she had no reason to stay. Now there was nothing to do but wait until her soul, which had been waiting and hoping all this time, found peace again, helped her accept her loss, and relieved her of her suffering and regret, so as to leave nothing within her which did not belong there — nothing, except herself. She did not want instant release, knowing that everything would turn out right, that in any case her lifeline had reached its appointed end, and all it had to do now was stop.

Her children talked on and on, imagining that she had got over the worst, and that their words had helped her. She did not answer, but the constant mention of Tanchora's name jogged her gradually out of her isolation. She was surprised to see the electric light, and it reminded her of the departed daylight in which Tanchora had not appeared, and which no amount of electricity could bring back. And at once her pain returned. In her anxiety not to suffer any more the old lady shook off her drowsiness and saw them all beside her: Liusia, Varvara, Ilia, Mikhail . . . Tanchora was not there. She could not be there.

"Something's happened to her," she said, as if repeating someone else's words, and only then becoming alarmed at them. "Something's happened to her," she said in a louder, more insistent voice. "You ain't telling me. You're playing me false. I know it."

"What are you saying, Mummy?" exclaimed Liusia in a surprised and injured tone, getting up from the bed. "What are you saying? How are we playing you false?"

"You are. You're playing me false." The old lady also stirred and tried to raise herself on her bed. Her shawl slipped off her head, revealing her short, thin, grey hair. "I know you are. You're keeping something from me. You don't want me to know. You keep saying: tomorrow, tomorrow. But there won't be no tomorrow. You think I'm stark mad and don't understand nothing." With her dishevelled head and quivering face she really did look mad. "If Tanchora was all right she'd be the first to come flying back to me. And I lie here waiting, like a little child . . ."

"Stop it, Mummy, please!" exclaimed Liusia. "Do you realize what you're saying? Nobody's playing you false. Can't you understand that? We don't know where your Tanchora's got to."

Liusia's voice and manner of speaking commanded obedience and silence from all, including the old lady. Frightened, she said nothing. Her open mouth quivered. Her lips tried to close, but could not.

"If anything's happened to her I won't have no peace, not even in the other world," she said mournfully.

"We don't know if anything's happened to her or not."

The old lady took away her supporting hand and gently lowered herself back into her hollow in the bed. The blood drained rapidly from her face and she turned visibly paler at once. In the silence Varvara's heavy, whistling breath could clearly be heard.

"That place she lives in now — did the war reach there?" asked the old lady, squinting fearfully at Liusia, and huddling, shrinking into her bed.

Ilia replied: "Kiev? Yes, the Germans took Kiev. I remember that well."

"So that's it," she nodded in the bitter certainty that she was right, and struck up a new lament. "Why's she like that? Why didn't she ask anybody? I'd never have gone there! What makes her so wilful? And I'm here waiting for her. She'll never get out of there now! Now she's gone and put her own head in a noose. Should have thought first."

"Wait a bit, Mum. Wait a bit," Ilia butted in. "You ain't just landed from the moon, have you? When do you think the war ended?"

"All the same . . ."

"What do you mean: 'All the same'?"

"Well, where is she then, eh? Why ain't she here?"

"Here we go again. You keep coming back to the same old song, Mum."

"Okay, that's enough." Mikhail slapped the table with his palm and lurched to his feet. "Your Tanchora ain't coming, and it's no good waiting for her. I sent her a telegram to tell her not to come."

The old lady shuddered.

"What did he say?" she asked in disbelief.

"I said I'd sent her a telegram to tell her not to come. There was no need."

"Oh, what have you done?" gasped Varvara.

"When did you find time to send her a telegram?" asked Liusia quickly.

"As soon as Mother came round."

"Then why did you keep quiet about it till now?"

"Slipped my mind. I forgot, what with all this booze . . ."

"But now you're quite sure you sent a telegram?"

"Quite sure."

"Or maybe you've dreamt it up. 'What with all that booze,' as you put it."

"No. I sent it. You can go to the post office and check. When you was talking just now I remembered I'd sent it."

"Well, there you are, Mum," said Ilia happily. "Nothing's happened to your Tanchora. She's alive and well, and I'm sure she wishes you the same, while you're at your wits' end here and driving us the same way. Didn't I tell you: if you just hang on it'll all clear up. It's always like that. You just have to wait, and not hurry. That's the main thing."

The old lady did not hear him.

"What did he do that for?" she whispered, and her face set in despairing curiosity. "What did he do that for?" she asked and shook her head, as if she still didn't believe Mikhail and was begging him, entreating him to admit he had been joking and hadn't really sent Tanchora a telegram. "What did you do it for, Mikhail?"

"What for? You were better, so I thought she'd be spending money and making the journey for nothing."

"But I wanted to see her. Why did you do it?" She started coughing as her hurt feelings mounted in her throat. "I wanted her to sit beside me for a bit, and talk to me, her own mother. I was all ready to say goodbye to her. I won't see her again. Why are you so contrary? I don't want nothing from her, no presents, nothing. I only wanted to have a look at her before the end, to see how she looks." The old lady did not cry, but her voice became a querulous, almost whining moan. "And what do you go and do? Take my last joy away from me, block out the last ray of light. You've left me to face death without Tanchora. You've no pity. You didn't notice I'd wore meself out waiting for her."

"Yes, Mikhail. You really had no right to decide all by yourself, without consulting us, whether Tania was to come," said Liusia irritably. "You were sober at the time, weren't you? So you should have known what you were doing."

"He ain't got no shame nor no conscience!" Varvara

chimed in. As she heard this support, the old lady's anger mounted. "He done it on purpose," she said slowly, as if remembering something, and sat up. Her uncovered hair was in disarray again, and her bony hands held fast to the bed. "You done it on purpose. I know. You wanted to hurt me. Right before I died you wanted to hurt me, you wouldn't let me go in peace. That's why you made Tanchora turn back, so's to have a bit more fun at my expense."

"Stop talking such nonsense, Mother! Why should I do it on purpose? What are you thinking of?"

"You done it on purpose." The old lady gasped for breath and clutched at her chest with her hands, gingerly rocking backwards and forwards to ease it. "Do you expect me to keep quiet? I won't. I'm not afraid of nobody any more. He's been looking for a way to put an end to me for a long time. He's sick and tired of having me, an old woman, in the house. He can't blame me, but he's got to feed me, and that gets his back up and he plays all these tricks on me."

"Come to your senses, Mother! You're talking out of the back of your head!" Mikhail took a step towards the old lady's bed.

Varvara screamed, "Keep away! Keep away from our Ma! Look at him! You've got to keep away."

"Back of my head, eh?" said the old lady defiantly, and paused, as if luring Mikhail into an argument. He was standing, swaying, in the middle of the room. "Forgotten how you scared me that time?"

"I don't remember nothing."

"He came in as drunk as he is now: 'Lying down, eh, Mother?' he says. 'Yes, waiting for death to take me,' I says. And he says, 'Do you know? Seventy years is all we're allowed now. More's forbidden.' I says, 'What do you mean — forbidden? People have always lived till their time comes, and nobody's stopped them.' 'Yes,' he says, 'they have, but now it's forbidden. I read it in the paper with my own eyes.' "

"That's the average life expectancy in the country. That's what he must have been talking about," guessed Liusia.

"Eh?"

"Well, er . . . We all live as long as we can, Mummy. Some of us live a long time, some not so long, and when they added it all up they found that in this country people live on average seventy years. If you, for example, live ninety years . . ."

"I don't want to. What would I do with all that time?"

"I'm just giving you an example. If you live ninety years and somebody else only lives fifty years, that makes seventy for each of you. And the average over the whole country comes to seventy. Understand?"

"Of course I understand that. If he'd said that to me I wouldn't bother to tell you about it. But I had old Mironikha all worried as well. When I passed it on to her, she said, 'Don't you fret, old girl,' but I could see she was scared silly. Scared silly she was. And we both sat there shaking. I says to her, 'You can walk on your two legs. Why don't you go and see Egor. He reads them papers too. He might have seen something.' And off she goes. But nobody ever got no sense out of Egor. He says to her, 'You know there ain't no soap flakes in the shops, Mironikha?' 'That's true, there ain't,' she says. And he says, 'There's going to be some soon. Orders from the top: boil down all the old women for soap flakes, because the housewives can't do their washing.' She says to him, 'Don't try and make fun of me, Egor. I'm not your Natalia, I won't put up with it.' And he gave her another scare, even worse. 'If you don't believe me you'll see for yourself. In Kliuchi the day before yesterday they boiled down all the old women, and they'll be coming here to do the same any day now.' Well, makes you think, don't it? It ain't very nice. Why should I make it up? There's me and Mironikha, two old women, half dead with fright. Mironikha not even daring to go home in case they catch her on the way. They've no right. We're good Christian folk."

Varvara threw up her hands and burst into sobs. "What an awful thing to do! Making fun of our Ma like that! What's the world coming to?"

"When did I say that to you, Mother?" Mikhail swayed and drew his palm across his perspiring face. He could hardly stand, and it was obvious to everybody that he felt sick. The accumulated nausea of today's and yesterday's vodka was rising to his throat, and he swallowed convulsively, trying to push it down again. His shoulders hunched, he shifted his weight from one foot to the other in the middle of the room, unable to remember whether he had stepped out voluntarily from behind the table, which he could hold on to, or whether he had been hauled out by force. His mother swayed before his eyes like a vision, and at times disappeared altogether. He had never seen her with her hair down, and he was afraid of her, but as soon as he shifted his eyes to one of his sisters the room would timidly stand still again and settle back into its rightful position, and his mother would lie down again in her bed, only to vanish again a moment later, rising in the air, and the room would swirl off again, creaking at its corners. But the story his mother had told seemed

to come as a surprise to him, and, with a glance at Varvara to stop the giddy swirl, he asked, "When did I say
that to you, Mother?"

"He can't even remember. Can't remember nothing.
He says things to make me sick with worry, and forgets
them at once."

"I really don't remember."

"What do you think you're doing, Mikhail?" Liusia
began in a tone which was wheedling and almost gentle, then suddenly raised her voice. "I said: What do
you think you're doing? This really is the limit. I don't
know any word bad enough for the things you do to
your mother. You behave like a little Hitler, if not
worse! What right have you to abuse her like this?
Answer me! And you, Mummy, why do you put up
with it? It's not as if you'd nobody to stick up for you.
He's not your only child. I'd no idea about this. I
thought everything was fine here."

"Listen, Ma, listen," said Varvara, tugging at the old
lady. "What our Liusia says is right. He's become so
shameless! Seems to think there's no law to stop him,
but he's wrong, he's wrong. Better men than him have
found that out."

"After all, you could have let somebody know what
sort of treatment you were getting here, and not just
put up with that sort of thing. You've done everything
to deserve some peace and quiet in your old age, and
we won't let anybody mistreat you, least of all your
own son. If he doesn't want you to live here you don't
have to stay. We'll make arrangements."

Mikhail suddenly flew into a rage: "What do you
mean? Maybe one of you will take her, eh? Go ahead.
You can have her. I'll give my cow to the one who
takes her. Well?" He stretched out his hand and

pointed at the old lady, with a mischievous, bitter laugh. "Well, come on. I'm offering my cow. Which of you loves Mother best? Take her. What's there to think about? I'm a low-down so-and-so, and you're all so good. Well then, who's the best of all? How about you?" he asked, approaching Liusia. "Will you take her home with you? Will you look after her? If you sell the cow you'll have plenty of money. Mother doesn't need much. You can see she hardly eats anything. The cow'll more than cover her needs. What she needs is your sense of justice. You're fairer than the rest of us. You know everything. You know how to look after Mother so that she'll be as happy as a lark. You'll see she has nice clean sheets, and read her lectures. Hurry up and take her, or somebody else will. What are you waiting for?"

"You're off your head!" spluttered Liusia. "You're mad!"

Nadia suddenly appeared out of nowhere and rushed up to Mikhail: "Stop it this minute! Stop it! You'll put us to shame. Get out of here!"

He pushed her away. "We were getting along fine without you."

"Don't listen to him, don't listen!" screamed Nadia. "Don't believe him."

Mikhail laughed again and felt the hangover which had been tormenting him whooping with joy and launching into a wild dance.

"So I'm crazy. I see. Mother shouldn't have to live with a lunatic. So maybe you'll take her?" he asked Varvara merrily. "You could use the cow, and it won't be dull for Mother in your family. And she'll have a much more peaceful time. Daughters are always better.

They don't get drunk, or abuse anybody. Well? Aren't you going to accept? Why don't you say yes?"

Varvara did not know what to say. "We've no room for her. Our Sonia's expecting again. Otherwise I'd take her."

"No room for her, you say? No room for the cow either?"

"Yes, there's room for the cow. In the cowshed."

"Room for the cow, but no room for Mother. You can't put Mother in the cowshed, or in five or ten years' time," he pointed at Liusia, "she'll turn up and tell you that really is the limit. And I'll back her up. I won't have Mother living in no cowshed. I want her to live decently as well." He turned to Ilia: "What about you, Ilia? What do you think of all this? Maybe you'll take Mother home with you and get your wife to look after her? If you're out at work the whole time, your wife's got nobody to say a kind word to. Mother would suit her fine. As you see, she can't talk much. After my place, she'd find your place nice and restful."

"You've had too much to drink, Mikhail," said Ilia nervously. "You don't know what you're doing."

"Can't you see that Mummy can't be moved anywhere now?" yelled Liusia.

"So nobody wants to take her?" Mikhail swung around and swept his wild eyes over them all. "Nobody. And nobody wants the cow. Then maybe someone'll take her without the cow? You won't? Right." He drew in air and hissed, "Then you can all get out of my house and go and get . . . And don't tell me I'm a wretch or a scoundrel, don't shout at me. And you, Mother, lie down and sleep. Lie down where you was before. They like you better when you're lying down — here."

He rushed out of the room.

In the strained, uncomfortable silence which came heavily upon them, the old lady's beseeching voice was head: "Oh Lord, set me free, and I will go. Let my death come to me, I'm ready."

In the darkness of the bath-house Mikhail drew out a bottle from the stove, his hands trembling, and fumbled on the hen-coop for a tumbler. With one finger holding the edge of the glass he poured vodka into it until it overflowed. Slopping the extra onto the floor, he drained the glass at one gulp, then flopped down on Ilia's bed.

10

That night the old lady made up her mind to die without further ado. There was nothing left for her to do in this world, and no sense in putting it off. Let the children bury her and see her on her way, as decent folk should, and let them do it now, while they were here, rather than make another journey for the purpose. Tanchora would come too. Mikhail would have to send her yet another telegram to tell her to come, but there was no getting round that. Now the old lady could think about Tanchora without pain, knowing that she would not see her again whatever she did. She had been wrong to punish herself and the others by hoping. By now she could have been laid out for burial, having forgotten that she had ever lived, forgotten everything, free of everything. Of course, if she had hung on and seen her Tanchora, her death would have been sweeter and happier — that was what she had been counting on. But let that pass, why torment yourself when it was time for your soul to depart and fly away in peace?

She lay in bed and waited for the house to fall silent, because she knew that her death was timid and would not come to noisy places. Everybody had gone to bed early that evening, straight after the scene Mikhail had created, but nobody could sleep. They were all sighing and tossing and turning. It wasn't that easy to put out of mind everything that he had said, and fall asleep. It wasn't a matter of simply pressing a switch. Ninka was probably the only one who was asleep, and even she seemed to be smacking her lips in her sleep. Either she'd gone to bed with a sweet in her mouth, or she'd so overworked her tongue by sucking sweets during the day that it still couldn't settle down for the night.

The old lady had often thought about death, and knew death intimately. In the last few years they had become good friends. She would often talk to death, which would find itself a seat in a corner and listen with occasional sympathetic sighs to her whispered, sensible thoughts. They had agreed that the old lady should depart by night: she would first fall asleep, like everybody else, so as not to scare death away with her open eyes, and death would then come softly, press up against her, lift away the short sleep of life and give her eternal rest.

It was not true that there was one and the same death for all — a bony, vicious old crone, almost a skeleton, with a scythe over her shoulder. That one had been devised only to frighten children and the gullible. The old lady believed that everybody had his own death, created in his image and likeness, as like him as a reflection. Each pair were like twins, always the same age. They came into the world on the same day, and they would leave it on the same day. Death would wait for its man and take him to itself, and they would never again be parted from each other. Just as each man was born for one life, so each death was born for one death. Just as people, having no previous training in life, lived chaotic lives, never knowing what the next day held, so their deaths, having no previous experience of their work, often did it badly, unwittingly frightening or worrying the people whose twins they were.

But the old lady knew that her own death would be painless. They had had time to look about them and see how others lived and died, and they had no reason to make things difficult for each other at the end — nor had they the strength to do that. The old lady would not put up any resistance, and death would not be angry with her for leading her such an endless dance: she hadn't meant to, and she had never been afraid of death, except when she was young and stupid. She had always regarded it as a release from suffering and shame. And if she had not yet invited death to come for her, neither had she tried to keep death at bay. She had not intended to live longer than others. But now it was time to invite death to come. Enough was enough.

The only thing she couldn't understand was why little children died. She thought it a sin that parents should have to lower their children into the ground, and she thought the sin was God's. A baby's twin death was also a baby, just as tiny and as innocent. It played with the baby, got carried away, and accidentally touched him, without knowing what it was doing. And where was God at the time? What was he thinking of? It was a sin when a new-born baby who didn't understand why he saw light in his eyes, or why he felt hunger in his belly, had to lose his life at once, not having an ounce of guilt to justify such treatment. Why had he been born at all, if he was to be so deceived? Why had he been shown the world and given human understanding?

The old lady herself had buried five of her children, and laid them side by side so that they should not be lonely. Four of them had died of illness, but the fifth, a little boy, had died of nothing at all. He'd been fit and well in the evening, had gone to sleep peacefully, but then he'd started crying in the night, as they all did when they wanted something, and woken his mother. She had taken him from his cradle and given him the breast, assuming he had woken from hunger, and then dozed off with him in her arms. Suddenly she felt that he had let go, but she sat on, holding him, to let him fall fast asleep. When she was about to get up it suddenly struck her, like a blow in the ribs, that no warmth was coming from him. She looked, and saw that his mouth was slightly open. She had supposed he wanted to suck, but all he wanted was to be taken in her arms, to die close to his mother, not alone. But why? For what sins? What sins could he be guilty of, if he couldn't even walk, but only watch others walking, if he couldn't speak, and only knew whether people were speaking kindly to him? What sins, if he had learned hardly any of life's skills except how to eat and sleep, and even these he hadn't learned here, by his own efforts, but earlier, when through no wish of his own he had been shaped into foetal human form?

Several times in her life the old lady had had to console herself with the words, "The Lord giveth and the Lord taketh away," but in this case they hardly applied. How could you take away something which, if you thought about it, you hadn't yet given, but only shown and promised? And furthermore, when you had only just begun to teach a child that he was alive, that when he fell asleep he would wake up again to learn more and more and grow bigger and bigger, how could you then tear him up by the roots which had only just taken, and throw him down? It was a sin.

The old lady had had no chance to bury the other three — the ones the war had taken. And the fact that she had not seen their deaths and did not know where they were buried was another punishment to her. She always felt that she had lost them herself, through her own negligence. To this day she had no idea what she ought to have done to keep them, but she felt sure she should have done something, and not just sat twiddling her thumbs and waiting for the sun to shine. Her waiting had been repaid by three burial notices, one for each of her sons. They had left home as fit, healthy lads, even men, and these three bits of paper were all that was left of them.

So if she had someone to leave behind, she also had somebody to go to. Apart from her children she would rejoin her father, her mother, and her brothers and sisters. Of her father's many children she was the last who was still here. Her last surviving brother had died the year before last. Her husband had gone the way of her sons, off to the war, but he had managed to die a natural death in spite of the bleak time. He'd been conscripted into the labour army, where he had fallen ill and not recovered, but, considering the times, he'd been lucky. He made his way home to die. It was summer.

The old lady accepted his death with resignation, as

something decreed by fate. There was nothing more to it. By that time she was used to running the family without him. You couldn't say their life together had been that bad, because many couples got on a thousand times worse, but it hadn't been that good either. It wasn't as if he drank, although it might have been better if he did: a man had to get the dirt out of his system sometimes, the same way you cleaned the fur out of a kettle, and for many vodka was the best medicine, as long as they didn't overdo it. A man would have a drinking session, sing a few songs, play the fool, and then he'd be better. He could go on functioning normally. But her old man didn't clean out his system for months on end, and he made life impossible for her. Nothing was to his liking. Whatever she did displeased him. She herself was surprised that she found the patience to endure the reproaches which he rained on her day and night. And then his mania would take a different tack: he would sulk, and he was capable of saying nothing for six months. It was just as well he wasn't at home much. If he wasn't away hunting he'd be away at some seasonal job. In winter he used to cart provisions from town out to shops in the villages, and in those pre-war days they used horses, and the journeys took time.

The thing that surprised the old lady most about his end was that he had been somewhere very close to the wholesale slaughter of the front, but had managed to return home and die in the peaceful silence of his own bed. In this she saw a hidden portent for herself, and at once made her peace with him. "Oh Lord, forgive us our sins . . ." she prayed, when she saw that he had gone. "Our sins," she said, not "his". And her tears and grief had all come from the heart, because, for all his faults, he was the father of all her children, living and dead. In any case, the fact was that she had somebody to go to, and somebody to leave behind.

She listened: somewhere outside a cow-bell was tinkling, and the house stirred with the breath of her children, which flowed in conflicting currents, but it was impossible to say whether they were asleep or awake. No, it was too early yet. It was best not to hurry.

The old lady knew full well how she would die. She knew this as if she had experienced death several times over. Although in fact she had not, she somehow knew. She could see the whole picture clearly before her eyes. Perhaps, just before the end of life, it is given to every man to see the last moments of his life ahead of him, right to the very end. Having been told about the beginning when old enough to understand, he would be cheated if the end were not shown to him as well.

She would fall asleep, not in the usual way, without noticing it, but in full possession of her senses, as if she were going slowly down some steps, pausing on every step to look about her and see how many steps remained. When she finally reached the bottom, where the ground was strewn with yellow straw, and realized that she was now fast asleep, another skinny old woman just like her would step off another staircase facing her and stretch out her hand, into which she would have to place her own. Going numb with fear and joy of a kind she had never known before, the old lady would start walking with short steps towards the outstretched hand, and suddenly on her right a vast expanse would come into view, clean, as if recently washed by rain, and bathed in bright, silent light. In her impatience the old lady would start walking faster. She would not have far to go, and almost at once she would see that she had arrived. At the last moment she would want to step back, or round the spot her feet were carrying her to, but she would be unable to do either. She would stop exactly where she was supposed to stop, and then, no longer able to control her movements, she would guiltily give her hand in greeting, and would feel how easily her hand lay in that proffered hand, glove-like, and full of relaxed, reassuring strength, which brought life to her enfeebled body. And at that moment from the expanse on the right would come the peal of bells.

At first it would sound loud and festive, as in times long past when the people announced the birth of a long-awaited heir, then it would abate slightly and flow over her head in a singing swirl of chimes. She would look about her in inexplicable agitation, and see that she was alone: the other woman had disappeared.

And then, afraid of no one, she would walk happily, devoutly to the right, in the direction of the pealing bells. She would keep going, on and on, leaving somebody behind who would watch with the old lady's eyes as the old lady walked away. The fading bells would lead her away after them.

As soon as she was out of sight, her eyes would look down and lose themselves in the straw. The staircase would also vanish, until the next time. The land would level itself out, and morning would come — a new, living morning.

No, she was not afraid of dying. Everything had its place. She'd been here long enough, she'd seen enough of life. She had expended all that she had within her, and now she was empty. She was drained to the very

bottom. Every last drop had gone. And what had she
seen in her life? There was only one thing she knew:
children, who had to be fed and washed, and for whom
you had to lay in things in advance, so as to be able to
feed them tomorrow. Eighty years was really too long
for one person, if you were so worn out you were ready
for the scrap-heap. But now, looking back at those
years from the threshold of death, she could not see any
great difference between them. They had each gone by
in haste to catch up with the one before. Ten times a
day the old lady had looked up at the sky to see where
the sun was, seen that it was already high or already
sinking, tried doubly hard to get everything done, and
never managed to. It was always the same: the kids
would pester her for something, the cow would be
mooing, the vegetable patch needed attention. And
there was work to be done in the fields, in the forest,
on the *kolkhoz*, in an endless giddying round which
gave her no time to catch her breath or look around and
keep an image of the beauty of the earth and the sky in
her eyes or in her heart. "Faster, faster," she would
urge herself on, flinging herself at one task, then the
next, and however much she accomplished she could
never see any end. That was the way her whole life had
flown by. In terms of years it seemed long and varied,
but when you looked back at it, poor: one thing after
another, year after year, worry after worry. She could
remember the days when the hut was lit by a lighted
taper. Later they'd gone over to paraffin lamps, but for
years now they'd just flicked a switch. Of course all
these changes took more time than it took to tell about
them, but still, no less than three kinds of light, some
brighter than others, had lit her way as she bustled
about her household chores, for which the daylight

hours were too short. When you had a big family there was no other way. And only when old age had got the better of her, and she had taken to her bed, did the years slow down and pass creaking over her head in long, sleepy winters, as if to say, "Be careful, and mind you don't say the years are getting longer. You've had more than your share."

But she had no complaints about her life. How could you complain about something that was all your own, given to you alone? You had to be satisfied with what you'd got, because there'd be no second chance. One life was enough for a person, because that was all you got. If you had two, you'd want more. The old lady had lived a simple life: bearing children, working, flopping into bed at the very end of the day, jumping up again, getting older — and all this in the place she was born in, and had never left, like a tree in the forest. Her life had been spent at exactly the same day-to-day tasks as her mother's. Other people travelled, saw the world, learned new things. She would listen to their stories when the opportunity arose, and wonder at them. She herself had borne children who travelled as much as anybody else's, but it never occurred to her how good it might be to change places with somebody in order to see more or live an easier life. You couldn't slough your old skin, like a snake. She never envied anybody, no matter how good-looking or successul they were. To her it seemed as senseless as wanting somebody else's mother to be your mother, or somebody else's child to be yours. Everybody's life had its own beauty. She had known her bright, joyful moments, which were dear to her and were hers alone, and she had had her moments of grief, which were equally dear to her and with the passing of time became even dearer, more a part of her. Without them she would long ago have dissipated her energies in all sorts of feverish and pointless activity. After each blow of misfortune she had picked herself up, put her old bones together again, and urged herself on: "Get along and live!" Nobody else would take her place after her, nobody would become her. You had to live while you still had the strength. There was no other way. Life for her was at once a joy and a torment, and she could not tell where the joy ended and the torment began, or which of the two was more beneficial to her. She accepted and absorbed them both, in order to live on and have her way lit by their hidden light.

The old lady lay still and listened to the even, alert breathing of the house in the night, lit by the magic light of the plentiful stars. She listened to the muffled, unconscious sighs of the sleeping earth on which the house stood, and the high, bright turning of the sky above it, and the whispers of the air about her, and all this helped her to hear and feel herself and what was leaving her forever for the vast expanse of night, leaving the flesh weightless and empty.

And suddenly it seemed to her that her life had been kind, meek, and successful. Unusually successful. She could hardly complain about devoting it all to her children, if man's business in the world was to see that it was never empty of people, and that it did not grow old without children.

She recalled the words Mikhail had said to her after the birth of his first child, Volodia. He was drunk, not with liquor, but with amazement at the fact that he, little more than a boy himself, had become a father, and taken part for the first time in the perpetuation of the human race. He had said, "There it is, Mother: you made me, I've made him, and he'll make somebody else." And he added with the wry, muted wisdom of a prophet, "That's what keeps the world going."

He had only just realized that this was what had always kept the world going and always would, until its end. It had only struck him now that this simple truth, from which nobody was exempt, had hitched onto him a new link in its endless chain. And at the same time, as a man, alone with himself, he had taken in the fact that he was mortal, like everything else in the world except the earth and the sky. And this was what had moved him to go to his mother and tell her what she had known for years, and had assumed he also knew.

For a moment she fancied she was in an old, dilapidated house, with little windows all covered from inside, and the spellbinding starlight entered through the walls and the roof. Each of the windows was a memory of one of her children: Liusia, Varvara, Ilia, Mikhail, and Tanchora. Above these was another row of tiny, boarded-up windows. These it was pointless to touch: they were her memories of those who had died. The old lady wandered like a sleepwalker from one window to the next, leaving no shadow behind her, and not knowing which window to open, where to look, whom to choose.

Her whole life was here, in these windows. Open them, and she would see what riches had gone to make it up, what memories would remain when she was gone to rustle the loyal blackberry bushes on the river bank and the birches at the edge of the forest, or to bring an evocative scent to somebody's nose, calling forth vague and troubling presentiments which could otherwise not have come. A bird in the forest tumbled sleepily from a high branch almost to the ground, but this was not yet her life being broken off. And it was not her memories but somebody else's which had turned into whispers, rustlings and indistinct falling sounds to trouble her sleep.

The old lady shifted her weight to relieve her pins and needles, and somebody in the other room also stirred as if in answer to her, begging not to be forgotten. For some reason she thought that it must be Ilia, who was sleeping in the house that night.

Now take Ilia . . . What should she pick out from her long maternal memory, what could she take to look at again without hurting herself or him? Today her reminiscences should all be gentle, harmonious, and bright. It would not do if any touch of bitterness, or any voice out of turn recurred to trouble the farewells of this last night. Soon, soon it would be time.

Ilia had been wild and unpredictable as a boy: when there was everything he could want in his own garden he would get into other people's gardens, yet when his own family had nothing to eat he would give the last crust to a complete stranger. There was never any telling what he might get up to next. Once he'd been set to guard a cartload of grain waiting to go to the mill. All of a sudden shots were heard from the place he was guarding, just as if war had broken out. Instead of sitting on the cart and shooing away the hens with a stick, Ilia had climbed onto the barn roof and was blazing away at them with a shotgun. He'd laid low two pullets and a piglet for no offence whatever. Another time, when he was a bit older, he'd gone one better than that. Some kind of inspection committee had turned up at the *kolkhoz*. Ilia and two other lads were doing the autumn ploughing on the far side of the Upper Brook. The moment the committee appeared he stripped naked and went on guiding the plough, whistling as he went, in his birthday suit. There were women on the committee, and they didn't dare come close, so they turned back without seeing how good or how bad the ploughing was. Apparently they took it out on the *kolkhoz* chairman afterwards, because he descended upon the old lady in a rage, as if she'd taught her son to walk naked behind the plough.

But now another recollection came. Ilia had also been drafted into the army, but right at the end of the war, so he didn't actually see action. The war ended, fortunately, while he was still in training. But of course they didn't know it was going to end when they saw him off.

It was a dry, windy day in late autumn. A cart stood ready in the yard with Ilia's things in it. The gates were open. It only remained for them to bid their farewells. Ilia came up to his mother. He was small in stature, and now dejected and yet elated at going off to war. But in this last minute he already seemed more like a stranger than a son. She made the sign of the cross over him, and he did not refuse her blessing. She remembered clearly that he had not simply endured it to please her, but accepted it, welcomed it. She could see that in his eyes, which wavered and lit up for a moment with hope. And at once the old lady felt easier about him.

This memory led to another, quite different one, which seemed to occupy a place beside it in her memory, although the two incidents had little in common.

Liusia had left for the city by steamer in the summer. They had come down to the quayside early in the morning, long before the boat was due, and camped there, lighting smoky bonfires to hold off the dense clouds of midges. Liusia was surrounded by her envious or pitying girlfriends, and little Tanchora hovered nearby. The old lady sat alone on a log which had partly sunk into the ground a little way off. Sadly, submissively she kept watch for the smoke from the steamer's funnel to appear in the sky above the inland. At last it appeared, but the sharp-eyed girls spotted it first and raised their voices in cries of excitement, tugging at Liusia, giving her all sorts of advice, all talking at once. The old lady sat in downcast silence.

When the boat was moored Liusia hastily gave her hand to each of her friends in turn, her mother last. The old lady squeezed her warm, lost hand and then guided her by the shoulders on her way. Then she walked a little way from the group, so that she could be seen more easily. The gang-plank was quickly raised, the paddle steamer cast off and began to turn its wheels, and Liusia went on her way with it, out into the mainstream. She was standing at the rail, behind a white-painted steel mesh, and waving to her friends. For some reason she didn't see her mother, although the old lady called out to her two or three times, and then started hopping up and down and waving her arms like one demented, in order to catch her daughter's attention.

The boat rolled so that it almost took on water, and the crew chased the passengers to the other side, including Liusia. The old lady was on the verge of tears. Then suddenly Liusia cast a last glance back at the shore, pushed past the young sailor who was shooing her out of her mother's sight, rushed back and started waving furiously, desperately, wretchedly to her mother with the shawl she had torn off her head. Her face was frightened, pale, and tears sprang to her eyes in a moment. The old lady rushed towards her, wading in water up to her knees, but the boat had picked up speed and started slapping forward on its paddles at full power, and behind it, dazzling, hurrying it along, and making it look like a sparkling toy, shone the bright sun.

The old lady had the feeling that they had said goodbye forever.

These memories of her children were unexpectedly interrupted, and she saw another day long, long ago, also on the river.

A short, drenching squall of rain, which had blown up without warning in one of those isolated summer clouds, had just passed, and the sun had already come out again. The woodland glades were steaming. Heavy, swollen drops were falling from the trees and bushes, and beads of water trickled here and there in the grass like beetles. The river was still carrying bubbles and foam. Everything was clean and had a jaunty sparkle, ringing with bird-song and the sound of water, and the air had a cool tang in it. The earth, drunk with rain, had laid itself bare, stripped itself naked, and was now breathing heavily, languidly. The sky above it was again clear, blue, and bottomless.

She wasn't an old woman then. No, she was still a young girl, surrounded exclusively by things beautiful, young, and bright. She was strolling along the bank, paddling in the water, which was warm and steaming after the rain, raising a low wave as she walked, on which tiny bubbles swayed and burst. The sand was dark and pitted, the bank low, directly opposite the island. The water was roaring somewhere at the point.

The channel was long and empty, and you could plainly see the powerful current surging in a straight, broad stream.

She paddled on and on, not thinking where she was going or why, or for what pleasure, but in the end came up onto the beach, leaving footprints in the sand with her supple, bare feet. She looked at them in surprise for a long time, assuring herself that she did not know their origin. Her long skirt was wet and clung to her, so she cheerfully pulled it up and tucked the hem under her waistband. Then she waded into the water again, laughing softly to herself and regretting that nobody could see her. At that moment she was so happy to be alive, to see the beauty of the world with her own eyes, to be amidst the vigorous, exultant, harmonious workings of life without end, that she felt a giddiness in her head, and a sweet ache of excitement in her breast.

Even now the old lady's heart stood still at the memory of that day. It was hard to believe that it had been, but it had, as God was her witness.

It occurred to her that such beauty could not possibly still be seen by people today, that it could not have endured without fading in all the years which had passed since that day. Could you, if you crossed to the spot on the far bank where she had been that day, still see it as it had been then, with the same freshness and joy? There had been so many changes in the world. Could this one thing have remained unchanged?

She felt a little hurt and sad, but she soon checked herself with the thought that she would be a fine one if she wanted everything in the world to grow old and die with her.

A long time ago, when Varvara was a little girl, the

old lady had found her in an alley-way, on her knees, scratching at the ground with a piece of wood.

"What are you doing here?" she asked.

"Digging."

"What for?"

"A hen was digging here, and a dog came and chased it away. I saw it. You won't chase me away, will you?"

"No, I won't."

"Then I'll just sit here for a bit and dig."

Her mother chuckled to herself and went away. When Varvara came home, she asked, "Did you find anything where you were digging?"

"I wasn't looking for anything. I was just digging. But a bull came and butted me away. Go and chase the bull away, and dig a bit."

"What for?"

"Just go and dig. You'll see."

"What'll I see?"

'I don't know. You'll see something. It's interesting."

That explained why, these many years later, the old lady had a sudden wish to squat down somewhere in the open and scratch at the ground, following Varvara's example, studying it with interest and excitement, looking for something in it that nobody knew was there. They laughed, old and young together, one who had taken leave of her senses, and one who was too young to have any sense yet. It was true that only the very old and the very young were alert to the wonder of their existence, and sensitive to the things that surrounded them at every step.

The night turned cold and set in firmly. Its clear, cold light, entering through the windows, drew patterns on the walls. The old lady had not forgotten how the heavens rang and played at this time, nor with what passion and promise the stars burned, nor how close and regally the new moon rode in the sky. But on earth all was still, lifeless, and motionless. Everything was wrapped in the deep, magical numbness of sleep.

With a shudder the old lady decided that it was time, the very best time. The night had entered its second half, there was no time to lose. The family were sleeping soundly, nobody would hear, nobody would disturb her. And the night was merry. That was good: the night would see her on her way.

Calmly the old lady made ready, without fear or panic. Softly she pushed back the covers from her breast, so as to make it easier to get started. Then she gingerly, noiselessly, rocked herself slightly, and found that she was carrying no extra weight. It had all gone. She had time for a fleeting moment of wonder at the fact that she was weightless, and at how easy it was to move her body, as if it was in thin air. Her body was still here with her, and she could feel her heart deceptively sending out its pulses to it. She stretched out her legs and made herself comfortable. Her legs would soon be at one with the rest of her body, and need no longer suffer in the knowledge that they had given out first. How many times had she told them it wasn't their fault, that she herself had worn them out with too much running, but they didn't understand. They would understand now. They had no choice.

Her eyes were still open and still held the deathly-pale nocturnal light — the last thing she would see. If that light came over everything that her eyes had seen before, it would be easier to accept the darkness from above. She suddenly felt cold and frightened at the thought that, having lived for nearly eighty years and always with time in hand, she was now hanging by a thread. At this moment she no longer had any future left, only a past. All her life was now in one piece, and in a few moments she would have neither future nor past. When she was gone her children would be left in the world, but she herself would have nothing and nobody, not even herself. Where would her life go? she wondered. After all, she could remember living only a little while ago. Who would receive the life she had brought to an end, like a job of work — perhaps done well, perhaps not, but brought to an end? You couldn't sew a pair of gloves out of her, could you? Somebody might mention her kindly, nod in her direction, and that would be all. The grass would grow over her memory, and they'd stop mentioning her altogether. That was a fact. What else did she want? She would have liked to know why and for what purpose she had lived, trodden this earth in a fever of activity, carrying the heaviest of burdens on her back. Why? Only for her own sake, or for some other purpose as well? Who had needed her for anything serious, or for any amusement? And was it good or bad that she was leaving other lives behind her? Who could say? Who could enlighten her? Why? Would her life produce even one drop of vital, long-awaited rain to pour on the thirsting fields?

In the farthest corner of the room she heard a creaking sound, like a garbled, indistinct answer to her question, and she waited, breathless: that must be for her.

And all of a sudden, just before the end, she had the feeling that she had been in the world before her present, human life. In what form, whether crawling, walking, or flying, she could not remember, nor even guess, but something told her that she was not seeing the world for the first time. If birds were born twice, once as eggs, and once when the eggs hatched, such miracles were not impossible, and she was not blaspheming. Long, long ago, at night, a violent thunderstorm had burst upon the earth. Thunder and lightning had flashed and crashed all around, rending the heavens, from which the rain fell in a solid sheet. The world had never before known such terror. It was quite possible that this thunderstorm had actually killed her, because she couldn't remember anything else before or after it, only the storm itself, and even this recollection came to her like an echo of some earlier memory, not her own.

Carefully she made the sign of the cross: may she be forgiven if there was something wrong about this memory. It came to her uninvited, and she did not want to annoy anyone by it. She did not know where it came from, or how it came to her.

Only now did she close her eyes, doing so at once, without a last look round. Before her closed eyes she saw swirling ringlets of smoke passing from left to right, as if somebody had decided to cleanse her by fumigation before her communion. She stretched and lay still, in tense anticipation of the first ticklish touch, from which a sorrowful state of somnolent well-being would spread all over her body. Her life as a person would be over, she knew the kingdom of man. Amen. She felt her mind growing dim and her hands turning numb. Or was she only imagining it, because she wanted it? The bells hung ready above the earth, ready to sound the promised chimes.

Minutes passed, and yet more minutes, with no change. As before, the old lady was fully conscious. She knew who she was, where she was, and why she was there. For some reason death was in no hurry to receive her. It was waiting for something.

She listened attentively to herself. Apparently everything inside her was still in place and still carrying out its duties. She could not understand the cause of the delay, and she groaned softly: I'm here, I'm here. Perhaps death thought she wasn't ready yet, and had to be told. To make quite sure she spoke again in the same groaning voice, scoring the silence of the night with her plaintive appeal: Come, don't be afraid. I'm waiting for you.

She felt ill at ease and was gripped by an uncomfortable sense of foreboding. Could she have given her death such a run for its money that it no longer had the strength to reach her? How many years had she been stringing it along behind her, even making it chase after her? If you weren't careful you'd soon bring death to its knees. What if this had happened, and death couldn't reach her, and she hadn't the strength to reach out to death? Would that mean she couldn't die? No, that never happened. The only people who didn't die were those who were never born. There must be some other reason. Death would not fail to do the task for which it existed in the world.

By now the old lady's breathing was anxious and troubled. She had only just accepted that she was rid of everything that held her to the world of men, and here she was having to start all over again.

She thought again: she had done something wrong. It wasn't that death had given her up but that she, more likely, had got in its way, by wanting to do death's work herself. Who would approve of that? For nigh on eighty years death had been waiting for its one and only hour of triumph, going over it time and again, working out the order of events. Death had its plans. You couldn't go interfering with them. That was the truth of the matter.

She decided that she ought to go to sleep, since night was for sleeping, and then, when she saw nothing and heard nothing, death would draw near, emboldened, and remove the most painful bonds still holding her to people and the world. Then perhaps it would wake her up, so that she could depart fully conscious. There wasn't that much night left, but it wasn't too late. There was still time before morning.

Now the old lady snuggled in her bed, trying to plunge herself into the ordinary sleep of the living, which she had enjoyed so many thousands of times in her life. She did not open her eyes, but let them relax a little, so that they lay easily and did not think about the light. That would do them no good. With her back gently touching the bed she started rocking herself, and her lips murmured indistinctly the words of a lullaby for children. She was at the very threshold of oblivion, she even felt as if she were being swathed in soft, grey material, and she was sinking deeper and deeper into it, burying herself with pleasure in its thick, soft folds and its spellbinding whispers, but something pulled her back, and went on bringing her back, mercilessly, again and again.

Sleep would not come. The old lady could guess why not: by this time of night sleep had set firmly and grown heavy and impenetrable, so that it was hard to get out of, but even harder to get into. It would not turn back for the sake of one person, and pestering it would be useless. A different approach was needed. It seemed you had to just lie still, and want nothing else, except to lie still, and demand nothing. Then perhaps she would be swept up accidentally and pushed towards sleep, exhausted from inactivity, and sleep would take her in, not knowing who she was. That would be nice. She must not hurry, and behave as if she had all the time in the world, as if the night had only just begun.

She started preparing herself for sleep: she made her breathing slow down and her body relax, she calmed her fluttering breast and folded her hands on it. She was lucky, just as she had hoped. She was caught up almost at once on a soft, sweet wave, which rocked her and bore her towards a blissful silence. She was practically there, only moments away, when suddenly, somewhere in the village, a cock crowed in a loud, hearty, shameless voice. This was so unexpected, so out of place, that an involuntary, stifled groan escaped the old lady, and her eyes sprang open. She shut them again at once, but she knew it was too late. It was hopeless now. Salvation had not come. Even if it had been close, it was now far away. After the first cock, a second began to crow, then a third and a fourth . . .

It had all been in vain. Now all hope was gone.

She opened her eyes, voluntarily this time, and she felt deeply ashamed. She had never before felt so ashamed: she had bade her farewells, said her last words, consoled herself with her last memories, lowered the shroud of darkness over her eyes — and she'd come back to life. It was unheard of. No, she wasn't afraid. She had never feared this, and she had no reason to deceive herself. She herself had died, and she did not know how her sinful, cowardly body, which had preserved its ability to move, would manage. On whose life, whose breath would it subsist?

The night was paling, the starlight had waned, turning drier, thinner, showing the daytime sky unfolding. The cocks had fallen silent, but after them the night was filled with creaking and trembling noises as it hurried to make its exit. It was that time when the stars withdraw to a greater height and look down dimly, wearily. The old lady took in all of this, like an empty, lidless pot left out in the open, with no will of her own to accept or reject it. She lay there lost and helpless, utterly numb, and no longer caring about anything.

She lay like this for a long time, until morning came, and then, when enough light had entered the room, she came to life and threw off the covers. She sat up, looked with revulsion at her legs, pulled on her stockings and pushed her feet into her slippers. She had learned how to do all this yesterday. But this morning was nothing like yesterday morning. Yesterday she had rejoiced at the approach of day, had great hopes for it, and thought about Tanchora. And none of the things she had looked forward to had happened. Even the night had withheld salvation and left her sleepless, even though the night was never short of sleep to hand out to all who wanted it. This time there was none for the old lady. Everybody was sick of her, nobody wanted her. If nobody else would give her a thought, why should she think of herself either?

Clutching the head of her bed she tried to stand up. Her legs bent under her, but she had no pity on them: If you won't die you can damn well do as you're told, and don't pretend you're so badly off because nobody'll believe you anyway. Putting her weight on her arms she straightened her legs, and with a desperate effort forced them to walk: If there's life in you, walk! Walk, like everybody else's legs, and don't dare fold up! Walk! Every bone in her legs creaked and groaned in protest, but she would not stop. Creak as much as you like, but walk! You can take orders from me, for once. Placing one hand over the other along the partition she dragged her feet along the floor. Anyone looking at her would have said she was crawling on the wall — she was almost lying on it, her arms flung out, searching for something to hold on to. She crawled through the doorway on all fours. There was no other way. At the porch there was another doorway to negotiate, a lower one, but she did not get up. She crawled out of the house on all fours, just like a dog, except that she didn't bark or howl. Her strength was almost gone, but with a great effort she managed to perch herself on the top step.

The fine morning sky was lifting higher. Even before the sun rose a deep blue could be seen swallowing up the pre-dawn gloom, particularly in the direction the old lady was looking in. Although it was early the forest had already shaken off its sleep and now stood bright and alert, each separate tree distinct. Even the foliage did not blend into one mass. Each tree's own gentle, living outline could be seen. Some hens flapped down on heavy wings from their perch behind the barn, shook themselves hurriedly, and set about jabbing at the ground with their bills, stepping quickly to warm up. It was cold. The raw air which had hung motionless over the river all night reached up to the village, and cold dewdrops glistened on the leaves in the garden. But the morning was advancing, ever changing. If a moment ago it had seemed slow, lazy, and grey, it was now as bright as day, playful, and active in its impatient, childish anticipation. Rainbow-coloured ribbons stood in the sky like narrow pillars, and before long the sun rose before the old lady's eyes, and the earth happily, loyally welcomed its light.

She had no idea why she had come outside. Perhaps she was hoping that her heart would not stand the strain and would give out on the way, thus completing the night's unfinished business. But it hadn't worked. She'd made it. She sat alone, lifeless, looking without interest at the garden, the forest, anything that met her eyes, looking and seeing nothing, finding nothing to look at. She was like a candle carried out into the sunshine, where it is no use to anyone. But she submitted to the sun: in her thin nightgown she was chilled and shivering, so even the feeble rays of the early morning sun were welcome. After all she was human, not some block of wood, and her body, she found, could still tell heat from cold. But still this was a day she could have done without, a day which did not belong to her. She had not wanted it, and had feared it from the start, feeling that if she was not fated to die that night, then something awaited her today. Nothing happened without a reason.

And so she sat and waited.

A milking-pail clanked behind her and Nadia came out. Not expecting to see the old lady here she started back in fright: "Mother!" That was what she called her mother-in-law. "What are you doing here?"

The old lady heard her, turned round, and nodded her head: I'm here.

"How did you get here? You're frozen! Let me take you back indoors."

The old lady refused with a determined shake of her head.

"But you must . . ."

Nadia ran back into the house and before doing anything else looked at the old lady's bed — it really was empty. Only then did she take a pullover from a hook and take it out to her mother-in-law.

"What are you thinking of?" she asked, still overcome with amazement. "Everybody's asleep, they don't know. Should I wake them?"

"Better not," replied the old lady. "You go and do your milking. I'll just sit here."

Nadia looked back two or three times before she reached the yard, and seemed surprised to see her still sitting there.

The sun had now broken clear of the forest and risen into the clear blue spaces that had been waiting to receive it. It remained a little to the right, just as it had done yesterday and the day before, ten years, twenty years ago. It was not too bright yet, and was clearly defined, not yet dazzling to the eye. Now there seemed to be even more dew in the garden, glinting everywhere in alluring, burning drops. The village was waking up, smoke was rising from chimneys, cattle were walking heavily, contentedly, down the street, making the ground tremble. Ill-fitting doors banged in the houses, and the first human voices of morning could be heard.

And there, lo and behold, at this early hour when nobody went visiting, who should appear unexpectedly out of the ground but Mironikha? Looking down at her feet as usual, she nearly knocked the old lady off the step. She sank back in disbelief and threw up her hands: "Gawd, is that you, old girl?"

"Yes," she replied, not even appearing very pleased to see Mironikha. Her voice was flat and feeble, and she said no more than she had to.

"You've come out?"

"Yes."

"Well then, old girl, how about running up over the ridge with me today? We'll be company for each other climbing the hill."

"No. I had enough trouble crawling out here. Some of the way on me hands and knees."

"And I was running here thinking I'd ask Nadia how you was today, and you're up and about and running outside."

"I ain't dead yet," said the old lady.

"Did you ask to die?"

"Yes."

"Not your time yet, then."

"What do you mean — not my time?" For the first time today there was some feeling in her voice — she sounded hurt. "My kids are here, and they won't wait long. Couldn't ask for a better time. But I'm still here."

"We're all in God's hands, old girl. It'll all turn out as He wills it."

"Well, I can't even walk in His hands these days. Thought I'd crawl out and show meself to Old Mother Death in case she's lost me, can't see me. She ought to see me here."

"Don't you fret."

The old lady did not try to keep up this cheerless conversation. Mironikha had not been with her that night, she wouldn't understand what a person went through in the hour of death, and what you felt like afterwards, when death, having taken your confession, cheated you. And you couldn't explain it to anyone either. Instead the old lady asked, "No news from your kids?"

"You asked me that only yesterday," replied Mironikha, surprised.

"Yesterday was yesterday. They could have written to you today. How do I know?"

"Sure, sat up all night long writing me a whole book. I don't know how I'll manage to read it all." Mironikha spoke without anger, but without any hope either. Her sarcasm was aimed only at herself. "What hard times could they have fell on to make 'em write to me?"

"It ain't like the olden days," said the old lady. "In them days you was born in a place and you stayed put in it. Nowadays they won't stay put for a moment. They keep on moving. But where to? What for?"

"It ain't for you and me to understand, old girl."

"Maybe it ain't. We're the last old-time old women left in the world, you and me. There ain't any more like us. The old women who come after us will be different — brainy, educated, able to understand what goes on in the world and why. We've got left behind, you and me. It's a new age now, not ours."

"You're right there, old girl."

"Course I'm right. You mark my words."

They said nothing for a moment. Mironikha heaved a sigh and stood up. "Nice talking to you, old girl, but I've got to be running along."

"Sit a bit longer."

"My cow still ain't back. The men say there's a couple of cows on the far side of the ridge. I've got to go up there. Nothing else for it."

"You won't make it up there."

"Maybe I won't, but I'm going to try. There's nobody I can send."

"What if you fall up there?"

"If I do, what difference does it make? I can lie up there, or lie down here. I'll be alone either way. Nobody to give me a glass of water."

"You ought to write to them yourself."

"What would I say to 'em? Think they don't know I was seventy-five last birthday. No, whether I write or not, it won't do no good . . . And I can't read or write no more than you can. They must be all right if they don't come and don't send no letters. If things were bad they'd write."

"Yes, that they would."

"Yes."

Mironikha shifted her weight from one foot to the other, anxious to be on her way.

"Well, I'll be running along, old girl. You just sit here and don't get up to no mischief. And when I get back I'll come and see you again. We'll sit a bit more and have a chat."

"Don't fall when you're up there."

She gave Mironikha her hand in parting. Mironikha gave a sudden start, bowed her head awkwardly, and pressed the old lady's hand to her cheek. Tears tumbled from the old lady's eyes. She made to get up, but Mironikha stopped her and turned towards the gate. She probably thought she was striding along at a great rate, almost running, but in fact she was straining to put one foot in front of the other, and it was obvious what an effort each step cost her.

The old lady dried her eyes and thought that that was probably the reason why she hadn't died in the night: she hadn't said goodbye to Mironikha, the only friend she'd had in all her life, and hadn't known the feeling she knew now — of a true, enduring friendship concluded with pure, perfect finality.

She knew she would never see Mironikha again.

There was one more day left to live through, an extra, unwanted day.

II

Nadia brought the old lady back into the house, virtually carrying her in her arms: the old lady's legs would not support her. Now she was lying in her bed again, looking straight ahead with sad, apologetic eyes, and listening warily to the sounds she heard about her. She felt she no longer had any right to do anything, to look, to listen, or even breathe, as if she was stealing when she did anything. Since the family had got up and Nadia had told them how their mother had made her own way out to the steps, they'd all oohed and aahed, surprised and pleased to hear that she was getting better by the hour, then gradually gone their separate ways, leaving her by herself. True they looked in often enough — Liusia, Ilia, and Nadia — but they only looked and went away again. Ilia said that if they waited a bit longer she'd start dancing, and they could all clap in time for her. The joke had pleased the others, even Liusia had smiled, and Varvara had taken it with her to the village, along with the news that their mother was walking again. Ilia had had time to warm up, his bald head shone with a warm, pink glow, and his eyes were alight with a sudden, devil-may-care sort of merriment. He was itching to do something, take part in something, but there was nothing for him to do. That was why he kept coming into his mother's room and repeating: "Still lying there, eh, Mum? Well, have a bit of a rest, and when you feel like doing a dance, just give us a shout. We'll come and watch. We all know you're going to give us a dance. Don't back out of it."

The old lady's only reply was a frightened, pleading look.

Later, when she was alone, Mikhail came in. He sat down at the table, where he had sat before yesterday's scene, lit a cigarette, and drew on it avidly, hurriedly. His usually ruddy face now looked unhealthily black and hot, and his eyes were puffy. He smoked, sighing, trying to find some relief from his heavy burden. He kept glancing at his mother, as though he was expecting something, hoping for something. The smoke irritated her and a painful fit of coughing seized her. She clutched at her breast, and her dry, aching coughs sounded as if they were tearing her throat to pieces. Mikhail hastily ground out his cigarette and left the room. They had not said a word to each other.

But when her coughing had subsided and Ninka came in, the old lady responded at once. She raised her hand and started stroking the little girl's shoulders, warming herself, warming her heart by touching the child's body. It was as if somebody were stroking her. She even closed her eyes, as she did at moments of special pleasure.

Without warning Ninka said, "Auntie Liusia's a fibber."

"Why do you say that?" The old lady opened her eyes.

"She is. She said she'd buy me some sweets. Everybody heard her. And she hasn't bought me any. She's a fibber."

"Well, go and remind her to buy you some."

"No, I'm scared of her. You tell her."

"Why be scared? She won't bite you."

"All the same, when she looks at me I feel scared. If she didn't look at me I wouldn't be scared of her."

"Don't be silly."

"I'll call her, and you can tell her," Ninka insisted.

"Better not. You don't need no more sweets. You had too many yesterday — sucking from morn till night."

In an offended gesture Ninka sprang away from her grandmother.

"You're scared of her yourself," she jeered. "If you wasn't scared of her you'd tell her. You're just a scaredy-cat!"

The old lady tried to smile, but could not. The corners of her lips twitched without any expression.

She evidently managed to doze off, because she did not hear Liusia come in. When she opened her eyes she saw Liusia standing there, looking at her searchingly. When their eyes met, Liusia asked, "How are you feeling, Mummy?"

"All right," she replied, not knowing what else to say. She felt she had left behind her the point where people felt well or ill. Even in her better days she'd never paid much attention to the question, distinguishing only between sickness and good health, weariness and energy, strength and weakness.

"Better than yesterday?" Liusia persisted.

"You ought to make it up with Mikhail, Liusia," said the old lady suddenly. "Will you? You shouldn't quarrel. It's my fault: I flew at him, and he was hurt. He lost his temper. And now he's suffering for it."

"Oh? That's interesting. He was hurt, and I wasn't? He said all those vile things to us, and I'm supposed to go and apologize to him. Do you know what you're saying, Mummy? Don't stick up for him, if you don't mind. I've no wish to discuss the matter further. I have feelings too, and I'd like other people to have some respect for them."

The old lady was at a loss for words.

"I ain't talking about him," she started to explain. "I ain't making excuses for him. No. He's one sort of person, you're another. There's no changing that. But whatever he's like, he's your brother. And whatever I'm like, I'm your mother — his as well as yours. And I'd like you to live in peace. Make it up, Liusia, for my sake. As soon as you make it up, I'll make my peace. That's the only thing that's keeping me now."

"Aren't you tired of harping on that, Mummy? You're practically well again, you're perfectly normal, you're even walking, and you go on and on about it. Can't you talk about something else?"

Ninka came in again. She could hardly have chosen a worse moment.

"Go for a walk, off you go," said the old lady, pushing her away. "Go on, I'll be waiting for you when you come back."

"Auntie Liusia's a fibber," retorted Ninka stubbornly, with a sidelong glance at Liusia.

The old lady felt there was nothing she could do but ask, "Why do you say that?"

"She is. She said she'd buy me some sweets. Everybody heard her. And she hasn't bought me any. She was fibbing."

"What on earth do you mean by this?" asked Liusia, flabbergasted. "You've no right to talk to me like that!"

"I'm not talking to you, I'm talking to Granny. Don't eavesdrop."

"Who gave you permission to talk to me as if I was one of your little friends? Don't you know you should show more respect for grown-ups? Hasn't anybody told you that?"

"Say you're sorry," the old lady whispered to Ninka.

"All right," said Ninka with a sniffle, all ready to burst into tears.

"Don't you dare cry," Liusia warned her. "Nobody will believe you. What an ill-bred girl you are! I don't like ill-bred children. I don't like children who talk to me like that. What a state of affairs!"

"She won't do it again," said the old lady cautiously.

"Wait a moment, Mummy. Is that the way you've brought her up? Saying, 'She won't do it again' and letting it go at that? Why's she still misbehaving? Let her explain. She'll be getting into worse mischief soon, I can tell you." She turned to Ninka: "If you *must* have some sweets I'll buy you some, but don't think it's a present — it's extortion. Do you know what extortion is?"

Ninka nodded quickly. Her aim had been achieved: Auntie Liusia was going to buy her some sweets.

When Liusia went out, Ninka darted out after her, no doubt to keep watch for her at the gate, or even to run after her to the shop, so as to pop out of the crowd at exactly the right moment and point into the shop window: "Auntie Liusia, buy me some of those. They're the ones I like."

That girl would look after herself anywhere. Whoever did she take after?

The old lady lasped into unconsciousness, and when she came to herself, half the room was bathed in sunlight. She started watching its progress, fearing and yet wishing that it would hurry up and reach her bed. It seemed to her that on this day which she had no right to see, something that was kept hidden from the living might be revealed to her. She gazed at the broad, bright sunlit patch on the floor, hoping to see a pattern in it, or hear a voice which would make something clear to her. So far there was nothing, but the sun was steadily drawing nearer, crawling onto her bed from the window on her right. In its silent, penetrating light the old lady sensed a taut, playful strength, which could only just be held in check, and it occurred to her suddenly that the sun might melt her, like some crumbly snowman dressed in rags. She would warm herself in it, feeling nice and cosy, and not notice that she was gradually shrinking, until she disappeared altogether. People would come to see her, and her bed would be empty. They would presume she had crawled out of the house again. Now she did not distinguish between her family and others: they were all just "people".

The sun at last rose onto her bed, and she laid her hand in it, absorbing warmth for her whole body. She felt as though she were absorbing not only warmth, but also weakness, but that did not alarm her: weakness was gentle and agreeable. She was anxious only to stay awake, and let it happen while she was conscious.

Somewhere close by the old lady heard Varvara talking to somebody, and it suddenly struck her that there was one thing she had completely forgotten. Straining her voice, she called out to Varvara, but there was no answer. Her voice was too soft and did not carry. She called again, louder this time. Varvara heard her and came in.

"What is it, Ma?"

"Sit down." She motioned with her eyes to a spot on the bed beside her. Varvara sat down.

"What is it, Ma?"

"Hold on." The old lady collected her thoughts. "I'm going to die . . ."

"Don't say such things, Ma."

"I'm going to die," she repeated, and added, "Somebody's got to wail over me."

"Eh?"

"Wail over me. The others won't. These days nobody even knows how to rock a baby to sleep, let alone lay somebody in the grave. They can't do nothing. You're my only hope. I'll teach you how. You're pretty good at crying, and all you've got to do is cry and sing a mourning-song . . ."

Varvara seemed to understand. Her face had assumed a terrified look.

"Listen to me. I saw my mother out this way, and you can do the same for me. Nothing to be ashamed of. The others won't do it." She heaved a sigh and narrowed her eyes as she mustered those age-old, half-forgotten words which nobody used any longer, then in a thin, lingering voice she began: "Oh, my darling Mother, my white swan . . ."

"Ma-a-a!" Varvara howled and shook her head, as if refusing to take any part in this performance.

"Don't yell," the old lady stopped her. "Listen for a while and learn this. No need to cry yet. I'm still here. Keep your tears for later, for tomorrow, or somebody will come in and interrupt us. Let's keep the noise down."

She waited for Varvara to calm down, then began again: "Oh, my darling Mother, my white swan . . ."

Varvara repeated the line after her, through her sobs.

"Where are you bound for, what have you made ready for?"

Varvara repeated this.

The old lady sat up in bed and put her arms round her, trying to calm her. Now her voice sounded firmer, and more urgent:

"What far country are you bound for?
By the high road
And the oak grove am I bound
For my beloved church of God
And its tolling bells,
And from the church of God
Into raw Mother Earth,
To join my own kith and kin."

The day wore on, sunny, warm, and relaxed. There was a heaviness in the air, with that tinge of bitterness peculiar to the beginning of a fine autumn. As before, the sky was blue, light blue overhead, and only at its edges, where the sun would set beyond the river, thinly veiled in a harmless-looking smoky haze. Higher and further to the left, rising in the sky, was a lonely little transparent cloud, too like a toy to cause any alarm. It was as if it had been put there specially for people to admire. For the rest, the sky was clear, deep, and filled with limitless peace. Under it, flooded with sunlight, lay the obedient earth.

Mikhail had been sitting for a long time at the barn door, his chin in his hand, smoking one cigarette after another. Ilia sat down beside him and enquired, "Not drinking today?"

Mikhail shook his head.

"I've just had a drop," said Ilia. "To keep my spirits up. Mother's up and about today, you heard?"

"Yes."

"She'll be dancing soon, that's for sure." He laughed and went on, "What about a drink, eh? The stuff's right here. No need to walk to fetch it."

"No," Mikhail replied. "No more. We had our fun yesterday, and that'll do."

"Yes, you overdid it a bit yesterday. Started going for the lot of us. Shouting at Mother . . ."

"I didn't shout at her."

"She lost her temper with you, good and proper. Especially on account of Tanchora. She was all ready to give you a hiding, make no mistake." He laughed again, and suddenly asked, "Look here: when did you send Tanchora that telegram telling her not to come? I've been with you all the time these last few days. You ain't been out of my sight. When did you fit it in?"

Mikhail flicked away his cigarette end and looked his brother in the eye while the hens raced to pick it up.

"I didn't send her no telegram," he said.

"What do you mean — no telegram?"

"Just what I say."

"But you said you'd sent her one? That was what all the argy-bargy was about yesterday. Don't you remember?"

"Sure I remember. If I hadn't said it, do you know what state Mother would be in? Better to deceive her than let her go on waiting."

"But . . . But where's Tanchora, then?"

"How should I know?"

"Well, there's a joke and a half!"

"Don't let on to them, though. Let 'em think I sent it," Mikhail hastened to add, because Liusia was coming towards them. He lowered his head, thinking, "Here we go." She would remind him of everything that had happened in the last two days, leaving nothing out. But it was no use trying to put him to shame now — he would reproach himself bitterly later on, and to greater effect. And listening to her scolding would make him sick. He felt sick enough as it was.

"Ilia!" Liusia called out before she reached them. She looked determined and agitated, as if something had happened. She didn't say what Mikhail feared she would say. "Ilia, do you know the steamer calls today? It'll be here soon. There won't be another for three days."

Ilia stood up, looking lost. "What should we do, then?"

"Suit yourself, but I've got to go. I can't possibly stay here any longer."

"We've got to go, then," Ilia nodded and glanced at Mikhail. "Mother seems to be all right now."

"You could wait a bit longer," said Mikhail timidly. Nobody answered.

They all went into the house together, but the moment they entered their mother's room they froze. Nobody noticed them. Varvara was bent low over her mother, almost lying on her chest, sobbing, and the old lady was intoning some eerie, doleful air. Her eyes were closed, but her face was lit up, almost exultant. They listened and made out the words — tender, hopeless words, which nevertheless seemed to have been turned inside out to acquire opposite meaning:

"Oh, my darling Mother, my white swan,
No more will you tread our oaken floors,
No more will you sit on our oaken benches,
No more will you look out of our windows . . ."

"What's going on here?" enquired Liusia in a loud and scornful voice. "What's this concert in aid of?"

Varvara and the old lady fell silent at once. Varvara

leapt to her feet and pointed at her mother: "Mummy here . . ."

"We can see it ain't Daddy," said Ilia, and roared with laughter.

"I'm going to die," mumbled the old lady mournfully, trying hard to explain something.

"Mummy, I'm tired of hearing all this talk about death. I really am. The same old thing, over and over again. How do you think we like it? There are limits, you know. Can't you talk about anything else. You've got a long time to go yet, and you keep on picturing the worst. It's not right."

"You'll make it to a hundred, Mum, no less," put in Ilia encouragingly.

The old lady said nothing, her eyes fixed on a spot on the wall.

"You can see for yourself, Mummy, that you're almost completely well again. So be glad and enjoy life. Be like everybody else, and don't think about burying yourself before your time. You're just as fit and well as anybody else, so behave as if you were." Liusia paused for a moment, then went on in the same gentle voice: "We've got to be leaving today, as it turns out, Mummy."

"You what?" exclaimed Varvara.

The old lady shook her head in mute disbelief.

"We have to, Mummy," Liusia insisted gently, with a smile. "The steamer calls today, and the next won't be for three days. We can't wait that long."

"No, no," moaned the old lady.

"You can't leave our Mummy today, you can't!" said Varvara excitedly. "You're like strangers. You don't care. Don't you see? You can't go."

"You might wait one more day," put in Mikhail in support of Varvara.

Liusia ignored them and spoke only to her mother: "We're not free to do as we please, Mummy. We have our jobs. I'd be happy to stay here a week, but then they'd start sending for me from work. We're not on holiday. Do try and understand. And don't hold it against us. We have to go."

The old lady burst into tears, turning her face now to Liusia, now to Ilia, and repeating, "I'm going to die. This very day. Wait just a little and you'll see. Wait. I don't ask for nothing else. Liusia! Wait. And you, Ilia. I tell you I'm going to die."

"There you go again, Mummy. You're going to live, and you keep telling us you're going to die. You're not going to die, so please stop saying you are. There's life in you for a long time yet. I'm glad to have seen you again, but now I must go. We'll come back next summer, I promise, and not for a hurried visit, like this one, but to stay."

"Next summer?" Ilia butted in. "We'll see you again before that. You'll get well, Mum, and walking again, and then you can come and stay with us. We'll take you to the circus. I live next to a circus. You should see the clowns! You'd have a great laugh there."

"Will one day make so much difference?" Mikhail persisted, trying to understand what the hurry was.

Liusia flared up: "I don't intend to discuss the matter with you. I think I know better than you what difference it'll make. Or do you still think we ought to wait for Mummy so that we can take her with us?"

"No, I don't."

"Thank goodness for that."

They started getting ready to leave, in haste and embarrassment. The old lady was no longer weeping, and seemed to be lying rigid, her face lifeless and resigned. When spoken to she said nothing. Only her eyes absently followed the bustle of activity.

Nadia hurried in, wanting to provide a meal before Liusia and Ilia left, but the others restrained her. Nobody felt like eating. Ilia whispered to Mikhail, "How about one for the road, eh?"

"No, I don't want any."

There was one thing Varvara had not forgotten. She said loudly to Liusia, "What about the dress?"

"What?"

"The dress you made the other night. You said you'd leave it to me."

Liusia pulled the dress out of her bag and tossed it disdainfully to Varvara.

At the very last moment Varvara suddenly declared, "I'd better be going too, seeing everybody else is. Best if we stick together."

"Varvara!" exclaimed her mother, in a scarcely audible groan.

"My kids could burn the house down while I'm away, Ma. I can't leave them alone in it. I don't know what they might get up to."

"Off you go, then," said Mikhail with a flap of his hand. "On your way, all of you."

They started taking leave of each other. Liusia gave her mother a peck on the cheek. Ilia pressed her hand. Varvara began to cry.

"Get well, Mummy, and stop thinking about death."

"She's a tough one, our Mum."

"I'll be back soon, Ma. Maybe next week."

Mikhail went out to see them off. The old lady

heard their footsteps under her window, and heard Ilia say something and give a laugh. Then all was quiet, and she closed her eyes.

Ninka came and nudged her into wakefulness. "Here, Granny, take this." She held out a sweet to the old lady, who waved it away. Feeling sorry for her, she said of the departing guests, "They're horrid."

The old lady's lips twitched into something between a smile and a grin.

Mikhail came in again and sat down on her bed.

"Never mind, Mother," he said with a sigh, after a long pause. "Never mind. We'll manage. We'll go on as before. Don't be angry with me. I'm a fool, of course. Oh, what a fool I am!" he groaned and stood up. "Just lie still and don't worry about a thing. Don't be too angry with me. I'm just a fool."

The old lady listened in silence. She was not even sure that she would be able to reply. She was sleepy. Her eyelids were drooping. She opened them a few more times before evening came, but not for long, only to get her bearings.

That night the old lady died.

Translated by Kevin Windle